Shakespeare's Daughter

A Novel

By
Susan Ronald

Cover Design: Andrew Balerdi

R&R Books, England in conjunction with CreateSpace
ISBN-13: 978-1533261625
ISBN-10: 1533261628

For Dr Matt Balerdi
for unlocking the past and setting me on the path of discovery

Prologue
Oxford, March 1615

A hush fell among the noblemen, orange-sellers, cutpurses and women of easy virtue as Will Shakespeare, their favourite playmaker, their poet and their friend stepped forward upon the thrust stage. The sun had set and they could see only his wizened face, lit by a single taper candle flickering brightly in his lantern. As he held it aloft, no one noticed that his hand trembled. Everyone was spellbound by his brown-eyed gaze. They had loved his plays for decades, and knew what would happen next. For this was an old play, a comedy, a well-beloved friend, and the intimacy of his words were written about them and for them. Though his face was heavily etched by a life well-lived, to his fellow players and votaries, he was at the height of his powers. After all, he was only fifty-one.

As he turned his head, slowly beckoning his audience into his magical world, Will Shakespeare knew this was a treasured speech. Satisfied that he had captivated them, his velvet voice rang out:

> All the world's a stage,
> And all the men and women merely players;
> They have their exits and their entrances,
> And one man in his time plays many parts,
> His acts being seven ages. At first the infant,
> Mewling and puking in the nurse's arms.
> Then the whining schoolboy, with his satchel
> And shining morning face,
> Creeping like a snail
> Unwillingly to school.
> And then the lover,

Sighing like furnace, with a woeful ballad
Made to his mistress' eyebrow. Then-

As he spoke this last word, he suddenly bowed. His audience erupted into cheers and applause. Many threw their hats in the air. Though they loved the Seven Ages of Man speech, no one seemed to care that it had been cut short. No one saw Shakespeare clutch at his right arm, much less hear his cry for help. By the time he fell to the floor, their poet idol would be a mere hair's breadth from death.

1615

Chapter 1

Run!

Susanna hared down the road, skirts flying. She clutched harder at her little dog bundled up in crumpled laundry, a huge satchel swinging heavily at her back. Run to the life you want to lead! Susanna shouted to herself. Still, curiosity got the better of her and she craned her neck to see if her husband, John Hall, was following. Her heart pounded. Just as she feared, there he was, rounding the corner up Chapel Street, hatless, his Puritan coat unbuttoned, arms scything as if he'd cut down anyone who dared stand in his way, puffing and panting like a pig fit to be stuffed for Christmas. Well, it's not Christmas! The Lenten season is already upon us. It's time to turn our hearts from sin. And me to turn away from you, husband.

Face front, she ordered herself silently. Lift your leaden legs, or you're done for. As she ran, she spotted Robert in the distance, loading up the cart – the cart that could take her away from this madness. Feet take wings, she commanded with a firm heart. Take wings and get me out of this godforsaken place. As if answering a clarion call from the Archangel Gabriel himself, her boots seemed barely to touch the ground. Robert. Concentrate on Robert, she chanted like a prayer. Ignore that gawping crowd gathering to watch the spectacle. This isn't one of your father's plays, Susanna. Run!

She knew that if her husband caught up with her – well, it didn't bear thinking about. She ran past neighbours she'd known all her life, willing herself to jump on Robert's cart and get out of

Stratford. As she sped past some of her so-called friends, it was Margaret Thompson, that busy-body with too little money and too many children, who asked aloud, 'What devil has taken possession of Susanna Hall?'

How dare she? Susanna's husband, Dr John Hall – that same man now pursuing her – had bedded Margaret, and dozens of other women, too, playing at 'doctor' together like schoolchildren. Even so, that was only one of her many reasons for running away. If she had to swear on a stack of Bibles, she couldn't say just why she'd chosen this minute of this day to declare her freedom. Other days had been worse, and other encounters with her husband more demeaning.

'I daren't think what could make her run for her life so,' Margaret turned, smiling beguilingly at Hall as he raced towards her.

Seeing that harlot standing with two of her husband's other paramours, Susanna hoped all Stratford would guess why she was running away, even if she was unsure herself. As she barrelled past, she heard a woman ask, *'Which one's at fault?'* A man answered, 'More important, which will end up in the stocks for disturbing the public order?' Further along, Lucy Babcock said, 'It's a sure thing Will Shakespeare's daughter must serve her penance.' That's when old Thomas Greenway pronounced with authority, 'Susanna must be riding at the reins.' As she bowled past, she held old Thomas in her steady eye, as if to toss some invisible spear his way. He withered under her stare. How dare he think *she* had been the one to commit adultery!

Everyone heard old Thomas's remark. Stratford's women giggled behind splayed fingers. Children were shooed away from her – the scarlet woman running in the road. Men hooted. Money passed hands. Most of the women were betting on the sure thing that it was Dr Hall at fault. Men bet on Susanna just to juggle the odds. Concentrate on Robert, she repeated to herself. He was nearly within hailing distance. Robert and that blessed cart were all that mattered.

It was part curiosity, part cussedness that made her peer over her shoulder again to see if her husband was gaining on her. The womenfolk of Stratford-upon-Avon suddenly took to jeering at him, having decided for their own good reasons that they'd egg her on. Maybe it was for their wagers with their menfolk, or maybe it was because they wanted to escape too. So, they cheered, 'Run Susanna! Run faster and leave the lecher!' Hall narrowed his eyes at them as he blundered up Chapel Street. Heartened, Susanna lifted her knees higher, picking up speed. He'd not catch her, not today, not ever.

The catcalls from the Stratford women grew into a roar. But their support set her wondering. Hadn't these same women been happy to have her husband wander his hands and lips all over their bodies? Hadn't they been willing him to carry on with his lechery? After all, he was the man who had ministered to their needs – medical and sexual – for ten long years, and some of those women he hadn't bedded as yet, had wanted him to. And now, these same women wished her freedom from him and the marital bed. How little they understood the man they toyed with, for she knew that one day – just like her – they would be made to pay for their insolence. John Hall would never allow a slight to pass lightly. He'd simply wait till they needed some of his doctoring. Then they'd pay dearly, of that she'd little doubt. She glanced over her shoulder again. All her idle wondering meant he was gaining on her. Stop thinking about him. Look at Robert.

'Harlot!' Hall cried out after Susanna. The Stratford women shrieked and booed at their doctor. The men of the town fairly split their sides laughing.

'Can't control yer wife, eh Doctor?' one of them jeered as he raced past.

'Strumpet of Babylon!' Hall shouted.

The men burst into louder peals of laughter.

'Quoting the Bible won't bring her back!' the vintner roared.

Susanna knew her husband thought she had nowhere to go, just as she knew she'd regret making a public spectacle of him if she were caught. But then again, as he'd told her often while beating her raw with a riding crop, the Shakespeares were good at making public spectacles. If he caught up with her this time, she'd be punished till her skin was lashed with a dozen streaks of blood. Well, since she'd decided her life was worth living a little while longer, she just wouldn't allow him to catch her. She had things to do before she met her Maker, and she was going to do them now.

Susanna spurred herself on, as if flaying Dr Hall's riding crop on her own haunches. Nothing and no one could stop her. She'd get on that cart with Robert and that was the end of it. Her father would have to give her some money, leastways until she could get a new start in life. He owed her that for all the years of misery he'd made by talking her into marrying Doctor John Hall. Susanna looked over her shoulder again. Her husband seemed as determined as she, and, for all her headstart, he was gaining ground.

'Obey me, woman! I am your master!'

Susanna heard the uproar of laughter from the townspeople and it gave her hope. Though near exhaustion, she found the strength to sprint faster. The crowd parted before her, cheering her on, until at last, Robert turned towards her. She could see that the cart was only half loaded with provisions. Surely they didn't need so much to travel the forty miles to Oxford? She tugged at the heavy satchel and glanced down. Her father's original manuscripts and his medicines were still tucked away safely.

'By God's wounds, suffer not the Lord's eternal damnation woman! Stop!' Hall bellowed.

The front door to her parents' home, New Place, swung open. Anne Shakespeare stood framed in the doorway, surrounded by the patchwork of thorny rose branches, taking in the spectacle. Susanna's sister, the dark and beautiful Judith, stretched on tiptoe in the shadows behind their mother, trying to see what all the fuss was about. Suddenly, Anne gasped. Everyone was gawping and laughing at her eldest daughter.

'Quick, Judith,' Anne commanded, thrusting a key at her. 'Check the manuscripts are still locked in the study cupboard.'

Anne strained to see over the crowd. 'Robert Whatcott!' she called out. 'What the devil are you playing at?'

Robert heard Mistress Anne's rasping voice above the hollering behind him. He looked 'round to her warily, mostly pondering on what he'd do if Susanna hadn't got hold of the manuscripts and how he'd get them for the Master if she'd failed. There Mistress Anne stood, waving her arms in that furious way of hers. If he didn't know no better, Robert could've sworn she wanted him to look behind him. So, he turned. Susanna was hurtling towards him, that big leather satchel of her father's at her back. He frowned at the sight of her, all dishevelled and breathless like, with that jewelled cloak she'd been sewing with such care all twisted up round her neck. That her dog of hers, Chaos, was poking his head out of some clothes, swaying to and fro in her arms, like one of them Arabian kings he'd heard tell of. Robert turned back to Anne. Behind her, Judith flailed her arms too, as if some grave misfortune had befallen her. Whatever Judith said it shocked her mother, for Anne cupped her hands to her mouth and shouted, 'Robert! Stop Susanna now!'

Robert turned back towards Susanna, wishing he had a hand free to scratch his aching head. Then he saw that husband of hers leggin' it up Chapel Street.

'Stop her, Robert! I command you,' Hall called out.

Robert had no need of any rhyme or reason behind that particular husband chasing his wife up the street. Susanna was in trouble, and he had vowed to Master Shakespeare long ago that he'd always protect her. It was his duty as the Shakespeares' trusted manservant.

Robert looked back to Mistress Anne and was suddenly overcome with one of them quandaries that so often plagued him. His job was to protect Mistress Anne too. And here she was, her thin arms pumping, powering herself up the garden path towards him. He couldn't tell if she meant to thump him, or stop Susanna, or lay into Hall. Maybe it were all three?

—

11

Still, Mistress Anne's latest black mood mustn't keep him from looking after Susanna, for she was his favourite. He turned and puffed out his chest at Dr Hall. And just then, a woman's booted foot thrust out from the crowd, catching Hall on the ankle. The doctor fairly well flew face down into the kettle dirt in the middle of the road. The townspeople shrieked and applauded with delight as Hall squirmed in the mire. Some wronged husbands were so delighted that they threw their hats up in the air for the sheer joy of it.

Susanna saw none of this. Her mind was set on only one thing: getting into that cart and leaving Stratford to the demons that tied her there. Robert held out a gloved hand, but she ignored it. She raced straight past, mounted the driver's bench and tossed the laundry, the dog and the satchel onto the footwell. She grabbed the reins and called out to him. 'If you're coming you'd best hurry,' she said, nearly breathless.

Her husband tried to stand up in the gutter, but slid and fell again. The crowd jeered and tittered. Finally, Hall rolled out and stood to his full height, dripping in muck.

'NOW, Robert!' Susanna cried.

Robert saw Mistress Anne running towards them.

'NOW!' Susanna shouted again.

He looked to the food and drink at the side of the cart. Without all his provisions, how could they make do?

Susanna hailed the horses and released the cart brake. Robert saw the wheels start to roll. He grabbed hold and climbed aboard as she gave a quick flick of the reins.

The townspeople hooted and clapped as if it were the best comedy they'd ever seen. Hall, a sorrowful figure of a man and stinking of muck, stood fuming. Robert turned round. It seemed to him that the doctor were clinging to his last gasp of dignity, when Hall cried out, 'Wife! By all that is Holy, I forbid you to leave Stratford!'

One of their neighbours called back, 'Bit late for that, friend!'

Anne stood near Hall in the road, shaking her fist at Susanna and Robert. There was an almighty cry of laughter from the townspeople.

Hall scowled at them. Anne turned, now shaking her fist at him. 'Standing there glowering won't get them back, John. Go after them! They've thieved away the manuscripts.'

'And my medicines!' Hall shouted back.

He searched to left and right. Suddenly, he spied a tethered horse – a fine mare – and leaped onto it, riding at a gallop after them. He spurred the horse on, crying 'Stop! Thief!'

Susanna looked back once more. Were they calling out to her as the thief? Her heart sank as she saw Hall whipping that pretty mare with a crop.

'Robert,' she shouted above the din, 'here.' She thrust the reins at him.

He did as she bade. His eyes widened as Susanna clambered over the seat into the back.

'Head for the London Road,' she called to him.

'But, there's –'

'Go!'

Robert veered the wagon to cross the bridge just in time. Susanna toppled over and all manner of things clanged and clattered in the back of the cart. But there was no time for him to fret over all that so long as Hall chased after them. He looked over his shoulder and saw that Hall, too, had just made the turning. Robert felt his heart rise in his throat and became sorely afeared that his days as the Shakespeares' manservant were over if Susanna's husband caught them up.

Robert flicked the reins, barking, 'Hurry, you nags!' But they were carthorses and couldn't outrun a fine mare.

Susanna rummaged through their meagre provisions and grabbed the nearest thing – a loaf of bread – and hurled it at her husband. Robert winced. There went one loaf of the two he'd loaded up. She reached down for some hunks of cheese and took aim. Despite her desperation, she'd never forgive herself if she hit any poor animal, much less a fine mare. She lobbed volley after volley of her homemade Cheddar, but Hall ducked from side to side then looked up smiling, unscathed. Robert's heart sank. They'd starve, that's what they'd do. They'd starve in some glade in the middle of nowhere if she didn't stop tossing food about.

But Susanna didn't stop. She scoured the back of the cart for what else she could throw, when she spied an old tankard. Grasping it, she closed an eye taking careful aim, then let fly. Hall spurred his mare on faster, and the tankard landed harmlessly on the road behind him. Her husband was only a horse's length behind them now.

'When I get you home, you'll wish you were dead,' he bellowed.

It was just what Robert needed to hear. With such a threat he'd be disobeying Master Shakespeare's wishes if he failed to drive the carthorses as hard as those Four Horsemen in that there Apocalypse. So, Robert flicked the reins harder, calling out, 'Run like the wind, you nags!' But the poor jades were already running as fast as they could.

Up ahead Robert saw the ford was still high, most likely coz a branch of the river had silted over again further upstream. He'd tried warning Susanna about that, but – well, but me no buts, as the Master would've said. Now their hopes rested on getting through the ford at full tilt, and pray Hall's mare would play her part well. Robert gave one of his elfin grins. With one last flick of the rein, he drove his carthorses forward. Only when he heard the splash as they sliced through the ford could he relax his grip. As the hail of water rose higher, he peered over his shoulder. Hall's mare reared up in a panic, catapulting him over its head and into the ford.

Susanna blinked, hardly believing her eyes. As they pulled away, John Hall stood dripping in the ford. His mare was already trotting back towards town. She turned to Robert, beaming as their tiny cart hared off into the open countryside. She'd done it. She'd escaped. Robert gave her a comforting smile. No, that wasn't fair – *they'd* done it. Still, she felt a sudden pang.

What if her father tried to force her to return?

Chapter 2

Susanna clambered back onto the driver's bench next to Robert. Chaos whimpered at her feet, all swaddled up in the laundry she'd grabbed off the line. As she reached down to untangle him from the clothes, Chaos stepped on the corner of the jewelled cloak still wrapped 'round her neck. What had possessed her to treat something of value as if it had none? If that cloak was damaged she'd never forgive herself. As she took it off, checking it over for rips and tears, she prayed she hadn't lost the gemstones and crystals she so painstakingly sewed on from those old costumes. All sizes they were too, just like the stars in the night sky. It had planets of pearls, faraway stars of crystals, some old rubies and diamonds that made up the constellations she could spy from her bedroom window. Question was, would it please her father? Would he wear it whilst quoting some king or other from one of his plays? Would he think of her as his princess?

The thought was more foolish than any fool's. She knew full well, she was no princess. She was the fool who'd listened to her father and married John Hall. She was even more a fool for staying with the brute. Still, it was the way of things: daughters married the men their fathers wanted them to wed. How could either of them have known that John Hall was a man who hungered so after the flesh?

Robert felt an ache in his heart. Poor mite, he thought. But what could they do? Sure enough they were heading to Oxford, just as the letter from Master Shakespeare said he should, but the letter were clear as glass: bring my manuscripts and my medicines and do as I bid, Robert, or you're done for – well, maybe not those words 'xactly. And now look at him, fetching along Master Shakespeare's headstrong daughter to Oxford. He turned his mind to the road, hoping somehow he'd see the way ahead for them. But so many thoughts were roaming about in his waggling head. They twisted and churned, making him dizzy. He just had to say something, anything, to get his mind off the mess Susanna had got them both into.

He cleared his throat. 'Ahem. Seems winter's gone early this year,' Robert said, like he were talking to some stranger instead of the girl he'd seen born and helped raise up.

Susanna nodded, stroking her dog. They had put enough of a ride between them and Stratford for her to know they were no longer being followed. But still, she feared what she'd done, and the future. Heaven only knew what Robert must think. Worse, what would he say to her father, the man who cherished his privacy above all else?

Maybe talking of the weather and suchlike, as Robert did, would make her problems seem smaller. She peered around her. Winter had ended early in this year of our Lord 1615. Though it was only the end of March, the spring blossoms burgeoned in the apple and pear orchards around town. Like everyone else, Susanna was thankful they'd survived another winter without plague or the long hoar frosts of her childhood, which killed the hedgerows and froze the livestock fast to the ground.

Susanna gazed at the beauty of the English countryside. Lapwings danced gracefully in the air. The rolling hills tamed by man's hand were bursting with spring. Even the neatly cut hawthorn hedgerows had grown new leaves. Soon they'd be beyond the furthest point she'd ever travelled from home. The hedgerows would give way to Cotswold stone walls. The mellow brick farmhouses would fade to marmalade then honey stone buildings. At least that's what her father had once said. She took a deep breath. There was something magical about this early spring, so different from all the years past. Maybe it was the scent of freedom. Or perhaps it was the sense of adventure. She looked over to Robert and smiled weakly.

'It surely seems so, Robert,' she finally replied.

He noticed the dark circles under her eyes for the first time. How long had her eyes been like that? Since when had she sprouted those tiny worry lines on her brow? She were meant to be in the prime of her life at nearly thirty-three, and look at her. The sleeve of her gown was all torn from her shoulder. His eye strayed warily to the laces of her bodice. They'd been ripped with some force, like someone'd tried to tear them clean off. His heart pounded, his mind suddenly raced razor-sharp. Though he'd little education and less of life's experiences, Robert knew the tell-tale signs. He spurred his carthorses on. May Dr John Hall burn in hell.

When they got to Oxford he'd tell Master Shakespeare. He'd tell him how Dr Hall shamed the whole family by his chasing after Susanna crying out his Puritan hell-and-damnation drivel, and then all would be forgiven. The Master will know how to fix it surely as the day is hounded by night. O, how his wriggling head ached. He harked back to the Master's letter. Fetch my original manuscripts. Where's the jewelled cloak? Don't breathe a word of your Master's plans – and 'specially *not* to Susanna. And above all, bring Dr Hall's medicines for the falling sickness. So what had he done? Robert closed his eyes, sick with how things had spiralled out of control and how nothing had gone the way the Master intended.

'I suppose the snow's gone for good this year,' was all he could think to say to Susanna.

She looked up at the clouds drifting lazily across the bright blue sky. Snow had fallen on high ground, she knew, but precious little had settled in the fields around Stratford. Whilst a mild and dry winter was feted by city folk, in Warwickshire the yeomen farmers and their kin knew that unless rain fell soon there would be a heatwave, drought, failed crops and little to eat by the coming winter.

'Now we must pray for rain,' she said, snuggling her dog to her.

'Course, Robert had heard many complain on the warmth of the season and how dry and dusty the highway to Oxford were. In an echo of his thought, his stomach rumbled like thunder. He cast a quick glance at Susanna to beg his pardon. But she was gazing up at the weaving red kites on the hunt and hadn't taken any heed. His stomach growled again. Well, it would, he told himself. He'd no breakfast really, what with the comings and goings of the morning. Only some fresh-baked bread and jam and two cups of warmed mead had passed his poor, parched lips. Why, it was hardly enough to keep his rounded body ticking over. How they'd make their way to Oxford with precious little food didn't bear thinking on. With half of it left by the roadside in front of the Master's home and the other half tossed out of the cart at Dr Hall, he feared they'd starve if Susanna hadn't brought enough money to pay for meals at an inn. He shuddered.

'You're not chilled, are you Robert?'

He kept his eyes on the road ahead. The shudder was for hisself, afeared that he'd starve. He shook his head and they rode on. Then another thought worried him like a blasted raspberry seed stuck between two back teeth. Some of the more mean-spirited townspeople would think that Susanna ran from her husband of these ten years to scarper with *him*. 'Course this made him see things in a light of a terrifying colour when it came to the Master. Just then, as if the gods were mocking him, he saw a deep rut in the road ahead and swerved the horses. This is just about the biggest rut in the road I've got myself into, he thought. By suppertime, the whole town will judge that Susanna'd run off with me.

'You feeling ill?' Susanna asked.

He heard the kindness in her voice. Couldn't she see what she'd gone and done? For the first time ever, he felt anger growing fast against her – she who he'd loved as his own daughter since forever.

'Susanna,' Robert began.

She tried to hold his gaze but he looked down at the dog.

'You sure named him well,' was all Robert could muster for now.

She stroked the dog. 'Chaos?'

He nodded. Chaos. That's what their situation was. Pure Chaos.

'Whoever heard of a dog called "Chaos" – though it's a good name for the mess we're in, aint it?'

Susanna turned her head away. Chaos was the only soul who loved her. He was a scruffy thing, found half-dead along the river one morning a few years back, mauled by the swans, she reckoned. She'd nursed him back to health, sneaking recipes from her husband's medical books on how to treat infections and dress wounds, never leaving the poor dog's side. John was livid, naturally. Claimed that the dog was causing 'chaos' in their lives and that Susanna was neglecting her family. So she called him Chaos, and promised her husband that once the poor thing was better she'd find him a good home. Yet Chaos stayed and had become the only love she knew.

'Chaos is a perfect name for a dog,' she shrugged. 'And what mess is it that you refer to anyway, Robert Whatcott?'

He could hear the edge in her voice. Nothing like her mother's or her sister's, mind. More like one of them paper-thin edges. But he couldn't blame her when she was treated no better than kennel dirt.

'Don't you see?' he asked, swerving from another rut in the road.

'I've eyes.'

'I mean, Susanna, don't you see how people have mistook it? I mean, you're running away from him and all – I mean how you left town – charging towards *me*?'

She thought for a moment. Would folk believe she was running into his arms? Why, that was just plain – oh.

'Only the evil-minded ones would dare to think such a thing!' she said, cross with herself that she hadn't cared if she'd be done to death by sland'rous tongues.

'And Stratford doesn't have such folk?' he asked.

Stratford had more than its fair slice of those who wished her ill, she reckoned. But surely no one thought poorly of Robert?

'They might believe it of me, but not of you,' she said.

'Just picture what they saw and how they all laughed. Then think on how you know Master Shakespeare don't take kindly to people knowing the family's business.'

Susanna pondered the problem. Just because she'd decided on the turning of the wind to run off, how did that change things for those she'd left behind? Her mother, her sister and even her husband all had a hand in her sudden decision. But not Robert. Robert was kind and brave and innocent. Robert was loyal and faithful. A king amongst servants. She smiled slenderly at him. Huge of heart, slight of paunch, slighter of height and hair but sweeter and more comely than the darling buds of May, Robert Whatcott was above all else her closest friend.

'What made you do it, Susanna?'

What indeed, she asked herself.

That morning, Susanna had opened the shutters to reveal the grey and indigo dawn. She sighed and recalled, like so many mornings past, at how unlikely it would be for her to travel down that dry, dusty London Road, as her father had done for the past forty years. Like all those mornings before, when she tended to miss him most, she thought on how she'd never left Stratford and its environs, and how she'd probably never have any call to do so as long as she lived.

Susanna opened the window and took a deep breath. The penetrating chill of the morning air had gone. What if this spring proved a false rebirth or no rain fell? The reply came to her as naturally as this becalmed dawn: many would soon lose their battle for life in this harsh English countryside. But we all lose our battles for life eventually, she mused. What was it her father had written all that time ago? *All the world's a stage, and all the men and women merely players; They have their exits and their entrances, and one man in his time plays many parts.* This morning, Stratford seemed somehow unreal to her, stage-like, or at least how she imagined a picture of a stage to be. After all, she'd never seen a play or been to a playhouse.

Susanna turned away from the first trails of pink and orange fringed with pale blue on the horizon and readied herself for the day ahead. The lark's birdsong had begun. The day was marching on. It was one thing for spring to come early and to fret about no rain, and quite another for the day's bread not to be baked, she thought, as she descended the stairs. A quick glance beneath the surgery door told her that a candle flickered within, and that her husband was already at work, preparing his potions, recipes and cures for the latest evil to befall the sick and dying. Susanna shook her head. Pity was, he didn't seem to care that their marriage had been dead for years. Then again, had it ever been alive?

And so, like all the other mornings past, she made her way into the kitchen and stoked the flames with fresh faggots under the cauldron. She felt like an unwilling and fresh-faced child, clinging to the tattered threads of the life that had been built for her. Today would be a day like any other; a day to brave the chill in her heart until evening came. Only then would sleep rescue her. Only then could she think back to the bank where the wild thyme blows, to the fairy stories her father once told her from his battered skiff as he punted them along the River Avon. But that was a past now buried. Buried with her brother Hamnet. Today was just another day, empty of the love and warmth of times long lost.

As steam began to rise from the cauldron of mead she was warming for her husband, Susanna pulled her smock over her head and tucked her hair under her cap. She recalled the time when she'd served her husband his warmed mead not long after they were wed, and how she'd neglected to put her cap on. How his eyes widened when he raised his tankard and saw one of her hairs across its rim. How he ranted about her being 'filthy' and 'unclean' and how her father and mother hadn't taught her the least little thing. When she protested, her husband tossed the warmed mead in her face. She shook off the memory. Lesson learned. Never again would she go near the cauldron or serving vessels without her hair firmly tucked under her cap.

As was her custom every morning, she brought the flagon of mead with a doorstop of bread and homemade cheese to the surgery door and knocked.

'Wait!' her husband's voice called out hoarsely.

Susanna bit her lip, then bent down to peek through the keyhole. He had his back to her whilst his arm moved up and down rapidly. She straightened herself with a start, knowing that he was satisfying his manly urges. Again. Wasn't once a day enough for any man? Well, he'd do as he must, and so must she. Swiftly, she placed the tray on the table in the passageway and made for the kitchen. It was high time she got on with baking the bread at her mother's home. Susanna grabbed her shawl from the hook, gathered it around her and flung open the kitchen door.

She didn't know or care, since she was long out of earshot a few streets away, that Dr John Hall eventually called to her, 'Come in!'

Chapter 3

The muffled bells tolled mournfully from first light. A solemn crowd well-wishers gathered in the quadrangle of Oxford's Magdalen College. Muffled bells for the dead or dying were a familiar sound, for the city had known many a tragedy since its first recorded history in 911, in the days of the Saxon king, Alfred the Great. From the time its first college was founded in 1249, Oxford had been the hotbed of new thought in the realm, with more than its share of treasons, burnings and bonfires. But this time was different.

This time every soul in the city mourned. As word of the latest tragedy was whispered on the lips of each passer-by, the crowd swelled inside the gates of Magdalen College until it could hold no more. Instead of the usual carnival atmosphere awaiting the death of a famous person, the townspeople stood in a reverent hush. Some seemed cowed by the imminent loss of such a good friend. Each mournful face turned to the huge oak door beyond which he lay dying. Each knew that so long as the bells tolled on, he lived. And where there was life, they had to believe, there was also hope.

All of a sudden, a murmur rose from the back of the crowd as a lone figure pressed past. Most let him by, recognising that only he could stop the inevitable. Others turned round indignantly to give the man jostling them a proper fig, until they saw that it was old Basil, the apothecary. 'Where physick had failed, old Basil would prevail,' a townswoman proclaimed.

Old Basil passed snail-like through the throng. Amid his 'pardon me's' and his muttered 'ahems', the crowd sensed the urgency in his slow progress. His furrowed brow and rabbit eyes, darting little arrows pricking at those who blocked his progress, seemed to shout louder than any spoken word. Occasionally, Basil was obliged to lay a wizened hand on the shoulder of someone he knew, until, after several minutes, he reached the studded oak door, grey with age.

Guarding it was a twelve-year-old boy with furtive chestnut-brown eyes, wearing worn breeches, scuffed boots and a faded green jerkin. But it was the hand-drawn badge of a falcon with outstretched wings holding a spear that gave him his authority, for it signalled he was William Shakespeare's servant. Old Basil knew the boy, just as the boy knew him. So when the apothecary broke through the front line of well-wishers, the boy's eyes lit up in relief and he gave the secret knock. Basil beamed down at him and touched the boy's sandy hair as if in benediction. The boy answered with a sad smile.

Seconds later, in reply to his knock, the great oak door creaked open. A heart-rending roar rose up from the well-wishers. A tall, dark man with piercing cornflower-blue eyes and a trimmed salt and pepper beard peered out from within. Seeing old Basil, a piteous sigh like a gentle wind, escaped his lips. He grabbed the apothecary by the arm and pulled him inside. As he made to shut the door, the man saw the forlorn look on the boy's face, as if he'd asked how he should explain Basil's arrival to the crowd. The man stepped forward and raised his arms to command silence. A hush fell like a stone.

'Friends, pray peace!' he began. 'Some of you may know me as a player upon the stage. I am John Heminges, fellow sharer in the King's Men and great friend of the man you all wish well. Master Shakespeare is thankful for your many kindnesses, but prays you not stand vigil for him, as there are others more deserving of your love. If you do wish to remain here, however, all I ask is that you do so in silence.'

A man's voice piped up roughly, 'Will Master Shakespeare live?'

Heminges hesitated, gazing with a watery eye from one expectant face to another. 'We can only hope and pray he does.'

With that, Heminges retreated. The boy turned his back to the oak door, resuming his post as Shakespeare's guardian angel.

Heminges and old Basil looked at one another. Only heaven knew if this man could relieve the malady. But since Shakespeare had refused any physician and had lost his power of speech, Basil's help was essential until the medicines arrived from Stratford.

The apothecary bent over his patient. Shakespeare had been lying ill for more than two days.

Heminges spoke in a hoarse voice. 'He's barely swallowed any broth.'

Henry Condell, another fellow sharer in Shakespeare's company of players, stepped forward from the shadows, as Basil poked and prodded his patient.

'How could we have let this happen?' Condell asked in a whisper.

'Blame me. You always do, Henry. But, we all played our parts. What I don't understand is why we didn't recognise the signs.'

'It's happened at least a dozen times now, John. Why did we let him go on stage when he was so ill?'

'You and I both know that Will never listens to anything we say on the matter of his health. Besides, didn't you think this was just like the other times?'

Both men stood silent for a moment, watching the apothecary carry out his craft.

'How long has he been like this?' Basil asked.

'Two days,' Heminges replied.

'So why didn't you call for me earlier?'

'The patient,' Heminges sighed. 'Before he lost the power of speech, he said he feared if we called for you, he'd die.'

'A common fear,' the apothecary said. 'Tell me, what purges have you given him?'

'None.'

The apothecary's reproachful look bore into him. 'I see... and bleedings?'

'None,' Condell said.

'And soothsaying? Stargazers, white witches or other manner of magic?'

'None,' Heminges replied.

'How about potions?'

Heminges shrugged.

Shakespeare's eyes briefly opened, darting between the men.

'We have sent for his medicines from home. It worked when he was like this in the past,' Condell said.

'So this has happened before?'

Shakespeare's eyes flickered again as Heminges nodded.

'This medicine is from a physician, I suppose?'

'His son-in-law,' Condell replied.

'I see. So why did you call for me?'

'We feared the remedies might not arrive in time.'

The apothecary motioned for Heminges to step aside with him. Shakespeare's eyes followed them.

'The son-in-law, I take it, has not been sent for?'

Shakespeare let out a sudden moan and the apothecary and Heminges rushed to his side. His body was shuddering, his mouth twisted in pain. The apothecary snapped his fingers at Condell. 'Quick! Those quills on the table!'

Condell snatched all the quills from the holder on the writing table and the apothecary bound them together with string from his cloak pocket. He shoved them lengthwise across the patient's contorted mouth to stop him swallowing his tongue. Shakespeare bit down on them, writhing.

'What if Will dies?' Condell whispered.

'We'd lose our soul.'

As suddenly as it had begun, the seizure subsided.

'It's the falling sickness,' the apothecary pronounced as he took the snapped quills from Shakespeare's mouth. 'How long has he had it?'

Condell and Heminges exchanged looks.

'For some time now,' Heminges said. 'But it's been worse of late.'

'I see. And you don't know what these medicines you sent for are made from?'

The two men shook their heads.

'Right. Send a trusted man with me to my shop for tincture of white peony. It will at least relieve his pain and the spasms in his hands.'

'And the seizures?' Condell asked.

'In the hands of God,' the apothecary replied. He turned away and was gone.

Heminges and Condell stood vigil, like desolate bookends at the foot of Shakespeare's bed. They had sent their lead boy actor, Nathan Field, to fetch the tincture to calm Will's excited humours. They stood frozen, gazing down at the sleeping patient.

'How much longer?' Condell asked, wringing his hands.

'For what?'

'Robert, of course.'

'Depends on the road. But the letter should have been delivered over a day ago.'

'So what could be taking him so long?'

Heminges shrugged. 'Perhaps he had trouble finding everything on the list? Perhaps Will's wife – '

'You don't think *she* read the letter?' Condell's eyes grew wide in alarm.

'You mean, if she read the letter she might destroy everything out of spite?'

Condell let out a gasp and began to wring his hands again.

'You must get hold of yourself, Henry. Whatever happened to Robert, whatever Anne Shakespeare did or didn't do, we'll need to grasp any problems and solve them for Will's sake. Understood?'

Condell, for the first time in months, if not years, closed his eyes to pray.

Chapter 4

It was a morning like any other in Warwickshire. The dawn chorus of wood pigeons had begun, when suddenly the swans gliding on the Avon were rattled, flapping their wings wildly to ward off some evil that hurtled unseen in their direction. In the distance, a rhythmic thud grew louder, until at last, the single horse's hooves with its rolling gallop drowned out nature's morning song.

A livery horse thundered north on the London Road towards Stratford, its nostrils flaring and its breath laboured, the rider hunched forward in the saddle gripping its matted mane. Time seemed to be the rider's enemy, for he whipped the poor beast mercilessly. As its hooves clattered onto the wooden bridge at Ettington, birds set off into scattered flight, and many a bedroom shutter flew open to see what was going on. A lone rider at dawn was never a good omen.

Several hours later, Susanna and Robert rode along in silence. She pondered again why she'd chosen today of all days to escape her life in Stratford. Was it the letter delivered by the livery rider? Or her husband? Or was it her mother and sister, Judith? Was it the playwrights seeking their own bubble reputation, hoping she'd deliver their plays to her father?

As always, Susanna had begun her day at her mother's home. She walked across the courtyard carrying freshly dried rushes when a window creaked open above her.

'By God's eyes, Susanna, stop frittering the day away!'

She looked up at her mother's scowling face and stared blankly.

'Get those rushes down, girl, and set the bread to rise. And when you're done with that, you've those playwrights to see to. Then I'll be needing you in the brew house.

Before Susanna could answer, the window slammed shut. She walked on. Why should today be different from the others? Well, her mother would have to wait till she collected her parcels from the market stalls. She could only run as fast as time could carry her, she mused, dropping the rushes onto the parlour floor. A cloud of fine flowers sparkled in the early morning sun. Instead of spreading them as usual, she grabbed her shawl and headed for the front door.

She flung it open and there they were. Framed in the doorway was a brace of playwrights waving and smiling.

'Morning Mistress Hall,' the tall skinny one said.

Susanna nodded to him and saw that he was fingering a roll of papers nervously.

'I'm sure you don't remember me but –'

Susanna smiled. 'O, but I do.'

The second playwright chirped, 'Morning, Mistress Hall.'

Susanna smiled and curtseyed. He was short and tubby with ruddy cheeks. 'Do I know you?'

The tub was taken aback, as if no one had ever forgotten him. 'Lammas Day last year? The Earl of Warwick's men? I played the role of –'

Susanna shook her head. 'No. Must have been my younger sister.'

Another voice piped up behind them. 'Perhaps I may be of assistance?'

The playwrights turned. A handsome man carrying a basket strolled up the path.

'I believe, Mistress Hall, that these parcels awaited you at the market stalls?' he said, elbowing aside the first two as he handed the basket into Susanna's arms.

'I thank you,' she said. It had been a considerate gesture from an attractive fellow with fine cobalt blue eyes. It merited a better return payment. 'Kind sir, are you another playmaker?'

The handsome man bowed low and swept his cap off his curly blond head. 'Aye Mistress, I'm not ashamed to admit that I follow the same craft as your good father.'

The tubby playwright butted in, 'I come to Stratford to see your good father too.'

The tall thin one jostled himself back to the front, waving his manuscript. 'The tale I have here is one to cure deafness! It's an ancient tale new-told, about a pirate queen and – '

'Interesting. I must see that one,' Susanna said.

The handsome playwright swooped under the tall one's arm. 'My play is a tale of woe, of love denied and a wicked king.'

The tall playwright shuffled in front of the handsome one.

Susanna shifted her basket of provisions to her hip and was about to speak when the little tub shouldered his way past. 'Mistress, old tales new-told and tales of woe? Puh! Such tales are told by idiots, signifying not a fig. Mine is about mistaken identities and children lost.'

'Sounds depressing,' Susanna shuddered.

'Ah, but it ends well,' the tall thin playwright interrupted, still selling his own work to Susanna.

'What? The children lost?' Susanna asked, craning her neck to see the tubby one.

The tall playwright crinkled his brow. 'No, mine's the ancient tale new-told about a pirate queen!'

She looked at the three of them in turn. The conversation was like bobbing for apples and made her dizzy following what each was saying. She'd toyed with them long enough. Soon her mother would call out for her to go to the brew house.

'I've no head for plays or playmakers I fear, but since you so kindly entertained me, and you, sir, fetched my basket for me, I'll take your plays and give them to my father when he's next at home.'

Each tendered his play into Susanna's basket, bowing and scraping backwards from the front doorstep.

The handsome playwright looked at her as he left his play on top of the pile and winked. 'You are an angel, Mistress.'

She smiled graciously at him and asked herself, does he truly think he can charm his way into my father's life?

And with that thought biting her mind, she smiled once more before kicking the door shut in his face.

Susanna looked down at the plays and sighed. All those playwrights. Every day. She stepped into the front parlour, where the fire roared, and with a twinge of conscience, tossed the plays onto the flames.

'Robert?' she called.

Within seconds, he appeared. He saw the fire blazing with the mountain of papers blackening and curling, and knew that they'd had a visitation from would-be playmakers. 'More works of genius to warm our hearths I see.'

She gave him a wry look and breezed past, handing him her basket.

'I'll need some time to myself, Robert.'

'But, you know your mother –'

Susanna turned back. Robert had been her helpmate in her small escapes for as long as she could recall. Dear Robert. 'I've strange and wondrous lands to behold if only for a few moments. Please?'

His eyes twinkled. What was the crime in Susanna stealing off for a short while to visit her father's words? He'd never understand why Mistress Anne were so against it. He smiled at a secret shared as Susanna hopped up the stairs as lightly as a sparrow to her father's study.

As she disappeared Robert sighed. 'And I've Lady Macbeth's tongue to pacify.'

Susanna entered her father's study. She had kept it just as he'd left it three long years ago, coming in only to dust and polish and put each quill, each cherished book and letter back in place with the loving care of a young mother for her child. Whenever she visited his study she was sure to leave it as if her father might stroll back in at any moment. She pictured his delight when he'd see his old fiefdom ordered high with his books – Ovid, Plutarch, Plautus and others – all in his unique jumble placed on shelves, in nooks and crannies and on his writing table, seemingly without the slightest thought. Yet, nothing could be further from the truth. He had left this place in mid-thought, and needed to return to it just as it was, so he could pick up the thread.

Sunlight streamed into the room where many of her father's plays and poems had been honed. She opened the small cedar chest that held his original manuscripts, reluctantly left in the family's safekeeping. Susanna closed her eyes. Where did she feel like travelling today? To fair Verona? To cold, windswept Elsinore in Denmark? Or back in time to greet Falstaff and Prince Hal? She opened her eyes and saw the knotted garden she'd planted with her father when she was a child. She resolved that today she'd travel to the French court where he'd planted his own knotted garden in a feast of words. She thumbed through the comedies until she found *Love's Labour's Lost.*

She took the manuscript over to her father's tattered armchair by the window overlooking the garden, cradling his tightly-handwritten pages. There were angry crossings-out and impatient notes that scarred the margins. She could see how his hand had hurried to get down his thoughts. This play, like so many others, had become her touchstone to her father's world.

She turned to the first act where he described how they had decided where to plant the knot-garden at home in Stratford all those years before. Through his imaginings, he had transformed the placement of their garden into a key part of the scene:

KING. So it is, besieged with sable-coloured melancholy. I did commend the black oppressing humour to the most wholesome physic of thy health-giving air, and as I am a gentleman betook myself for a walk. The time, when? About the sixth hour when the beasts best graze, the birds best peck and men sit themselves down to that nourishment they call supper–

Susanna lifted her gaze from the page. She thought she heard a shrill voice calling out her name and tuned her ear for her mother's steps. It was a sure thing she would be tossed into a harridan's fury if she saw Susanna reading her father's plays. She held her breath until the voice trailed off into the distance. She resumed her journey that had begun in their knot garden in Stratford:

KING. Where, I mean, I did encounter that obscene and most preposterous event that draweth from my snow-white pen the ebon-coloured ink, which here thou viewest, beholdest, surveyest, or seest. But to the place, where? It standeth north-north-east and by east from the west corner of thy curious knotted garden: there did I see that low-spirited swain, that base minnow of thy mirth –

COSTARD. Me?

KING. That unlettered small-knowing soul.

COSTARD. Me?

KING. That shallow vassal –

COSTARD. Still me?

Susanna looked up and smiled at their curious garden glistening in the morning dew. How her father could write such emotion into so few words filled her with wonderment. She thought, not for the first time, how often the university men had mocked him as an unlettered small-knowing soul, a crow pretending to don the cloak of the mighty peacock. A thunderous voice interrupted her thoughts.

'If you're amongst his plays again, I'll –'

Susanna's pulse quickened in her throat. Before she could close the manuscript and put it away, her mother tore into the room like some banshee wailing its mournful cry in search of her dying son.

'I knew it!' she screeched.

Susanna blinked in fear. Her sister Judith stood behind their mother, her face ablaze with a sinister smile.

'Didn't I tell you I needed you?'

'Yes, Mother.'

'Didn't Robert repeat my message?'

'Yes, Mother.'

'So why didn't you do as you were bid?'

'I'd done my morning chores and –'

'I decide when you've finished your chores.'

Judith smirked. Susanna narrowed her eyes at her.

'Stop that, you marble-hearted girl. Your sister's done nothing.'

Susanna was speechless. Why was their mother blind to Judith's malice?

'I rue the day *he* taught you to read. I –'

'Not again, Mother, please.'

Judith laced her arm through their mother's.

Anne's cheeks were flushed with anger. 'I rue the day as heartily as the day I married him.'

'Mother,' she began in a voice as mellifluous as the sweetest dainties, 'He's my father as you are my mother.'

'No. You're *his* daughter,' Anne looked at Judith. 'Just as Judith is her mother's glass.'

Susanna's heart burst. No matter how many loaves of bread she baked, or meals she cooked, or household accounts she prepared, or provisions she bought, or toiling on the family's farm holdings scything and winnowing, or keeling the mash into ale, or brewing mead from their honey, or pretending to be kind to would-be playmakers then destroying their dreams, or sewing, darning or anything else that could be expected of man, woman or beast – her mother hated her. Nothing could erase the shame of her being the babe who had forced the eighteen-year-old Will Shakespeare to make Anne Hathaway, eight years his senior, his wife.

So Anne never forgave Susanna and doted on Judith. Judith – that poor surviving twin– had whatever she wanted, as if it somehow made up for their brother Hamnet's death, aged twelve. The hours she spent primping and preening in front of that Venetian mirror their father had bought her, daydreaming of marriage to some local swain, when as Shakespeare's younger daughter, she could aim higher. But she was always one for looking at a pretty face instead of a warm heart or a full purse, and Judith would clearly marry badly. Yet, unlike Susanna, Judith would be allowed her choice of husband.

Meanwhile, none of them was aware that the express rider was barrelling into town from the London Road. He was in a terrible hurry, rattling across the Clopton Bridge, then north to the Market Cross, narrowly missing the muckraker wheeling a cartload of manure to the tannery on Henley Street. In his haste to make way, the muckraker's cart was overturned, but by the time he'd muttered his anger, the rider had reached the Shakespeare home on Chapel Street, dismounted and banged on the front door knocker.

Susanna heard the knock and made to reply.

'Don't think I've finished with you,' Anne warned.

Susanna heard Robert open the front door.

'You think you're so smart, Susanna,' Judith piped up, 'just coz father taught you to read!'

'He tried to teach you too, but you wouldn't learn.'

'She's more sense than you. Knows her station, does Judith,' Anne scoffed.

Judith agreed. 'Reading fills your head with tosh.'

'Is that why you go off with any handsome swain who'll have you?'

'She's more to offer any handsome swain than you ever had,' Anne's acid tongue bit back.

'Maybe because she wasn't married off to the first comer, like me.' The words escaped Susanna's lips before she could stop them spilling out.

'Nor will she be,' Anne answered.

'Father was poorer then. You got the best he could get for you, seeing how plain you are and all.'

Susanna looked sadly from her mother to her sister. 'Seems to me he's all the poorer now than he was back then. Mother, please, this anger doesn't suit the mother of my childhood. Let the past go?'

Anne stood still, speechless for some seconds. 'That was before.'

'Before what, Mother? What has made you so bitter?'

'What happened between your father and me is our affair.'

'It drove him from the family home,' Susanna said. 'Tell us, please? If we can't help, at least we can understand better and give you our compassion freely.'

Anne shook her head. Tears welled up in her eyes. 'Agreed we'd never talk about it.'

'Please, Mother?' Susanna went to hold her mother's hand, but Anne pulled away.

She wiped the tears from her cheeks and shook her head again. 'No, Susanna. It's my secret, and I'll take it with me to the grave. So will your father.'

They all jumped at the knock at the door. 'Sorry to disturb, Mistress,' Robert bowed as he entered. He held out a letter to Anne.

'It's addressed to me, Mistress, but I knew I'd best show it to you,' he said.

'Humpf!' Anne snatched it away. She mouthed the words as she read. 'Wants his manuscripts, does he?'

'And the jewelled cloak Susanna was making up and his medicines,' Robert added. 'But, it's meant to be, uh, hush-hush-like.'

Anne waved the letter at him. 'He writes most of his secrets. A secret written can be published.' She cast a withering glance at

Susanna. 'Well, he can't have the manuscripts. That wasn't the bargain.'

Robert's jaw dropped. 'But Mistress Anne, I–'

'Mother, please,' Susanna interrupted.

Anne rounded on Susanna and took the manuscript from her. She marched over to the desk, placed it back in the cedar chest and banged down the lid.

'No. Gave me his word he did,' Anne said.

Susanna drew near. 'Mother, he's not breaking his word. He only asks for his manuscripts.'

'Broke his word before when he had those filthy poems published. I'll not have that shame again. Surely you see that much?' She took a key out of her pocket and locked the cedar chest.

'Mother–'

'Made up my mind,' Anne interrupted, returning the chest to the corner cupboard. She turned the key in the lock and placed it onto her household key ring.

She crumpled Robert's letter and shoved it into Susanna's hand. 'No one reads the manuscripts now. Not you. Not your father.'

Susanna stared dumbfounded.

Anne wagged a finger at Robert. 'Tell Master Shakespeare what I said. Susanna, go fetch his medicines and that cloak. He can have those.' And with that, she was gone.

Susanna opened the creased letter and read:

Robert, I greet you well! We're playing at the festival of plays in Oxford. Come to Magdalen College in all haste with my handwritten manuscripts from the cedar chest with the brass hinges. Ask Susanna to give you the jewelled cloak she's so kindly been making for me and to beg her good husband the doctor to make up some more of my medicines. Come quickly – and no dallying over a pint to tell everyone Master Shakespeare's business. And above all, come alone! WS

'A festival of plays?' she muttered. 'If only …'

'Pray, tell me,' Robert pleaded, 'how can I bring the manuscripts to your father now? He'll roast me if I go to Oxford without them.'

But Susanna thought only on how she longed to see her father perform. How she wanted to know what had driven him from home. If she could see one of his plays performed, then maybe she would understand him better. Then she recalled that he shouldn't need more medicines for at least another three months.

'You leave that to me, Robert,' she said, walking to the desk. 'Now go pack up the cart with the provisions you'll be needing.'

'But what about Mistress Anne?'

'I'll handle my mother.'

Robert headed out the door, shaking his head. Susanna grabbed her father's satchel and the letter opener. She went to the corner cupboard and twisted the blade into the lock until it gave, then placed the cedar chest on the floor. She forced the letter opener behind the escutcheon and stomped on it with her boot until its lock broke off. Smiling to herself, she shoved her father's manuscripts into his enormous travel satchel.

Chapter 5

'Susanna?' she heard a voice ask. 'Are you feeling poorly?'

She looked up at the sapphire-blue sky, blinking.

'Susanna,' Robert said softly, 'd'you want me to stop for a spell?'

She gazed at him with unseeing eyes. Slowly he came into focus.

'I'm sorry,' she said, 'I was thinking back again, nothing more.'

Robert nodded. There was sadness in those eyes of hers. Sure as he was about his place in the world, he couldn't imagine how hard it was to be the daughter of the most famous man in all Warwickshire. Why, with playmakers on the doorstep every day – High Days and Holy Days too – and people coming back from London with tales of this or that play of Master Shakespeare's, he reckoned she felt the Master belonged to 'most everyone but her.

He saw how this morning when that rider came it had to be a shock to her, though she never said. He heard the racket once again when that rider banged on the front door in his addled brain. The noise were near loud enough to stir the dead from their graves. He recalled how he dropped those rushes he'd been laying down to give whoever was banging so, a piece of his mind. But when he saw the dusty rider standing before him, he knew there'd be trouble. Express riders from the Master always made him fret.

When Robert dug into his pocket to tip the man, the rider's eyes trailed down to the Shakespeare badge of service emblazoned on his chest.

'The boy what gave me this letter yesterday in Oxford wore the same badge as you,' the rider said, taking the money.

Robert knew he was mistaken. There were no boy in Master Shakespeare's service, and certainly no boy who wore his badge. 'Livery's just at the end of the lane,' Robert pointed. 'You'll find food and water there and a fresh horse. Tell 'em Robert Whatcott said to put it on Master Shakespeare's account.'

The rider nodded his thanks and turned away. Robert stared at the letter, wondering who that Oxford boy could be, and why the letter was addressed to himself. The rider walked back along the garden path to Chapel Street, biting down on the coin. Everyone knew it was easier to pay an express rider in counterfeit coin than to thank him properly for a job well done, and Robert took no offence.

He leaned against the door, weighing the letter in his hand, hesitant. What if it was bad news? He tore it open with fear in his heart, and read it as fast as he could, sounding out the words in places. Despite the Master's orders, there was no doubt. Mistress Anne must see it. O, how he dreaded talking to her when she were in one of her rages at Susanna. And how her raging voice bellowed!

They'd been driving through Warwickshire for a fair few hours, so Robert felt it was safe enough to stop. His throat were as parched as if he'd eaten a barrel of salted fish and his tongue stuck to the roof of his mouth each time he swallowed. When he spotted a grass clearing shaded by a high hedge near the river it seemed just the spot to pull off the road and mull through their predicament over a drink or two of small ale. Well, maybe three...

Robert looked at Susanna fearing she'd beg him to carry on, so it came as no small relief when she pointed to the glade ahead, 'Let's stop there, please?'

He couldn't help smiling. They hadn't spoken for a good long while, probably coz each were wondering how to handle the fine muddle they'd got themselves into. As he turned the horses off the road, the dog sprang from Susanna's arms and ran off, trailing some of her laundry in the dirt behind him.

'Chaos!' she grumbled.

But the dog kept running.

'Come here boy!' She shouted and ran off after him.

A minute or so later, whilst Robert mined for hidden treasures in the back of the cart, he heard a whimper and Susanna scolding the dog. If there were too little to drink, they could only last another few hours in any comfort, and he'd have to divert to a farmstead or hamlet to beg for the mercy of strangers. A rustling in the bushes brought him back to the here and now.

'Is that you, you damned dog?'

'No, Robert.' Susanna's voice cut the air like the angry winter.

He'd never known her to get cross as long as he could recall. But there was the rub. Robert felt shamed and downright flummoxed about the mess Susanna had got them both into.

So, Robert being Robert, he only said, 'You found Chaos then?'

'Aye.'

'Susanna, I–'

'Go about your business, Robert. I'm mending my gown here.'

What happened this morning made no sense, he shook his head. Best just rummage for some provisions, he thought, and forget the whys and wherefores. He hadn't far to look to see the Master's leather satchel and his manuscripts were still there, and the box of quills and ink. He tossed back the burlap cover some more, and felt the jewelled cloak all tucked up in a corner. At least the Master's things were all accounted for. Robert flipped the cover back over the side of the cart, and like a pigeon aiming for home, his hand fell on three jugs of small ale. He breathed a mighty sigh. There was one loaf of bread left and a little cheese, not sufficient for them to keep going long, but enough to make do until he could get them to a town or village that evening, maybe Shipston-on-Stour or Chipping Norton.

He took a jug with him as he hopped down. For now, he'd set aside his worrying. He needed a drink and so did their horses, he reckoned, as he unhitched them from the cart.

'Come, my beauties,' he said stroking them. 'You did just fine before and I'm sorry if I hurt your feelings back there when I called you "nags".' He led them to the edge of the river and the horses quickly dipped their heads.

He felt miserable. So, he took a long swig from the jug and thought. His whole world had gone topsy-turvy-down. But the more he thought, the more he drank, and the hotter under the collar he became. He found himself wondering if it was an unseasonably hot day, or if he'd let his anger rise so that his blood boiled over. He lifted the jug up high and took another long, cooling swig of small ale, savouring its tangy sweetness. And the more he thought on things, the more storm-struck his meanderings became. He picked up a flat stone from the river's edge and skipped it across the water. Five bounces. Dear Lord, didn't Mistress Susanna see what she'd done? He looked at the jug and thought he deserved another cooling sip.

'They'll call me a common churl, they will,' he called out behind him, wiping his mouth with his sleeve and hoping Susanna would reply. Surely, she'd see how unhandsome she'd been to him?

But no answer came, other than a rustling in the bushes.

Robert picked up another flat stone and tossed it. Only three bounces. He upturned the jug and gulped down the last of the small ale. As he did, the horses stopped drinking, lifted their necks and shook their heads. Robert jumped back, but not quickly enough. The jug flew from his hands and smashed against a rock.

'God's bodkins!' he swore, gazing down at the broken jug. Even worse, horse slobber dribbled from his shoulders to his boots.

As he wiped himself down, he thought back to how he had hoped that after they ran away from Stratford, he'd be able to talk some sense into Susanna. Get her to go back straightaway. But no, she'd not hear a word of it. She was coming with him to see her father, and never going back home ... ever. He should've hogtied Mistress Susanna and carted her home when he had the chance. That's what the Master would've wanted.

He heard a rustle again and looked up.

'Why, I bet our neighbours'll be thinking I've run off with another man's wife!' Robert cried out in frustration. 'They'll be planning to pillory us or worse when we get back – maybe even cage us!' His eyes widened in horror at the thought of being put in a cage like some wild beast for obeying his mistress's orders to flee.

'I'd like to see them try,' Susanna called back at him.

'And you can count on your husband to chivvy them along. Why did you have to run off so, well, so theatrical like and all?'

'I am my father's daughter,' she replied artfully.

'Ah, Mistress, you know all married folk have their tiffs, but they don't go stealing half-loaded carts and manservants, do they?'

'Now don't laugh,' she warned, coming out from behind the bushes, ignoring him.

Susanna stood before him wearing her mother's gown. She saw the smashed jug and Robert's drooping eyelids and knew he'd spoken out with false courage bought at the bottom of the jug.

But all Robert could think was how Susanna looked the sorriest excuse for a woman he'd seen in a good while wearing that gown. Anne Shakespeare had once been as lithesome and lovely as young Judith, but the years had given her a few spare pounds to warm her empty bed. Susanna had gathered the dress in as best she could without needle and thread by tucking and folding its fabric, but her pale shoulder peeked out from the collar. And, she stood there with her hair loose like a maid's, only wilder. She were right comical looking, but it would have been cruel of him to make merry of her predicament, 'specially as her own clothes were ripped beyond repair. Still, she looked like a little girl dressing up in her ma's clothes.

Susanna looked unhappily at him.

'Sorry, Mistress,' Robert said, suppressing a smile. 'It's time to move on, I reckon.'

Susanna took the reins. 'I'll hitch them. You drive.'

They rode on in silence. Chaos was asleep in her lap and she stroked him absentmindedly. She told herself she wasn't running from Stratford. She was clutching at the overwhelming desire to see her father perform in one of his plays. That's what had caused her to bolt like an unbroken foal.

'Robert, you've been in our family's service since my grandfather's time, isn't that so?'

'I have.'

'D'you know if my mother was happy when she first married my father?'

Robert gulped and looked away.

Susanna thought she should change tack. 'She was a great beauty in her day, right?'

'Aye. And the Master were too – all six foot of a strapping youth with those chestnut-brown eyes of his and his sugared tongue.'

'I bet folk said he'd bewitched her.'

Robert hadn't the heart to tell her that folk thought Anne Hathaway – an heiress and all of twenty-six – was mad to marry the penniless teenager Shakespeare.

He cleared his throat. 'I don't remember. It were a long while ago.'

'But I relive it every day, Robert.'

He couldn't bear to tell her the litany recited by both her parents of the rights and wrongs of the story. 'Sides, it weren't his story to tell. Without knowing why, he suddenly burst into song. The birds fluttered from the trees, taking flight from his washboard singing voice. Chaos hid his head beneath Susanna's skirts.

Chapter 6

Warming her face in the spring sun, Susanna had to admit that the lark's song in her heart had faded long ago. Thinking back through the annals of her life, all joy had gone when Hamnet died. That's when her father started staying away longer too.

'Robert?' her voice sounded strange to her ears.

He turned, his eyebrows raised in innocence.

'Tell me, have you really ever seen his plays?'

'More than once – don't you recall?'

She shook her head. Susanna had never seen her father's plays because her mother insisted they were unmeet for her daughters.

'Let's see, there was the time I went with the Master to London just before Hamnet–'

'Hamnet?' A quick pounding in her chest always followed the mention of her dead brother.

Robert closed his eyes and saw the sweet twelve-year-old boy, with his brown curly locks, full of promise and brimming over with words, just like the Master. The stench of the sweating sickness filled Robert's nostrils, just as it had on that blustery night the boy died. He should never have spoken of that ill-season when poor Hamnet was given up to the Lord.

'And when else, Robert?' Susanna asked, drawing him back to the present.

'Uh, ah… let's see,' he needed time to think. Dipping back into such an evil time was like some poison or the taste of bitter wormwood on his tongue.

'Why there was that time the Master took ill up Worcester way.'

Susanna wrinkled her brow.

'You remember. That were when your husband first came among us, carrying home Master Shakespeare in that old rick-cart?' Robert bit his lip. How could he be so foolish as to mention Dr Hall only hours after he'd shamed Susanna so! He closed his eyes cursing himself for his knavery. Why you're nothing more than a varlet Robert Whatcott, he scolded himself. And a common rascal, a churl even …

Susanna nodded at the memory. Her father had been poorly as far back as the summer of 1605. She could still hear the bells jingling around the neck of Lulubell the donkey that fine summer's day. She recalled how she'd peeked out of her bedroom window to look down the lane. There he was, the great Will Shakespeare, all laid out in a rick-cart pulled by a donkey, with Robert at the reins.

Shakespeare's friend Henry Condell had sent word to come fetch him as they were playing only twenty miles to the northwest up Worcester way. It seemed Shakespeare had what they feared might be the falling sickness, so the family was to send someone quick. Without so much as a minute's thought, Robert hitched up his Lulubell – all decked out with her battered straw hat laced with gillyflowers for the Morris Dancing fete – and hared off in the cart towards Worcester.

For two long days they waited, praying for some sign. Then on the afternoon of the third day, they heard Lulubell's chiming, followed by Robert's caterwauling, as he was want to do when he was worried. She ran to the door and threw it open, just in time to hear Robert slaughtering another country ditty. Then the cart came into sight and Susanna saw a tall stranger in Puritan dress, sitting bolt upright scribbling in a brown leather book. As they drew closer, she saw her father's head resting in the stranger's lap. It was the first time she'd clapped eyes on John Hall.

He cradled her father as though he was accustomed to doing it hundreds of times. But suddenly, her father lifted his head, all wobbly-like as drunkards do, and said, 'Weep not, ladies! I'm but hung over on the horn of abundance! Ah, see my wife, the Lady Anne! How now? What? See the love she wears so lightly upon her workaday sleeve!' And with that, his eyes twirled 'round in their sockets and his head fell back into Hall's lap.

'Humpf!' Anne scoffed. 'The only man I know who uses his good wit to conquer his disease 'stead of potions. D'you know what ails him?' she asked the stranger.

It did seem odd to Susanna that the stranger was just sitting there scribbling. Anne looked to Susanna. The stranger wasn't taking any notice of them. A few moments later when he was finished writing, he closed his brown leather book.

'See how his face twitches? It's not a palsy, I think… rather some kind of perturbation of the brain. I've read of this in Galen, you know.' He was talking at them like they were his pupils or some such nonsense. It was gibberish as far as she could tell.

'Then there's the deafness that comes and goes, and his confounding smells-'

'Confounding smells?' Susanna asked.

'Aye. He mixes the sweet smells of summer with vinegar or manure. Why, only a while earlier he was sure the mead I gave him stank of foul meat.'

'I see,' Susanna nodded, not seeing anything at all.

'Then he speaks nonsense sometimes. Things like "to wake a wolf is as bad as smell a fox" or "your drams of drugs stink of scruples"… and there was the time he said "his quick wit was wasted in giving reckonings." All nonsense, see? Then between times, he's bright and right as rain.'

Anne curled up the corner of her mouth. 'Best bring him inside then, so we can see to him, Mr–?'

'Doctor, actually. Dr John Hall at your service ladies.'

'Mistress Susanna?' Robert asked timidly.

Susanna sighed. 'Just rick-cart memories crowding in on me again.'

'Ah. I've been chiding myself. I shouldn't have made mention of that either. Not with this morning and all.'

She hadn't any right to make him uncomfortable. Robert was her only friend. 'You did no wrong, Robert. I was asking what times you'd seen his plays, and you were answering.'

'That's kind of you, Susanna.'

'No kindness in it, just the truth Robert.' She turned and saw how he shied his head away from her. 'So, tell me, which ones *did* you see?'

'Truth to tell, not many. Just the ones about the Scottish king, the mad son and the wicked daughters.'

'Let me test you. What were they called?'

'I know the Scottish king were Macbeth. The mad son – let me see – were something Lear,' Robert knitted his brow. 'And the wicked daughters' one – that were your brother's name. Leastways I think so.'

Of course, the mad prince was *Hamlet* and the wicked daughters and foolish king was *Lear,* but Susanna hadn't the heart to correct him. Besides, she couldn't help feeling a twinge of envy that Robert – like so many others – had seen what she'd been denied. How she hungered to join in with the groundlings and become one of her father's greatest votaries.

Susanna suddenly felt quite empty inside. She had no mother or sister to miss her, other than for her housework. No husband either – well, at least that was a blessing. She looked down at her wedding ring. It had never been a symbol of love, more like a brand as you'd put on any sheep or a cow to keep them from straying. She wrenched it off her finger. She glanced over to Robert. He was busying himself avoiding the ruts in the road. As he swerved to miss a boulder, she tossed the ring into the undergrowth. And with that, she felt an overpowering urge to plunge into one of her father's plays.

'Let's pull over once again when you can, shall we?' she asked Robert.

'Soon, Mistress,' Robert replied, pointing to the road ahead with his chin. 'There's a lake nearby here if I'm not mistaken.'

They stopped at a dark blue lake sheltered by willow trees and surrounded by the rolling hills of the north Cotswolds. Newly planted crops had already turned the fields green, Susanna thought, looking into the distance, pretending she was idly gazing at the countryside, when her head was full of worry. Robert, meanwhile, stole off to heed a call of nature.

She fetched the satchel from the cart, searching for a spot where she could sit quietly with Chaos at her side. She would read beneath the bright green arbour of nature, remembering her father's love of the colour green. *Green is the colour of lovers. Spring is near when green geese are a-breeding. A green goose a goddess. His eyes were green as leeks. How green you are and flesh in this old world! It was the green-ey'd monster which doth mock! It was so sir, she had a green wit.*

She had every right to look and read and understand her father's work, she thought in defence of her actions. One day it would be her father's legacy to them, and their family heritage to pass on. Her calming thoughts were interrupted when Chaos ran over to a rabbit hole, burying his head inside. His muffled bark echoed in the ground. His bottom was raised up high, his tail wagging madly. Susanna smiled as she opened the flap of the satchel and pulled out the first manuscript that came to hand. It was *Love's Labour's Lost* once again. That's when she noticed beneath the title the words written in her father's scrawl *green is the colour of gardens, of jealousy, of loves of life – breathe colours into words, fool.* Why hadn't she seen it before?

She turned the page to continue to read on about the escapades of Berowne, Longaville and Dumaine and the ladies attendant on the princess of France – Rosaline, Maria and Katharine – and their friends. She had entered a foreign yet familiar land. Set in

Navarre, the play was a feast of high-born and low-brow words, just as her father spoke. A mint of phrases from his brain coloured each page from the tawny-coloured Spanish knights to the loftily daubed conviction that *green indeed is the colour of lovers* were painted recklessly from her father's palette upon the page. Susanna was filled with pride and awe that he could create such a feast of languages woven into delicate taffeta words. Still, as an unlearned woman, she knew she hadn't understood all the play's meaning. She squirmed inside. She'd stolen his words like a dog thieves scraps from its master's table.

Susanna called Chaos to her side. Still mesmerised by her father's silken phrases she gazed out over the lake. She wondered what it was about the people in the play that seemed so familiar to her. She flicked back to her father's scrawled notes. These were his afterthoughts – perhaps after having seen it performed several times. Her eyes fell on a particularly tidy bit of writing beside the couplet,

a lover's eyes will gaze an eagle blind,

a lover's ear will hear the lowest sound.

Carefully written were the words *Mary, my love.* They shone in Susanna's uncomprehending eyes. Susanna blinked. Who was Mary?

Her heart pounded as if it might take wings and beat out of her chest. Was Mary some lost love or a present-day mistress? Suddenly, her ear tuned back to the present, where all she could hear was the rustle of the breeze. She looked up with a start. Chaos was gone.

Her eyes darted around. She examined the rabbit hole and saw that he'd been unlucky in digging it out. Had he gone off in search of food? Her stomach growled back at her in reply. The dog could hardly be blamed. They were all starved. Susanna carefully put the manuscript away in the satchel.

Robert dreamed of a feast worthy of a king. Capon, pigeon, lark's tongues, roast pig and a table full of dainties made from candied cherries and sugared apricots. In his handmade confectionary of a delicious dream, he'd already had quite a bit to eat, but still craved more. All round him sat Shakespeare's company of players, the King's Men, feasting happily. Robert took hold of a perfectly-roasted pigeon, his mouth ready to savour its succulent flavour, when it turned its head at him and cooed. Its browned and crisp skin changed into feathers and its wings began to flap. Robert woke up with a start.

The sounds of cooing wood pigeons in the trees echoed above. His heart banged in his head. Imagine eating a live pigeon – puh! He shook himself and made to stand. Then he saw Susanna and the dog were gone. He'd left her unguarded. He'd dozed off. And now they were lost in the midst of this wild English countryside. Dear Lord.

'Calm yourself, Robert,' he said. He drew his dagger from his belt and began to pace, alert, looking for brigands.

'For pity's sake, where's she gone? Should I call out her name? If I do, and she's been taken by some highway man, or worse still, his lawyer, then what?'

Just then, there was a rustling in the bushes. Robert pointed his dagger at the noise. The branches parted and a thin, filthy, bearded man in a ragged uniform trudged forward.

'Halt!' Robert cried out. His dagger trembled.

'Pray peace, friend.' The man held up his hands in surrender.

Robert eyed him up and down. He was hatless and wore a tattered militia jacket and stank from thirty paces away.

'I'm but a poor soldier seeking a crust of bread,' he said.

'A ruffler then? Where's your licence to beg?' Robert asked, in a quivering voice.

The ruffler patted his jacket and rummaged through its pockets.

'Must've lost it.'

'Then be off with you and don't think you can trouble us none,' Robert ordered defiantly.

'Us?'

The ruffler edged towards him, smiling. 'Have you no food to spare for a soldier returning from the wars?'

'And which wars may they be?' Robert asked. He cursed himself for saying *us*.

'Why, Punic, of course.'

'Punic? Which battle?'

'Carthage.'

'O, Carthage,' Robert nodded. 'We won that one, didn't we?'

'With General Hannibal at the van,' the ruffler nodded, inching ever closer, forcing Robert to either stand his ground or move back. He stepped back, his mind racing. He could do all sorts – he could charge at the ruffler – he could shout for help – why he could even warn Susanna with a cry. But instead, he stumbled over a rock and fell backwards. Before he could right himself, the ruffler was astride his chest battling to wrest away his dagger. Robert swung at him with his fists and kicked and struggled to push him off, but the ruffler was too strong. A poor soldier, indeed, Robert thought, grinding his teeth.

With a deft twist, the ruffler stole away his dagger and held it to his throat. Robert gulped. He closed his eyes to pray for deliverance. Then he heard the cocking of a pistol. His eyes shot open to see it pointing straight into the ruffler's ear.

'If you don't want to hear bells ringing in the one good ear you'll have left after I pull this trigger, you'd best climb off my manservant,' Susanna warned.

She winked at Robert. Chaos stood at her side, growling viciously.

Robert couldn't resist taking his revenge for the shame the ruffler had heaped on him. He hauled him off and punched the man on the nose. The ruffler slumped off to the side, holding both hands to his face.

'That hurt!' he cried out.

'Get up!' Susanna shouted, waving the pistol madly.

The ruffler obeyed, struggling to his feet. Robert had bloodied his nose, but other than that, it seemed only his pride was hurt.

'No call to pull a pistol on me like that!' the ruffler exclaimed.

'Why ever not? You'd have done the same to us if you had one! You should be ashamed of yourself!' Susanna shouted, waving the pistol at him as if it were her finger.

Robert stood and dusted himself off.

Susanna looked him ... her hapless protector. Truly, no matter what kind of gloss she painted on it, this had been a very bad day.

'You know, you – you, ruffler, you,' Susanna blathered, 'I've had a gutsful of men today.'

Robert's eyes widened.

'The last thing I needed was for the likes of you to come into our lives,' she huffed. 'Besides, who gave you the right to come barging in on us like that, huh? Scaring my poor little dog and my friend here?' She pointed her pistol at Chaos, then Robert. Robert ducked, fearing the pistol would go off.

Susanna paid no heed. She was sick and tired of everyone taking advantage of their good natures.

'Life's hard enough for honest folk without the likes of you thinking "O, there's a likely pair of conies, I think I'll steal their horse and their food," she spat. 'It's enough to churn a decent woman's stomach.' She pointed the pistol at her gut.

Robert waved his hands at her, his eyes huge with fear. 'Susanna, the pistol!'

'O, not that we've much to rob, mind you,' she ranted on. 'It's the principle. It's your lack of common decency.' Without realising it, she pointed the pistol once again at the ruffler. He flung his arms up in surrender. Robert breathed a sigh.

'Why, I ought to truss you up and ruffle *you*! Then we'll see how you like it, huh?'

'I'll take that now, Susanna,' Robert said as he gently took hold of the pistol.

The ruffler's knees buckled. He collapsed, crying. Susanna looked at Robert, regret filling her heart.

'Please,' she pleaded with the ruffler, bending down beside him. 'I don't know what came over me. Please stop crying.'

Yet the ruffler wailed on. Susanna looked to Robert for help.

In all the years he knew Susanna, he'd yet to see her lose her temper like that. Maybe it were good she got it all out of her head. Maybe it would do her heart some good too. But, no matter what, he was sure he'd not seen the last of this new Susanna.

Chapter 7

John Heminges was staring at Shakespeare's sleeping face, when a soft knock at the door jolted him from his reverie.

'Come,' he said.

The door inched open. The twelve-year-old boy who had been guarding the door to the college peeked in.

'Come on in, Will,' Heminges said.

The boy Will slid through the crack in the opened door and closed it silently behind him. He wore no shoes, no hose, and his grubby breeches were frayed at the cuffs. He wore the same jerkin of the roughest forest-green broadcloth as before, only this time he had no badge of service. Heminges looked down at the boy's dirty feet and shook his head.

'Where are those boots I gave you, Will?'

The boy stopped dead. 'Do I *have* to wear them with those itchy woollen socks?'

Heminges grinned. 'If you want the boots, you do.'

Will rubbed his bare feet together.

'I've not come coz of the boots but coz the Master of College wants to know if Master Shakespeare there,' he looked over at the playwright's still body, stifling a sob.

'Yes?'

Will took a deep breath to compose himself. 'If Master Shakespeare will recover for the King's Men's performance at the Festival.'

Heminges looked upwards for divine intervention. 'Tell the Master I simply don't know. None of us do. We are all in the hands of God.'

The boy gazed with glistening eyes at Shakespeare. 'The world would be poorer if he didn't.'

Heminges nodded. 'Aye, that it would be. These many years have been good to us all.' He blinked several times in disbelief. 'I've known Will Shakespeare almost thirty years.'

'Then, you must have a hundred tales of your times together.'

Heminges stared at his old friend, thinking back to a world gone by, about the time when he nearly falsely took away Shakespeare's life.

Will tugged at Heminges's sleeve. But Heminges fixed Shakespeare firmly in his gaze, still and silent. The boy took Heminges's hand in his and squeezed it to let him know that he wasn't alone in his sorrow.

A tear fell on his cheek and Heminges cleared his throat, smiling at a memory. 'I'll tell you one tale, Will. It was just before the harvest of 1586, though that harvest wasn't in our green and pleasant England. It was in the Netherlands, the Low Countries blighted by a bloody war with its overlord Spain for over twenty years by then. And dear Lord, that war still rages another twenty-five years on. I often ask myself, when will it end?'

Just then, Shakespeare stirred. Heminges leaned forward. The hazy afternoon sunlight streamed in through the mullioned window, casting an eerie shadow across Shakespeare's face. The corners of his mouth twitched and seemed to dance faintly as if he heard Heminges speak.

'What does that mean?' Young Will asked in a quivering voice.

'I'm no expert, despite my years of caring for him on our travels. Sometimes it passes in an hour, sometimes in a day. This is the longest time I can recall.'

Heminges eased himself into the chair beside the bed. 'You know, Will, he always loved life on the road. The joy of meeting the unexpected head on was one of life's great jokes to him. He told me that in Holland.' He stopped talking and stared blankly at Shakespeare.

After a few moments, the boy urging him to continue, placed a hand on Heminges's shoulder. 'I'd been an apprentice for nearly nine years,' he sighed, 'since Candlemas of 1578, to the kind and generous James Collins of the Grocers Company. Though old Collins had died in 1585, before my apprenticeship was completed, his good lady wife kept me on when she took over the business.'

Heminges shook his head. 'Though I was relieved, it turned out to be a bit of a jumble. I'll never forget the day that crow-like alderman in his black robes swooped down on our home in Honey Lane late one evening five months after old Collins died. "The time has come," the alderman said in his scratchy voice to the widow Collins, "for the livery companies of the City of London to support the Queen to help the Dutch."'

The boy's eyes widened, sensing an adventure.

'That meant that the widow's apprentices, wagons and know-how on feeding a city like London would be put to better use in the field of battle. And as her most trusted employee, I was made a captain of the victualling company, under the command of a Welshman. By the autumn of that year, I found myself leading my 125 so-called *volunteers* into the Low Countries to feed the Earl of Leicester's army.'

'So, Master Shakespeare was a soldier?'

Heminges smiled. 'Not yet. He was one of my volunteers. We'd had a chance meeting in London the night before I was due to leave, and when I told Shakespeare where I was going he asked to come with me. Unlike most, he didn't need to be hoodwinked into taking the 'Queen's Shilling' by downing a tankard of ale. No, he saw the war as a great adventure, a way to feed his growing family and get that start in life so many men crave.'

Heminges stopped and stared ahead at some distant memory. The boy nudged him as if to say there was nothing worse than a story half told.

'The evening after Shakespeare had agreed to join me,' Heminges continued suddenly, 'I learned that the parish muster officer had made a large addition to the volunteers in my company from the Mermaid Taverne – over twenty shillings were spent gathering them with the Queen's Shilling for what many believed to be Leicester's War rather than the Queen's.'

Heminges smiled at the memory. 'Shakespeare was – to say the least – a wondrous complement to our band of brothers, always laughing, save when he had to fight. And then, when we did, we were thankful to have Will Shakespeare by our side.'

'Why's that?'

'You mean, besides his being a master swordsman? There was always something about Shakespeare that was forever young, forever energetic. He had an eternal twinkle in his eye, like the child who sees the world crystal clear even in the most blinding fog.'

Heminges gave a wry smile. 'He often set about doing the most unexpected things in the oddest of circumstances. But, once he took you to his heart, his world became your golden oyster. Words you never dreamt of, philosophies yet to be written, spoke to you through his very thought and deed, never mind his phrases. In a look or a sentence, Shakespeare captured your heart and mind and made you the richer for surrendering to him. Even that time, when I nearly had to hang him from the highest elm for treason.'

'What?' the boy gasped.

'The Grocers Company of Victuallers to the Queen's Royal Army had been set the task to make our way to Flushing in the Netherlands to bring relief food to its governor, Sir Philip Sidney, and his embattled men. We were meant to reach the town by September. But it was already early October, and we were still at least two days' ride away. We made camp for the night in a part of the country held by the English and Dutch. The next morning, when I ordered the roll call before breaking camp, I had a sudden panic. Over forty of my men had deserted in the night.'

'Surely not Master Shakespeare?' the boy asked.

Heminges stared at Shakespeare, lost in the past. 'I quickly mounted up. I called to my sergeant-at-arms and a handful of trusted horsemen with pikes. We'd need to recapture my men before another company discovered them and took decisive action. Desertion was a hanging offence, punishable by summary execution for treason. The only benefit to the wrongdoer was that there'd be no drawing and quartering, or cutting out of hearts to throw into the guilty man's face. In the battlefield, hanging was all the Queen's army had time for.'

'Bodkins!' the boy cried.

Heminges narrowed his eyes at him.

'Sorry, Master Heminges.'

Heminges nodded. 'It was a terrible punishment for terrible times. So we mounted up to find the deserters. I recall cursing back then, too. I was cursing my men for being so pig-headed and stupid. But of them all, I cursed Shakespeare the most. I kept asking myself, "What could they have been thinking? Surely they'd seen the dangling bodies swinging from the elms lining the road?" I couldn't understand it. It wasn't our job to fight the enemy. Our job was to feed the troops. And I needed every man I had with me. I suspected Shakespeare of being their ringleader. I was smart enough to know I was no captain of men, whereas Will Shakespeare was. I was just a purveyor of food. So when my new and dear friend Shakespeare ran off like that, all I could think on was "How dare he do this to me!"

'But I hadn't far to look. When we reached the crest of the first hill, we spied a great number of men bringing in the last of the corn harvest. Some were wearing the Grocers' livery. My horsemen cantered towards the harvest carts, calling out for the victuallers to halt at once. That's when I spied Shakespeare wearing his Grocers' cap and livery driving the last cart, rich with corn.'

''Swounds Master Heminges, he must've been quaking in his boots, right?'

'Not at all. Seeing me and the sergeant-at-arms, Shakespeare gave a white-toothed smile and waved his arms in welcome. I saw all my missing men in their uniforms, mixed in with the Dutch country folk. So I signalled to the sergeant-at-arms to halt. Pikes were poised, waiting for my orders.'

'Then what happened, Master Heminges?'

'"What the Devil d'you think you're doing? I fumed at him. I was so furious I had trouble steadying my mount. The horse danced from side to side, half ready to bolt. "Soothe him by stroking his mane," Shakespeare called back. I was near speechless at his assuredness. Still, I leaned forward, instinctively obeying his command. The horse settled in seconds. I was struck then, as I'd be many times in our adventures, by his audacity. How could such a man be so carefree facing certain death? D'you know how he answered my question? "Why, the harvest, what else?" Can you believe it?'

The boy stifled a giggle.

'I nearly laughed too, save that I was convinced he was mocking me. Just as I was sure that Will Shakespeare was *my* superior. That was when he saw my face cloud over in anger. I can still hear his voice ringing out like a crisp bell of common sense in that desolate landscape. "Corn is love, and if we've come here to help, they'll need to love us. We need to be of service where we're most needed," he said.

'I looked around us. The fields had been cleared with only the shortest straw stubble remaining. In normal times, there would be the ceremonial burning of the straw, and then the harvest festival. Then the backbreaking work of tilling the soil to sow the winter crop. And so the cycle turned. But these weren't normal times. For a dizzy moment, the Dutch landscape seemed just as it should. Farmers with their long-handled scythes slung over their shoulders were heading towards the nearby village with some unpronounceable name. Their Dutch maidens drove wagonloads rich with harvested grain that waved lazily with the motion of the wagon. My victuallers, weary from weeks on the road, walked alongside them, laughing and joking with the women. Corn stored for the winter meant no one would starve. Corn was the best love an invading army could give to those they were meant to protect.'

Heminges smiled. 'I remember Shakespeare's wispy hair flew wildly from beneath his victualler's cap. I remember his eyes, too – that rich brown colour of roasted chestnuts flecked with gold twinkling up at me. There was something else in those eyes of his, something I couldn't put my finger on until much later.'

'What was it, Master Heminges?'

'He saw I was unsettled and reflected it back at me. That's a rare gift, making people see themselves better. But I was young and looked away. In the back of Shakespeare's wagon, I saw the booty of corn, bound up in sheaves and crowned with a garland of flowers, as was the habit of the English at harvest time. Bringing in the corn before winter was an imperative of life. And so it dawned on me: Shakespeare is right.'

'So why all that unsettled feeling?'

'Because I should've had him executed.' Heminges mimicked how he'd barked at his friend, "For being absent without leave," I told him, "and taking a third of our men with you." Why, the cheek of it! But he just tucked his chin to his chest. "It seemed the moral thing to do, John, uh, Captain Heminges. The Dutch aren't the only people who'll starve if we don't help them bring in the harvest. Besides, this wagonload of corn is their gift to us for our many kindnesses."

'I saw my victuallers were heading towards me across the fields, laden with offerings of food and beer. My horsemen followed, pikes still poised to run them through on my order. I hadn't the stomach to punish any man who was so right for doing so wrong.'

'But why did he do it without permission?' the boy asked, stunned.

'For the joy of meeting the unexpected head on. "Isn't that one of life's great jokes?" Shakespeare asked. And all I could think of was if I'd done as I was meant to do, then the world would never know of all those poems he'd never write. The thought fairly pierces my heart still.'

Heminges and the boy stared at each other in silence, each understanding the other. Neither of them saw a faint smile glowing on Shakespeare's lips, as if he'd heard every word.

'And so I disobeyed orders. Here was a man who, in another place and time, I knew with absolute clarity would make his mark on the world. There was something to this Shakespeare. He was some mysterious and wise soul through whose eyes I suddenly yearned to see life better. It was only then that I realised he had a way with people and words that set him above all others. To hang him would be the greatest crime of my life, even though I had the law on my side.'

The boy gave a devilish half-smile. 'The law is an ass.'

'Well put,' Heminges said. 'Very well put indeed. You must tell Shakespeare those words when he recovers.'

The boy beamed up at Heminges. Shakespeare lifted an eyelid, unobserved.

'You know, Will Davenant,' Heminges said, 'you have a gift with words. You have that same half-smile that Shakespeare gave me back then when I told him to bring that corn to the sergeant-at-arms to store it properly.'

'It's a fine tale, Master Heminges,' the boy smiled.

Shakespeare swiftly shut his eye.

'All true,' Heminges agreed.

Will Davenant turned to Shakespeare.

'He won't bite you know.'

'You mean, Master Heminges, I should …?'

'Go ahead, he seems to like the sound of nice voices, and you have a very nice voice.'

The boy blushed and took a few steps towards the bed. Suddenly, as if something magical had happened, Shakespeare stirred. The boy's eyes shot wide open, half in fear, half in expectation.

Heminges leaned forward. Shakespeare's eyes batted opened and closed several times.

'Does it mean he will be fine again?' the boy asked.

Shakespeare stared at the boy. Heminges looked from Shakespeare to Will. He made a sign for the boy to follow him away from the bed so they could speak privately. Yet as soon as Will turned to follow Heminges, Shakespeare's hand reached out and grabbed him by the wrist. They both gasped.

Heminges leaned towards the bed.

Shakespeare's eyes were trained steadily on the boy.

'Speak to him, young Will,' Heminges urged.

The boy swallowed. 'So, you don't want me to go?'

Shakespeare's wintry stare softened. A smile grew unevenly on his lips.

'Truly?' he asked.

Shakespeare's grasp slowly eased around Will's wrist. His hand slid back onto the bed, his ink-stained index and middle fingers patting the boy's hand, before his eyelids fluttered shut again and he eased into a peaceful sleep.

The boy looked to Heminges. Without a word, Shakespeare had spoken volumes.

Heminges motioned for them to let him sleep. Together they walked silently towards the door, Heminges's hand on the boy's shoulder. As Heminges reached for the door handle, he could swear he heard Shakespeare's voice, as thin as a gossamer thread, whisper, 'Hamnet.'

Chapter 8

Susanna and Robert made the ruffler undress at gunpoint. Robert tied him loosely to a tree whilst Susanna hid his uniform by the lake so he couldn't follow them once he broke free. As they rode off to the wailings and laments of the ruffler, she couldn't help but feel a twinge of pride at her bravery. Robert had told her she'd been quick-witted to find the pistol in the cart and rescue him.

All too soon, Robert began to caterwaul a country ditty. She turned her head away, since one ear hearing was better than two. The broad views across the Warwickshire countryside had closed in on them. They were now enshrouded in a dark wood of sycamore and elm. Susanna gazed into the bright green-leafed branches towering overhead. Starlings chattered madly. Only a sliver of the afternoon sky could be seen every now and again as they passed beneath the canopy of trees. She took heart at a pair of swallows darting between the sycamores. Their return meant that this was no false spring, as some people feared. There would be good weather ahead, she mused. Good weather to balance the tempest beating in her mind.

She heard Robert take another deep breath, preparing to sing another verse. Susanna sighed and gazed at the passing woodland.

His scratchy, tuneless melody rang out:
> Under the greenwood tree
> Who loves to lie with me,
> And turn his merry note,
> Unto the sweet bird's throat,

Come hither, come hither, come hither ...

She tried to listen again for the birdsong. Poor Robert. He loved a good tune, but had a screech owl's voice. He was ruminating on what he should sing next, when Susanna became aware of something strange. She put her hand on his arm, pricking up her ears.

'Listen,' she whispered.

Robert let out his deep breath, eyes wide.

The woodland was utterly silent. It was as if all the animals and birds had fled.

'What could it mean?' she asked.

'Odd, isn't it?'

She'd never been in a wood that was silent. She remembered how, as a child, she used lie down with her head resting on a log, and how the woods were always alive with wildlife, even if it was only a beetle scuttling on fallen leaves. This wood had died. There was no breath of a breeze in the trees. No more birds on the wing. Even the bright spring leaves seemed darker and more sinister. The low branches overhung the road, making it hard to see the way ahead without ducking to avoid them.

Without warning, Robert pulled up hard on the reins. Susanna grabbed onto the side of the cart. Chaos let out a deep growl. Robert tugged fiercely to keep control. The horses whinnied with fright, yet turned sharply to Robert's will as he struggled to keep them from bolting. But, suddenly there was a jolt and the cart listed on its side.

'Robert?'

'It were nothin' Mistress,' he said, righting himself.

'Nothing?' Susanna looked down at the rear wheel. They'd rammed a huge tree branch that had fallen cross the road. It looked to her like the wheel rim was bent.

'I just need to swing the branch off to the side of the road,' Robert explained, 'then we'll be on our way.'

Before she could protest, a tall dark man on a black and white piebald horse rode out from the shadows, his gleaming silver pistols drawn. Susanna sat still. His eyes were magnetic, holding her stare against her will.

Robert didn't see him as he tied the reins to the hand brake, muttering to himself, 'Whoever heard of trees falling into the road when there's been ne'er a drop of rain?'

'Ahem,' the highwayman said.

Robert looked up slowly.

The highwayman smiled. In different circumstances, Susanna would have thought him a fine figure of a man. He was well-dressed in a long brown leather cloak. His horse's reins were studded with ruby gemstones. This was a man of substance, even if his substance was gained at someone else's loss, she thought.

Two horses – a grey palfrey and a sturdy brown jennet – emerged from the eerie wood behind him. To Susanna's surprise, they carried a brace of young doxies, dressed scantily with most of their bubbies showing and much of their legs, bare. Still, that wasn't all that was indecent. They rode astride like a man, hugging the beasts with their knees. She looked into their painted faces and was shocked to see them smiling as if they were pleasured. Susanna ran her eyes over their bawdy clothes, suddenly feeling old. Though these were no ladies, they had a certain style and knew their place in the world. Susanna couldn't help thinking she had neither.

Suddenly, there was a judder behind them. Then another, and another. Robert and Susanna wheeled round. Standing behind them were three of the highwayman's accomplices brandishing daggers and pistols. They oozed menace. The oldest and fattest one leered, revealing a single front tooth. The one with a huge bulbous red nose narrowed his eyes at them and grinned with a hard, flinty smile. The third, their muscle man, stared blandly about him, as if he were in some market stall deciding which ornament to choose as a gift for his wife. His sole concern was to thieve, leaving the others to tend to their prey.

The muscle man's eyes fell upon the satchel containing her father's manuscripts. Susanna's heart pounded. If they stole the satchel, her father's medicines and his words that he held most dear would be lost, most likely forever.

'Teacake, what d'you see there,' the handsome highwayman called out in his milky, posh voice.

'Loads o' stuff … tons!'

'Then, my little Teacake, let's unpack the heavy load from our poor travellers here, shall we?' The highwayman smiled, his straight, white teeth shining brightly. Susanna reached out along the bench and felt for Robert's hand. It was cold and clammy. She squeezed it tightly to stop herself trembling. Robert squeezed her hand back.

The man with the single tooth laughed good-naturedly. 'Poor travellers, I like that! Poorer-by-the-minute travellers, that is!'

The handsome highwayman motioned with his pistol for Susanna and Robert to step down. They reluctantly let go of each other's hands. Her head banged in fear like a drum. Just as she stepped down, the doxies rode past her. She heard a thud, and instinctively turned to look for Robert. But, he had vanished.

'Wonder if she's got nice clothes hidden in there,' the blonde doxy asked in a thick Cotswolds accent. She had dismounted and hopped onto the cart, searching among their things.

'Well, if she does, it'd be a surprise, just have a look at her!' the red-headed doxy said with a giggle.

Susanna glared at them. Who were they to talk about her in that way? The doxies found her torn dress and held it up. Susanna stood, narrow-eyed. She wasn't sure how, but she'd get her own back on these brigands if it took a lifetime. And whilst she was plotting her empty revenge, the doxies kept ferreting through their things abetted by the wide-eyed muscle man Teacake. Susanna furtively looked for Robert. She hoped he'd run off into the wood unnoticed and made good his escape.

Suddenly, the cold steel of a pistol turned her chin to the side. The dashing highwayman had dismounted and stood tall before her, smiling as if he were asking her to dance at the harvest festival. Please dear Lord, she prayed, let Robert get help.

'We're searchers,' the highwayman told her.

The lie was too much to bear. 'You don't say?' Susanna couldn't keep the defiance out of her voice. 'And these,' she waved an arm at the doxies, 'are your wanton queens?'

The highwayman smiled even more broadly. 'Mm. We're searching for your licences to travel from your parish. Tell me,' he asked, eyeing Susanna's attire and stifling a titter, 'which parish might that be?'

Neither she nor Robert had obtained their licences to travel. If a real searcher happened on them, they'd be hauled off before the magistrate of whatever godforsaken place they were in.

'Since you don't know where you hail from, perhaps you might be so good as to tell me where you've put your licences?'

'I, er, um—'

The highwayman's smile flashed again. He raised his brow in displeasure, moving closer to Susanna. 'You *do* know the penalty for travelling without licences don't you? The pillory, that's what … if you're lucky.'

She could feel his breath on her cheek, and cursed Robert for saving himself. How could he just leave her alone with these … *people?*

Anger filled her heart. 'We've been asked to bring all we possess in this cart in haste to my – er, employer,' she lied.

The highwayman slowly nodded and began to circle around her, appraising her value as if she were a side of beef.

'And just what do you *do* for this *er*, employer?'

Susanna closed her eyes. He didn't believe her. She heard the sound of bottles tinkling and a fluttering of papers. They had found her father's medicines and manuscripts in the satchel.

'This *er*, employer wouldn't be a writer of filthy ballads and scurvy rhymes perchance?'

'Hey Ratsey! Lookey here!' the blonde doxy shouted.

Susanna opened her eyes wide. Ratsey! Gamaliel Ratsey? The most notorious highwayman in the country?

Ratsey leaned forward seductively and whispered, 'Ah, so you've heard my name?'

She felt weak at the knees. What could she do against a highwayman so beloved by the poor? As Shakespeare's daughter, everyone would think she was rich and fair game for the likes of Ratsey. No one would lift a finger to rescue her – that is – if she could find any help. O, Lord, how could Robert have just left her?

A doleful moan rang out, unexpectedly. Everyone stopped dead, straining to hear where it came from. Then another anguished cry, followed by strange noises and someone babbling.

'Ratsey!' Teacake called out, motioning for him to come to the far side of the cart.

'Fang!' Ratsey cried to the great hulk with the one tooth. 'Hold on to this country Joan!'

Fang lumbered over to Susanna, smiling that daft one-toothed smile at her. She cringed inside but stood proud.

At the far side of the cart, Ratsey gazed down. She stretched up onto her tiptoes and saw Robert, lying on the ground, writhing and drooling.

'The book of burning brooks ...' Robert babbled.

Ratsey leaned forward and sniffed at Robert.

'Bubble, bubble, toil and trouble ...'

Ratsey warily approached. Robert gave a huge writhing spasm and he jumped back.

'Must be possessed of evil spirits,' he diagnosed, looking to Teacake. The doxies leaned over the side of the cart. The robber with the huge snout resumed his frantic search for riches. No need to let someone possessed of evil spirits to get in the way of a good robbery, Susanna scoffed to herself.

'Teacake, bring that country Joan here,' Ratsey ordered.

Teacake grabbed Susanna roughly by the arm and hauled her over to him. Robert was rolling on the ground, as if he were having one of the falling evil spells that afflicted her father. His eyes and mouth twitched wildly. Teacake, forgetting all about Susanna, leaned forward next to Ratsey, sniffing at the air above Robert.

'Smells mad enough to me,' Ratsey said.

Fang, Snout and the doxies came alongside Susanna to see better.

'You think, Rats?' Teacake asked, still sniffing for the smells of madness.

'Seems that way, don't you think?' Ratsey asked.

Robert suddenly let out a howl like a wolf. Ratsey, Teacake, Snout, Fang and the doxies all jumped back together, as if dancing a jig. Only Susanna stood her ground. Then again, only Susanna knew that Robert was playacting.

'How long has he been like this?' Ratsey asked Susanna urgently.

'A fair ol' while I'd have to say,' she quickly answered.

Ratsey nodded, thinking. 'Is it catching?'

'Some say so. But you know what they say about madness …'

'He's been goin' on somethin' fierce, Ratsey, 'bout feet tasting of ash,' Snout grimaced.

'Aw, Ratsey, let's shoot him and be done,' Teacake suggested.

'No!' The command escaped Susanna's lips before she could think.

Ratsey turned back to watch Robert writhing and frothing at the mouth.

'You've surely heard how killing a madman brings an ill-wind down on you?' Susanna asked in desperation.

Ratsey reflected before he said, 'Look. You know my name, country Joan. So you'll know I'm a fair high lawyer, and not without pity for poor dumb beasts.'

He turned to his mob and ordered, 'We'll leave them with one horse and their lives, such as they are.' He shook his head at Robert. 'Poor dumb beast.'

Ratsey and his brigands swung into action. Fang and Teacake joined the others to bag up their booty. Susanna raced to Robert's side, patting his head with a cloth. He opened a clear eye and smiled.

Then she turned and saw Teacake stuffing her father's medicine and some of the manuscripts back into the leather satchel. Snout brought the rest of the manuscripts over to Ratsey. He leafed through them with a grin, before shoving them into his saddlebags. Fang had unhitched the horses from the cart and eyed them up to see which one he preferred. The dapple grey was an old mare and quite a way past her best, whereas the chestnut was a two-year-old gelding. Naturally, it was the chestnut Fang decided on, and he tied it to a rope. He walked it over to his own horse and secured the rope onto his saddle. They all mounted their steeds and beckoned their horses to leave.

'Just know, country Joan, there'll be other searchers along – real ones – and in these woods, without your licences...' Ratsey made a gesture with his finger as if to slit his own throat.

Susanna glared at him. Ratsey smiled, tipped his hat at her in mock deference, and they all rode off at a gallop.

'Cowards! When my fa – er – master hears, he'll–'

She was still screaming at their billowing cloud of dust when Robert stood alongside her. Susanna jumped.

'Robert! You scared me!' she cried, clutching her hand to her thudding heart.

'Sorry, Mistress.'

She turned back to the disappearing dirt cloud. Robert's ruse of pretending to have falling sickness only served to remind her that her father feared he was growing poorly again, though perhaps by now he'd recovered. She remembered her mother's turn of mind as well as half the folk in Stratford. Shakespeare was forever play acting, they claimed, just like Robert had done, when there was never a solitary thing wrong with him. His claim for the medicines may just have been another of his tricks, they'd say. Well, that's as may be, but her father had sent for those medicines and he must need them more than anything else in his life presently – even his blessed manuscripts. And now both the medicines and his life's work were slung across Ratsey's black and white piebald.

'We must go after them,' she whispered.

'Hold on there, Mistress Susanna,' Robert began, eyes wide with fear. 'We've come away with our lives and a horse to boot and–'

'Not a very good horse, eh Robert?'

'A jade some would say, but a horse just the same, and you know what they says about gift horses ...? Any road up, Mistress, we've come away with one horse, which as far as it goes, is no bad payment from Ratsey. So why would you want to go after him?'

'We have to.'

'Now Susanna, I'm no righter of wrongs you know that.'

'We have to.'

'Or hunter of highway men.'

She stared silently at the road ahead.

Robert knew better than to argue further. They were going down a road to perdition, most likely to end up in Ratsey's lair. He walked back to the cart, hoping he could mend the damaged wheel. Even with the old dapple grey mare on her own, they could still reach Oxford in a few days. He gazed down at the rear of the cart and gave a heavy-hearted sigh.

'Axel's broken, Mistress Susanna.'

She tried to calm herself. But try as hard as she could, all she saw in her mind's eye was her father having a turn, and her husband ministering to him. What would become of them all?

'Mistress, did you hear me? The axel's broken.'

Susanna took a deep breath. 'We must go after them ... on horseback.'

'In the Devil's name, why?'

'They've taken the medicine – all the manuscripts – our money, the lot. We've no choice, we're going.'

Robert knew from long experience of Susanna Hall that arguing would get him a headache, pure and sure. Come what may, he resigned himself to the terrifying truth that they would give chase to the most notorious outlaw in the kingdom, armed only with their wits and an old dapple grey mare.

Chapter 9

'So now I'm a pursuivant of highwaymen,' Robert moaned to the mare. He threw the blanket onto her back in a huff. Then he heard a twig snap. He turned quickly, fists held high, ready to defend what little they had left.

Susanna held up the horse's feed bag. 'Sorry. I've been foraging. It's just what we need to make our brew.'

Within the hour, they had filled their bellies with a nourishing soup of nettles, roots and elder flowers. Susanna nodded to Robert that it was time to go. She grabbed hold of a charred stick and passed it to him.

'You call. Charred side up, you ride first,' she said.

Robert held the toss, and Susanna rode.

They inched along in the tracks of Ratsey and his mob – never sure if they'd come upon them in the woods or clearings. The fear of another surprise attack made them edgy, but at least, she thought, Robert wasn't singing. As the sun set against the nearby hills, Susanna mused, it was the end of their first day. They were late. She pondered back on the mystery of things and what a muddle it had all become. Fact was she was afraid to think forward. The future held no touchstone to the past, save her father.

'Robert? Tell me truly, d'you believe in my father's falling evil spells?'

Robert peered down at Ratsey's tracks. 'It's not for me to say, but they seem real enough to me.'

'Like yours back there?'

Robert raised his eyes to her, wounded. 'In all these years of service with your family, I've had many a doleful day with your grandfather, then with your uncle, then lastly with your father, watching their falling sicknesses. Whatever–'

Susanna glanced to right and left nervously. His voice seemed to cry out their deepest family secret. 'Sssh!'

'D'you think the trees will tell?' he asked acidly. He saw Susanna redden and was sorry for his sarcasm. 'I beg your pardon. I shouldn't have said that.'

Susanna let the awkwardness between them pass. 'Some say he has them for sympathy. To avoid answering burning questions, my mother claims. Or, well – just to be theatrical, others say.'

'Folks will say what they will. But the doctor believes your father's got them, and by all I've seen the Master does take ill, just like his father and his brother before him, may their souls rest in peace.'

They both crossed themselves silently, more in superstition than belief.

'Master Shakespeare believes that your husband's found some cures in his potions, so that's all that counts for me.'

At heart she believed her father must have the falling evil most times, just as her grandfather did. What she didn't dare say was that she feared someday soon, the same affliction would strike her too. After all, it seemed to run in her family. But it was a strange illness where you could be bright and busy for days or months on end. Then, without warning, you'd fall over or talk gibberish or make an ass of yourself anytime anywhere. Problem was, if she had her way, her father would need to find another doctor with other remedies to cure him in the future, for she had no intention of setting eyes on Dr John Hall again.

She was struck once more by how it had all started. From the moment she decided to take the manuscripts, the die was cast. She'd gone home intending to bring them to her father personally – hoping he'd invite her to stay to see him perform. For some daft reason she thought she could sneak away without anyone caring. After all, no one ever paid her a blind bit of notice, save Robert and Chaos.

When she walked down the way to her home she had a spring in her step. She had the manuscripts, now all she needed was the cloak and her father's medicines. As she passed through the garden gate, Chaos greeted her with licks and a wagging tail. Together they ran up the stairs to her bedroom. In the oak chest at the foot of her bed was the jewelled cloak, all wrapped up to give to her father on his long hoped-for return. Now she would be giving it to him in person – in Oxford. She tingled with excitement and looked down at Chaos. 'Course her dog would have to come with her. If she left him behind, her husband was sure to poison him.

And so they went downstairs to Dr Hall's pharmacy. She knew how there was always a box of medicines standing at the ready in case her father needed it. All she'd have to do was find it. Standing there, she marvelled at the pretty blue and white porcelain bottles labelled with natural remedies, poisons and magical herbs and how such vile things from wormwood to arsenic could cure the sick. Running her finger along the shelves of prepared potions, she was mildly surprised that none of them were labelled for her father. She rummaged through the clutter of smaller bottles on his workbench, knowing that whatever she touched needed to be put back exactly as she'd found it. Long ago John Hall had laid down the law that this was his domain, his kingdom, and no one – not any servant, nor even his wife – could enter with the purpose of setting it to rights. Over the years Susanna had been allowed into his inner sanctum, in the main to fetch and carry, so she'd come to know his foibles and filing away of things. On the sideboard, his brown leather casebook for the acutely ill was stacked tidily upon the black leather one for the dead or dying. But search as hard as she could, her father's medicines were nowhere to be seen.

Had her husband set her father's potions aside carelessly or had he hid them away from prying eyes? Chances were, she thought, since John knew her father would ask for them one day or another, they were somewhere safe. After all, her husband took considerable pride in being Shakespeare's physician for his secret and mysterious malady. Though prone to parsimony, John had invested in a new red Moroccan leather notebook just for Shakespeare, which remained about his person at all times. 'Close to my heart,' John had once said to her as he tapped it beneath his doublet. She recalled how her father had sworn him to secrecy when he'd first tended him all those years back. Unlike her husband's other patients, there would be no public reading at the Royal College of Physicians from her husband's casebook of William Shakespeare's illness. It was their most precious family secret, for those who suffered from the falling evil were shunned and cast out.

As Susanna scoured the room, she wondered – not for the first time – if her mother and husband might be conspiring against her father. It was an unhandsome thought, she knew. But the truth was she couldn't be sure that either of them wanted to see William Shakespeare alive and well again in Stratford. The pretence that Shakespeare was in health and jetting about in his silks allowed her mother to be pitied, whilst conveying on Dr John Hall all the rank and circumstance of being Shakespeare's physician without having to work at curing the great playmaker for one narrow minute. The myth of him seemed far better than the man.

Her eyes fell upon a skull sans teeth, glass jars of all manner and shapes with pickled body bits floating inside, including a tall thin jar containing a man's severed thumb with the letter 'T' tattooed on it. She shuddered and wondered what the 'T' stood for. Had its owner had it tattooed there so he could recall how he made his mark when signing important papers?

She furrowed her brow. There were two pine boxes John used for her father's ready-made medicines: one held six bottles and the other a dozen. Surely they wouldn't be hidden among his books? Still, if John and her mother had agreed to keep the medicines from her father, anything was possible. She ran her finger along the shelf as she read the book titles. Carefully, she lifted out *The Uses of Mugwort, The Bleeding of Men with Leeches* and *The Bleeding of Women with Leeches*. Only these were wide enough to hide either box behind them on the higher shelf. Empty. As she put the last of them back in place she frowned. She repeated her search on the lower shelf, taking out *Meadowsweet and the Falling Sickness* and *Physick for the Falling Sickness*. Nothing. Surely, the boxes were here somewhere? Her heart sank. Her husband's special concoctions, which he called his 'efficacious remedies', were nowhere to be seen.

Suddenly, she heard moaning in the surgery next door. John. Her heart leaped into her throat. Susanna pointed at Chaos to stay. John must be seeing to a patient. She listened at the oak-planked door that separated the pharmacy from the surgery. It was a man's moan, low and dull and rhythmic. Somehow, it didn't seem to be the sort of moan a patient made when being examined. If John was in there she was sure he was up to no good. But before her mind caught up with her hand, she'd unlatched the door silently and inched it open. There, on the elm sideboard just inside the surgery, alongside some of her husband's medical tools, sat the smaller of the pine boxes marked 'Shakespeare's Potions'. He must have been filling the box when a patient called at the surgery door, and put it down there for the moment. Now that the door was opened, the heavy, pulsating breathing sounded more like sighs. John was busy with his patient. So, she resolved to steal into the surgery, take the box and head off to Robert and Oxford.

She inched the door open wider and reached across to take the box. Just as she laid her hand on it, the door creaked open wide enough for her to see her husband astride young Sally Caldecott. Sally was sprawled the length of the examination table. Susanna's eyes rested on Sally's legs spread-eagled, skirts raised, bodice unfastened and breasts bouncing up and down to the pumping motions of her husband. John stood, eyes closed, breeches around his ankles, driving into Sally harder and harder. So hard, that Sally began to slide along the table some ways, until he clutched her back to him. Within seconds, though it seemed like an eternity to Susanna, he climaxed, shaking and stirring in ecstasy before he shouted, 'Hallelujah!'

Sally's eyes shot open, surprised perhaps at the use of a holy word for such a sinful deed. Then Sally saw Susanna staring down at her.

'Amen,' Susanna said without emotion. 'You're meant to say "amen", Sally Caldecott. That's the way the good doctor likes it.'

Hall looked up, agog. Sally tried to pull her bodice around her but Hall still weighed her down.

'Uh, Susanna – ah – I can explain – it's not what you think,' Hall called out as he bent down to yank up his breeches, releasing Sally. He didn't see that he had the laces from the girl's bodice entwined in his shirt points. As he bent, he wrenched the bodice free and catapulted it into the hearth.

'My bodice, it'll catch fire,' Sally shrieked, sitting up and hiding her breasts with her arm.

Susanna closed the door behind her. What her husband did no longer mattered. She set the box down whilst she took the jewelled cloak from the satchel. Quickly, she put the box inside and closed the flap. She slung the jewelled cloak across the top of the bag. Her feet were running out of the house before she realised it, pursued by her dog Chaos.

'Susanna, wait!' John pleaded, following her into the garden. 'Truly, it's not what you think!'

Susanna glanced back. He hopped after her, still buttoning his flies. He hadn't seen the shirt that dangled like a lifeless white flag of defeat at the front of his breeches. She looked away quickly to blot the sight out of her mind, only to see Sally clambering through the surgery window, still half-dressed.

'Weren't you able to fetch Sally's bodice from the fire before it burned?' she asked coolly.

'How often have I told you, never enter the surgery without knocking!' John blustered. A good attack is the best defence her mother always said. And that's what he was doing now, just as he'd done in the past.

Chaos jumped up and tore off the bit of shirt hanging from Hall's flies. He cried out, as if the dog had bitten off his manhood. He kicked at Chaos but missed.

'Your damned dog could have done me mortal damage, Susanna!'

Chaos shook the bit of shirt in his jaws as if it were some animal he was killing. She went to pick him up, but John grabbed her arm. She saw from his dark look that he meant to hurt her.

'You can't mean to beat me here and now, husband. In our own garden? What if Sally saw?'

He stopped to think for a second or two. Susanna wondered if Sally thought she was special. Then she asked herself what if Sally or any of his other paramours saw her husband hurting her? Even if they did, it wouldn't matter. Susanna belonged to her husband. She was his chattel to do with as he pleased. Still, the threat that Sally might see them had worked. John turned his head.

Susanna tore her arm free and ran off. He raced after her, grasping at her skirts. 'Where do you think you're running to?' he called.

Just as she reached the steps that led to the back gate, Hall gripped her arm and spun her around.

The potion bottles jangled inside the satchel.

Hall's eyes bulged. 'What's in there?'

When Susanna didn't answer, he glowered, 'Are those my potions?'

Still Susanna said nothing. Keep him guessing what you're thinking, she urged herself, or you'll lose your moment to escape.

She could see his mind whirring, and realised that her mother hadn't told him yet about her father's letter.

'Why are you home, *good wife*? Shouldn't you be doing your chores at your mother's?'

As Susanna wrestled to free her arm, he ripped at her bodice, then her sleeve. She looked down at her torn dress, sickened by what he'd done to it and what he was about to do to her. She recoiled. 'Have you no shame, John?'

'For what?'

She could see he was truly puzzled.

'O, *that*?' he motioned with his head towards the surgery window. 'No.'

'You swore "never again in our home," husband.'

He shrugged. 'Seems I lied.'

He revolted her. She needed to go – now. She struggled to free herself again and scowled at him, 'Leave go my arm, husband!'

Thin-lipped and full of fury, he whipped his other arm back and struck Susanna with his all his might. She reeled, stumbling on the steps. The bottles rattled again inside the satchel as she fell.

'Give me the satchel,' he repeated.

He held out his hand, more in menace than in peace. Just then, there was a loud knock at the surgery door. Susanna looked back, seeing Mistress Evans, young Sally's grandmother, doing the banging. She couldn't help but smile.

'I think you may want to answer the surgery door, husband.'

'Surely you don't expect me to fall for that old ruse a second time? The satchel,' he growled, wriggling his fingers at her, in a signal to give it back.

Susanna glanced back to the surgery. Mistress Evans was gone. Her heart sank. John would beat her. She looked up at him, anger growing like a wild weed in her heart.

'Where do you think you're going with that satchel?' he asked.

'Robert's asked for it.'

'You mean Father Shakespeare asked for it,' he spat.

'Don't spit his name at me, Dr High-an'-Mighty Hall. It's Will Shakespeare that bought you this house and all you are!'

'Just as I bought you!' He yanked her to him and bent down to kiss her roughly. 'Though I sometimes think I'd be better off with any old heifer.'

Susanna struggled to turn her head away.

'You dare refuse me? You're my property, good wife. And if I wish to take you here in this garden, so I shall!'

Hall pinched Susanna's jaw and turned her face back to him. She was a living, breathing woman who wanted love, understanding and above all, harmony in her life. She'd been raised, like every other girl, to believe that the family was everything, and that her husband was its heart. She had long ago given up on love and understanding, but still prayed daily for peace. But even that had been denied her.

John bent down and gave her a fierce, brambly kiss on the mouth. Should she thrust her knee into his groin and make a run for it? The world seemed to spin round and round until, at last, all her fine thoughts of resisting her husband passed. She saw the Promethean fire in his eyes.

'Do your worst.'

He gave her a wry smile. 'I'm a man and you're my *good lady* wife. You have denied me long enough.'

'Since yesterday?'

He looked at her. 'Considering your advancing age, you're not a bad-looking woman, Susanna.'

She turned her head aside and stared at the stone wall. She was near on thirty-three and her life was over. Her husband, twenty years her senior, thought only of two things: medicine and sex, though not always in that order. If her mother were to be believed, sex was the only thing men thought about. What was her phrase? Such is the simplicity of man to hearken after the flesh. Women were necessary to sex, and that was what gave women their place in the world, her mother said.

John ripped again at her sleeves and her bodice. Susanna knew what he intended, and forced herself to look at him as he raped her.

'Dr Hall!' a craggy voice called out. He stopped dead.

'Dr Hall!' the old woman's voice echoed across the garden. 'Haven't you violated enough women for one day? First my granddaughter, then–'

Hall pulled away from Susanna, smoothing down his clothes.

Mistress Evans, though well into her seventies and somewhat frail, had a voice that rang out like Gabriel's horn. She walked with a stick and was bent with a granny's hump, but she was still a force to be reckoned with.

'And now you're violating your good lady wife?'

'My dear Mistress Evans,' John said in a tone that oozed like a sweet cordial, 'you're mistaken.'

Susanna brushed herself down. Her dress was badly torn and her bodice laces ripped. Mistress Evans gazed over to her. 'My poor dear,' she sighed, shaking her head.

Susanna felt as though she should fling herself at Mistress Evans's feet in thanks.

John slid his eyes from her to Mistress Evans.

'You're wondering how you can make me believe you're the injured one, Dr Hall?' Mistress Evans quipped.

'But, dear lady, you're mistaken as I've already said. I–'

She stepped closer. 'Mistaken? 'Bout what, doctor? You're a fornicator! A sex fiend, hear? Now leave your good woman alone!'

He blinked, dumbfounded. 'That's no woman. That's my wife.'

'No woman?' Mistress Evans asked, wintry-eyed.

He shrugged. 'Mere chattel.'

Mistress Evans inched closer. 'You wouldn't like it if I called you a mere quack?'

John opened his mouth to speak, but Mistress Evans silenced him. 'A charlatan maybe?' she asked.

Susanna's eyes darted between them, while behind, she saw Chaos slink into the house.

'Mistress Evans, I'm a Puritan!'

'Puritan? HAH!'

'My dear woman, I'll have you know that I'm respected for my beliefs.'

Mistress Evans grimaced and raised her stick. She thumped John over the head.

'Ouch! Have you lost your mind?'

Just then, Chaos waddled out of the house with Sally Caldecott's charred bodice between his teeth. He padded over to Mistress Evans, laying her granddaughter's property at her feet. Mistress Evans hooked the bodice onto the end of her stick and held it up in the air, waving it in John's face. 'No more than my granddaughter lost this?'

She took hold of the bodice and whipped Hall with it. Susanna stood back. This was her moment. She ran towards the garden gate, pulling the jewelled cloak around her neck to cover her ripped gown. She grabbed what clothes she could from the line and ran faster.

Run! She cried to herself. Run from this hell!

'Susanna?'

She looked around her abruptly with a start. Robert was standing beside her.

'You were gasping for breath,' he said.

'Was I?'

He could see the fear in her eyes.

'Let's rest a while. We've still a long way to go.'

Susanna agreed and dismounted, feeling most strange.

Chapter 10

Darkness had fallen some while before they tracked Ratsey and his mob to their riverside inn hideout. Susanna motioned for Robert to unbridle the dappled grey mare and set her loose. The horse was wheezing so badly that Susanna feared she'd give them away. Someone was sure to take charge of the poor beast soon, for if it had life in this workaday world, it had a use. As the horse ambled off, Susanna still felt a pang of regret.

She looked at Chaos. A yapping dog would be a danger too. She gave him the command to be silent, tapping her finger to her lips. He slunk down low. He had never disobeyed a command yet and if he did now, then she didn't know her dog.

Susanna, Robert and Chaos stole into the inn yard. Ratsey's black and white piebald grazed, tethered near a side window of the inn, his coat glistening in the moonlight. Soft yellow candlelight flickered from within. No wonder Ratsey was such a successful thief, Susanna thought as she untied the horse's reins from the metal ring. The highwayman always had his escape at the ready. The piebald horse was enticed away by Robert waving some grass at it. By the time he returned to the window, Ratsey's distinctive voice echoed inside.

'Teacake!'

Susanna's heart pounded. Robert flattened himself against the stone wall, holding his hand to his chest. But all went quiet again as suddenly as Ratsey's bellowing had begun. She bent down, unlaced her boots and took them off. She tied them together and passed them to Robert. He hung them around his neck and motioned for her to move forward.

When she peeked inside, she saw the ruggedly handsome highwayman seated at a scrubbed pine table, with stacks of coins set out neatly in front of him. Behind him was a large four-poster bed, its blankets all in a heap. Teacake stood before him, head slung low.

'We've managed less than twelve pounds between all of them,' Ratsey scolded. 'It's hardly enough to keep us in malmsey and women for a week, now is it?'

Teacake shook his head, fingering his cap.

Ratsey turned his head to the foot of the bed and gazed at Shakespeare's jewelled cloak.

'No, Ratsey,' Teacake mumbled in a mouse's squeak.

All of a sudden, brash voices were raised in song from another room:

> My masters and friends and good people draw near,
> And look to your purses, for that I do say,
> And though little money in them you do bear,
> It cost more to get, than to lose in a day.

Ratsey grinned. 'Off with you and join the others. Tomorrow must be a better day.'

Teacake scuttled out. Ratsey stood and stretched. He grabbed hold of his candle and took it over to the bedside table. He held up the jewelled cloak to the light, the small diamonds reflecting greedily in his eyes.

It was several hours before the bawdy songs died down, and the candles were extinguished. And all the while, Susanna and Robert had waited, stiff with cold, beneath Ratsey's window. Earlier, they'd tossed a coin for the privilege of retrieving the satchel, and again, Susanna won.

She gazed up at the full moon and the stars. By its position, she reckoned there must be only a few hours of darkness left. She listened to the cacophony of snores which had rung out steadily from the darkened inn for well over an hour. It was as safe as it would get, so she nudged the dozing Robert, signalling that it was time. She looked down at Chaos and patted him, bringing her finger to her lips once again. In the distance she could hear the river gurgling. Soon, they'd either be sailing to Oxford on that river, or they'd be dead. But without her father's manuscripts and potions, she'd prefer death to seeing his reaction if they arrived Oxford empty-handed.

Susanna stood before the darkened window, her moonlit silhouette reaching across the floor. With a tool Robert had found in the stable, she prised open the window. It creaked as it gave way. She froze, half-expecting Ratsey to rise up from the darkness, pointing his pistol in her face. The seconds ticked by like pouring treacle from a jar. Then, just as suddenly as the snores had stopped, she heard the reassuring melody of heavy breathing once again. She pulled the casement window open wide and climbed into Ratsey's den.

As she tiptoed over to the pine table, a shaft of moonlight fell onto some papers. One of the doxies stirred, raising her head and stretching her arms, before falling back down with a sigh. Ratsey slept on his back between the redhead and the blonde curled up in his arms.

If only her heart would stop banging like some shutter in a storm! Do what you came to do and get out, Susanna urged herself. She inched out her arm and felt for the papers, silently sliding them towards her. It was her father's play *Othello*. She dabbed her hand softly on the table, feeling for other plays, but none were there. As she rolled up *Othello* and stuffed it into her skirts, she thought, only thirty-eight more to find.

She turned and stared down at Ratsey. He was a fine specimen of a man she had to admit, even if he was the most notorious highwayman alive. And those doxies … without a stitch of clothing, not even a shift. The redhead's leg lay across Ratsey, and the blonde had her hand resting on the redhead's thigh. Susanna found herself wondering how it must feel to make love to a real man. But straightaway as she thought this, her face burned with shame. She'd come to get her father's things, not to admire a handsome, dangerous rogue. She looked away and saw a large chest on the floor beneath the bed.

Just then, Ratsey sat bolt upright. 'Get him! Over there!' he barked.

Susanna dived under the bed.

'Now there, Ratsey,' the redhead cajoled, 'we're not robbin' anyone.'

'No, Ratsey, we're beddin' each other,' the blonde added sleepily.

Susanna's ears pounded. She had dashed underneath the bed without thinking. Now what? Ropes held the mattress aloft, but despite the crisscrossing and knots in them, the mattress sagged, poking and prodding her.

'What?' Ratsey said dreamily.

'We're abed, Ratsey ... the three of us,' the redhead told him.

Susanna heard a rustling.

'That's better, love. I can feel you know what I mean,' the doxy purred.

Susanna heard kissing and felt the whole bed sway as they made love.

'My go now,' the blonde complained.

Ratsey turned, hitting Susanna squarely on her backside. The unmistakable sounds of lovemaking made Susanna flush with heat. She stared blinking, trapped; when unexpectedly, she spotted a wooden chest dead ahead. She reached forward to prise it open. It was locked. Then, without warning, the ecstatic writhing above her head stopped. Seconds later, Ratsey was snoring.

'Aw,' the blonde whined. 'I never get my go.'

The redhead dropped her legs over the side of the bed, feeling for something with her hand. Panic filled Susanna's head. The doxy must be in want of the pisspot. Susanna grabbed hold of the pot beside her, and lifted it into the doxy's searching hand.

'Ta very kindly,' said the redhead.

Surely this couldn't be happening to her? The tinkling sound of the doxy weeing told her that it most certainly was. She felt like screaming. The pisspot re-appeared, wobbling in the doxy's hand.

Susanna grabbed hold and placed it on the wooden floor. Then, she heard a loud snort and the cocking of a pistol.

'Who's there?' Ratsey snarled.

'Just me, love – call of nature,' the redhead cooed.

Ratsey laughed.

'Come here, "just me".'

The bed began to creak and sway again.

What could be taking her so long? Robert asked himself. And why did he let her talk him into all manner of trouble? Couldn't Susanna just do as she was bid for once? When the Master hears of what's been going on he'd be sure to flog him – who'd been his poor obedient manservant – to within an inch of his worthless life. Although, he had to admit, that weren't the Master's way. More likely he'd rhyme him a rhyme and tell Robert how he'd let him down. Then he'd look into the Master's sad dark eyes and feel the whole world's weight bearing upon his shoulders. Sure as anything, the Master wouldn't truly blame him for all their ills, but he'd still make Robert feel he'd disappointed him. That is, if they reached ever Oxford. Robert peered in the window for Susanna.

Truth were he loved her like the daughter he never had. It pained him to see her so sad and lonely all rolled into one. Why couldn't Mistress Shakespeare see what she'd done to her eldest child? O, he didn't expect Judith, spoiled creature as she were, to see how she could catch more love with honey than vinegar, as they say, but Mistress Shakespeare should have seen better. And what would the Master say when he saw his well-beloved girl and the state she'd got herself into? O, it were a curse to love a child from afar, as the Master did. Many was the time he'd heard the Master say, it were a curse to love a thankless child, and Robert always put those words against Judith's name, not Susanna's. But what if the Master thought Susanna was thankless for her boldness? Sure as dawn will follow this moonlit night, there would be a reckoning in Oxford. He only hoped that he'd not be the one to pay the bill.

Susanna jumped when she heard a tinny sound. Ratsey rolled over. There it was again. She raised her eyes. A set of keys dangled between the head of the mattress and the wall. As she craned her neck, she saw the keys were attached by a leather strap to Ratsey's wrist. She slid forward just enough to ease the leather strap off him. Asleep, his wrist was smaller and limp, and the knotted leather loosened easily. The keys fell into the palm of her other hand. She slid on her belly towards the wooden chest. She tried the first key, but the lock wouldn't give. Then the second – again nothing. The third key was her last hope. The lock clicked open.

She lifted the lid and felt inside. Relief spread over her like a blanket. She'd found the satchel. Opening the flap, her fingers touched the manuscripts and bottles, then slid out from beneath the bed. As she stood, she looked back at Ratsey and his doxies. They slept like babes, mouths ajar, and she wondered again what it felt like to be made love to by a man like him. She turned and saw Robert at the window, pacing back and forth. There would be time enough to wonder upon the mystery of things from a safer distance. She slung the satchel over her shoulder, but it brushed against something that fell like loose coins to the floor.

Ratsey stirred. Susanna turned. It was the jewelled cloak, crumpled in a heap. Ratsey sat up, eyes wide. She snatched up the cloak, ran for the window and dove out, head first.

'Scurvy caterpillar!' Ratsey growled.

The doxies awoke, snatching the bedclothes to their breasts. Ratsey pushed the redhead doxy onto the floor. He reached under his pillow and turned back, brandishing his pistols.

Outside, Robert pulled Susanna to her feet. Swathes of papers fell out of the satchel. She stooped down and snatched them up, clasping them to her.

'Run, Robert!' she cried.

She sprinted ahead. Chaos dashed off into the darkness after them, collecting a paper as it flew away.

Ratsey ran to the window waving his pistols. Suddenly, he let out a shriek, dancing from foot to foot. He dropped to a squat, moaning. Embedded in the soles of his feet were gems from the jewelled cloak.

'You all right, Rats?' the redhead asked.

Ratsey grumbled and hauled himself to his knees at the windowsill. He took careful aim at Susanna's back and fired.

The shots whizzed over her head, just as she bent down to get the paper from Chaos's mouth. She looked back and saw Ratsey, scowling as he crouched in the window frame. He held her stare, engraving her image in his mind to exact his revenge at a later date, should she escape. All Susanna could think of was getting into a boat and rowing all the way to Oxford. She turned and darted off again.

As they reached the riverbank, they heard noises. Ratsey had flung open the front door of the inn. Wild-eyed, half-dressed, he shouted, 'Varlet! You'll pay! You'll rue your ruffling Gamiliel Ratsey!'

Chaos ran past Robert and Susanna and hopped aboard the boat. Susanna followed. Robert cast them off with a push. Then he untied the other boats moored at the landing stage, giving them a shove downriver.

'Robert!'

'Coming,' he called back as he waded to the boat. Climbing aboard, Susanna saw he was grinning like a cat who'd just had the most almighty dish of cream. 'Well done,' he said. He took the oars and rowed to the far side of the riverbank, where they hid under an old crumbling brick bridge. They heard all manner of hooting and hollering from Ratsey and his mob in the distance. Susanna looked behind her but saw only the flickering of candlelight.

'You hurt Susanna?' Robert asked softly as he rowed further beneath the bridge.

She shook her head. She felt that old heart of hers beating at a gallop again. Stupidly, for the first time, she truly recognised that this was no game. She had endangered her life – and Robert's – for the sake of her father's medicines and manuscripts. The folly of what she'd just done made her see that everything had always been for her father and his art. All the family's sacrifices, all their labours, day in and day out, paled – her father and his work always came first. Until that very moment, she hadn't realised why she'd risked everything to save them. It wasn't for any selfish motive to buy herself an escape from Stratford. It was her gift of love to her father. Though she still longed to see him perform his plays to her, she'd pursued Ratsey for *him*. He needed his plays and medicine. She gazed across at Robert, who waited on her answer.

'No, Robert, I'm not hurt. Are you?'

Chapter 11

Robert looked up at the easterly sky. The stars were fading into a rainbow of purples, pinks, and oranges. As it was spring, he reckoned it must be around four-thirty in the morning. Soon the colours would fade into tender hues of blue and it would be dawn. He'd been rowing for hours, or was it days? His arms ached just like they did after threshing wheat, and his eyes stung from straining to see in the pitch of night.

He gazed over to Susanna, all curled up in a ball, eyes shut, clutching that satchel to her whilst she slept. They had rowed a fair few miles since the Oxfordshire inn and Ratsey. Surely, they were out of danger now? Just then his tummy rumbled. O, how his eyes were gritty and his belly empty and hollow! Best keep your mind to rowing, he urged himself half-heartedly.

But his thoughts wandered to Master Shakespeare and what he'd say about their adventures, and how he'd best explain himself, and why he brought Susanna to Oxford, and what'd happened back in Stratford to make him do such a thing. Robert heaved a weighty sigh. He needed a little sleep, not much of one, just some twenty or thirty winks, before he faced the Master. The truth of it was, he couldn't clearly remember any of those things that sat so heavy on his mind, much less how or if Susanna'd talked him into coming along. He pulled the oars up and quietly placed them in the rowboat. Just twenty winks and he'd be fit company. Maybe only ten would do the trick. Robert pulled up his rough cloak around his ears and scrunched down into the boat, resting his neck against the bow. As his eyes batted opened and closed, as he puzzled through for the hundredth time how he'd explain about their scrapes and escapes.

Susanna was awakened by Robert's snores. She gave a good long stretch, wondering where she was and why her back and neck ached. When her fingertips skimmed the water, the night's adventure flooded back. Her eyes shot open. She was curled up in a boat – not much more than a skiff – with her face pointing to the morning sky. The first blues of a fine dawn washed over the evening stars, the full moon faded into the day. Swallows swooped down onto the river, scooping up insects in their beaks. The wood pigeons cooed in the lime trees along the riverbank. They were floating downriver peacefully with the current, the only people on the landscape. The grassy banks seemed nearly a quarter of a mile distant on either side. She quietly propped herself up and took a deep breath. It was the first time she'd felt safe since their encounter with the ruffler. They'd escaped the wrath of Ratsey and his mob by hiding under the arches of that ruined bridge whilst Ratsey blundered upstream, thinking he was outwitting them. Bluff and double-bluff, she smiled to herself. With the river's swift current, she knew there'd be no need to lie low in their bedraggled rowboat now. Ratsey was gone from their lives, and they had lived to tell their story.

But then, as if she simply must have some bone or other to worry, her mind turned to their lives in Stratford. They had been ruled by the great Shakespeare and his plays. The rhythm of her daily chores began with fending off would-be playwrights, then, on her mother's orders, destroying their life's work and dreams in the fire. Anne Shakespeare claimed it was to save innocent families from a ruinous fate. Even their Stratford neighbours had remarked that life would never be the same because of Will Shakespeare and his fame and fortune. Some were happy that the town would forever prosper because of him. Many others were not.

Susanna wondered why *everyone* flocked to them on the wings of some lonesome dove, praying for favours. Because folk were simple and sought out … what had her father said? Ah, yes – they sought the 'bubble reputation'. They wanted to be close to fame and fortune hoping that some might rub off on them. That's why they had all those young playmakers on their doorstep each and every day. That's why all Stratford cared where Will Shakespeare was playing and what he was writing and how he fared. He was no longer theirs – her mother's, hers and Judith's. He belonged to the world. In the words of her mother, his family must seem an almighty inconvenience to him now, other than to tend to the hopeful 'bubblers.'

But was she a bubbler too, peeking glimpses of his plays whenever she could? As Will Shakespeare's daughter she had some claim, maybe, in his thoughts and dreams. After all, she gladly worked in his home, sewed his special costumes, like the jewelled cloak, fended off those who came to his door – just to be some small part of his life. He was her adored father who snarled himself up in the string when they made their knot garden. He was the father who punted with all three children along the Avon, playing silly games, chasing them through the woods, hugging them to him and laughing. Susanna gave a jagged sigh. Her father was the only person – aside from Robert – who'd ever made her feel loved. And that – not his plays – was why she was going to Oxford. To feel a father's love once more.

Of course, she could see as clear as crystal why strangers loved her father too. He'd found a way of stitching his words together into a beautiful garment that spoke to them of their everyday lives – whether he was writing about kings or queens or fools. Where most people talked in sackcloth and ashes, her father arrayed his words into a sumptuous quilt of gold and silken tissue. Where others possessed one or two sober-suited phrases, Shakespeare enjoyed an entire shimmering wardrobe of words. It stunned her that this was the same man she fondly remembered whiling away his days all stacked up end-to-end playing children's games with them by banks of the River Avon.

Even more incredible, all those plays he wrote from his vast wardrobe of words had found some practical way of putting a roof over their heads, clothes on their backs and food on the table. She'd been told myriad times by the wishful playmakers that her father was the first of them to support his family by his words alone. But his words also took him away from them, making home a dismal place. It was a mystery to her how she could love his plays so powerfully and yet pine for him to come home. She gazed down at the satchel.

She propped herself up against the stern and opened it. She must count the plays out, all thirty-nine of them. Smoothing them on a large oilskin that lined the bottom of the rowboat, she saw his tightly packed scrawl with margin notes. She thought back to how his manuscripts, with all his notes, had come to live in Stratford when he was so little there. She recalled her mother's fury when those two big poems of his were published in the plague year of 1592, and how she shouted of her shame that he'd written about his betraying her with someone else. But when all his sonnets were published six years ago in 1609 ... she winced remembering her father's anguished cry to her mother: *Hell is empty and all its devils are here!* How her mother carried on like the Furies! Everyone had that book of sonnets in their hands in the marketplace, at their dinner tables, in church or tucked under their pillows in bed at night. O, how her mother was shamed, and how Susanna felt pity for her. It was bad enough, Anne had cried in great heart-pounding sobs, that her husband travelled so much, but to write in poetry things like 'Hate-away' for Hathaway and about his tortured love for 'dark ladies' and 'young men' was too much to bear. It meant her mother daren't venture out into the street without someone sniggering behind splayed fingers at her. No wonder Shakespeare had stormed off.

Shortly after the sonnets were published her father came home. There were days on end of slammed doors and muffled cries, of him raising his voice for all to hear, swearing that he'd never authorised that varlet printer in London to publish them. He told anyone who'd listen how his poems were stolen, his words changed, then published without a by-your-leave or a penny crossing his palm. But when folk in Stratford asked if he'd written them, he owned the sonnets as his work alone, despite the printer's changes. Each day Susanna saw him, she felt the pain in his soul. She believed him when he vowed to her that he never wished those poems to be published. And she knew why. For all his strutting and fretting upon the stage, William Shakespeare was a most private man.

But much of his innermost thoughts were now printed for the world to see. Her mother was right to be shamed, even *he* owned to that. Still, it was weeks if not months before her parents were speaking to one another again. The solution, which pleased him and made her mother take some comfort, was that he would henceforth live at home in Stratford and she would become the guardian of his original manuscripts. These precious papers would never again leave the family home.

The problem with the solution was too much water had travelled under that bridge and they were used to living apart. Susanna recalled one day how plates flew and her mother's shrill cry rang out when her father said he had to away to London to sign some papers to purchase the Gatehouse at Blackfriars. Why did he need a London home after all these years? her mother shrieked. Susanna never heard his response because a pewter charger hit the wall just as he answered. Within the hour, he'd packed a bag, hired a horse and rode off. Since then, he kept in touch by letter now and again. And that's how her mother came to keep his manuscripts and her father won his freedom.

Susanna finished counting. All thirty-nine manuscripts were there. The play that lay on top was *Much Ado about Nothing*. She'd read it many times before, but each time she visited her father's plays, she discovered something new – in them and in herself. Its heroine, Beatrice, and the hero of sorts, Benedick, loved to hate each other. At times, Benedick seemed like some hovering albatross, at others like a sighing Romeo. Yet it was a tale to please all audiences, she imagined. At several points, Susanna stifled a giggle so as not to awaken Robert, still curled up so at the bow. When she came to the beginning of scene three of the second act, she read the lines:

> I do much wonder, that one man seeing how much another man is a fool, when he dedicates his behaviours to

love, will, after he hath laughed at such shallow follies in others, become the argument of his own scorn by falling in love ... I have known when there was no music with him but the drum and the fife, and now had he rather hear the tabor and the pipe.

Susanna read her father's margin note. It looked like 'the Countess', then her own name, 'Susanna.' What could he mean? She decided to read on without peering at his notes. She could always puzzle them through later. What mattered now was to meet up again with Dogberry who was the mirror of Constable Brearley of Stratford, and to enjoy reading how Benedick would get his Beatrice.

As the morning sun warmed them, Susanna passed from *Much Ado* to *A Midsummer Night's Dream*. Again, she felt as if she were in the Forest of Arden where she had played so often with her father, brother and sister when they were young and green. And again, she saw margin notes with her name scrawled next to Helena's. Then she read Oberon's lines:

> I know a bank where the wild thyme blows,
> Where oxlips and the nodding violet grows,
> Quite over-canopied with luscious woodbine,
> With sweet musk-roses and with eglantine.

Her eyes filled with tears as she recalled the first time she'd heard that verse. She'd taken a tumble by the river and her father was dressing her wounds with dock leaves. She was five.

Susanna gazed up at the morning sky, feeling as if a tremendous weight had been lifted. Her father hadn't forgotten the good times, and somehow hadn't forgotten her, as her name was scrawled in many places in the margins of many plays. So, it had never been a case of out-of-sight-out-of-mind after all. It seemed more likely to her that he'd become too big for Stratford to hold.

Time passed effortlessly, floating downriver. Susanna had dipped in and out of a dozen manuscripts. Now, her father's dramatic masterpiece, *The Tragedy of Hamlet*, lay on top of the pile. Though she loved it, she had to feel strong inside herself whenever she delved into it. The story was about a mad prince bubbling over with a sharp wit poisoned by thoughts of revenge. It made her tremendously sad. Hamlet was a grown man of eighteen who hated his uncle for killing his father. Without a conscious thought she suddenly remembered the hot row between her Uncle Gilbert and her father over her mother shortly after Hamnet's death. Then she remembered how Gilbert brought her mother fresh-cut pansies in the spring and how her face lit up. Was Gilbert the Haberdasher, as he was called about the town, her mother's lover? She pushed the malicious thought from her gossiping mind.

She turned the page and came to the curious passage where Polonius told his son Laertes how to behave on his travels, she bit her lip to stop from sobbing. These were the words her father lamented he'd never be able to say to his own son Hamnet, the son who would never find his way in the world:

> Give thy thoughts no tongue
> Nor any unproportion'd thought his act.
> Be thou familiar but by no means vulgar.
> The friends thou hast and their adoption tried
> Grapple them to thy heart with hoops of steel …
> Beware of entrance to a quarrel …
> Give every man thine ear, but few thy voice:
> Take each man's censure, but reserve thy judgment.
> Costly thy habit as thy purse can buy
> But not express'd in fancy; rich not gaudy:
> For the apparel oft proclaims the man …
> Neither a borrower nor a lender be:
> For loan oft loses both itself and friend;
> … This above all – to thine own self be true;
> And it must follow as the night the day,
> Thou canst not then be false to any man.

Such wise counsel had been given to the world because it had been denied her father to give his dead son. She placed the play upside down among the others on the oilskin.

Now it was she who was making her way into the world for the first time, without any such wise saws. When she'd see her father in Oxford, he wouldn't speak words like those of Polonius. His words to her, she feared, would be to return to Stratford, to her hearth and home and the husband she'd never loved. That was a woman's lot, nothing more, nothing less. O, if she had only been born a boy! The wonders she might behold! Alas, she was but a woman, unloved and uneducated, aside from her reading.

Robert dreamily opened an eye and saw tears streaming down Susanna's face as she read his Master's plays. Beauty personified, Shakespeare's good friend Richard Burbage had told him once. That's what Shakespeare's plays were, beauty personified. No wonder she cried. Best leave her to her loving thoughts of her father and the good care of his words. Robert closed his eyes to dream of feasts yet to be eaten and women yet to be loved.

Chapter 12

Susanna's senses filled with wonder. So this was Oxford. Though they were still some distance from the city's centre she was awestruck by the dreamy spires that seemed to nudge the ambling clouds. She'd heard of the spires, of course, but had never imagined that there would be so many bells. Hundreds – no, thousands of them – and each one pealing a different note.

Marmalade-coloured stone buildings lined the riverbank. They were old, much older than anything she'd seen in mostly timber-framed and wattle and daub Stratford. These buildings spoke of grand history and wealth. They had all manner of decoration around the windowsills and gargoyles perched beneath the rooftops scowling and poised to spew out rainwater onto hapless passers-by.

Robert tapped Susanna's shoulder and pointed to the bridge ahead. 'This is where we get off.'

Still absorbed in the stunning beauty of the place, she asked, 'Where are we, Robert?'

He glanced at her. Poor mite. Didn't she know it was Oxford? Never been out of Stratford. Never seen a *real* city. He shook his head. What would happen if the Master decided to bring her on to London with him? Why, she'd either flee back to Stratford, vowing never to leave again, or more likely, fall in love with it. Any road up, he ached for the Master to take charge and help her. Things were all topsy-turvy down. He just wanted to be a plain old manservant again with his Master telling him what he wanted done. That's not to say that he didn't still love Susanna, he did. It was more that he was troubled by the thought of Master Shakespeare's flinty eye casting a spell on him for bringing her along unbidden. Then he feared the Master would reproach him for being a lowly churl. Robert could hear him in his head: *You ought to have stood up to her, stopped her from rustling your cart away.* But the Master hadn't seen Susanna's eyes as she ran towards him. He didn't care if it was a home truth that she ought to be in Stratford, managing two hearths and homes. The boat wobbled and he felt her prod his arm.

'I asked "where are we?"'

'Sorry, Susanna, I were miles away, travelling in them circles in my head again. Why, it's Oxford.'

'I know that much, Robert Whatcott. But where in Oxford?'

'That's Bookbinder's Bridge,' he pointed. 'It's where we have to leave the boat.'

They glided through the jumble of rowboats, skiffs and barges moored by the old stone bridge. Robert caught the eye of the boatman with his soiled oilskin greatcoat, motioning them to a landing jetty. A young boy, probably no more than twelve or thirteen, waited for them at the top of the steps. When the boy caught sight of them, he gave a great wave as if they were old friends, and pointed to where they should get off. Robert tossed him the rope. The boy skilfully caught it and tied them to the jetty.

'Hello, strangers,' he greeted them with a bright smile, trying to hide his sideways glances at Susanna's peculiar gown.

'We're no strangers, I'll have ye know. We're English,' Robert protested, his hands dug onto his hips.

The boy ignored him and held out his hand. Robert sized him up, and judged him not to be a danger. He gave him his hand and the boy hoisted him out. Though he might be after their money, Robert imagined, he could beat him in any fair fight.

'I can hear you're no foreigners, but you're strangers to Oxford, aren't you?'

Robert turned to help Susanna out of the rowboat. As she stepped off, clutching Chaos in her arms, it swayed awkwardly.

'Yes,' Susanna replied.

'She is. I'm not,' Robert said in a slight huff.

'No offence intended, sir,' the boy said, lowering his chin to his chest and looking straight at Susanna.

He had eyes the colour of roasted chestnuts, she reckoned, and brilliant white teeth. His jerkin was of the poorer sort and his breeches were sorely mended, but he had shiny new boots of fine black leather. He was no urchin. Someone cared for him.

'We're no conies for you to trap, I'll have you know,' Robert said. Susanna pinched his arm to make him hold his tongue. It was no good starting off on the back foot in a new place, rubbing people up the wrong way and all. Besides, a willing lad might be useful.

'Name's Will. Will Davenant at your service, Mistress. My parents run the Taverne on Cornmarket. Need a room for the night?' He looked sideways at her dress and added, 'Maybe some clothes?'

So that's his wheeze, Robert thought, pursing his lips. He saw Susanna looking at him, eyes as wide as a little girl's at a village fete. She didn't know anything of the world and nothing of the Master's plans. Then again, what little Robert knew of the world you could fit into a thimble. As for the Master's plans, if he were speaking plainly, all he had was an address, somewhere, that is ...

He thrust his hands deep into his cloak, then his breeches pockets. All he knew was where to bring the Master's things. But the where of it was on that letter. By the wrath of God, where had he put it?

'Why thank you – er – Will. But the thing of it is we've got rooms. As for the Mistress's gown, well–' Robert stopped talking, still fumbling through his pockets. He bent in two, reaching deep within his cloak for his secret money pocket, but all he came up with was fluff balls. Robert scratched his head. Only one other secret document pocket, he thought, lifting his sleeve, but again, it was empty. Robert flapped down his cloak sleeve and frowned. God's death! Where had it gone?

Will looked at Susanna. She shrugged and rolled her eyes.

'I don't suppose you know the way ...' Susanna began. She couldn't remember the name of the college.

Suddenly, Robert jumped. He delved into his jerkin and next to his heart he felt Shakespeare's letter, hanging in a pouch around his neck. Victorious, Robert beamed at them and whipped it out. The letter was so crumpled he had to smooth it against his knee so he could read it. 'To Magdalen College. We've some things to give to the King's Men – to Master Shakespeare to be exact,' Robert said, puffing out his chest.

The boy's face grew dark at once. 'Shakespeare?'

Susanna was puzzled by his reaction.

''Course. All Oxford knows where Master Shakespeare is! Follow me.'

Whilst they wended their way through Oxford's bustling streets, Susanna looked skywards. She'd never seen such tall buildings. Why, they must be three storeys above ground and the rest. She hugged Chaos to her. They were in a city where stray dogs were two a penny. Mangy beasts most of them, she thought, as they weaved amongst the people and their animals. A lurcher of sorts caught Chaos's scent and sniffed menacingly at Susanna's skirts. The sniffing grew into a loud growl.

'Shoo!' she cried holding Chaos higher in her arms. If the brute stood on his hind-legs, he'd surely be able to nip at her dog. Chaos cried softly, peering down at it. Just then, Will turned to see the lurcher worrying them. Without hesitation he ran at it, arms flailing and making noises like a lunatic. Susanna's heart leapt in her chest. What manner of boy was this? She looked around for Robert, who had walked on ahead of them. O, why had they so gullibly agreed to follow this mad boy?

Will saw the look on her face. 'Have no worry, Mistress. I'm just scaring off the flea-bitten thing.'

She lowered her eyes, ashamed. Having been robbed twice in a day made her nerves jangle like a tambourine.

Robert and Susanna followed swiftly in Will's footsteps. The streets were finely cobbled and the houses in the lanes were prosperous, yet there were beggars in nearly every doorway. As they passed, some – like the ruffler – claimed to have been injured in the wars, whilst others sat with their tin cups shaking at all who walked by, even stray animals. As they passed a stone doorway further on, a beggar glanced at Susanna and handed her a penny, smiling toothlessly, 'You look to be in more need than me.' Speechless, she accepted it with a gentle nod of thanks.

They walked on a spell, with Susanna turning her head to left and right and up to the buildings hemming in the lane. Suddenly, she heard music playing, and raced forward. Was it the festival of plays, she asked herself. As they rounded the next twist in the lane, they came upon a shabby band of strolling players and their musicians playing a bawdy tune. The singer danced a jig whilst he made up a new rhyme to the old ballad *Return of the Prodigal Son*. When they got to the refrain, a mother dressed in Puritan drab covered her son's ears. The rhyme was as lurid as any Susanna had ever heard. Most people just laughed and sang along – save the mother and her son. Once the tune was over, the singer passed his hat around to be paid something, anything, for their performance.

The singer came up to Susanna, eyeing her from head to toe. He winked at her. 'Fancy a tumble?' his eyes glistened with the hope of a 'yes.'

She frowned and was just about to give him a well-deserved part of her common-sense mind when Robert led her away by the elbow.

'Mustn't linger,' he wagged his finger at her.

Turning the next corner, the lane narrowed and became darker. The penthouses loomed above, projecting over the road and sheltering passers-by from both sunlight and rain. The upper storeys were so close that the householders must be able to touch hands from across the way.

Just then, Robert tripped and lunged forward. A chicken squawked and feathers flew high into the air. Chaos sneezed. Robert caught himself against Will's back, and the boy helped to steady him onto his pegs again. Robert glowered at the shrieking chicken as it scurried off in a zigzag and under a market stall nearby.

He brushed himself off. 'Chickens only cross the road when they can cause the most mayhem,' he said.

Will grinned and motioned for them to walk in single file behind him. 'Just in case,' he smiled.

It was only a little way further before the lane ahead widened again. They'd come to a small square with a huge crowd of people lining the market stalls. Susanna gawped. A stargazer's apprentice decried a special 'See-three-for-the-cost-of-two festival of plays discount' to all and sundry from her makeshift shop, whilst the stargazer herself beckoned with her gnarled fingers for conies to peer at her magic crystals. With an Arabian-style turban, her frazzled silver and red hair peeking out beneath, her hoarse voice, leathery complexion and bangles and beads, she seemed more of a witch than a soothsayer.

Then, suddenly, Susanna heard Will shout, 'Make way!'

The crowd parted like a wave, to reveal a stilt-walker juggling and a tumbler rolling between his legs. Susanna flattened herself against a wall, agog. In their wake were theatrical hawkers handing out leaflets and crying over and over, 'Come see the great Ben Jonson's *The Alchemist*! Come see the world's greatest playmaker perform!'

Robert nudged Susanna to move on, but she was still spellbound. 'I thought Shakespeare was the greatest playmaker,' she mused aloud.

Robert narrowed his eyes at the performers. 'Not to Ben Jonson. Come.'

She allowed him to take her by the arm like a child. She'd never seen such a spectacle in her life, not even when the travelling players came to Stratford. Every street corner had some playacting taking place. Whether it was jugglers or fire-breathers or actors speaking their lines or reciting poetry, all Oxford seemed one enormous play of life to her. Leaflets littered the streets proclaiming some performance or other. Above, she heard an unexpected cry of pain and looked up. From a penthouse window, came another scream. Beside the window was the sign 'Otis, Expert Toothpuller.' Yet something niggled at her whilst Will expertly laced them through the entertainments. Something felt amiss, as though there were a thousand eyes trained on her movements.

Just then there was a tug at Susanna's arm. Chaos growled. Will turned and ran past her. She looked over her shoulder to see him tackling a boy cutpurse who seemed no more than seven or eight years old. When Will stood tall, he held a small money purse aloft in his hand. He strode back towards Susanna, a smile lighting up his whole face. Somehow he seemed familiar to her, like an old friend long ago forgotten.

His eyes trailed down to her side. She saw her skirt was slashed and her money purse, gone. Robert had been next to her all the time, but hadn't seen a thing.

'Yours I think, Mistress?' Will said, holding out the money purse.

Susanna was amazed. 'I hardly felt him take it.'

He looked at her torn and shabby dress. 'It will mend,' she said lifting a shoulder and smiling at him.

They carried on, Robert hugging to one side of Susanna whilst Will guarded her on the other.

'Is it true, as Robert there just said to me, that you're a relation of Master William Shakespeare?' Will asked.

Susanna felt warmly towards him. He was hard working and dared to stop a thief from stealing her money.

'Aye, Will Davenant. I'm his eldest daughter.'

Will pointed his finger at a huge archway.

'That's Magdalen.'

'College?' she asked.

He nodded back just as they spied a crowd of people milling about in the quadrangle beyond.

'Are those people assembled for a play?' Susanna asked expectantly. Perhaps she'd be able to see one of her father's plays today? The thought made the hairs on her arms tingle.

Will looked down, brushing his new boots in the dirt. 'Not exactly,' he muttered.

Susanna and Robert exchanged quizzical looks and made their way through the archway into the quadrangle. Will trailed after them, less eager to join them now that they had been safely delivered. Susanna turned back and felt a pang for him.

'The King's Men are through that archway there,' he pointed to the far corner.

She reached into the money purse he had rescued and took out a groat. 'Here, Will, with our thanks for your kind help,' she said, holding out the coin to him.

The boy pulled back as if he'd been scalded. 'No, Mistress. I can't take money from you – you being Master Shakespeare's daughter and all. No … never!' He backed away several steps before he turned and broke into a run.

Robert looked sternly after the boy. I should hope not, he thought, shaking his head.

Chapter 13

As Susanna and Robert stepped through the archway she gazed up to the stone-ribbed ceiling festooned with brightly coloured shields and liveries of people and places she could barely imagine. She lowered her eyes reluctantly, only to be ever more awestruck by what she saw. Before her was the most wondrous, discrete courtyard surrounded by ancient cloisters. It was a place of calm and contemplation. Its blue wisteria was in full bloom, clinging lazily to the rich golden stone. A gentle breeze perfumed the air. She raised her eyes slowly to the sky, drawn there by the vertical line of the cloister, as if its maker had anticipated this divine discovery on behalf of those who came here. For one giddy moment, Susanna thought she heard celestial angels singing amongst the passing clouds. Then she recognised the well-beloved hymn sung by an earthly choir nearby. She stood motionless, breathing in the heavenly scent, hearing the angelic voices and feeling as if she were tasting a beauty that she had never thought possible.

Some minutes later she saw a group of seven or eight men dressed in rich costumes from the old Queen's day. Three of them were more lavishly arrayed than the others. A teenage boy with huge dark eyes looked directly at her, expressionless at first. Then, without her moving, he graced her with the most enormous gleaming smile. Behind him, other actors were busy cutting and thrusting, rehearsing their swordplay.

Susanna watched the three men huddled together as if they were planning some sort of military campaign. The boy with the admirable smile had run over to them, gesturing back at her and Robert.

A tall man with salt-and-pepper curls and a neatly trimmed beard seemed perplexed at the sight of Robert and Susanna, who still clutched at her dog. Did he think they were common churls? Whilst he peered quizzically at them, the actors' sword fighting became livelier, with thrusts and parries clinking like music to an ever faster rhythm.

Suddenly, the bearded man's eyes widened. He smiled. Susanna looked to Robert, who had already stepped forward. She followed timidly in his shadow, leaning into the wall, instinctively fearing that she didn't belong. Dread enfolded her like a shroud.

The bearded man approached, smiling. Susanna had already observed that he had a fine figure and shapely leg. What she hadn't seen was his eyes. Though he had a Celtic countenance, his eyes were a piercing cornflower-blue. As he looked at her, she couldn't help thinking that his were eyes she could gaze upon for a long while.

'Robert!' he exclaimed, clapping him on the shoulders. 'We'd nearly given up on you! Fortune smiles on us at last!'

The others pricked up their ears and rushed over too, greeting Robert as a prodigal son. Though she knew it was wrong of her, at that moment, Susanna felt like an interloper. She was pleased that the family manservant should be welcomed as a hero amongst her father's friends, but had to avow that she was a bit envious. After all, she was Shakespeare's daughter and should be greeted with some degree of cheer.

A balding, shorter player gripped Robert by the arms. 'Tell me you have the medicines?'

Another player, with eyes that sparkled like stars added, 'And Will's manuscripts?'

'Or we'll boil you in civet piss,' the teenager with the admirable smile, laughed.

Robert nodded at them all. He was mightily relieved that they had found the Master's friends at last. 'My good King's Men, yes, we have all he asked for, though we did meet bountiful trouble along the way.'

'We?' Henry Condell asked.

Robert wheeled round, fearing Susanna was gone, and saw how she lurked in his shadow like some scared fawn. He doffed his cap and bowed to her. 'Mistress Susanna, these gentlemen are your father's friends and fellow players in the King's Men. Masters John Heminges, Henry Condell, Richard Burbage and Nathan Field. Gentlemen, this is Master Shakespeare's eldest daughter, Susanna.'

All smiles faded. The players stood motionless.

'Can't be, Robert,' Henry Condell spoke up at last, tugging at his ring, 'she's dressed no better than an almswoman— '

'You're having us on, Robert!' the teenager with the admirable smile said and shook his head.

Susanna hated to admit that Master Condell was right, and so, thought it best to ignore his remark.

'Gentlemen,' she said in a threadbare voice, 'I'm pleased to meet you.'

John Heminges collected himself first and made a low bow. The others followed his lead soon enough.

'The pleasure, Mistress Susanna, is ours, I assure you.'

She inched towards Heminges of the cornflower-blue eyes. 'I've come to see my father. Is he near?'

All the players exchanged worried looks. Susanna felt her heart bang like a pistol firing in her chest. Something was wrong. Robert looked at them, bemused.

'Pray, what's wrong?' she asked.

Heminges looked at her sidelong. 'Prepare yourself, Mistress. Your father has been poorly.'

She stood very near to him now. His eyes penetrated her gaze. 'Please, take me to him. I have his medicines in here,' she patted the satchel.

Heminges nodded and led Susanna away. Robert gazed at the two of them walking back to the cloister, fearing their journey had been for nought.

Henry Condell broke the spell when he leaned into Robert's ear to ask, 'What were you thinking of, you knave? How could you have brought her *here*?'

Robert glared at Condell. Why, he had nothing to be ashamed of. They'd braved hellfire and damnation, rufflers and Ratsey. He was proud of Susanna. So proud in fact, he'd shout their adventures from the rooftops of Oxford. Besides, if he didn't tell one and all, these players with their loose ways and wicked quips might think all sorts of wrong-headed ideas.

'Me? Bring *her* here?' Robert bellowed. 'Why, it's she what brought me! I were whisked away from my hearth and– '

Susanna heard Robert begin their tale of escape. She glanced back to him and smiled thinly. It was a smile that begged him to say nothing of her husband. Then she turned round and prayed that they hadn't been too long in coming.

The bedroom where Will Shakespeare had been for the past three days was dark, despite the sun shining brightly outside. Heavy curtains were three-quarters drawn, and a shaft of sunlight fell upon his bed and glinted across his face. He was sitting up, as alert as ever, thinking, when he heard voices in the next-door study. He swiftly lay back, smoothed the bedclothes and closed his eyes.

Meanwhile, Susanna and Heminges stood at a round oak table near his bedroom door. She had opened the satchel and taken out the box of medicines. The manuscripts were a trifle travel-sore around the edges, but it was nothing a heavy weight couldn't sort out. Before she'd finished, she stopped and looked up at Heminges.

'How long has my father been ill?' Her voice cracked.

'About three days now, I fear.'

She looked away and nodded. That was very long for one of his turns. She clutched the box of medicines and walked towards the bedroom. Heminges made to follow, but she looked at him, begging him with her eyes to let her go on alone. He nodded to her, and she smiled slenderly in thanks. She opened the latch, praying her father would be resting peacefully, and closed the door quietly behind her.

When she walked towards him, she couldn't help but give a short gasp. It seemed to her that he'd shrunk to a shadow of his former self. O, how thin he was! Plucking up her courage, she went to the bedside table and read the potion labels on the bottles. Red peony. Meadowsweet. Tincture of French mercury. Some apothecary was trying to kill him, she thought.

She set the box of medicines down on the table and opened the lid. Taking out a phial and uncorking it, she stared down at her father. Had it really been three years? Perhaps it wasn't the illness but age that shrunk him? Then she saw how his right hand was curled up in spasm and his face twitched. His hair had thinned and greyed. His cheeks had sunk in near his mouth and his skin was pale and sallow. Breathing seemed to be a heavy labour for him too. There was little doubt that he had all the hallmarks of a sick man. She regretted questioning Robert about the falling sickness. O, why did her father have to leave them time and again, when he could stop work and rest comfortably at home? He'd no need of more money, surely. Then her mother's face loomed in her mind's eye.

She bent over and slid her arm under his head, holding it steadily. She gently emptied the medicine into his mouth and was relieved that his swallowing reflex still worked. She straightened and replaced the bottle in the pine box. On the inside of the lid, she saw a folded paper wedged in. She dislodged it with her finger, opened it and read:

> Take 6 bruised leaves of white willow to 20 drams of white willow bark. Burn both to ash. Add four crumpled meadowsweet leaves, two inches of common mallow stalk and cook slowly in claret wine.

Susanna disbelieved her eyes. It was her husband's recipe for making up her father's medicines. No wonder John Hall had pursued her. His recipes were more precious to him than sex. Any doubts she'd had about hurting her father if she left Hall vanished. She placed the paper into her skirt pocket. Any apothecary in the land could fill this recipe. Suddenly, the sadness of her husband cherishing his recipes more than his own wife washed over her. And now that she gazed upon her beloved father lying in such a state, it nearly strangled her heart.

'O, father!' she sighed, 'I had no idea you were so poorly.'

She collapsed in the chair at his bedside and laid her head down. Shakespeare slowly opened his eyes.

'And here I was, running to you for help,' she breathed. 'How selfish I am. I should have been worrying about you and your turns. Instead, all I could do was think of myself ... O, you might have forgiven me if you knew my misery and shame, how mother's shrewish ways made me steal your manuscripts from Stratford – and how everyone must think I've taken Robert for my lover! Mother, Judith and my own husband hate me. And why?' she asked. 'They think I'm a person of no worth. Why you ask, Father? Because I read and love your plays. If you only knew how I can sit and read them and do nothing else day and night – how I long to see you perform – how I dreamed of seeing you again. Why sometimes I even fancy I'm playing Ophelia or Cordelia or–'

'But never a Juliet,' Shakespeare's velvet voice whispered.

Susanna's eyes widened in horror. He knew she'd never felt the passion of a reciprocated love? She straightened. She blinked stupidly at her father, whose chestnut eyes were wide open. He smiled.

'You heard?'

He nodded. He opened his mouth to speak, but before he could utter a word, Susanna scraped back the chair and bolted from the bedroom.

Run! Run away you fool, the words echoed in her head. You wear your shame too brazenly. Yet as she tore into the study next to her father's bedroom, Susanna came upon a large, burly man with a thick head of sandy-coloured hair rifling through the satchel. Her feet were suddenly glued to the floor. Some of her father's handwritten manuscripts were strewn on the table. This man, whoever he was, held a wad of papers in his pudgy hands, reading the pages avidly, almost as if devouring the words like some feast. Without thinking, anger overtook her shame.

'Who are you and what d'you think you're doing? Susanna burst out.

The man peered over his shoulder at her as he coolly slid the manuscripts back into the satchel. He grinned.

'Ben Jonson at your service,' he said, bowing theatrically.

Susanna's anger was unsatisfied. 'That only half answers my questions.'

Jonson turned towards her as he would a man, prepared to brawl. 'When someone presents himself, you're meant to respond in a like manner, Mistress–?'

The outer door opened and John Heminges entered. Henry Condell, Richard Burbage, Nathan Field and Robert followed in his slipstream. Robert glanced to the round table and the manuscripts and made a lunge for Jonson. Nathan held him back.

'This Ben Jonson person,' Susanna pointed excitedly, 'was fiddling with my father's manuscripts.'

Heminges raised his brow and turned to Jonson for an explanation.

Jonson shrugged. 'John, you know I'm a writer, not a fiddler.'

Heminges suppressed a smile. 'Mistress Susanna,' he said, turning to her, 'Ben Jonson is a fellow playmaker.'

'A friend,' Nathan piped up.

'A foe,' Burbage grimaced.

'Both,' Condell added, his eyes darting between Jonson and Susanna.

Jonson let out a deep guffaw.

Robert tried hard to make a smile of friendship, fearing Susanna would think he was making sport of her like the others. She looked away.

Susanna felt clay-brained. If Jonson was a friend, a foe, and both, why did they pay her no heed? As sure as apples weren't pears, as she always said, there was something wrong with the way Jonson read those plays. Yet if she kept hard to her point, she was sure her father's friends wouldn't believe her. What she couldn't decide was if she was somehow being knotty-hearted, curious-minded or just plain blunt-witted. She felt pique rise in her throat. 'I need some fresh air,' she murmured shouldering her way through them all.

Robert saw how they all stared after her, bemused. Couldn't they see how greenly they treated her? 'Course he knew they meant no harm, but then again, they hadn't known all she'd suffered of late.

'An odd girl,' Jonson said, shaking his head and smiling. 'Is she Will's?'

Robert glared at Jonson. 'His eldest and most precious daughter.'

Jonson raised a brow at him, as if he could somehow make that brow a dagger pointing at his eye. Slowly, Jonson turned his stare to Heminges and Burbage. 'She's odd all the same. But no never mind. I've come to see Will!'

They all stood near the bedroom doorway, speechless. Robert felt as if his heart would rent itself in his chest. Master Shakespeare, a mere shadow of his former self, stood crooked like a man in his seventh age, clinging onto the bedpost for dear life. His hair had gone from the crown of his head at long last and hung wildly about his ears. Robert wanted to rush to his side to help, but just as he made to move, Shakespeare commanded him with his dark eye to stay where he was.

'Will,' Heminges said, 'thank God you're better.'

Ben Jonson looked at Heminges. 'Will looks like a cocky-monkey,' he said loudly.

Shakespeare squinted at Jonson. 'Still constipated, Ben?'

'Don't start, Will,' Henry Condell cajoled.

Shakespeare's eyes softened. Clinging to the bedpost to stand, he said, 'John, I must find Susanna.'

'That violet hard-faced girl?' Jonson needled.

'She's full of wise saws you'll never see, Ben,' Shakespeare replied tartly.

Jonson smiled smugly. 'You murder the English language, Will.'

They all looked at Shakespeare and Jonson volleying insults.

Shakespeare shuffled towards Heminges but faltered. Heminges rushed to his side, gripping his arm.

'I need to find Susanna, John.'

Jonson laughed. 'That brass girl?'

Robert turned quickly to the others. His wit were too slow to help in a battle of poets. He heard Burbage mutter to Condell, 'He makes a cipher of insults.'

Nathan nodded in agreement. 'Like most pocket poets.'

'Been boiling gold to turn into brimstone again, Ben?' Shakespeare asked.

The King's Men tried to stifle their laughter. Jonson leered at them.

Robert bit hard on his lip to keep from laughing aloud. Brimstone to gold? The Master still needed no help from his friends to parry and thrust words, despite his illness.

'Now, Will,' Heminges began, trying to control his mirth, 'don't add fuel to his fire.'

Shakespeare raised his eyes to Heminges. The fire had gone out of them. 'Find me Susanna, John,' he pleaded quietly.

Robert saw his Master's pain and rushed to his side. Couldn't they see he was failing? That he was near fainting with weakness? And these men called themselves his friends? Why, it was too much for any loyal manservant to bear!

'I'll find her, Master,' he said boldly, helping Shakespeare back to bed. 'First,' Robert waved his finger at the others, 'you lot... OUT!'

Robert glimpsed his Master peering at him with a melancholy eye, but he wouldn't be drawn away from the task at hand. Shakespeare needed to be abed, and he'd tuck him in good and proper to make sure his amblings would be kept at bay.

'There,' Robert said, proudly tucking his last tuck.

'I should give you sweet musk-roses to soothe your worried mind,' Shakespeare smiled.

Robert was taken aback. He never liked it when the Master mocked him, and even less when he was reciting poetry at him.

'Old friend, d'you know that old friends are like fine wine?'

Robert felt his cheeks suddenly hot with embarrassment. He bent down again to avoid Shakespeare's gaze, feigning to tuck him in some more. Yet he knew his Master was waiting for a reply. He thought a spell, fishing for some witticism before he blurted out, 'O, full-bodied? Thick with sentiment?'

Shakespeare shook his head, his eyes brimming over with kindness. 'No, Robert, old friends are like fine wine because they are trustworthy. They never disappoint.'

Robert felt all skimble-skamble inside. Well, if he was trustworthy, then he'd have to spell it out plain as day that he'd done wrong. 'Then Master, trust this. Susanna is starved.'

There. He'd said it. So why didn't he feel any better?

'I send money.'

Robert rounded on him. 'Starved of love, Master. She ran away, or were it that she ran to you? I can't say which.' He scratched his head, wondering.

'Find her, Robert. Bring her to me, please?'

Shakespeare wore a wise eye now, he could see. Still, something wasn't right. The Master spoke clearly, without a slur, not as other times when he had one of his turns.

'Answer me this first, Master – Are you really ill?'

Shakespeare smiled at him. 'Illness is part of God's good plan.'

'But—'

'Please. Go.'

Robert nodded in obedience and turned away, scratching his head some more. O, how he disliked it when the Master answered in riddles!

Chapter 14

Susanna slowed her pace. Behind her, she heard players' voices and turned. These were no King's Men like her father's troupe, but mere boys, jetting about in their silks.

She looked beyond them to the marmalade stone buildings and wondered how all those years ago – long before she was born – her father had come, much like her, to Oxford on a whim. It was a whim that changed his life, no doubt, and made hers what it was today.

Perhaps she'd come because of that uneasy feeling she had about her father's illness. If he'd been ill for three whole days, it was different from the other times she knew of. The most he'd ever been abed was a day. Still, there was that bad time he rose up only to sway like a drunken sailor even though he was sober. Somehow that wobble never quite got better and soon he began to walk with a limp. Susanna put her hand in her pocket, fingering the recipe for her father's medicines.

The truth was simple. Her father saw through her with his remark – *but never a Juliet.*
She knew she wasn't young and beautiful or passionately in a requited love like Juliet. Did he see her as the plain daughter and Judith as the pretty one? Could it be that her father never saw her as giving rise to a burning love as Romeo had for his Juliet?

She reached the river's edge and ran her fingers along the tops of the rushes. She thought back to her adventures with Robert and their escape from Ratsey. She saw the greedy glint in the highwayman's eye as he held up her father's plays. Suddenly, she knew. Ratsey had the same envious sparkle she'd seen in Jonson's eyes. She sprinted towards the college. She must find her father's friends and convince them.

Where is she? Robert asked himself, twisting his head this way and that, straining to find Susanna. And why had she run from her father when he were the self-same reason she'd come to Oxford in the first place? The way she were acting these last days reminded him of when she were little and she'd run off on the least little excuse of unkindness from her mother. Any escape were better than give Mistress Anne the angry words she should hear. That's what made Susanna so special to him. She were a gentle soul with the courage of a lion in want of a friend or three. As he strode through the cloisters, Robert swore to himself once again that he wouldn't let her down.

'Robert!' a little voice called out.

He heard the quick, small steps of boots bounding towards him. Susanna, he thought as he turned. His heart sank when he saw it was just that little rapscallion from earlier on.

'Afternoon, Robert,' young Will Davenant said, beaming up at him.

Robert didn't want the disappointment to show on his face, but knew it had, for Will's smile faded as quick as the sun peeks from behind a cloud. 'Sorry if I seem churlish. It's just that I'm looking for Susanna, and–'

'I just spied her down by the river,' Will said and pointed through the cloister doorway. 'Come I'll show you.'

It was one thing to find her on his own and quite another to bring along a young boy to see her unhappiness. Robert might have been blunt-witted, but he was sensitive to her plight.

'Will?'

The boy looked at Robert, eyes twinkling. There was something about this boy that looked familiar, but he couldn't put his mind to what it were.

'I'll check down by the river. You look in the buildings for her,' Robert ordered.

'But–'

Robert swiftly stepped past, patting the boy on the back. 'There's a good lad.'

Susanna followed the path from the river back to the main gateway of the college. A round porter with ruddy cheeks passed through the archway jiggling a large key ring at his side. He inserted one of the keys into the chapel door and pulled on the handle to check he had unlocked it before he moved on. He tipped his hat at her as he passed. Seconds later he had unlocked the door to the clock tower. Susanna looked to the chapel door.

'May I go in?' she called out to the porter.

He turned and replied, 'Afternoons are for visitors.'

'I'm a visitor,' she said.

He nodded at her and walked off.

She ducked through the tiny chapel door. She had an overpowering urge to pray.

It was quite the most beautiful chapel she'd ever seen. With its alabaster columns stretching high to the stone-ribbed ceiling, its chequerboard flooring, linen-fold elm panelled walls, dark-stained oak pews and the sun streaming in through stained glass windows, it seemed a picture of godly perfection. She fell to her knees before the altar and clasped her hands in silent prayer: *Dear Lord, give me the strength to find a way back to my father and the wisdom to help him. Make his friends believe me and protect his life's work from scoundrels and thieves.*

Before she could say her 'amens,' the door opened behind her. Susanna sprang to her feet, pretending to admire the chapel like any other visitor.

'There you are!' Will Davenant's voice rang out in an echo. 'Robert's been looking for you.'

Susanna turned to Will.

'You alright, Susanna?'

'It's just the shock of seeing my father so unwell,' she lied.

Will knitted his brow. He reached deep into his breeches pocket and pulled out a pair of dice, holding them underneath Susanna's nose.

'They're liar dice. Always roll sixes!' he beamed at her.

She was all a jumble inside. She must have looked it too, for Will stooped down and rolled the dice to show how they worked. Of course, they came up sixes.

Susanna laughed. 'You wouldn't cheat anyone, would you, Will?'

He shoved the dice back into his pocket, shaking his head of brown curly locks. He tipped his chin up at her in a familiar way, smiling. But how could it be familiar? Without warning, an image from the past flooded over her. She was twelve again. Judith and her twin Hamnet were ten. They were playing by the River Avon with their father. Hamnet ran up to her, smiling, his chestnut-brown eyes twinkling with merriment, as their father dashed after him at a breakneck pace. Hamnet shoved the ball he had under his shirt at her, and raced off. He called back over his shoulder, waving both arms wildly, laughing, 'See? I don't have it, Father!'

Susanna hid the ball behind her back quickly. Shakespeare winked at her as he darted past her. 'Hide that ball well, my girl. Don't let him take it back again.' Then he called out, 'Come back, Hamnet, you cheeky monkey!'

'Susanna?' A voice tugged at her mind from the present.

She looked at Will Davenant, searching her face with his big, beautiful chestnut-coloured eyes – eyes that were so like Hamnet's.

'What's wrong?'

She felt dazed. It couldn't be. 'I'm not sure,' she said in a whisper.

Will's face was etched with worry. 'I'll fetch Robert,' he said as he made to head off.

'No, Will. Stay. Please? Let's talk a while.'

He approached her timidly, she thought, though he should have known he'd nothing to fear from her. She wondered what his parents were like and if his mother loved him. Then she wondered if his father knew he wasn't Will's real father.

'Tell me, what path would you like to follow in this life?'

'Why, a playmaker, just like Master Shakespeare. It's what I want more than boiled sweets or breathing.'

'Why?'

'To take people away from this workaday world, don't you see?'

'But we are what we are and none of us can change that.'

'O, so that's why we pray in church, to magic away our sorrows?'

Susanna smiled wistfully at him. 'My brother Hamnet used to talk about how he'd magic away our sorrows.'

Will looked at her, puzzled.

'Hamnet died some time back, when he was a boy. Sweating sickness or typhus. We're not sure which.'

Will gazed at his boots and scuffed at the ground as if he were ashamed. 'I'm sorry to hear that.'

'It was a long while ago.'

He turned to leave the chapel, head hung low. She felt she had to stop him – to make him feel less sad, and to gaze upon his face one last time – just to be sure.

'Don't go. Please? Tell me about how you'd magic away our sorrows?'

Will raised his eyes to her, smiling Hamnet's smile.

'By being a player and playmaker I'd breathe magic into people's lives, just for a few hours. It would be a gilded gift as good as summer sunshine to lift the darkness from our hearts.'

Susanna wanted to say that was precisely what he had just done, but she couldn't find the words.

As she made to leave the chapel with Will, she was unaware that Robert still scoured the college and Shakespeare paced his bedroom like a caged animal – both hoping to find her soon.

Chapter 15

Susanna walked briskly through the cloisters, her footsteps echoing against the stonework. Though the afternoon shadows lengthened, hundreds of people still kept their vigil for Shakespeare. Some chanted prayers, whilst others recited poetry. A man bedecked with flowers and a black fustian cloak stood to sing,

> When daffodils begin to peer
> With hey, the doxy over the dale,
> Why then comes in the sweet o' the year,
> For the red blood reigns in the winter's pale.

> The white sheet bleaching on the hedge,
> With hey, the sweet birds, O, how they sing!
> Doth set my pugging tooth an edge.
> For a quart of ale is a dish for a king.

It was Autolycus's song from the fourth act of *The Winter's Tale*. Then a peculiar thought struck her. Like Susanna, these people were strangers to her father. Like her, they sought to speak to him through his own words. It seemed to her that somehow, she had to set herself apart from them – to stop being an admirer of her father's words – and find her own words to gather herself to him.

Shakespeare heard the door to the study open and close. His eyes widened. He hobbled smartly back to bed, smoothing the bedclothes down as best he could. He shut his eyes and took several deep breaths. As the bedroom door inched open, he turned his head towards it. His face lit up at the sight of Susanna.

'We are not the first, who with best meaning have incurred the worst,' he whispered awkwardly.

So, he sings me Cordelia's lines to her father in *The Tragedy of King Lear,* she thought. He wants me to respond with *his* words, the words Lear spoke to Cordelia as they awaited their fate, imprisoned. Only moments earlier, she would have had no hesitation in responding: *We two alone will sing like birds i'th'cage: When thou dost ask me blessing, I'll kneel down and ask of thee forgiveness*. But she'd resolved to find her own words, not his.

Yet, no words of her own came to mind. All she could muster in response was a slight tilt of the head and a lifting of a shoulder.

'It was such a surprise to see you,' he said. When Susanna made no reply, a puzzled look fleeted across his face. 'Yet a pleasant one, nonetheless, Susanna...' his voice trailed off.

She plucked up her courage. 'Father ...'

'I'm sorry, Susanna ... so very sorry. Please tell me all.'

She felt her throat grip tightly, as if willing her to be silent. 'There's too much to tell, I fear.'

'Then let me help. Start with your mother.'

Again, a shrug was all she could muster. Why, she asked herself angrily, when she was brimming over with words in her head?

'Still bitter?' he asked, as if to coach her in her lines.

Words failed her. She closed her eyes and nodded.

'Still mistrustful?'

Suddenly the words came. She opened her eyes and stared at her father. 'She thinks you want your manuscripts to publish them like the sonnets.'

'How many times–' He stopped himself. The rest of his thought remained unsaid. 'I never agreed for that varlet Thorpe to print them. She should know by now I never earned a penny.'

His words flowed freely, his eyes were bright. Was it possible he was well enough to try to out-think her?

'How long have you been ill, Father?' The gossips accusations against his sickness being nothing more than playacting flooded back into her mind.

Shakespeare's eyes trailed to the two empty phials by the bedside. Susanna frowned. She had given him only one.

'Not long,' he shrugged.

'The truth, Father. Mere weeks ago, you were sent enough medicines to last for months.'

His face darkened and he turned away.

Susanna swallowed. She had seen a flash fleet across his eyes. He feared he was dying. 'You wanted the manuscripts to pass to your lawyer to make your will?'

He tucked his head to the side like a scolded child.

She understood now. 'To bequeath them to Will Davenant, your son?

He sat bolt upright and peered at her, his mouth ajar in shock.

'Susanna, I can explain–'

'You always could.'

'Don't act like your mother.'

'When have I ever?'

'You seeing young Will has made you jump to all the wrong conclusions,' Shakespeare blustered. 'That's just like your mother.'

'I'm no shrew, Father,' Susanna said. The tears began to sting her eyes, so she turned away. She'd not let him see he'd wounded her.

'Wait! I've not finished,' he called out.

'Ah, but I've finished listening,' she said calmly as she walked out, closing the door quietly behind her.

His words had unleashed a sudden, crashing hurt that tore her heart in two. She bowled past the satchel on the table. How dare he compare her to her mother? Just as she touched the door handle to make her way back into the cloisters, she stopped. Why was it always she who controlled the stormy emotions that raged inside her? Was it because others – her sister, mother, husband and father – never controlled their own? Why did she have to be the mistress of all reason for everyone? She shut her eyes, praying for deliverance from the crushing anger she felt. But no manner of talking herself to be calm could extinguish the flame. She saw the satchel and gave a devilish, sly smile. Without a whiff of reason, she snatched up the satchel and dashed from the room.

She walked briskly through the cloisters fearing someone from the crowd would see her clutching the satchel. But they were too absorbed in their vigil to take a blind bit of notice of her, much less what she carried. Still, it dawned on her that taking the manuscripts was a daft thing to do, even in the heat of anger. Besides, who was she angry at? Herself or her father? She stopped and rested against a statue, thinking she'd best return the manuscripts before someone took note they were missing. Then a still, small voice inside her head whispered for her to hold them safe. Hadn't that Jonson leered greedily at them? And no one had believed her when she said he had an evil intent? And why was no one guarding them? Perhaps that was her father's plan, to have Jonson supposedly steal them? But why?

Just then, she heard quickened footsteps at the far end of the cloisters. Without a beat, she wedged the satchel on its side behind the statue as Robert turned the corner.

'Susanna!' he called out, relief etched in his voice. 'There you are. I've been searching up and down the college for you. They've found you a room and a change of clothes.'

She stood mute. All she could think of was whether Robert saw her lying heart pounding and leaping out of her chest. She gave a slight nod and led him away from the hidden satchel.

He saw that she was still troubled. 'About your father–'

'Later, Robert, please.' She held up her hand as if to ward off some evil. 'Now that he has his medicines, he's in want of nothing.'

'But–'

'Where's my room?'

He had rarely, if ever, seen anger flash in Susanna's eyes and was saddened to see it now. How could he make this right again for all of them? He'd served the Shakespeare family near all his life.

He'd ministered to the Master just as his own father had seen to John Shakespeare in his time. *O, Lord,* he prayed silently as he showed Susanna the way, *I know I've been a foul-weather Christian, preferring the pub to the pew, but the Master can't move on to you without setting things to rights here on this earth, now can he? Dear Lord, make him better... even if only for a while? Leastways for Susanna?*

In the stillness of her room high above the cloisters, Susanna laced up her stomacher. It was cruel of her, she knew, treating Robert as silently as a deep, dark, starless night. But what else could she do? If she owned up to him about her foolhardiness in taking the satchel, then he'd be all woven up in her deception, or worse, make her own up to theft. Then that little voice piped a tune in her head again that – maybe – she wasn't telling Robert because she knew she couldn't lie to him about discovering her father had another child? And a boy at that.

Was she jealous of young Will? She asked herself as she tugged nervously on the laces of her stomacher. Perhaps – but he had the name of Davenant and had obviously not been owned by her father. Was she upset for Will, who could have been Hamnet reborn? Upset for him that he didn't have the Shakespeare name? Hmm. Could well be... Or was she angry that her father had been unfaithful to her mother? She'd have been a fool to think he'd remained faithful to her.

Or maybe it was none of those things.

Robert busied himself tidying up his Master's writing table, not knowing how he could make Shakespeare see just how troubled Susanna was. He gazed at him, sleeping all innocent-like, propped up on his feathered pillows. But all he saw was how Susanna got all tangled up inside like some poor lamb struggling in brambles to break free. Robert picked up the quill from the blotter and put it back in its inkstand. It was peculiar to him that a man of so many words could find none to help his own daughter.

As he brushed the table clear of sand, his palm was streaked with ink – fresh ink. How odd, he thought, as he cleaned it with his kerchief. Surely the Master wasn't writing? He looked around at the telltale signs of writing, piecing them together: the sand on the table, the quill left lazily out of its inkstand, the fresh ink splattered. He leaned forward and saw there were other new ink stains on the writing table.

'What's wrong, Robert?' Shakespeare asked as he stretched, freshly awakened from his slumber.

'You've been writing, Master?'

'I'm a writer, am I not?'

'You were writing just before I came in?'

'What if I was?' Shakespeare fidgeted in his bed then quite unexpectedly, threw back the bedclothes with a flourish.

'So you're better, Master?'

'For now … the medicines you brought seem to have done their deed once again.' He tried to stand.

'I'm so happy, Master Shakespeare,' Robert said joyfully. Then straightaway a thought clouded his mind. 'But where's the writing?'

'Posted. Nathan took it to the livery.'

Robert suddenly felt brain-sick. His eyes slid to the bedside table and he saw the two empty phials of medicine. Six phials were all they'd brought with them.

'To Dr Hall, Master?' he asked, wincing inside.

'Of course!' Shakespeare shouted as he stood. 'You didn't bring enough medicines with you, now did you?'

'O, Master Shakespeare! How could you?'

'What's wrong?'

'O, Master … you've set a plague upon your own house.'

'Stop quoting me and tell me what I've done.'

'Did your letter go by express rider?'

Shakespeare nodded.

'With instructions to deliver no matter what time of night?'

Shakespeare stood motionless except for the tiniest nod.

'When did he leave?'

'Near on two hours ago.'

Robert began to pace and flail his arms as if he were trying to take flight. 'O, Master, what have you done?'

'That's what I'm asking you, knave!'

'Forty miles from here to Stratford by express rider,' Robert paced, tapping his finger on his lip. 'That means if there's no hold up, he could be with Dr Hall by midnight–'

'And?'

'Forgive my speaking plainly, Master, but we must leave,' Robert ordered. 'We must leave Oxford before Dr Hall gets that letter!'

Shakespeare frowned. 'No … that is, not unless you tell me why you're babbling on so.'

'You truly want to know?'

Robert poured some of the poisonous bits of Susanna's life with Dr John Hall into his Master's ear, ending with her being chased out of town by him and the obvious question, 'Hadn't you noticed the manner of her dress – for if you hadn't you were the only one!'

'I confess I thought she looked poorly turned out,' Shakespeare whispered in a slender voice.

Shakespeare flopped back onto the bed, covering his face with his hands. 'O, Robert, what have I done?'

Chapter 16

Susanna heard the murmur of voices as she walked into the chapel. She turned to leave, disappointed she couldn't be alone to think things through. But just as she did, she recognised the deep tones of Richard Burbage's commanding voice.

'Right then, from the top. Nathan, this time you be "Shadow". Henry, I'll play "Falstaff" instead of you, and see what you think.'

Susanna inched back hoping to peek at their performance unnoticed.

Burbage cleared his throat and puffed out his chest. He threw his shoulders back and suddenly appeared a much larger man, just as she'd imagined Falstaff to be.

'Shadow, whose son art thou,' Burbage as Falstaff asked.

'My mother's son, sir,' Nathan replied.

'Thy mother's son! Like enough, and thy father's shadow. So the son of the female is the shadow of the male. It is often so, indeed, but not of the father's substance.'

It was as if they'd stabbed her with her father's lines. No, it was her father stabbing Will Davenant with his words. She stumbled backwards, as the room seemed to spin, and knocked against some baskets lined against the wall.

Condell, Burbage and Nathan stopped and peered at her in surprise.

Susanna stepped forward, embarrassed and confused. She was imagining more in her father's words than he had intended, she told herself. Besides, hadn't her greatest wish been to see one of his plays performed? Before she realised it, she said, 'Don't stop on my account, please… you're rehearsing *Henry IV Part II, Act III, scene 2*, right?'

Burbage and Nathan smiled. Condell nodded in appreciation of her knowledge. All her indecision, her anger and her feeling like a usurper vanished. To see her father's company of players – the King's Men – rehearse privately, even if it wasn't for her, was more than she could have hoped.

Burbage elbowed Nathan then Condell. 'Shall we?'

The three players smiled.

'Right then, I'll play "Justice Shallow",' Condell began clearing his throat, 'from …but not of the father's substance!'

They took their places and began again.

'Do you like him, Sir John?' Condell as Shallow asked Falstaff, pointing to Nathan playing Shadow.

'Shadow will serve for summer. Prick him, - for we have a number of shadows to fill up the muster book.'

Just then the door to the chapel opened and John Heminges bowled in. 'Sorry to interrupt,' he called out breathlessly. He glanced at Susanna and tipped his hat at her.

'What is it?' Condell asked with his eyebrows knitted in a peak like a church steeple.

'I've just been to see the Master of the College. The festival has been cancelled.'

'What?' Condell, Burbage and Nathan cried in unison.

'No!' Susanna exclaimed.

'What d'you mean, *cancelled*?' Burbage demanded striding towards Heminges.

'Just as I said, Richard. The Master of the College just came from the Chancellor of the University. It was agreed that there are too many sturdy beggars and cutpurses roaming Oxford's streets–'

'Drawn to the city by us playmakers, I'll wager,' Burbage spat. 'O, when will these accusations cease that we players are an affront to the godly?'

Heminges shrugged. 'You know the Puritans. It's no use bewailing our fate. To keep the peace, the Puritan bailiff of Oxford has insisted the festival be called off. We players are to be gone by midday tomorrow.'

'Is there no hope?' Susanna asked.

It seemed everyone felt the desolation in her voice, for they all turned a sympathetic eye to her. She searched John Heminges's eyes and felt him looking deep into hers. The warmth rising in her cheeks made her feel suddenly hot.

'Come,' Heminges said to Susanna, holding out his hand, 'let's all break the bad news to your father together.'

She tore her eyes from his face and looked down to his outstretched hand. She placed her palm on his wrist formally, and they walked out together.

Shakespeare made them repeat their news several times. Robert thought it sounded like he were running his men through their lines at rehearsal. Leave tomorrow, the Master said. Sorry, repeat that … Why? Sorry, I don't understand and so on and so forth. What weren't there to understand? They were being booted out of Oxford as breachers of the peace!

'Sturdy beggars and cutpurses, puh,' the Master said. 'They always say that when too many of us foregather. Either that or there's plague. To be a Puritan father is to fear that someone somewhere is having a good time! Damn them all!'

'We're just as angry as you, Will. Nonetheless, we must away first thing tomorrow,' Heminges said.

Shakespeare nodded reluctantly. 'Perhaps we'll tour the provinces?'

Susanna could see his mind whirring. 'Not back to Stratford?' she heard herself ask.

'No. Let's see… perhaps you'd like to see Norwich?'

Her heart skipped a beat for joy. 'Norwich is good,' Susanna smiled, surprised . Norwich was as goodly a distance away from Stratford as you could get and still remain in England, she thought.

'You'll like Norwich,' Shakespeare nodded at her.

She could hardly believe her ears. Her father was inviting her to go along with them.

Robert stopped packing up his Master's belongings and stared at him, confused. He could see plain as the nose worn on his Master's face that Susanna appreciated that sweet invitation to Norwich. But how would she take it if their paths crossed her husband's on the morrow? How could the Master have been so blinded to her plight? O, woe is the house of Shakespeare!

'Robert?' He heard Susanna's voice, but daren't look her in the eye for fear of betraying what he knew and, worse still, what he thought he knew.

'Robert, you look unwell,' she whispered.

'No, Susanna, just busy packing up,' he lied.

'Right then,' Shakespeare began. 'Nathan, you're in charge of the players' parts and printed plays. Put them with my manuscripts from Stratford.'

Susanna wheeled round. The manuscripts ... O, dear Lord.

'Richard, you and Henry settle up for breakages and our food and drink.'

Burbage and Condell turned and left the room swiftly. Heminges hovered at Shakespeare's shoulder, his eyes on Susanna.

'And Susanna,' Shakespeare said, turning to her.

She looked inquiringly at her father, pleading that her eyes wouldn't give away her brain-weariness.

'Yes Father.'

'If you could start packing up the racks of our wardrobe in the prop room,' Shakespeare smiled at her. 'Nathan will be able to help you shortly.'

'But I don't know where–'

'I'll show you,' Heminges said.

Susanna's head thundered as if a hundred horses galloped through it. John Heminges, her father, an unknown brother, the manuscripts ... what *was* she to do? How could she fetch the manuscripts *and* put them back without anyone knowing the damned fool thing she'd done? She'd gone from being a nobody to a somebody in their eyes, but once they saw her for all her blundering ways, she'd be a nobody once more – heading back to Stratford in shame.

She swallowed hard. At least she could right one wrong. 'I'm not certain I should go with you to Norwich.'

Robert raised his eyes. O Lord, he thought.

Shakespeare sat up straighter. 'Why ever not?'

Robert inched forward. I'll bet she knows the Master has sent for her husband, he wagered with himself.

'Because … because …' she turned to Robert with a pleading eye.

Robert stared at her, helpless.

'Because, Father,' she smiled sweetly. 'I believe you've forgotten someone.'

'Who?' Shakespeare, Heminges and Robert called out together. They looked from one to the other. Robert scratched his head. He weren't thinking Susanna would say that in a year's worth of snowy Julys.

Shakespeare frowned. 'Who, Susanna?'

She tucked her chin to her chest as she would if admonishing a child. Shakespeare held her stare, and she could see his mind churning like a river's weir, clicking and sputtering names in his head. Then he smiled. 'Where's young Will Davenant?'

'At home, I should think,' Heminges replied, furrowing his brow.

'John, go to the Taverne please. Pay my compliments to Will's mother and finalise arrangements for his apprenticeship.'

Susanna beamed at her father. If her plan for Will succeeded, she would have done a fine thing. But she'd still have to turn her mind to retrieving the manuscripts, unseen by a soul, and put them back where they belonged before Nathan discovered they were missing.

Robert paced the length and breadth of the room. Shakespeare watched from his bed, his head moving backwards and forwards until he could take it no more.

'Robert, stop.'

Robert did as his master bade, but the anger in his heart found words, nonetheless. 'You can have me whipped and caged if you will, but I must speak my mind.'

Shakespeare raised his eyebrows.

'How could you let your own daughter go off thinking you'd done no wrong?'

'D'you want to poke a stick in my spokes, Robert?'

'D'you want to drive a stake through her heart, Master? It's a loveless match you made for her.'

'It's what fathers do.'

'He beats her.'

Shakespeare frowned, but remained silent.

'Dr Hall is Mistress Anne's pet.'

Shakespeare gave a wry smile.

'Hall takes other women in their home … anytime, anywhere.'

Shakespeare's eyes grew wide with horror. 'You didn't say that before. You only told me that he was cruel, but I took it that he was cruel like me – too busy with his work.'

'What Master? Cruel in ignoring her? Cruel in pretending she didn't exist like you? Susanna would be lucky if her husband treated her as her father does.'

'You think me a perfidious father … that of all those in the world I should have loved, I have loved Susanna least instead of best?'

'Aye, Master,' Robert said with false bravado.

'That I have neglected all her worldly needs?'

'I wouldn't say that. You have provided well.'

'Or that I have dedicated myself to my folly – the theatre?'

Robert tilted his head, fearing to say yes.

'That I am a truer friend to my fellow players than to my devoted daughter?'

'I mean that you as good as sold her, Master, to a man unworthy of the prize.'

Shakespeare looked away, his face darkened by Robert's truths. 'How was I to know?'

'You didn't see with your heart, Master, though you should have. Dr Hall is a damned Puritan, to use your words.'

Shakespeare closed his eyes and breathed deeply. Robert knew he'd hit his mark at last. It was time to drive a cart and horse through with his point.

'Hall mocks Susanna and your good self in public. He calls her the whore who Will Shakespeare sold for his medicines. He mocks your playmaking as mere fripperies.'

'He what?!' Shakespeare shrieked.

'Without Susanna, all Stratford would know your private affairs – that you are afflicted with the falling sickness, too. She stays with Hall to keep your secret, Master.'

Shakespeare hung his head low. 'Why did no one tell me just how bad it was, Robert?'

'Coz you ordered us to keep silent on all things from home. Coz Susanna didn't want you to share in her shame, and coz we didn't know how to tell you so you'd hear.'

Shakespeare shook his head. By the time he looked up, tears were streaming down his face.

'I'd rather die than take Dr Hall's medicines again. Let's away at first light, Robert. We'll lay a false trail for Hall, too.'

Robert gave a weary smile. Perhaps there were some hope for Shakespeare and Susanna after all.

Chapter 17

Susanna looked up at Heminges, thinking all the while how she could retrieve the satchel.

'Your father has bragged about you these long years,' Heminges said.

Susanna nodded coyly. They were walking towards the statue. She could just make out the satchel wedged between the plinth and the side of the cloister. If he kept looking at her he might spot it, she thought. Swiftly, she dropped back to adjust her boot. Heminges waited, peering over his shoulder at her. She caught him up, walking on the opposite side.

'Where are the well-wishers going?' she asked, bemused. College officials were shepherding them away from the grassy quadrangle. A porter swept up the apple cores and orange peel strewn on the lawn.

'If we go, so must they,' Heminges shrugged.

Susanna pressed on, ever nearer the statue.

'I know this has been a difficult journey for you, but I'm happy you have come. I've wanted to meet you for some time. Tell me, has your father ever mentioned me or the King's Men?' he went on.

If her heart hadn't risen in her throat from fear, she might have smiled. John Heminges was flirting with her. He was the first man to do so for more years than she cared to remember. There hadn't been many men in her life, and it seemed to her the only ones who showed any interest were really more interested in her father and his shining fame and fortune. All except John Hall – or so her father told her at the time. Her husband was a man of means, Shakespeare had said. He had a profession. Surely he'd be no churl or varlet of a playmaker unable to feed his family, he had reasoned with Susanna.

She looked at Heminges. He was a fine-looking man, of that there was no mistake. Still, she couldn't shake the feeling that he must be like all the others, wanting something from her. She'd never been the object of any man's desires and there was no cause to make her think that it was so now. Perhaps he hoped she might influence her father in some matter or other. But how could that be? Surely he held more sway with her father than she did?

'You asked if my father ever spoke of the King's Men?' she asked, avoiding his other remarks.

Heminges made to speak, but merely nodded.

'Whenever my father comes home, which as you know is in a plague season or not at all, he never speaks of London or the theatre or his friends,' she said, toying with him. 'Extraordinary, wouldn't you say?'

Heminges smiled thinly. 'Your father is an extraordinary man.'

Susanna turned to see the last of the well-wishers ambling out of the quadrangle. Soon she'd be able to retrieve the satchel unseen.

'Tell me, John, please,' she asked, 'how did you two meet?'

Heminges's eyes seemed to cloud over at the memory. He sighed.

'It was my last evening before taking my command to fight in the Low Countries back in '86,' he explained. 'I had run out of candles and could not see well enough to finish writing out my will.'

He trained his eye on her. Was it to make sure she'd understand how important an encounter it was? Or was it something else, she wondered.

'To go to war without a will, is an anathema to any man who seeks a good death with all his affairs in order. But the hour was late, so I had to rush to the chandler's before closing time. As I crossed the threshold, Will barged past me shouting, "A tallow end, an inch of candle, a wick and wax!" How urgently he pleaded, with his hair all uncombed, his shirt points untied and no doublet.'

'The chandler covered his ears with his hands, for you see, Will had already honed his actor's voice and it was loud enough to wake the dead from their slumber. Then the poor man apologised to us both saying he had but one candle left since his next batch hadn't quite cured. Will, like a flash of lightning, proposed we should vie with words for the shopkeeper's favour, and I, thinking myself quite the poet despite being a mere grocer, agreed. Of course, Will composed a sonnet off the top of his head about the glory of candles casting a magical beam into the pitch of night, lighting fools the way to dusty deaths. I tried a sonnet too – one that I had written and committed to memory. Alas, I was the poorer poet.'

Susanna gazed at his face. It was a fine face, kind and yet strong.

Heminges resumed his story with a faraway twinkle in his eye. 'It was clear that the candle maker had made up his mind for Will, and I'm not proud to admit that I pleaded like a sore loser to his loyalty to Queen and country. I appealed to his good reason not to let a man go to battle without having made out his last will and testament. After all, I was to leave for war at noon on the morrow. Though I've no doubt the shopkeeper was a true and loyal Englishman, and he was sorry for his decision, Will had won the day fairly.'

Heminges turned to Susanna, giving her a sorrowful half-smile.

'Will grabbed the candle and rushed out into the street. I was doomed to return to a darkened room and leave my affairs in disarray – potentially staring at a bad death.'

What he described fit with her own memories of her father – an actor to the last. His were the antics of a selfish man. So, how could Heminges think so well of him?

'But, when I left,' Heminges shook his head, 'I often recollect those salad days... there was Will standing before me ready with a compromise. He had thought upon the weight of my circumstances and returned to offer me the candle. It wasn't a fair match he said, as he intended to be the greatest poet of our day. I thanked him and said I dare not deprive him. The thought that I might keep the world from even one line of his sonnets would be a crime I wasn't prepared to commit.'

'That was very noble of you, John,' Susanna said, softening towards her father in her mind.

'Not as noble as you think. He wouldn't accept his victory. Instead, he walked with me to my lodgings and waited until I had finished writing my will. I sealed it and handed it to my landlady. Then we chatted and laughed some more as we walked back to his rooms with our shared candle. He wrote whilst I read his poems. By the dawn, he'd agreed to join my regiment as a volunteer. Yet, in spirit I was already his disciple.'

She admired Heminges for his generosity and scolded herself at the same time, for she couldn't help but feel a tad envious of the relationship that had grown from that spark nearly thirty years earlier. After all, she had no great friend – only a mother who hated her, a sister who begrudged her everything, a husband who abused her and envious neighbours. It must bring untold joy to have someone who loved you for who you are – with all your faults observed and forgiven – and who you loved in return.

But above all, she wanted to believe in this vision Heminges portrayed of her father. Not for herself, but for Heminges. He'd been a true and trusted friend, and seemed the kind of man to her who would never rest until a wrong was righted – the kind of man who would chase after the missing manuscripts for however long it took to find them. How could she think that he wanted to befriend her purely to curry some small favour with her father? It was mean-spirited of her.

'You speak of him with such love.'

'I'd not be the man I am without him,' Heminges said and paused in front of a door. 'We're here.'

Susanna looked at the closed Gothic door ahead of them, wanting to linger but knowing she must hurry to retrieve the manuscripts if she hoped to avoid discovery. The cloisters would not remain quiet for long, she was sure. She peered into the darkening courtyard. Only the porter was there, stooped over, picking up the last of the leavings from the well-wishers.

'I could show you how to fold the costumes into the chests,' Heminges offered hopefully.

'If there's one thing I know about it's how to care for clothing, John Heminges. I thank you kindly for your offer nonetheless.'

They stood close to one another, Susanna feeling a physical longing for this man. Yet it was something strange to her, an unknown sensation. She shook herself loose from this wondrous attraction. She was a married woman. Badly wed it was true, but a wife in name for all that. Besides, there was work to do.

'You've a job at the Taverne,' she smiled up at him.

'So I do.'

Heminges bowed and took his leave, his eyes lingering on her in unspoken affection. He's drawn to me too, she couldn't help thinking. Imagine, someone likes me without reference to my father. She opened the prop room door a crack and waved to Heminges as he glanced back at her. How could she be so stupid to have taken the manuscripts and ruin everything?

The moment he turned off towards the town, Susanna shut the door and hurried back to the statue. She reached down and tugged the satchel free with a grunt. It was only fifty yards to her father's rooms, she told herself. No distance at all. She merely needed to place the satchel back onto the round table in his sitting room, and no one would be the wiser.

Just then a man appeared around the corner of the cloister nearest to her father's rooms. Another man followed on, dressed as a justice of the peace in a livery she couldn't make out in the gloaming, but he dragged some hapless well-wisher forward by his elbow. Others rumbled back into the cloisters and over the wall to the quadrangle of grass, tossing leaves and flowers in the air and prancing about like pixies.

Susanna froze. The justice of the peace and his friend were standing in front of her father's door, barring her entry.

'I tell you,' the justice said, 'the bailiff will make this a matter of the Star Chamber if you're not careful, my boy. Imagine accusing his lordship of *giving* you the ill-gotten gains!'

'But I'm no Gamiliel Ratsey, or even a Sir John Falstaff!'

Susanna's heart leaped in her chest at the mention of Ratsey's name.

'No,' the justice agreed. 'You're no Ratsey or Falstaff for sure. You're just a younger son of his lordship's enemy, without a penny to your name – why you've no dozen white luces in your coat!'

'It was an old coat!'

'You stole it nonetheless, dear boy, and were caught.'

'But to be held over in custody?'

'Them's the rules!'

The young man, who apparently was no friend but rather the justice's prisoner, struggled free and broke into a run, bolting directly towards Susanna. Half in dread of discovery and fearful she'd become embroiled in their battle, she dashed back to the prop room door, ran inside and closed it behind her. Breathless, she leaned against it, listening to the great tumult rise up outside.

There was nothing she could do in this sour turn of fortune's wheel. So long as a justice of the peace was roaming the college scouring any nook he fancied for his prey, she'd be unable to return the manuscripts for some good long while. There was nothing else to do but wait, she told herself, leaning over to light the lantern hanging by the door. Maybe there was another solution? But what? If she did nothing and waited, surely Nathan would soon discover that the satchel was missing? She mulled the problem over and over to herself as she lifted the lantern aloft. It took a few moments for her eyes to grow accustomed to the light, but when they did, what she saw astounded her.

The prop room was a treasure house beyond her imaginings, dashing her worries about the manuscripts from her troubled mind.

She marvelled at the shining weaponry, the body armour and rich costumes. She strolled down the aisles of theatrical props in wonderment until she came to a large rack of clothes, filled to overflowing with glittering jewelled gowns. Susanna stretched out her hand and ran her fingertips along their shoulders. She had never seen such an array of rich dresses anywhere, ever. Suddenly, a meek thought found its voice, blurting itself out under her breath, 'These beauties are wasted on young boys.'

She smiled at herself and looked round just to be sure she was alone. Dare she? She gingerly lifted the tags from the sleeves of each of the magnificent dresses, reading 'Desdemona,' 'Juliet,' 'Kate,' 'Rosaline,' 'Beatrice,' 'Titania.' There were more, many more, but such a collection of finery was too much for her to take in.

Before she knew what she was doing, Susanna slipped out of her mother's gown, wearing only her shift, and studied herself in the silvery mirror nearby. Was she truly as plain as she believed? Of course, Judith was the pretty one. That she knew. Still, John Heminges seemed to like what he saw. She searched for hairpins on the table beside her and loosely tied up her hair. Had John Heminges seen a long and gracious neck, she wondered, as she turned one way and then the other. She certainly did not. Had he thought her shoulders were softly rounded? Hmm, perhaps. Did he find her arms not too fat, nor too thin? Or her hands slender and refined? If he did, then he was blinder than a bat. Hers were workaday hands, strong and honest, not beautiful. Granted, her cheek was less sallow than when she'd left Stratford, and her eye seemed more alive to her mind. Perhaps that's what John Heminges admired, and was why she seemed less plain than she'd been told, or allowed herself to believe all these years.

She cast her eyes back longingly to the costumes. Never before had she been so close to so many sparkling gems of gowns. Perhaps, if she were found out, she might never be near them again. The shouts and racing footsteps raged on between the justice and his prisoner, reminding her that she was herself a captive until they were gone. Susanna bit on her lower lip wondering if she dared try one on.

She reached out, her hand hesitating for a moment, before she grabbed hold of the 'Rosaline:' a russet velvet and silk gown with cream slashings of taffeta and pearls sewn onto the sleeves. She would be Rosaline from *Love's Labour's Lost*, she mused, clever and witty, a woman worth loving.

She squeezed into it and instantly felt transformed, though she lingered before daring to turn back towards the mirror. Would she look like some mutton dressed to look like a lamb? Better to know the truth than believe a lie, she scolded herself, and turned. Her heart seemed to dance. Surely the image in the mirror could not be hers? The woman staring back at her was beautiful, with dark green eyes, dark hair and a fair smooth cheek. Her careworn face blushed with pride. She decided she must test this image to be sure it was truly her, and so stood proud to recite Berowne's lines to Rosaline:

'O, never will I trust to speeches penned,
Nor to the motion of a schoolboy's tongue,
Nor never come in vizard to my friend,
Nor woo in rhyme, like a blind harper's song!'

Susanna smiled that she had remembered this and more. She gave a twirl to the woman in the mirror and continued:

'Taffeta phrases, silken terms precise,
Figures pedantical; these summer-flies
Have blown me full of maggot ostentation.
I do forswear them; and I here protest,
By this white glove – how white the hand, God knows! –
Henceforth my wooing mind shall be expressed
In russet yeas and honest kersey noes.'

She beamed at her reflection. Then she wondered how she could dare to talk of wooing minds and taffeta phrases? She thought back to when she'd run from Stratford, back to her sorrows, to their trials on the journey to Oxford. Back to what she had done with the manuscripts.

Unexpectedly, the woman in the mirror was no longer beautiful or clever, but rather someone with an umbered soul and ebony secret. She should be racked – no strappadoed with her arms strung up behind her back and raised up high for what she'd done. Then her father's words from *King Lear* rang out in her head: *'who can tell me who I am?'* How slenderly she had known herself these past days. Had she suffered some kind of madness or brainsickness, like others in her family?

No. She was unlike them. She'd suffered some error of the mind, of judgement certainly, and gone down some false trail from which she had to backtrack to set herself on the right path again. She was no thief, no murderer, no jealous Oberon or bell-weather, no builder of bubble reputations, no possessor of pride and self-will. She was Susanna – sinned against, not one who wronged others. In her pursuit of a father's love and honour, she had hurled herself towards self-destruction. *Who can tell me who I am?* The burning shame of concealing her crime one moment longer shot like darts of blinding light through every guilty fibre of her being.

The echo of boots running outside and shouts for help from Richard Burbage interrupted her self-admonishments. Her heart thudded in her ears, for she feared she'd been discovered. It would be the end of her time with her father – an end of Heminges's admiration for her. She would be shamed forever, sent back to Stratford to the husband from hell and his gatekeeper, her mother. Without a conscious thought, she wheeled round and opened a clothes chest, laying the satchel at the bottom. She piled her mother's dress on top, grabbed another and began to lay it out in neat folds just as the door to the prop room flew open.

'Susanna!'

It was Nathan.

She placed her hand to her throbbing throat to calm herself. 'Back here!'

'Where?'

She quickly snatched another costume and began to fold it too. 'By the rack of gowns.'

Nathan raced towards her. 'Have you seen…,' he panted, 'the satchel?'

'Satchel?' The word sounded so innocent tripping off her tongue.

'The one you brought from Stratford!'

'Uh, ah–'

'Think, Susanna. It's important!'

How could she think? There was no time. 'Uh, no. Not recently. Why?'

'It's gone,' he breathed as if it were his last breath.

'Gone? O, no!' It was all she could think to say. Did she look genuinely surprised?

He held his lantern aloft and saw there was much left to do. 'I'll finish here. Your father asks for you.'

'But, I, uh–'

Then Nathan's stare quickly hardened. He raised and lowered his lantern the length of the Rosaline gown Susanna was wearing.

'That's my dress,' he hissed at her. 'Take it off. Now.'

'But–'

'Now.'

'I'll not take it off with you standing here, Nathan,' Susanna blustered.

'Ahem.' Standing in the doorway, John Heminges cleared his throat. 'What's going on?'

'She's wearing my Rosaline, John. I've told her to take it off.'

Heminges raised his lantern to see Susanna better. She was so nervous she thought she'd faint. It wasn't enough that she'd stolen the manuscripts. Now she'd be accused of stealing a priceless dress as well! She pictured the justice of the peace trailing the hapless prisoner. That would surely be her end, too – imprisoned in Oxford gaol for theft.

'It suits you,' Heminges said.

'I'm sorry?'

'I said "it suits you," Susanna.'

She stared speechless, before that inner troublesome voice of hers asked in an astonished tone: *He's not going to scold me? He likes what he sees? The dress suits me?*

Nathan began to tap his foot loudly.

'Only, you might want to choose something more practical for the journey? Please take your pick,' Heminges added.

Susanna felt the warmth of his gaze on her cheeks. She nodded, fearing her words would give away her jumble of emotions. Moving over to the wardrobe, she wondered what to do. Should she own up to taking the satchel? Should she pretend she'd just found it in the chest? No. Everyone would suspect that it was her who put it there. Her father would feel betrayed and, at best, she'd be forced to return to Stratford. At worst – it didn't bear thinking on.

'John, haven't you heard? The satchel's missing,' Nathan blurted out.

'Are you certain?'

Susanna peeked at Heminges. He looked pale.

'I've checked everywhere.'

'I'll check again. Meanwhile, Nathan, you go find Ben Jonson, and bid him to come and see Shakespeare.'

And with that, they dashed off, leaving Susanna in sore regret for all that she'd done and not been able to put right.

Susanna passed through the cloisters, eyes widening at the dozens of flickering lanterns weaving in and out of the college's rooms in the search for the manuscripts. The King's Men called to one another in despair, crying out that perhaps they were in the chapel or the Master's Lodge? Meanwhile, she feared a mere gaze from one of them would give her away. She walked on, eyes fixed on the stone pavement. With each desolate step, she felt as if she were walking to the execution block.

When, at last, she entered her father's study, he was sitting in an armchair beside the round table. His face was drawn, his eye flinty. She saw that his hand trembled again. She had done this to him.

'I'll fetch your medicine,' she said reassuringly as she made to pass.

He reached out and gripped her wrist. 'No. I'm rationing myself. Did you hear?'

Susanna nodded. His knuckles were white and his grip cold as a winter's morn.

'Mm. Nathan said.'

Shakespeare raised his face to hers. His dark eyes seemed to deep-search hers hoping to see into her soul. 'You need to know something, Susanna.'

She closed her eyes for a split second. It was the end of their time together. And it was her fault.

'About what?' she asked coolly.

'Will Davenant. Though he's my son, he can never replace you or Hamnet or Judith in my heart.'

Susanna sighed in a near swoon, and knelt down beside him as she tried to hide her relief. 'Father, promise me something?'

It seemed a long while before he nodded at her, though she was certain it was only seconds.

'Please, don't abandon Will as you did me.'

His eyes shone with tears. 'I never abandoned you, Susanna. Please see that the playhouse is no place for a young lady, and it's at the playhouse that I earn my crust of bread.'

'I do see, Father. But I'm no young lady and I desperately need you. You're the only one who has loved me for who I am, and even for who I am not.'

At that moment, the King's Men burst into the room. Robert trailed behind and saw Susanna kneeling close to his Master. As he made his way across the room, she slowly stood up. Shakespeare let go of her hand, his arthritic fingers softly stroking her palm.

'It must be Ben Jonson,' Condell shouldered his way forward next to Heminges, rubbing his hands. 'After all, he was looking through your manuscripts. Isn't that so, Susanna?'

'Ah, yes,' she said. Had they heard the quiver in her voice?

'When?' Shakespeare asked her.

'Just after I gave you the medicine this morning.'

'And you said nothing?'

'I knew too, Will,' Heminges murmured, 'and it never occurred to me that Ben'd actually take them.'

The door flew open and Nathan stormed in. 'Jonson's gone.'

'Gone?' Shakespeare seemed winded by the word.

'Already?' Susanna asked.

'What's going on, Mistress?' Robert whispered in Susanna's ear.

'The manuscripts have been stolen.'

'How?' he breathed.

Shakespeare clasped his hands tightly in front of his mouth as if in prayer. 'Where's the court now?'

'Greenwich,' Condell pronounced.

'Then sorry lads. Norwich is out. Jonson will be with the King at court. We're off home to London.'

Everyone looked utterly dumbfounded.

'Come on,' Shakespeare urged, suddenly blooming with a forgotten vigour. 'Be not so dull and heavy ... we are fashioned for this journey! Jonson is the usurper and it's Jonson who steals nature's breath and frightens its trees and fields and animals as a tyrant. Come my tortoises: The hook is well-baited, and by God we fish will bite!'

Chapter 18

Robert tried to busy himself by tidying away his Master's clothing. The facts of it were, he were mightily shocked at the anger in his heart. O, how that beetle-headed stubbornness that nibbled away the goodness in the Shakespeare family were enough to make all the milk in England turn sour! Puh!

He slid his eye to Shakespeare, sitting up in the high-backed armchair next to his bed, and nearly jumped out of his skin to see his Master eyeing him, too, mischievously.

'A penny for them, old friend?' Shakespeare smiled.

And there he goes sweet-talking me again, Robert said to himself. Spending time and his honeyed words on me, when he should be holding out his begging bowl to his Susanna and praying forgiveness for how he's acted. He'd fairly had enough of all this sweet wordplay and playacting. It weren't right.

Robert tossed the jerkin he'd been folding into the chest of clothes. 'Enough, Master. Enough!'

Shakespeare tilted his head.

Fit to burst, Robert blathered, 'Don't you think it's high time you went to talk to her? By all that is holy, it's wicked not to tell her the truth. Master, how you can keep on like this?'

'Not so much wicked as cowardly, Robert.'

'It must be done... I says this as an old friend. And as a friend to your daughter.'

Robert saw his Master retreating into some dark place in his mind. O Lord, had he gone too far? Was his Master going back to that ill-winded chamber of his brainsickness?

Shakespeare sighed, 'I'd rather my eyelids be weighed down to steep my mind in forgetfulness, than to embark aboard the ship of her impetuous winds. No, I am a coward, Robert. For the truth lacks the gentleness she so needs and deserves. The truth will have her run from me.'

'With respect, Master, the truth will out.'

'In good time. Yes, in the end, the truth will out,' Shakespeare said, focusing on Robert. 'But pray, dear friend, let me find my own time for that end.'

He saw the grief etched on Shakespeare's face. It were the pain of a man weakened by sickness. The Master needed to control his world in the precious little time he had left. Robert felt the agony of a great man pleading with his manservant not to repeat a word of what he knew, so the anguish of the father for his daughter could remain their secret a while longer. It weren't the sorrow of a man who feared death.

Regretting his outburst, Robert signalled his agreement, and a truce between them was finally declared. It was an understanding from which Robert would not retreat.

Shakespeare gave a silken smile. 'Was it not just yesterday that she bounced upon my knee and I sang sweet songs to her?'

'Good Master,' Robert said, placing a gentle hand on his master's shoulder, 'She will hear you if you sing again – only to her.'

'Ah, but I sing best to a large audience. I've become a blind man who fears he's rendered her deaf … or worse still that she only hears some crow. I'll need the good service of my friends to help her hear my voice again.'

'She is like her father, stubborn as the night. Neither of you are deaf though you both feign deafness.'

Shakespeare slowly nodded. 'Perhaps. Then again, perhaps not. But I thank you for giving me succour so she may hear my poem above her woes.'

Robert looked down at his Master. Shakespeare held his gaze, his pain melting into a lifetime of regret and sadness.

Susanna rested her arms on the windowsill, searching the night sky for answers. They had all jumped to the wrong conclusion. So why couldn't she just say so? No, it wasn't Ben Jonson, it was me. Eight little words, no more. What a fool she'd been to give free rein to her anger! After years of enduring outrageous misfortune, why had she chosen that moment for a fit of pique? And now, her anger had given way to an unrelenting sadness. Though she knew it as she ran through Stratford's streets, it was only now – truly for the first time – she saw she had nowhere else to go. Stratford held heartache, her husband and her old life. Surely life was meant to hold more than pain and drudgery? But she alone brought this cursed path upon herself the moment she stole that satchel for the third time, and she only she could make it right, or must bear the consequences. Her eyes followed a silvery cloud billowing like a veil masking the crescent moon. If angels were sat upon that cloud would they say she'd been so wicked to deserve this fate? Would they disapprove of this journey of hers and all she'd undertaken to achieve?

She jumped as a knock at the door brought her back to the here and now. She turned away from her stargazing, still feeling imaginary angels sitting on high, passing judgement upon her as a bedevilled woman for all she'd done and all she planned to do to set things right. She padded over to the door and opened it a crack.

Will Davenant beamed up at her, holding an armful of clothing. She heard a little bark and saw her faithful dog Chaos wagging his tail by Will's side.

'Will?' she asked, surprised.

'Sorry to disturb, but I've …' he looked down at Chaos, 'I've brought you fresh gowns for the journey.'

She was moved by his simple kindness. 'O, Will, that's very fine of you. So, has Master Heminges been to see your parents? It's been fixed? You'll be coming with us?'

Will nodded. 'They're just the scullery's,' he said, thrusting the clothes at her.

She took the gowns, stomachers and sets of sleeves from him. 'Come what may, I shall wear these proudly. It is a kindness I shall never forget, Will.'

'Mistress Susanna, Master Heminges tells me I've you to thank for my apprenticeship,' he beamed. 'I hope these clothes go some small way as thanks.'

'There's no need for thanks, Will. But tell me, are you happy to go? What do your mother and father say about your good fortune?'

He shrugged. 'My mother is pleased coz I'll have a future. My father grumbled – said I'd never amount to nothing.'

Susanna was hardly surprised. Did his father know that Shakespeare was the boy's real father? 'I suppose they'll be seeing you off?'

Will looked down and shrugged.

Her heart broke for the boy. What would happen to him if her father tossed him aside, as he'd done with her and Judith? Aye, there's the rub. But there was another. Could she protect Will?

'You admire Master Shakespeare, don't you, Will?' she unexpectedly heard herself say.

'O, more than anyone in the world.'

'Yet, what if things shouldn't turn out as you would wish...' her voice trailed off.

'But they will.' His face showed all the eagerness and fear of what lay ahead.   Susanna bent down so she could look him in the eye. She held his chin between her thumb and forefinger. 'It is admirable to be so sure of life, but experience teaches us to be on our guard.'

Will furrowed his brow. Susanna let go of his chin.

'From what I've seen, playacting can acquaint us with strange bedfellows. People could disappoint you. Even people you admire above all others.'

He thought for a moment then looked down to his breeches pocket and took out his liar dice. He turned them over and over in his fingertips.

'Playacting isn't only on the stage,' Susanna continued. 'Sometimes the people we think we can trust the most are merely playing a part.'

'I know we all have a part to play,' he said looking squarely at her. 'Well, I choose this life, this part. I can think of no other better written for me.' He stood tall and determined, like a man who knows he must make a stand.

Susanna smiled at him, disarmed, and more than a little envious   of   his   insight.

Henry Condell paced the room, as he addressed Shakespeare.

'You can't be serious, Will.'

He looked to Richard Burbage, then Nathan Field and finally John Heminges. Heminges stood by Shakespeare, still sitting in the high-backed armchair. Robert boiled over with resentment at what Condell was saying. His eyes read like an entire library of reproach.

Burbage sighed. 'Will, we can't take her with us.'

Shakespeare motioned for Robert to continue with the packing up.

'Why not, Richard?'

'Because she's not … one of us.'

Robert saw his Master studying them all. Shakespeare cleared his throat before asking, 'She makes you feel awkward?'

Burbage turned to Heminges and nodded vigorously. Shakespeare's face was alight. 'Get used to it, men. She's coming.'

Robert looked down to keep from grinning. Heminges suppressed a smile.

'But we're not set up… to have a *woman* amongst us.' Condell began to pace again.

Shakespeare smiled mischievously. 'You think her sharptongued?'

'No! She's quite sweet, really,' Condell said.

'She's no Kate from *Shrew*,' Nathan piped up.

'Nor Queen Margaret from *Richard III*,' Burbage added.

'She's more tragic, Will,' Condell turned to him. 'Something of an Ophelia.'

'I caught her wearing my Rosaline!' Nathan exclaimed.

'D'you blame her?' Heminges said. 'She's hardly been arrayed as a daughter of Will Shakespeare should be, now has she?'

Shakespeare grinned. 'She's not imperious, a votress, a vengeful enemy, a vulnerable child or even a woman on the prowl, is she?'

They all shook their heads.

'She's intelligent, pleasant-looking, sharp-witted?'

They nodded.

'Is she not amenable and kind?' Heminges asked the others.

Shakespeare's eye judged Heminges's thoughts, and smiled.

Robert turned his back on Heminges, pretending to fold a cloak of the Master's. He bit on his bottom lip to stop himself from falling about, laughing. Master John Heminges were in love. In love with Susanna!

'So you don't like her?' Shakespeare taunted the others.

After a moment's hesitation, Burbage said, 'It's complicated.'

'Pray, how so?'

'How so? Will, don't you feel how the stars have shot madly from their spheres?'

'Don't quote my words from *The Dream* at me, Richard. How so?'

Robert peeked round and saw Shakespeare smiling like some cat with cream round his lips.

Condell sighed, eyes trained on Heminges. 'There could be unintended consequences ...'

'Like?' Heminges asked, anger rising in his voice.

'Why do you taunt me into saying something I've no wish to, John!' Condell cried. 'Something none of us wishes to?'

'I only want you to say what you mean, Henry,' Heminges replied.

Stunned, Condell looked for rescue from the others, but none budged. Flapping his arms against his sides like some flightless bird, he blustered, 'I don't know what I mean!'

Robert crossed the room to fetch the Master's points for his shirts and saw that all-knowing, exasperating smile of his. It was what he called Shakespeare's 'I-see-through-you-clear-as-glass' smile.

'Good, then it's settled,' Shakespeare said. 'She's coming. Now goodnight. We leave first thing.'

Burbage, Condell and Nathan exchanged glances. Heminges was the first to leave. The others shuffled out behind him. As the door closed, Shakespeare shot a look at Robert. 'Well, well! Now that was interesting, was it not, old friend?'

Chapter 19

Though it was early the next morning, it seemed that all Oxfordshire had gathered to wish them God Speed. The shops had shut, as their shopkeepers came to gift fine victuals to the King's Men for their journey. Others showered Shakespeare with warm cloaks and blankets, soft downy pillows and candied fruits. The good housewives of the city rushed forward to the wagon with cakes and ale they'd been saving for after the Lenten season passed, but would only hand them over for a kiss from Shakespeare. He warmly complied. Susanna was so taken with the love these people showed him – people who neither she nor her father knew – that she was speechless.

Burbage shook his head and sighed at Heminges. It was a look that said, *If someone doesn't bundle Shakespeare into the back of the wagon, we'll still be in Oxford next Christmas.* So Burbage decided to join the fray, thanking one and all profusely, and bestowed the odd kiss or two before he whispered into Shakespeare's ear. Reluctantly, he allowed Burbage to lead him towards the wagon as he nodded and theatrically blew kisses to the ladies. But, a pretty little housewife pushed her way forward and grabbed Burbage by the arm.

'Here Master Burbage, you must take these.' She held out three large beans. 'When you get to your destination, throw these over Master Shakespeare's left shoulder and he shall be restored to health,' she predicted with a wide-eyed gaze.

'I thank you.' Burbage smiled and closed his hand into a fist around the beans.

As they mounted the steps into the back of the wagon, the crowd parted and a woman pressed forward holding tightly onto Will Davenant. She waved and hailed Shakespeare, 'Will!'

Shakespeare looked back at her. His eyes softened and his lips parted as if to say something, but no words came. He stepped down awkwardly and walked slowly towards her. Susanna watched intently.

The woman had been fair in her youth, of that Susanna was sure. Even now her figure was lithesome and her features held an exotic beauty. As the woman and Shakespeare looked silently, and searchingly at one another, Will Davenant gazed up at them. Susanna thought that it seemed as if the relentless clock of time had stopped for them. The woman leaned forward and spoke softly into Shakespeare's ear. He nodded and whispered back. She hugged him tightly as her reply, and he haltingly hugged her back. It was she who stepped away first, teary-eyed and smiling. She bent down and kissed Will Davenant, clutching him to her. So this was the boy's mother, Susanna thought. The moments passed in what must have seemed an eternity between mother and son, before she stood tall once again. Shakespeare held out his hand to Will and the pair mounted into the back of the wagon. Susanna stretched onto her toes to see Will's mother better, but she had melted into the crowd.

At last the victuals and baggage were loaded. Robert appeared with the horses, handing the reins of the black one to Burbage, then those of the palfrey to Heminges. He tied the third horse to the rear of the wagon. Shakespeare winked at Robert, taking in the mayhem of well-wishers and actors performing in their homage to him. As he sat down with Will, there was a roar from the well-wishers as Shakespeare snatched up a handful of quills from a nearby box and tossed them like rose petals to the crowd. With each quill tossed, the people bellowed 'over here' or 'send me one' or 'me please!' Children hurried to the wagon's side to ask for some token, any token, of his affection. Others held up their arms, fingers outstretched, longing simply to touch Shakespeare. He turned to Will, inviting him to join in the lark of tossing quills. Will beamed and stood up, hurling quills to their adoring public. Just as he did, a woman crept beneath Shakespeare's waving arm and took a shears to his cloak before sneaking off with her snippet, unheeded. She ran off waving it gleefully at the crowd.

Then Shakespeare called out, 'Robert, more quills! My kingdom wants my quills!' Robert darted behind Shakespeare and Will, cradling Chaos under his arm, searching for more.

Heminges and Susanna watched intently, shaking their heads. 'Is it always like this?' she asked.

'Not always. I imagine they feared for Will's life and that makes them frenzied.'

Just then, a pistol shot rang out and the crowd gasped. Susanna defended Will Davenant with her body, whilst Shakespeare grabbed his staff to wield as a weapon. Chaos growled. Robert went for his dagger. Heminges, Nathan, and Burbage dismounted – swords drawn, ready to protect Shakespeare, Susanna and Will. Condell ran in the direction of the pistol shot, but was suddenly reeled around. He had a pistol pointed to his head.

Susanna glanced up and muttered to Robert, 'Not again?'

John Heminges stood proud, his sword still drawn. 'What is the meaning of this?'

The unshaven townsman who held the pistol, scratched at his beard with it. His cloak was moth-eaten and spotted with grease. The well-wishers stood silently.

'Plays is the meaning,' the unshaven man said. 'Or rather the lack of 'em.'

Suddenly, other pistols were drawn by ten or so men huddled closely behind him. They motioned with their weapons for Condell, Burbage and Nathan to rejoin Shakespeare.

'I'm sorry?' Heminges asked, bewildered.

One of the bandits whispered in the unshaven man's ear, and he nodded in reply.

'We queued all night to get our tickets,' the man called out. Heminges stared blankly.

The unshaven man's eyes widened as he jogged Heminges's memory, 'To the festival? Or rather the lack of festival?'

Heminges turned to Shakespeare, who shrugged back at him.

The well-wishers looked just as puzzled as the King's Men were at first, until a whisper grew to a roar, agreeing that this must surely be some play about to commence. Like a huge swell of the ocean, they sat down in an obedient wave.

The unshaven man rolled his eyes in disbelief at the blank looks from Shakespeare and Heminges. He scratched his beard again with his pistol and called out for all the world to hear, 'We queued for the plays?'

Robert glanced to Shakespeare, then Heminges, then the other King's Men. They just stood there, though heaven only knew why.

'We're theatre-goers,' the unshaven man groaned, lowering his pistol. 'And it's all coz of you, there's no plays. No players. No festival even. All cancelled – see?'

The irony was not lost on Susanna. She glanced at her father and saw that his eye shined merrily.

A second theatre-goer stepped forward. 'So we want a performance, see?'

'Proper-like,' another said.

'A comedy,' said yet another.

'By William Shakespeare, there,' a fifth one pointed.

'Not by wots-'is-name,' a sixth man nodded.

'Jonson,' the crowd shouted, joining in.

'That's it.' The sixth man wheeled round smiling, arms raised for applause.

'Oi,' the seventh man shouted and elbowed the sixth. 'We agreed on blood 'n guts.' He turned to Shakespeare, and grinned a toothless smile. 'I voted *Macbeth*.'

'And I, for *Henry V*,' the seventh piped up.

'Those aren't comedies!' the fourth one scolded, shaking his head. 'Now, *Merchant of Venice*! There's a comedy!'

All heads turned from side to side as they watched the theatre-goers' spectacle.

John Heminges stepped forward. 'Sorry my good men, but we must away.'

Before anyone could move, the unshaven theatre-goer raised his pistol in the air and fired again. 'A play! Nobody moves till we've got our play by Shakespeare there!'

The well-wishers roared with laughter and applauded. The King's Men looked to Shakespeare, and he, glanced to Susanna. Her face brightened with expectation. Robert tugged at Shakespeare's sleeve and whispered, 'The doctor?'

Shakespeare turned to Robert. 'We'll be gone before he's out of his surgery door,' he breathed.

Minutes later, Shakespeare stood holding his staff, alone in the road. Behind him, the jewelled cloak that had been so beautifully sewn by Susanna was stretched on poles as a makeshift curtain. In front of him sat his expectant audience, with the troublesome theatre-goers cross-legged on the cobbles in the front row.

Shakespeare gazed upon them all, ending his sweep of the audience with his eyes trained on the unshaven man.

'You,' Shakespeare pointed. 'What's your name?'

'Jasper?' the unshaven man replied, as if asking his approval.

Shakespeare laughed.

'You, next to him. What's your birth month?'

'June.'

'Quickly!' Shakespeare pointed to the third man. 'Your wife's name?'

'Margery.'

'Your favourite food?' Shakespeare nodded to the next man.

This theatre-goer seemed to have a need to ponder the question, as if there were so many foods and too little time to sample them in his brain.

'Quickly!' Shakespeare commanded.

The poor man jittered. 'Uh, mead.'

'That's a drink,' Shakespeare laughed again. 'You, your favourite food?'

'Cakes.'

'Glad it's more than one!' he mocked. 'And you, next to him. Your favourite play of mine?'

'Hmm. That's stumpin' me...'

'Come on! We haven't all day!' he urged.

'Romeo and Juliet.'

'Good. It's my daughter's too,' Shakespeare peeked over his shoulder at Susanna and winked.

It was, she wondered? If he rattled those questions at her, she doubted she could answer as quickly as the theatre-goers. What *was* her favourite play, she wondered?

'Right, now you, my good man,' Shakespeare nodded to the next theatre-goer. 'Your favourite character?'

'Falstaff!' he cried out to great applause and hoots. He stood up to take a bow.

'Sit down! This is my show!' Shakespeare ordered, swiftly turning to another theatre-goer.

'You.'

'Me?'

'Yes. Your favourite line. Quickly.'

'Uh, "My kingdom for a horse!" that'd be it.'

'Good. Now you with the red hat, your favourite baddie.'

'That'd be King John.'

The pace quickened. 'Next, your favourite colour?'

'Green.'

'You, your favourite woman's name?'

'Rosaline.'

'Me too.' Again, Shakespeare peeked back at Susanna and smiled.

Without further delay, he turned to his audience and banged his staff on the cobbles to signify the show was beginning. A rapt silence spread like a shroud, warm with the expectation of a longed-for performance.

His velvet voice rang out:

> Our pair of star-crossed lovers, Jasper and Rosaline,
> sigh away as cuckoos in June,
> unaware that King John has ordered,
> at Rosaline's parents' sad behest, for Jasper to die.

Susanna, like everyone else, was captivated.

Shakespeare continued:

> But Jasper's mate, Falstaff,
> rescues their dark fate,
> with falsely poisoned cakes and mead
> that very night, late.

The theatre-goers, bug-eyed, gasped.

Shakespeare suppressed a smile, and waved his arm theatrically:

> Jas must take the draught and pretend to die,
> Whilst Rosaline waits in the wild wood, seeing green.
> Not as the colour of lovers, nay my friends,
> But as that of the green-eyed monster.

'Jealousy!' the unshaven theatre-goer cried out. His friend in the red cap poked him to be quiet and the audience hissed, 'sssshhhh!'

Shakespeare raised his brows conspiratorially:

> For in the glade where Jasper lies,
> a maiden Margery is spied.
> Rosaline thinks Jasper's been untrue,
> And runs off – woosh!

As he spoke the final line, Shakespeare retreated behind the jewelled curtain and with Susanna's help clambered aboard the cart. He turned back to his dazed audience and cried out with gusto:

'A horse! A horse! My kingdom for my horse!'

With that, the cart rolled off. Robert grabbed hold of the jewelled cloak as Shakespeare gave a deep bow to his adoring audience who were hooting and shouting and throwing their hats into the air.

Holding on to her father's arm, Susanna glowed in the reflected sunshine of his words. Somehow she'd get the manuscripts back to him before any more wayward accusations were levelled against Jonson. Somehow, she'd find a way to stay amongst them… at least a while longer.

Less than an hour later, another spectacle was brewing at the porter's lodge of Magdalen College. A dusty Dr John Hall dismounted from his breathless chestnut mare, and slung his saddle bags over his shoulder. He strode up to the porter's window, plain for all to see, that this was an angry man for whom time had run out.

He pounded on the entry lodge window. A bowler hat slowly rose from below, until at last, the face of the college porter was visible.

'Master Shakespeare,' Hall commanded.

'What about him?' The porter answered blankly.

Hall rolled his eyes. 'His rooms.'

The porter, without expression, pointed to the far side of the cloister, and without a nod or a thank you, Hall marched off. The porter smiled wryly and took his ease in the nearby chair. A good five minutes later, Hall was back, spitting fire and brimstone.

'By all that's holy, man, I asked for Master Shakespeare!'

The porter shrugged. 'I begs to differ, sir. You asks for "his rooms" now didn't you?'

Hall's mouth thinned into a taught line. 'Let's start over.'

'If you wish, good sir.'

Hall took a deep breath. 'May I see Master Shakespeare?'

'You may, but you can't.'

'Stop talking in riddles man! Come here!'

The porter stood and shuffled over to his window. Hall grabbed him by the scruff of his neck.

'Where is Shakespeare?'

'Ah, now that's more like it,' the porter nodded approvingly.

'WHERE?' Hall was bright crimson with anger.

'Gone.'

'WHERE?'

'O,' the porter frowned and scratched his head. 'They did tell me... it's on that tip of mine tongue...'

Hall gripped the porter's robes tightly and pulled him so close that their noses touched. 'How's your tongue's memory now?'

'Less good, sir.'

Hall narrowed his eyes and reached into his pocket with his free hand. He handed a coin to the porter, who promptly bit on it.

'Any better now?'

'Hm. It's only a penny's worth better, sir.'

'So far your memory's not been worth more.'

The porter stared at Hall, his hand extended for another penny.

'I could fix that memory of yours,' Hall threatened. 'I'm a doctor, I'll have you know, and I have ways of making patients scream that you'd never dreamt on.'

'Now, I remember!'

Hall released the man and thrust him backwards.

The porter spluttered. 'Norwich. Yep that's it. Leastwise that's what they called out to the carter.'

Hall held out his hand. 'I'll have my coin back.'

He gently placed the penny into Hall's palm. Then the doctor swung round and a jingling sound like glass breaking came from his saddlebags.

The porter gave a great grin at Hall's back and took out a pouch from his doublet, rattling it by his ear. 'God bless ye, good ol' Master Shakespeare,' he sighed wistfully. 'May that doctor rot in a bog in the Anglian fens!'

Chapter 20

The wherries criss-crossed the water, their lanterns swinging drunkenly aft. Susanna gazed on in awe. Tawny stone buildings with their standards unfurled lined the port shore in greeting. People milled about the quayside, their laughter and cheers echoing on the water. Ever lower in the sky, the setting sun nudged the treetops, peeking out from behind the great houses like some huge vermillion orb that teased them with its splendour. As the shadows lengthened, one by one the wherrymen leaned over the side of their boats with a taper to light their lanterns.

In the houses along the shores, candles flickered in the windows. And through it all, the hundred barges and wherries that sailed on the Thames rowed to their destinations, oblivious to the beauty enshrouding them. Susanna watched the oars of their barge rise and fall, slicing the water to the rhythm for the oarsmen's stroke. Somewhere in the distance Susanna thought she heard flutes that sang like lapwings.

So, this was London.

She looked about her, stunned at its grandness. She revelled in its splendour and understood its hidden squalor. Its vastness and rich tapestry of people were unlike anything she'd imagined. She looked west, then eastwards – absorbing it, wondering if her eyes deceived her. As they rowed towards her father's London home, she was thankful he had insisted on making the final leg of their journey by barge from Maidenhead.

She silently recalled that conversation. There was something in his eye that told her this was how he wanted her to see London for the first time: sailing on its lifeblood, the river. O, how his eye glinted with mischief ... How she hung on each of his honeyed words and his charming ways he so carelessly used to persuade them to travel by river. Once Shakespeare had decided he wanted to hire a barge and leave the horses at the post livery, the King's Men bowed to his wishes without dissent. This was no whimsy, but rather a fond dream to show her London, in his own particular way.

They glided past the fine houses that fringed the river's edge. Gazing over to her father, she saw how his hands trembled more than they had the day before. She wanted to give him a smile of thanks when she saw how his eyelid drooped lazily. Was he sickening for another turn? And if so, why wasn't he mindful to take his medicines? After all, six phials should last for a month at least. Then that unkind thought niggled at the back of her mind: or was he playacting to gain her sympathy?

Yet, in her heart, she knew he lived in terror of those turns. Perhaps that was why he'd resisted to overnight at an inn: fear that the world would know William Shakespeare suffered from the falling sickness and would brand him as possessed of evil spirits? Perhaps she'd known this ever since that summer of '05, but her own life – such as it was with her husband all these years – had clouded the memory.

Susanna reflected back to her grandfather, John Shakespeare. Had she not seen him hide himself away from the world? Hadn't everyone believed him to be a drunk, with his wobbly gait and talking gibberish? Still, Grandfather Shakespeare seemed to take longer to heal up from his turns than her father. Suddenly his words rang in her ears: 'I far prefer being branded a drunk and layabout than possessed by the Devil.'

And what about her father's brother, Gilbert? He, too, had his turns, but they were more like dizzy spells. Gilbert would fall over and become confused, but he never talked nonsense to her mind, and his falling seemed to be some perturbation of the brain that simply made him feel faint. Unlike their feelings towards grandfather, everyone in Stratford felt sorry for Gilbert, who was as goodly and kindly a soul that ever was. Most thought Gilbert's dizzy spells were for his overworking in the family glove-making business, and acting as the man of the house for her father in his absence.

She sighed as they rowed past a bevy of wherries heading upstream. Her father's sickness – that is, if he wasn't playacting – was modelled on her grandfather's. It was sudden and violent, sometimes coming on with wild rhymings and such, and at other times, his legs would give way beneath him and he could no longer speak. He covered up his brainsickness with theatrical and extraverted behaviour, where her grandfather's illness had been marked by sullenness and rumours of drunkenness and her uncle's, by overwork.

Whether he was playacting or suffering just now, Susanna thought she'd probably never know. She shielded her eyes from the setting sun. As she turned her gaze to the other side of the barge, she spied her father, quiet, eyes shaded under his broad-brimmed hat, staring at her as if he could see into her soul. She shuddered as though a phantom had walked upon her grave, and looked away. Was he or wasn't he ill?

On the far side of the river, she saw a householder was gathering wild pink valerian along the shore with his young daughter. He showed her the plant, most likely explaining its calming benefits, Susanna imagined. Another fished and dozed as dusk drew in. A small group of men stood chatting on a doorstep, smoking tobacco in their clay pipes and drinking from flagons. Susanna's eyes trailed down to the river. She could see the reflection of their richly upholstered barge mirrored in it, as if the river were a looking-glass. Entranced, her eyes glided back to her father. Shakespeare sat quietly, staring at her.

'Why do you stare at me so, Father?'

He jumped slightly, as if awakened from a dream.

'Words roll 'round in my brain,' he said.

Heminges, Burbage and Condell all turned to scrutinise Susanna.

'What words, Will?' Heminges asked.

'The barge speech by Enobarbus.'

Heminges shone his eyes on Susanna. They seemed to glaze over as he recited the lines:

> The barge she sat in, like a burnished throne,
> Burned on the water: the poop was beaten gold,
> Purple the sails, and so perfumed that
> The winds were lovesick with them: the oars were

silver,

> Which in the tune of flutes kept stroke, and made
> The water which they beat to flow faster.

'A pretty speech,' Susanna nodded, trying to pretend she wasn't flattered at being compared to Cleopatra, the queen of Egypt. Fact was, she'd never heard such blandishments from a man before and was keenly embarrassed. She looked away, feeling the warmth of his words reflected on her cheeks.

She fixed her attention on the hustle of people ambling about and selling their wares along the river. Some leaned from their ground-floor windows, hanging out their handiwork for all to see. Hawkers cried out for people to buy their wares which they wore upon their backs, like country pedlars selling chapbooks or linen from their packs.

But this was the only similarity Susanna could see with the countryside. Looking beyond the vast throng to the stone and brick buildings, she felt the history of this place. Many houses had family crests over the doorways. As they passed downriver the buildings became ever more sumptuous.

'That home was Sir Thomas More's,' Heminges pointed out to her.

Susanna looked to her left at the old brick building, thinking it exceedingly fine. 'I see,' she replied. She recalled an unfinished manuscript pages amongst her father's papers which referred to

More, though she was unsure who Sir Thomas was, other than he had lived back in King Henry VIII's time.

And so they continued ever eastwards, downriver, into the dusk. One by one, candles were lit inside the homes and inns along the Thames. Soon it would be evening, and they would be back at Blackfriars.

A cry of *Westward ho!* rang out as a wherry steered so close to them that its wherryman had to push himself away from their barge with his filthy hand.

The boatman from their barge cried out, 'Oi! Watch out for my upholstery!'

'I barely touched it!' the wherry man shouted back with an obscene gesture.

The boatman rushed to the stern. 'See that?' he muttered, pointing to the greasy mark. In dismay, he looked to Susanna then Heminges then Shakespeare, adding, 'I mean, really! Gone are the days of the polite "pardon" and "by your leave". What is the world coming to, I ask you?'

Susanna touched the grease mark lightly. 'You might try a poultice of Shepherd's Purse mixed with salt … apply some gently, let it stay a goodly while and then brush it away without rubbing it in. That should do the trick.'

He tipped his cap at her. Robert saw how Heminges and Shakespeare looked on admiringly.

But Susanna remained oblivious. They had rounded a bend in the river, and it seemed there were twice as many wherries on London's busiest thoroughfare. People boarded in the west, whilst wherries returned empty from the east. In the distance, she spied a magnificent bridge with twenty stone archways and fine homes and shops built across it.

'Goodness!' she exclaimed. 'What bridge is that?'

'London Bridge,' Heminges said. 'There are rapids beneath it, but we'll be docking shortly and won't suffer from the current.'

Susanna gazed at the wherries again. 'And, where is everyone going?'

Heminges looked to the Southwark side of the bridge.

'The bear-baiting most likely. The Globe is closed just now, and I doubt anything's on at The Rose, given...' his voice trailed off.

'Given what?' she asked.

'Its new owner isn't quite sure what to do with it,' Shakespeare answered.

Robert saw Shakespeare look at Heminges, as if to say, *Not yet... don't tell her anything just yet.* Did Heminges share the same secret as he did, or was the Master making new ones?

As the barge turned into shore, Susanna felt her heart race in anticipation and fear. She must as privately as a whisper return the manuscripts before more damage was done in wronging Ben Jonson.

A tired Richard Burbage separated from the others at the little stone church on Blackfriars Street, and he gave a weary wave. Susanna, Heminges and Condell walked on together for a while before she heard a cart rolling on the cobbles behind them, and turned. Shakespeare was perched precariously between Robert and Nathan, lurching from one side to the other like a rag doll. He laughed merrily.

Henry Condell tapped her on the shoulder. 'Would you like to see something that's pure London?' he asked.

He motioned for her to stand against the cool stone building. Heminges walked on, unaware they'd stopped. Condell pointed with his chin to the tiny building on the corner next to the church. 'See that school house?' he asked her.

She stretched up onto her tiptoes to see above the heads of the passers-by. A discrete stone building was tucked away from the street. Boys were rushing out purposefully. 'Aye,' she replied. He tapped the side of his nose with his finger then placed it to his lips.

'Watch carefully,' he said, his eyes sparkling with mirth.

Two of the schoolboys walked past and smiled sweetly at Susanna. Their faces were angelic and they were probably aged no more than seven or eight. Whilst gazing across to her, the darker-haired one accidently walked into a good housewife and apologised profusely. The startled housewife looked him up and down. Seeing he was smartly dressed she nodded her forgiveness to him. The fairer-haired boy with an even more angelic face moved behind her briefly before he rejoined his friend and doffed his cap at the woman. He led his dark-haired friend away admonishing him for his clumsiness.

'It's so rare these days to see youngsters with such good manners,' Susanna said softly to Condell.

'Wait,' he said.

As they rounded the corner, the dark-haired boy lifted a woman's purse from his doublet and smiled at his friend.

Susanna's jaw dropped in astonishment.

'That's no ordinary school over the road. It's a school for scoundrels. They're being taught to lift a purse without ringing the bell on the wrist of their teacher. Those two have a way to go before they can become Public Foisters or Judicial Nippers,' Condell said shaking his head.

'But if you know what they're up to, why aren't they stopped?'

Condell grinned, 'You've much to learn of London ways. Come,' he said, taking her by the arm. Susanna looked at the other boys who'd come out of the school house, all of them smartly dressed in goodly cloth. The youngest of them couldn't have been older than five. It was hard to believe they were being trained in the art of thievery. But then she saw the 'schoolmaster' stand on his front stoop, paying the watchman who was meant to keep the peace, and she understood. He who pays, earns your loyalty in London.

Condell tapped her on the shoulder again and she turned round. He pointed to a timber and brick house opposite. She looked at the astrology hawker sitting by the open window of her front room. A banner was hung beneath the sill proclaiming *whatever dies was not mixt equally* then below it advertised *the elixir of life, only 3d* and *white stone, your fortune!* As odd as her advertisements were, it was the astrology hawker herself who enchanted Susanna. The woman wore a silken turban with golden threads and flowery designs and matching robe from some exotic land. Her face was wizened by the sun and her eyes were pinpricks of light blue. Just as Susanna was about to remark on how extraordinary the woman looked, the astrology hawker's eyes sparkled with joy. 'Will!' she cried and pointed.

Susanna saw her father's cart turn the corner into Blackfriars Street. Shakespeare sat bolt upright, waving and smiling. All signs of his illness had vanished. His friends and neighbours crowded around the cart, cheering and carrying on something fierce.

'Sing me a sonnet, Will,' a householder called out.

'One of love,' a stallholder bid.

'Or beauty!' the astrology hawker laughed.

'Yea,' a neighbour cried, 'so we can give her some of her own white stone to smooth her wrinkles!'

They all roared in merriment. Her father joined in too, drinking in their love of him as if it were some magical potion.

Then another cry of 'Will' rang out. It was John Heminges waiting by a huge grey-stone gatehouse. Susanna read its sign 'Blackfriars Gatehouse'. As she peered up at it, her first thought was that her father's London home was sinister. Then she realised that the building seemed all doors and windows and no house at all. It wasn't in the least like her parents' home in Stratford.

'It looks like a gated entry to some dark country,' she mused aloud.

Heminges looked up at it and shrugged. 'It serves its purpose.'

Susanna thought it was more like a great hulk or some forbidden ship about to whisk them off to a distant shore. The cart pulled up, and Robert and Nathan helped her father down.

'My bones shake,' Shakespeare grumbled. Slowly he unfolded himself to his full height and walked stiffly towards Susanna.

'One day, all this shall be yours,' he proclaimed proudly.

Susanna wasn't sure if it was meant to be a blessing or a curse.

Chapter 21

The air inside was still and thick. Susanna felt baubles of sweat trickling down her spine as she mounted the stairs. Straddling a passageway for horses and carts, the Blackfriars Gatehouse had two old winding wooden staircases that spiralled to the rooms above. John Heminges mounted the stairs ahead of her, Henry Condell behind. Shakespeare, Robert, Nathan and Will Davenant followed, struggling to help her father up the narrow, snaking staircase.

At some turnings, there were doors onto the landings, while at others, there were only windows. The higher they rose, the more foetid and stale the air became. As they climbed Susanna felt dizzy, as though all the air had been sucked out of her. She grabbed hold of Heminges's back fearing she'd fall, but when he turned and his lantern aloft to look at her, it was as though his smile breathed life into her again.

'Come,' he said, holding out his hand. 'It's just beyond.'

She took it gladly and climbed again. Only when she heard the jangle of keys and the click of the latch could she feel her breathing ease. Heminges swung the heavy oak door open and she tumbled in after him.

'O, Lord,' was all she could say as she tried to catch her breath. She gazed up at the hammer-beamed ceiling hundreds of years old.

'Precisely. The story goes that this was a house of the Lord in Henry VIII's time,' Heminges said, opening the shutters and windows. 'I often imagine the monks rolling in their graves at the thought of a player and playmaker owning it.'

He whipped off the covers from the chairs, cupboards and tables. A shower of dust sparkled orange and violet in the last gasps of twilight. On the far wall was a large stone fireplace with two more doors leading only heaven knew where. Blackfriars, of course, she thought, stifling a cough from the dust. It had been part of the Dominican monastery until the Dissolution eighty years or so back. It was little wonder this hall felt as if it were filled with ghostly shadows whispering secrets of a world long vanished.

Her musings were interrupted by cries from the stairwell.

'Ow! You churl! That's my head!' Shakespeare barked.

The door was flung open with a thud. In the centre of the doorway stood Shakespeare, gasping for air, held up under his armpits by a winded Robert and Nathan, sweating under the weight of their charge. As soon as Shakespeare saw Susanna, he straightened and tried to walk with a smidgen of dignity to the armchair.

'Humpf,' he grumbled, collapsing thankfully. 'Staircase is hardly wide enough for three men abreast.'

Susanna shook her head. That tottery old staircase creaked of rotten oak under foot, with woodworm making the treads soft as pine. She thought back to her childhood when her girlish fears made her tremble at the thought of staircases. Then she recalled how her father would sweep her up into his arms and race down the stairs with her, then back up again to show how there was truly nothing to fear. It was just the wood creaking under foot saying 'ouch' he'd tell her. Fancy her remembering that now …

'Watch what you're doing, Robert!' Susanna heard her father bellow.

Robert was manhandling a heavy trunk into the hall. 'I'm watching,' he huffed back. He placed the trunk down with a thud and wiped his brow.

Unless Susanna was sorely mistaken, it was the trunk where she'd hidden the satchel.

'Not here, Robert,' Shakespeare waved from his armchair throne. 'The costume chests go to the prop room. John?' he asked, turning to Heminges. 'Make sure all the trunks go to the prop room?'

Heminges nodded and helped Robert back down the stairs with the chest.

'Nathan?' Shakespeare asked.

'Go with young Will to buy provisions?'

Nathan rose and headed out, ruffling Will's curly brown hair. Will ran after him.

Susanna needed to see where the prop room was, so she could steal away to it later for the satchel. Thinking quickly, she called out, 'Wait up. I'll come with you.'

'Mind you don't get that ale from the tavern opposite,' Shakespeare called after them. 'It tastes like feet.'

'And you, Will Shakespeare,' Condell wagged his finger, 'are going to bed.'

Susanna peered back to see Condell helping him to stand and walking her father away.

'Tell Robert to bring me my quills and paper, Henry,' Shakespeare ordered.

'You threw them all to your adoring friends, remember?'

'Then tell Robert to go buy some more.'

Susanna made her way down after the others, admiring him for trying to maintain control of things, yet worried, she'd brought on this latest bout of sickness. As she turned the corner of the winding staircase, she spied Heminges and Robert carting the trunk off onto the first floor above the main entrance.

Whilst they were making their purchases across the way at the market stalls, Susanna pondered about how difficult it would be for her to get to that chest. In her mind's eye, she saw the key ring dangling in the lock as they passed into the prop room. Heminges must hold the keys. After all, he'd unlocked the front door and the great hall.

'Bet you've never seen a sight like that?' Nathan tapped her on the shoulder.

A gaggle of playwrights had already gathered at the entrance to the Gatehouse.

'They're my daily chore for my mother,' she said. 'I greet them, then take their plays. Lately, she has me burn them.'

Nathan took off his hat and scratched his head. 'Blimey.'

'We usually have three or four playmakers a day. Sundays maybe more.' Susanna nodded to the stallholder in thanks, taking her parcels.

Will cried out suddenly, 'MAKE WAY!'

Everyone flattened themselves against the buildings. A thin, barefoot boy wove past, herding his enormous spotted Gloucester pig. But the boy was no match for his animal and the pig ran squealing out of control into a vegetable stall, knocking down the cabbages and trampling them. The smell of mashed cabbage filled the air, mingling with the stench of the market. The stallholder let out a cry at the boy and his pig as they ran along, cabbages rolling behind them. Soon enough, the Londoners went about their business, as though this happened all the time. Susanna shrugged and turned to find Will.

Instead, beyond the gutted stall, she saw Ben Jonson flounce off, waving a fist at Richard Burbage. It seemed Nathan had spotted them too, for he shot off calling out, 'Ben! Richard! Wait up!'

Will tugged at her sleeve. 'We need to get back and tell the others,' she said, walking off swiftly.

Fear gripped Susanna by the throat. The keys were no longer in the lock of the prop room. She scolded herself once more for her stupidity as she laid out the table settings. She hadn't thought that they'd find Jonson today. Damn him!

Her father sat in front of the fire, flanked by Heminges and Condell, with Nathan and Burbage panting from their dash home.

Robert approached Susanna, carrying the plates. It didn't take any stargazer to see that she were upset. 'Now there,' he whispered. 'No one blames you.'

'I know,' she said, thinking all the while that they should hold her to account if there was any justice in the world. 'But I left the manuscripts on that round table in plain sight, so it's really my fault. And–' She bit on her lip, just as Will ran past with two full tankards for Nathan and Burbage. Robert patted her on the shoulder. Seeing her so fretful for what she'd done wrong, when she only knew how to do right, was too painful for him.

'Is that all Jonson had to say?' Shakespeare asked, frowning.

Burbage swigged his small ale. 'He said he's insulted.'

'Says he doesn't have them,' Nathan added, wiping his mouth on his sleeve.

'But I *saw* him with the manuscripts, Will,' Heminges said.

Susanna stepped forward, wishing away their wrong-headedness. 'All Jonson was doing was reading, not stealing, John.'

Heminges gazed at Susanna, puzzled. 'But it was you who said he was acting oddly.'

'Well, maybe I was wrong. We'd just got into Oxford after a harrowing few days and Father was poorly and–'

Shakespeare cut across her. 'Invite Ben round, John. We need to talk.'

'I've done that, Will,' Burbage said, putting down his tankard. 'But he says he needs a written apology first.'

'Never!' Shakespeare shouted.

'Richard,' Condell piped up, 'what if Jonson's lying? Wouldn't be the first time–'

'Nor the last,' Shakespeare added.

'What if,' Condell placed a calming hand on Shakespeare's shoulder, 'he's planning to publish Will's work as his own?'

'No one would dare believe him!' Shakespeare cried, outraged.

'Surely not?' Burbage said.

'O, wouldn't they?' Heminges asked. 'You all know how greedy those printers are. Remember Will's sonnets?'

Young Will Davenant cried, 'Kill all the printers!'

Nathan smiled at him. 'The line's "lawyers", Will.'

'Same thing,' Condell added

Shakespeare looked at them in turn, pondering the problem. He's looking at everyone save me and Robert, Susanna thought. None of them existed for her father, other than to slide back into their players' hides as fetchers and carriers, she mused uncharitably. Was it for the loss of the manuscripts that he ignored them? Or, worse, had he guessed she had a hand in this new drama?

'It would make sense, Will,' Burbage nodded.

'I don't understand,' Susanna said in exasperation. 'Aren't there printed versions of the plays already, and players' parts too?'

'True,' Heminges answered. 'Those printings have been authorised by our company. But, only twelve plays have been printed. The other twenty-seven only exist as manuscripts or players' parts.'

'And no printed play or player's part contains my handwritten changes, Susanna,' Shakespeare interrupted. 'The manuscripts are different from all the rest – better I'd say.'

'Besides, if Jonson brings the manuscripts to a printer,' Burbage ventured, 'whether he's honest or no, the printer would be mad to question him. Money's money after all. If Jonson claims them as his own, the printer has no duty to call him a liar and risk his wrath.'

'And speaking of money,' Condell began, 'there'll be no money for Will or us either if Jonson has the plays printed.'

Shakespeare had grown puce with anger. 'Find Jonson.'

'Jonson said he's off to the king at court to tell of our effrontery,' Nathan said, as quiet as a wren's chirp.

'What? The court? At this time of day?' Shakespeare's eyes widened in disbelief.

'More than likely I'd bet he'll be at the Mermaid,' Heminges scoffed.

Shakespeare nodded. 'Ah, a court of a different colour.'

Susanna felt her heart sink and her arms go limp. She turned back to laying the table, feeling she was broken inside. Even if she could get to the satchel that very evening, she'd done the damage: Jonson had been wrongly accused to his face of stealing the plays.

Robert gazed across at Susanna, thinking he had to say or do something to give her cheer, even if it were just to let her know she weren't alone. He eased up to her and took the spoons and bowls from her with a gentle tug. She nodded in thanks with a slender smile and dashed away. Poor mite, he thought, she blames herself, she does, for all these troubles 'bout the manuscripts. And she's the one who'd saved them in the first place!

Chapter 22

The sign of the Mermaid Taverne creaked on its hinges as it swung. A storm was brewing in more ways than Robert could get his mind around. It was past nine o'clock at night, yet despite the weather people were only just gathering in the taverne. Clearly, word had spread that the playing companies had returned from the festival in Oxford. Clearer still, Robert were sure they'd come to see Shakespeare and Jonson at one of their wars again. There were great rumours flying as to why. He'd heard some speculate that it were over a woman, whilst others wagered it were about money. All Robert knew for certain were those people pushing to get inside preferred casting off the truth in favour of salacious rumours. To the rumour-mongers the truth hardly mattered. For the others, all they hoped for were a free spectacle with some good ale and a haven to cut some purses in – maybe shift some stolen goods even.

Of all the haunts for drinking and gambling in London, the Mermaid – so he heard tell – were the most delightful and dangerous, attracting nips, foists, swindlers, conycatchers, players, ladies of the night, ladies of the court, musicians and tourists into its parlour like that famed churl of a fly to the spider's web.

Robert glanced over to Susanna. Her eyes were ablaze. She'd been warned of this and more before they foregathered outside the Mermaid with the King's Men. In mirror images of Oxford, and again at Blackfriars, the crowds swarmed round to wish Shakespeare 'Good Health' and asked a bookful of questions about his health and when he'd play again. Propped up by his stick and Will Davenant,

Shakespeare nodded graciously to all, replying as best he could. But given the leer in their eyes, Susanna wondered if it was 'Good Health' they truly wished him so much as to see a brawl of words between him and Ben Jonson. To her mind, the air was thick with anticipation.

'Come, my roaring boys,' Shakespeare bid the King's Men. 'And girl,' he smiled at Susanna. 'It's show time.'

The barmaid leaned over their table with a heavy tray of drinks, showing more of her breasts than she hid. Without a care to splashing or no, she passed around the tankards more as if she were dealing cards than serving valued customers. Nathan and Robert frowned at theirs suspiciously before Robert had the wit to swap them round. Condell sniffed at his and passed it on to Burbage.

'Hey there, Joan,' Burbage shouted. 'We ordered malmsey, not ale.'

The barmaid straightened up and narrowed her pretty eyes at him, her hand firmly placed on her rounded hip.

'Now look ye here, Master Burbage. First ye says three malmseys, two small ales and four perries. Then ye changes it to two malmseys, four small ales and two perries.'

'Ah but Joan–'

'Don't go "ah Joanin" me. Besides by the time you takes a swig o' one or 'tother, you're liable to change yer minds again!'

The whole table, save Susanna, looked down at their tankards, mistrustful. They sniffed at them and shifted them round to their neighbours. Susanna had her perry and she held fast to it before it got snaffled away.

'See? You'll just do what yer doin' any road up and swaps them round with yer neighbour!'

Burbage tried his rough charm once again. 'Ah, Joan–'

'If you want to win me favour, Master Burbage, you'd best call me by me own name for once!' the barmaid mocked.

Just then a battered old soldier scraped back his chair and stood, crying out, 'Mine host! Mine Host! Wherefore art thou, Mine Host!'

The barmaid turned round, swishing her skirts and headed towards the old fellow. 'The name's Nell, Master Burbage!'

Burbage stood to beckon her back. 'Nell! Nell! Wherefore art thou, Nell!'

The taverne rang out in peals of laughter.

Nell looked back briefly with a raised eyebrow before turning her attention to the old soldier who swayed like he was aboard a ship.

'Now, Cap'n, it's mighty early for ye to be pie-eyed, don't ye know?' Nell tried to take his flagon from him, but he raised it high above his head.

'Mine host!' he breathed at her, nearly falling into her arms. Nell reeled back and shook her head to clear it from the stench of his breath.

'I've a plaint,' he pouted. 'This ale is as thick as Tewkesbury mustard and as sour as pickled onions!'

'Cap'n, it's the same ale as you've been drinking since opening,' Nell replied from a safe distance.

The captain rocked to and fro, until he tucked his chin into his chest to steady himself. 'This ale is stale,' he muttered.

The patrons of the taverne hooted gleefully at the drunken soldier. Susanna looked at her father. Shakespeare returned her gaze, sadness welling up in his eyes. The captain reminded her of the gibes her grandfather had had to endure. His words, *better a drunk than suffering from the falling evil,* rang in her ears.

Nell snatched away the captain's flagon. 'Let me be the judge of this ale, stale or otherwise.'

She took a short swig and clicked her tongue against the roof of her mouth. 'Hm. No... tastes more like...' Nell stopped to take another swig – this time a long one, tipping up the flagon until it was emptied down her throat. 'Ah, yep. That's it, Cap'n.'

'What's it?' the captain reeled forward again.

'It's not stale. It smells like a smelly old drunk's toes! Now pay up and be gone with ye. And don't head towards the river or you'll drown you daft, dappled fool!'

She turned on her heels, carrying the empty flagon away with her. The captain suddenly wound his arm up over his head and took a swing at her with such force that when he missed, he twirled round and round until he fell over, breaking his chair.

'Why you! Hit a man when he's down, will you? Why I'll – I'll make a pretty picture of you!'

The whole of the Mermaid, save Susanna and Shakespeare, were falling over themselves in fits of laughter.

Quick as a flash, Nell stormed back towards him, and yanked the old man to his feet. She wound her neck out at the old soldier. 'Hold tight there, Cap'n. I'll beg ye some paper and an inkhorn from our friend Shakespeare there, shall I?'

The captain inched backwards, as slow as a tortoise. For a few seconds, all was silence. Then the captain's eyes batted several times before he swooned to the ground, fast asleep, and began to snore.

'That wasn't exactly the show I had in mind,' Shakespeare shrugged.

For nearly an hour they sat without further entertainment or incident, occasionally whispering in each other's ears. Susanna had taken to wringing her hands like Condell, though peering across at him through the haze of smoke he seemed extraordinarily calm for such a nervous man, only betraying his emotions by the darting of his eyes.

Susanna studied the Mermaiders. Smoke from their clay pipes hung lazily in the air like a fog. Tobacco, they said, soothed the spirit and made your food taste better. But Susanna would have none of it. To her taste, it smelled like burning leaves and the smoke parched her throat. Through the haze she judged that most of the men seemed to be gamblers, and indeed many of the women. A fair few of the women looked like careworn prostitutes taking a rest from their duties, whilst others seemed to be practised card sharps.

Will Davenant tugged at Susanna's arm, his eyes sparkling. 'They've got liar dice,' he said and pointed with his chin at two women, who were the only ladies resembling harmless housewives. They were fleecing the men at their gaming table.

Heminges leaned across to Susanna. 'There. That's the Admiral's Men, just arrived.'

She quickly turned and saw the Admiral's Men strutting like peacock players, as they just walked by without a word, giving a desultory nod to Shakespeare's table. Susanna frowned.

Robert nudged her. 'They smell a players' war.'

'Is that why they said nothing?' She gave Robert a worried look.

Just then, the front door of the taverne blew open. An astonishing looking woman – probably as old as her father – stood framed in the doorway, gathering her Oriental rug cloak around her throat with her gnarled fingers. Her hair jutted out at all angles from her crimson and gold headdress like fire pokers, and was coloured grey, red, pink and blue.

'Who's that?' Susanna whispered.

'Agnes, my patron,' Shakespeare answered.

'Agnes Henslowe, owner of the Rose Theatre, now her husband's dead,' Heminges added softly.

'And the brothel next door too,' Condell added.

'Thinks she owns your father as well,' Heminges said.

'Evening all!' Agnes cried.

All heads twisted round, their necks outstretched like kites closing in on their kill. As soon as they saw it was only Agnes, a few answered listlessly, 'Evening.' Susanna was sure they were disappointed it wasn't Jonson.

'Is that the best welcome my Court of the Mermaid can give me? Are you suddenly taken ill with polite manners? Or do the bold ladies and debauched gentlemen of my here Court of the Mermaid wait on some other entertainment besides me?'

The Mermaiders carried on with their drinking and gaming, undeterred and uninterested in her words.

Agnes narrowed her falcon's eyes and stepped further in, slamming the entry door to the taverne behind her.

Everyone jumped.

'Ah! Now I got you by your noses! So–'

There was a sudden beating on the door. Agnes peered over her shoulder then reeled round quickly. 'Shall I let in the folly that beats at the door?'

'Yes!' they cried out like schoolchildren, wriggling in their seats. Susanna thought it might be some sort of playacting. She glanced at her father and Heminges and saw they were captivated.

Agnes strode to the door. 'Folly beats again on the door, and I shall let it in ... while at the same time I'll let your judgement out!' she cackled at them.

A huge force pushed at the door just as Agnes unlatched it. It was no great wind that blew in but that vast edifice of a man, Ben Jonson, standing proud, and scouring the room with his mean eye. When he spied Shakespeare, he raised the corner of his mouth into a wry smile.

'No time like the present,' he barked, 'for us to have it out, right Billy?'

Agnes, bent over like a crone, squeezed past Jonson. He patted her on the back for luck, like you'd do any hunchback, and slowly made for Shakespeare's table.

Susanna gazed around her. Every eye in the taverne was trained on Jonson. The Mermaid became as silent as a churchyard before dawn.

He stood at the corner of their table. 'Well, it if isn't Quiverstick.'

The Mermaiders roared like lions at his pun on Shakespeare's name. Jonson slid his eyes to left and right, nodding his thanks and milking their appreciation.

Shakespeare, meanwhile, coolly eyed up his prey. As the hoots died down, he tilted his head at Jonson. 'Evening, Ben,' he said quietly.

'I've come to settle scores,' Jonson growled.

'Settle them? More likely you wish to be paid than do the paying,' Shakespeare replied.

'Don't go making a meal of me, Billy. You have within you books of undivulged crimes as yet unwhipped by justice!'

The crowd gasped, Susanna amongst them. O, Lord, don't let him convince the world he hadn't stolen the manuscripts, I pray you!

'It is man's nature to deny his guilt,' Shakespeare said.

'You are a perjured villain, Billy. A scoundrel, a varlet who with convenient scheming has practised on a man's life – my life! Why your close and pent-up guilts should split open your concealing continents of shame to cry aloud that you are a sinner, and I am a man more sinned against than sinning,' Jonson raged. He trailed his eye away from Shakespeare to Susanna.

The crowd remained hushed. Susanna's throat was dry, her heart raced. Though the room overflowed with Mermaiders, she could still hear herself swallow. Jonson knows, she shouted in her head … somehow, he knows it was me! And soon, so will the world!

'Not bad, Ben, for a first attempt, but paraphrasing my words and citing them as they were meant to be said are horses of varying colours. The speech goes:

'Tremble, thou wretch,
That hast within thee undivulgèd crimes
Unwhipped of justice: hide thee, thou bloody hand.
Thou perjured, and thou simular of virtue
That art incestuous: caitiff, to pieces shake,
That under covert and convenient seeming
Has practised on man's life: close pent-up guilts.
Rive your concealing continents and cry
These dreadful summoners grace. I am a man
More sinned against than sinning.'

The Mermaid was silent – not in fear, as after Jonson's speech – but in awe. One of the gamblers dropped his cards, and he alone applauded Shakespeare's performance. Soon he was joined by another, then another, until most of the Mermaiders erupted into raucous cheers for Shakespeare.

Jonson turned puce. He rounded on Shakespeare like a mad dog. 'Go! Vomit up your hard words against me in front of all our roaring boys and girls here. I dare you!'

The applause ceased. Everyone's eyes grew wide with anticipation. There was a mass scraping of chairs against the floor as the Mermaiders moved round to see better. They'd finally got what they'd come for: a poets' brawl. Heminges made to speak, but Shakespeare put his hand on his arm, a clear motion to silence him.

Jonson turned his icy gaze to Susanna again and leered down at her. Her mouth was as dry as if someone had stuffed it full of chicken feathers. Then, he rounded on Shakespeare.

'You, o' wondrous Will, with your spy-like suggestions and privy whisperings that cut like a thousand other sleights, how dare you accuse me, the mighty Ben Jonson, of petty crimes and thieving your worthless manuscripts?'

There was a sharp intake of breath from the audience. Some whispered 'Manuscripts?' Susanna looked at Robert. He sat stunned, his mouth gaping like the rest of them.

Jonson nodded repeatedly, victoriously, Susanna thought.

'Why, I was just saying to your scribe Ralph – now my scribe Ralph – that there's even a malicious tale hopping from pillar to livery post about how I bribed him to ruin you. How his printer friend, Thorpe, was printing up your manuscripts as my own,' Jonson snarled.

Another sharp gasp from the Mermaiders filled the air.

Shakespeare shook his head in sad lament. 'You never were a good actor, Ben. Should have spent more time ambling with a company of players by a play-wagon.'

Jonson slammed his fist on the table.

'I am all that I am in arts whilst you flit and strut your hour upon the stage in your silks and soon will be no more! I am the King's masque maker, the King's darling. I am all he desires in art! I am to travel to Scotland in his company and regale him with my wit and words, then where will you the great visionary Shakespeare be? Six feet under with the worms fit only for the Isle of Dogs.'

His words made Susanna want to burst to her father's defence. Whatever cruelty this man wanted to inflict on him in public humiliation was, she was sure, undeserved, especially as he was foretelling her father's death. Manuscripts aside, it was vile of him to mock Shakespeare so. She squirmed in her seat, itching to make a lunge for him. No wonder the King's Men called him 'the bricklayer'. Yet she knew instinctively that if she spoke out, she'd only make things worse. She was a simple country girl, for all that she was Shakespeare's daughter. She hadn't the words at her fingertips the way these players did. Compared to the high-flown phrases Jonson and her father used, hers were a pale and flimsy mist of a lowly alphabet strung together to make country sounds.

Susanna glanced over to Robert again and saw his anger etched deeply into every furrow of his brow. She peered across to Heminges and Condell, and saw they were looking daggers at Jonson. Burbage, Nathan and Will looked on as if a rotten smell had settled in the room. Finally, Susanna gazed at her father. He remained calm, as if someone had asked him the way to a local shop or for the time of day. What was he really thinking? Then she noticed the faintest glimmer of a smile slowly glow on his lips.

'Ah, the Isle of Dogs ... where you were once tried for lewd matters handled upon the stage in the reign of the old Queen?' Shakespeare asked sweetly.

'Apologise, you cur,' Jonson growled, 'or I'll tear you piece by bloomin' codpiece.'

Shakespeare pushed back his chair from the table and slowly stood tall. It was the length of time it took him to stand proudly that perhaps made him seem taller and more commanding than Jonson, Susanna thought, even though he was several inches shorter and more slender. With equal care, her father looked from one anxious face to another in the taverne, until everyone had seen the calm of his eye.

He banged his stick on the floor as if a play were about to begin.

'Roaring boys and girls, our friend, Ben, my fellow playmaker and poet has quoted liberally from his plays – and mine – in response to the accusation that he has stolen my original manuscripts and notes of all *my* plays for the mean and green-eyed purpose of publishing my life's work under his name.'

The Mermaiders booed, knowing full well what was expected of them. Jonson leered.

'My life's work is still missing, but …' Shakespeare leaned forward and held the gaze of the patrons nearest him, 'the show must go on! I'll not let Ben's companion Envy and his overworked engineer Jealousy keep the truth from you. Despite it all, I've finished a *new* play.'

Again they gasped, but this time with happiness. Susanna heard the whispers 'A new play by Shakespeare' and 'What joy' ring throughout the Mermaid. Jonson's jaw dangled in shock. Susanna felt a surge of pride course through her body.

Shakespeare twirled round to everyone, holding his arms up invitingly. 'So, come one, come all. Bring your sisters, brothers, wives and mothers! Come to The Tabard Inn in Southwark at the week's end for the premiere of William Shakespeare's final play! O, and before I take my bow, there's ten pounds in it for whoever finds my manuscripts and notes.'

The crowd burst into cries of joy. Hats were thrown in the air and someone cried out to give Shakespeare three cheers. A group of fiddlers struck up their song and the taverne's customers rose to dance a jig. Even the drunken captain stood to dance, but alas, his legs were still like gelatine and he wobbled under the table once more.

Meanwhile, Shakespeare eyed Jonson coolly. All Jonson could do was snarl back at his knowing smile. Where Jonson had to milk the audience's reaction, Susanna realised that her father drank in their adulation, appreciative of their support and love. How odd, she told herself ... only days earlier, she wouldn't have known the difference.

She looked at Jonson, who was trying fruitlessly to regain everyone's attention. The Mermaiders celebrated that Shakespeare would not be vanquished – by Jonson or illness. But she worried. The manuscripts must be returned – somehow. But how, without everyone – her father especially – discovering that she'd committed a crime and compounded it by not owning up? She knew full well that they'd never see the world through her eyes. If she owned up, she'd have to leave. And then where could she go, besides back to Stratford? No, she must return the manuscripts without anyone finding out about her shame.

She saw Agnes standing hunched amid the crowd, jabbering at Jonson, pointing her gnarled finger at his face. Susanna glanced at her father and noticed again how his hands trembled, for all his calm and bravado. If he had a fatal turn, she knew she could never forgive herself for her part in it. A weighty sadness welled up in her heart. She worried her mind to a frazzle as to how she could make things right again. To her surprise and delight, her father looked across to her, holding her eyes with his loving gaze. At that moment, all else faded. What mattered was that she had found the father she had been searching for and she wouldn't allow anyone or anything to take him away from her again. Even her own stupidity.

Chapter 23

Susanna lay awake fully dressed in her bed, waiting for the house to quieten down.

'Robert!' Shakespeare called out. 'You're taking a thieve's eternity!'

'Thieve's eternity my arse,' Robert mumbled. How long had it been since he'd helped the Master write at this time of night? Never, that's how long! When he'd finish a performance, there was carousing and merrymaking, but never writing! Why, it must be near two in the morning or more … and here he was lugging Shakespeare's writing box and papers as if he'd had a night's rest.

'Robert!'

'Your creative juices grow an evermore impatient mistress, Master,' Robert huffed, setting down the box on the writing table.

Will Davenant trundled in behind Robert, holding the inkhorn and a clutch of quills.

Shakespeare grinned mischievously at Robert. 'I'll turn his blasts from hell into sweet airs from heaven.'

'Don't say? So,' Robert said, setting out his things to write, 'you've not written that play yet, have you?'

'No.'

'But, Master–' Robert huffed.

'Ssh,' Shakespeare ordered dipping his quill into the ink.

Will leaned forward until his face met Shakespeare's just as he was about to write. He smiled slenderly. 'Is that your writing eye I see, Master Shakespeare?'

'Aye, young Will,' Shakespeare grinned at him tussling the boy's hair with his other hand. 'That it is.'

With that Shakespeare wrote the words:

He was the hush of his father's eye, and no mother's son. Come quickly, Will, sit by me and rehearse your part, for yours shall win all their hearts.

The boy's eyes were alight with wonder. As Shakespeare dipped his quill, he tried to read the words upside down.

'Ah – ah, Will,' Shakespeare teased, 'no peeking!'

Robert was heartened to see his Master writing again, yet feared this lack of sleep and overwork would bring on another turn. When Will left the bedchamber to fetch Nathan, he took the liberty of saying so. 'Master, you must rest.'

Shakespeare kept on writing. 'Nonsense,' he said without looking up.

'You've no more medicines, and–'

Shakespeare set down his quill and peered at Robert. 'We'll have no more talk of medicines. I told you, I'd rather die than take anything from Dr John Hall ever again!'

'Then take care of yourself. Rest, Master.'

'I've a play to write, Robert. I've no time for maladies or manservants who remind me of them.'

Robert studied him carefully. He'd been put in his place before over Master Shakespeare's turns. It was a sore point. Question was, when he saw the hand tremble and the face droop on one side, as it did now, should he or shouldn't he tell his Master what he saw? Shakespeare returned to his writing with the fever of someone hastening to get to the end of a thought. No, Robert mused. He should say nothing. The Master was a man more than full grown, in the autumn of his years, and it was plain to see that he had made up his mind to write one last play before his end came. Who was he to stop him?

And so Shakespeare's writing of his new play began and went on, long into the night. Susanna waited, listening. Just as she thought everyone was asleep, her father would groan or crumple paper or call out for Robert or Will again. Nathan entered the fray a few times to help Robert fetch and carry or to prepare some warmed small ale with bread and cheese. With her eyelids closed, Susanna listened to the rhythm of the murmurings from her father's room and fell into a deep slumber.

The bells of St Paul's chimed six o'clock as Susanna stretched the sleep from her body. Her eyes shot open and she jumped out of bed. It was clear daylight. She'd slept for hours and missed her chance! You knave, she shouted to herself. How could you be so treacherous in the first place? A thief. That's what she was ... and weren't all thieves common churls? Shouldn't I hang like any highwayman after a bootless inquisition by my father and his peers as any lowly thief would be? Don't I deserve to be treated as Caliban – filth – unworthy of his attention?

She gazed out of the window at the dawn. She couldn't let another day go by without returning those manuscripts to their rightful place. Still, with the house awake, there was no way she could come and go unnoticed. If she told anyone she wanted to unpack the costumes, or even gaze upon them a while, some helpful soul would come with her. Some helpful soul ... as much as she hated the thought, there was nothing else to do. Only Robert could help her now.

She found him in the stables, grooming the horses and singing:

> When icicles hang by the wall,
> And Dick the shepherd blows his nail,
> And Tom bears logs into the hall,
> And milk comes frozen home in the pail,
> When blood is nipp'd and ways be foul,
> Then nightly sings the staring owl ...

Robert saw her rushing towards him. He carried on his song, thinking something had gone seriously awry:

> Tu-whit, Tu-who, a merry note,
> Whilst greasy Joan doth keel the pot.

As she eased neared, he saw that her face was tear-stained, her hair uncombed, and she wore the same sleeves and dress as the day before. In fact, if he didn't know better, he'd swear she'd slept in them.

'O, Robert!' Susanna blustered, 'It's – um, I've ...'

'Bad news?' he asked, stopping his grooming. A lump in his throat kept him from swallowing. 'Is it – your father?'

Susanna blew her nose with her kerchief. Her lovely green eyes were ringed with dark circles from lack of sleep.

'O, Robert!' she wailed again.

He felt his heart leap from his chest. Dear Lord. It's the Master. Robert felt an overpowering urge to bawl his eyes out. Still, he knew his place and hugged her to him before giving way to tears. 'There, there, child–'

'O, Robert! What am I to do?'

He pulled away from her and gave her a good hard look. He had to be brave for them all. He was the manservant, and had to take charge. If the Master had gone to meet his Maker, then there were things to do, people to tell and suchlike.

'Now, you have no need to handle anything on your own,' Robert reassuringly said. 'I'll help with all the necessaries.'

'You will?' Susanna asked, wrinkling her brow.

'For your father, of course.'

'My father?'

'He's ... I mean ... coz he's ... dead?'

Her eyes widened with horror. 'Is he?'

'Isn't he?'

She rubbed her aching face. There must be some confusion, surely. Though her heart pounded fearing Robert was telling her something she didn't know, she prayed he had simply got the wrong end of her intended confession. 'I've not come to tell you anything of my father,' she whispered.

'You've not?'

'I saw him just ten minutes ago at table.'

'You did?'

She nodded. 'I've come to avow something … about me.'

He gave his head a good scratch.

'It's not about him, leastways not directly, leastways we shouldn't think of it like that … I mean, it's more about me, though it's about him too, but he's not dead and–'

'Just spit it out!' Robert ordered. His head spun in circles trying to understand what she meant.

'Spit it out?'

'Just say what you have to say!'

Susanna swallowed hard and closed her eyes. 'It's not Jonson.'

Now Robert felt dizzy like he were befuddled. He dropped the grooming brush in the straw and leaned his head against the horse's haunch.

'It's like you're speaking in tongues, Susanna,' he moaned wearily.

She realised she'd just have to spit it out as Robert said and straightened up to take whatever medicine he'd mete out to her. 'It's not Jonson who stole my father's manuscripts.'

Robert's jaw dropped.

She couldn't quite yet say the rest, so she pointed to herself.

'Why, Susanna?' Robert breathed, as though someone had winded him.

'I thought we were getting close – my father and me …'

'And you weren't?'

'He compared me to my mother. I wanted to prove I wasn't her.'

'So you stole his plays? His only fair copies of all his plays?'

Susanna shrugged. 'I suppose I was angry – I know I wasn't thinking straight.'

It didn't take a genius to see how distraught she were, Robert told himself. And how she'd been burdened with this lie since Oxford, too … How could the Master compare his gentle Susanna to her mother? Had he forgotten all he'd known of them both?

He patted she on the back. 'There now. You thought he knew you better.'

'It was cruel of him, Robert.'

His mind raced ahead. 'Do you still have them?'

Susanna blew her nose once more. She feared if she spoke, she'd burst into tears again. Instead, she nodded.

'Where?'

'In the chest in the prop room.'

Robert thought a moment. Well, that should be easier to put right than he could ever have hoped. 'Good. Let's go. Now. I'll stand guard at the door whilst you fetch them. Are they still in the satchel?'

She saw how his eyes twinkled with devilment and she felt herself take cheer just looking at him.

'Yes, Robert. But afterwards? How do we let everyone know we've found them?'

'Let's see to first things first,' he said.

In no time at all Robert had snaffled the keys from the peg in the hall without anyone asking why. By the time he reached the first floor prop room, Susanna was waiting.

'You go in,' he said, unlocking the door. 'The chests are just to the left, after the inner archway. I'll stand look-out here.'

Susanna nodded.

'And I'll hold the door ajar, so if I hear someone come I'll slam it shut, then make to lock it—'

'But I'll be —'

'No. I said I'll make to lock it, not that I *would* lock it,' Robert wiggled a kindly finger at her.

She ducked inside the prop room, wondering not for the first time or the last, what she had done to deserve such a good friend as Robert Whatcott.

With her lantern held high, for the room had no windows, she prowled her way through the treasure trove rich with plumed hats, shining brass helmets trimmed with silver, swords, rapiers and elm bows with their rainbow fletched arrows. As she passed through the vaulted stone doorway into the room beyond, her eyes travelled over the stone-ribbed ceiling with its latticed brickwork woven in between the gothic arches. In times of yore, this would have been some kind of root store, sealed off from the rats and other vermin, high, dry and clean. She imagined the ghostly sight of the black monks chanting their melodious psalms, fetching carrots or onions for their evening meal or morning broth. Then it struck her how very odd it was that her father – a man who shied away from all religion in favour of the new philosophies – should become the owner of this Dominican house of prayer.

Susanna lowered her lantern away from the vaulted ceilings to the chests of clothing, just where Robert said they'd be. She ran her finger along each one, examining and prodding, concluding that this one or that couldn't be the chest that held the satchel and manuscripts. Then she realised that as it was the first chest into the hall, it must be the last one in the serried rank in the prop room. She dashed to the end of the row and sighed. It had the same scuff marks as the one in Oxford.

Susanna bent down and hurriedly opened its lid. She recognised the gowns. Swiftly, she took them out, one by one, and placed them carefully onto the table beside her. At last, she came to the Rosaline gown, and knew she was only inches away from salvation. She lifted it out as if the dress were a cherished babe, and laid it on top of the other gowns. Next came her mother's frock, she nodded as she grabbed hold of it, tossing the dress impatiently onto the brick floor then …

She stared at the bottom of the chest. The satchel was gone.

She sat on the floor, mouth open, eyes wide in disbelief. This was the chest. The dresses were the ones she'd placed on top of the satchel. Disbelief grew into sheer fright. She stood and turned to the next chest, prising open its lid. Perhaps someone had swapped the clothes inside? One by one, she hurled the gowns onto the floor. Again, no satchel. Blinded by panic, she heaved the next chest round, and again, after flinging the doublets and hose out, she sat back. There was no satchel to be found.

Time were marching, Robert told himself as he paced to and fro on the landing. What could be keeping Susanna? Someone was sure to come up or go down or call out for him soon. He gnawed on his cheek, thinking. Best see inside, he told himself, closing the door quietly behind him. When he came into the prop room where the clothes chests were kept, it looked much the same as that day their belongings were strewn about the road after Ratsey robbed them. And in the midst of the clothing carnage sat Susanna, desolate, wide-eyed. She turned her chin up to him and shrugged sadly, 'The satchel is gone, Robert. The manuscripts are gone.'

He gulped and gazed at the tempest of costumes blown about the room. 'I'll tidy up,' was all he could think to say.

Susanna slowly stood. 'And I'll own up, Robert. It's the only medicine to cure this evil.'

'Susanna, wait–'

'No. I'd be grateful if you'd fix this mess for me whilst I own to the other. The manuscripts are gone, and that's that.'

'Don't you see?' he said, pulling her back. What possessed these Shakespeares, always going for the grand gesture?

'What?'

It seemed like her eye were dead – like she were no longer interested in this world.

'They've been stolen.'

'I know that, Robert, because I was the one who'd done the stealing!'

'No. You know it coz they've been stolen from you!'

It was as if he'd smacked her between the eyes. Of course. Someone knew somehow that the manuscripts were in the clothes chest and had taken them. Someone had seen her taking the satchel into the prop room in Oxford? But who? Nathan? Heminges? Surely not.

Susanna gazed into Robert's troubled eyes. 'You're right.'

'Tell me just how it all happened. The when and where of it. Everything you saw.'

Susanna nodded. Robert was helping to clear the fog in her brain. Still, even if they could guess who'd stolen them away, that didn't mean they could retrieve them before–

'It had to be Jonson,' she blurted out.

'Jonson? Are you sure?'

'No. But who else would prey on my father besides Jonson?'

Robert scratched his chin. Who else indeed?

Chapter 24

Robert worked hard to convince Susanna that it would be best if she told John Heminges first. Maybe with Heminges's help, they could find the manuscripts. After all, who knew her father's enemies and friends better?

So whilst Robert had the chore of folding the costumes back into their trunks, Susanna mounted the stairs to the great hall. She tiptoed up to Heminges, who was still asleep in the armchair by the fire, legs stretched out. Yes, he was a fine man. Not only in his manner and appearance, but also in his soul. Robert was right, if anyone could help her, it was John Heminges.

His eyelids opened as if he sensed he was being admired, and greeted her with a sleepy smile. 'Must have dozed off in front of the fire,' he yawned. 'With your father calling out to us all halfway through the night, somehow it didn't seem worthwhile going to bed.'

'John, may we speak?'

Heminges sat upright, straightening his doublet. 'Of course. What is it?'

'I've been troubled these last days,' Susanna began. She stopped dead when she saw how he was looking at her with such love. Her heart melted. How could she tell him that she was a liar and a thief? Whatever he felt for her – and she was sure there was something in his heart – it would sink like a small ship in a sudden squall.

But before she could speak, there was a stomping on the stairs and Robert shouted out, 'Oi! You can't go in there!'

'I go where I wants to, manservant!' a woman's voice rasped back.

The hall door flew open, cracking against the plaster wall. Agnes Henslowe stood framed in the doorway, just as much a fright as she had been the night before, and still wearing her Oriental carpet-like cloak and extravagant headdress.

'Where is he?' Agnes glowered.

Heminges sprang to his feet. 'Agnes, dear.' He walked over with arms wide as if to hug her, but she brushed him aside.

'Where's that barnacled cozener!' She stopped Heminges from coming any nearer by thumping her fist on his chest. 'So he's lost my treasure, has he?'

'Are you mad?' Susanna piped up. Anger rose sharp as a dagger in her overheated brain.

'Ha! You must be the daughter.' And with that, Agnes swooped around the room, like a bird on the hunt for food, pulling open drawers, thumbing through papers, even poking behind paintings on the walls.

'Stop,' Susanna blustered.

'Agnes,' Heminges cajoled sweetly.

'Don't you "Agnes" me, John,' she commanded. Her falcon's eyes darted around the hall some more before she swept off to the corner cupboard where Shakespeare kept his dry sherry sack.

'How dare he steal my manuscripts,' Agnes muttered, as she flung open the cupboard door.

'Just who do you think stole them?' Susanna asked, fearing the answer.

'Your father, who else?'

A breathless Robert bowled into the room. 'I'm sorry, but she just swatted me aside and–'

'Scurvy gnat!' Agnes cried at him.

Susanna knew anger had only done ill by her, but it boiled over into every inch of her being. 'How dare you claim my father stole his own manuscripts!' she raged. 'And how can you call them your manuscripts when *he* wrote them?'

'It's what they call "work for hire" dearie, so they're mine,' Agnes glared at her, eyes like blazing fiery darts. 'For money. Paid for by my dear departed Henslowe. Six pounds a pop. A ruddy fortune as plays go, mind you, too!'

'Now Agnes–' Heminges began.

'Don't!' she ordered him, wagging a gnarled finger in his face. 'You and your sugar-coated tongues, you're all alike the lot of you players and playmakers. Actors, puh! Wish we theatre-owners could make do without you! My Henslowe paid for them, and I'm his bene-fishery. Will had no right to horn-thumb them away without so much as a "please and thank you" to Stratford-upon-bloody-Avon. Why, I've a mind to call in the law!'

'On what charge?' Robert shouted.

'What charge, the brave manservant asks?'

'No one's ever accused a Shakespeare of stealing.' Susanna's anger spoke, though the words nearly burned her tongue.

''Cept the Lucys and that little matter of your pa's deer poaching–'

'YOU, IVY,' Shakespeare barked from the corner of the great hall, 'you which sucks the lifeblood from us actors and playmakers! If you howl about me once more, I'll tear you apart like a great oak, limb from withered limb!'

Agnes turned and considered Shakespeare for a moment, picking at her teeth with a finger nail. She narrowed an eye and said, 'Prospero? Right?'

Shakespeare suppressed a smile. 'Who told you *I'd* stolen those plays? Jonson? I saw you two all hugger-mugger last night, don't forget.'

Agnes lifted a brow but said nothing.

'I told you last plague season that I was redrafting them.'

'Will, that was donkey's years ago. Five at least.'

'No, three,' Susanna interrupted clearly recalling the last time her father was at home. That said, she'd have to admit that the plays had been held in Stratford longer than that – at least since '09 and the publication of the sonnets.

'Then three,' Agnes shrugged.

'Agnes, you know all my handwritten manuscripts must remain with me. It's in the contract, darlin'. Remember?'

'But not in Stratford-upon-bloody—'

'To keep them safe from that horn-thumbing printer of my sonnets?' Shakespeare reminded her.

A light seemed to glimmer in Agnes's mind, for she reddened before spewing, 'I don't recall any such bargain with you, Will.'

'Humpf!' Robert muttered to Susanna. 'I'll bet all her bargains catch cold and die.'

'That and more,' Susanna breathed softly. 'What are we going to do, Robert?'

But before he could think of an answer, Shakespeare had inched closer to Agnes in that commanding way of his that made everyone stop and stare.

'Don't go playing the player with me Will Shakespeare,' Agnes said, wagging her crooked finger again.

'It's no matter now, Agnes,' he replied. 'My manuscripts have been stolen. We suspect that bricklayer, Jonson.'

'Ben? That love?' Agnes shook her head. Her headdress swung to and fro as if it would tumble off. 'Couldn't have.'

'Why ever not?' Heminges asked, frowning.

'With all your balking about Jonson,' she said, casting a sharp eye at each of them, 'I searched his house myself, even brought along the nightwatch to make an arrest.'

'Just because you searched, it doesn't mean he hasn't hidden them somewhere else!' Susanna blazed.

'Susanna's right,' Shakespeare agreed. 'Why would Jonson hide them in his rooms? And besides, he's hardly likely to admit to you where they are, is he?'

'There you go again, Will, with your reasoned compass and your charming ways,' Agnes leered.

Shakespeare nodded as if taking a bow for a performance. 'Perhaps we should join forces? After all, we're both the poorer for this escapade.'

'Join forces? I heard tell your forces are spent!' she cackled.

Heminges, Susanna and Robert gasped. Shakespeare's face darkened. Just then Will Davenant entered the room.

'What's all the–' he started to ask, then shut up, seeing Agnes glaring at him, then Susanna, then Shakespeare.

'Quaint. Father. Daughter. Son,' she spat.

Susanna glanced at Will. His eyes widened in wonder.

'You mark my words, there's a plague in your house, Will Shakespeare. A ruddy plague, hear?'

Laying her bombshell and prophesy at their feet, Agnes flicked her Oriental cloak and swooped out of the room.

Susanna held her breath, waiting to see young Will's reaction.

Shakespeare hugged the boy to him, and looked him straight in the eye. 'Would you be unhappy to learn that such a thing were true?'

Will shook his head, speechless.

Susanna stooped in front of the boy. 'Will, I don't know what to say ...'

He turned to her and curled his fingers around hers. 'Would you be happy to have me as a brother?'

'I couldn't be happier,' she said.

A few hours later, after Shakespeare and his children had spent time in private, everyone assembled in the hall to discuss what they should do next. Since Agnes's visitation, Susanna's intention to own up to her theft of the plays had vanished like grey smoke on the wind. Also gone was the anger that had risen up in her for the second time in less than a week. Of course, she'd been lonely, sad and frustrated, but she had never recalled having a real temper. Though she owned she might have spoken in anger to Judith, she felt mostly envious of her mother's love for her sister. Maybe it seemed like anger to them? Perhaps her father had held up a glass to her in Oxford after all. Could he have been right and she had crafted some of her mother's shrewish skills as her own?

'Don't you agree, Susanna?' Shakespeare asked.

She'd not been listening. 'Are you saying, Father, that all this has been some grand plan?'

'Aye. That I am. Someone didn't want my plays to survive. Someone still doesn't.'

'But only the most perfidious of friends could do such a thing …' she said in a thin voice.

'Or the greatest of enemies masquerading as a friend,' Shakespeare nodded, finishing her thought differently than she would have done.

'Isn't Ben Jonson both? Does he not change his guise with the faces of the moon?' Heminges asked rhetorically.

Susanna looked from Heminges to Shakespeare. 'It's true, Father, I've heard you speak of him as both.'

'Yes, it's true. At times we're testy enemies, vying for the laurels of greatest playmaker … then 'tween times, we're happy rivals competing to make the farthermost conceits of language. Sometimes his arrows are the swiftest, as from a Tartar's bow; then at others, mine, when loosed, prove the fleeter.'

'Until these past days I've always thought on your relationship with Jonson as a friendly rivalry,' Heminges said.

'Still, something has changed …' Shakespeare stared at the fire. 'When friendly rivals become enemies it's a tricky game to see when it's best to fight and when to lay down your arms. It's a rough magic, and one I'm unsure I can still conjure.'

With that pronouncement, he slumped down in his armchair, his palms facing upwards in surrender. His right hand and arm trembled. To Susanna, it seemed as though his body had shrunk, as if all the winds from his book of common bravura had gusted away. His dark eye gazed hollowly at the grate. His cheek sagged with age, or perhaps it was concern, his facial expression seemed a blank canvas. Within seconds, he had sunk away from being the mighty

Shakespeare, the righter of wrongs, the optimist extraordinary, the magical jester with words. This was a man grown old with worry and infirmity, a man who would be happier to slumber through his days, and prowl his room at night. Unless the Shakespeare of old returned to them, at least in some spirit, Susanna feared that even if he recovered the manuscripts, he'd be unable to write more or direct Heminges as to his wishes. Worse still, he may never know how very much she wanted to say sorry for any part she played.

Robert stood at Shakespeare's shoulder seeing a man in Heminges compelled to befriend Susanna, just as he'd done since she was a babe. If the Master died before father and daughter made their peace, she would need good friends and strong counsel like John Heminges. She'd need to make her way in the world away from Stratford. And as Will's oldest friend and closest ally, it would be a considerable relief, to Robert's mind, if John Heminges were there for her.

Yet if he were strictly honest, Robert prayed that Susanna gave rise to greater feelings deep within Heminges's heart. She were a woman in sore need of love. But these were thoughts he must never give voice to. They were wrong. She were married, and no matter how badly married, Dr Hall's wife she must stay. Then again, Heminges needed love in his life once more. He were a widower, with children grown. But would he see it as a betrayal of his friendship with Will if he was to love Susanna? Robert prayed they'd find a way, for both their sakes.

Shakespeare narrowed his eye at Heminges then purposefully turned to study to his daughter. Was he also reading something into Heminges's gaze, Robert wondered? Was his Master giving Heminges his blessing to tell Susanna how he felt? Or had he seen a warning in his tired eye?

'It seems to me that we need to think through who'd want to steal Shakespeare's manuscripts,' Heminges reasoned aloud. 'Then we can decide who was the most likely person, or even persons, to have stolen them.'

Nathan hung his head. Condell wrung his hands and stared at Shakespeare with hangdog eyes. Burbage scowled into his drink. Heminges looked at them with a careful gaze. Only Shakespeare seemed to place some value on what he'd said.

'Perhaps you have a point, John. But who?' Susanna asked.

'Anyone could have taken them for infant-like doings or treacherous feats, but if we open this up so each of us can scratch at our opinions, all we'll succeed in airing are our ancient bickerings – one playmaker with the other,' Shakespeare said.

Talking in that high-blown way, Susanna feared he might be sickening again.

'To my mind, what we need is someone to divinely interpret these doings without misquoting the deed,' Shakespeare nodded.

Susanna murmured, 'Amen.'

'Tronco?'   Heminges   enquired.

Condell was the first to smile broadly, followed by Burbage then Nathan. Will Davenant looked to Susanna for understanding, but she could only shrug.

'Who or what is Tronco?' Susanna asked.

Heminges turned explain, but Shakespeare chimed in, 'All in good time, Susanna. All in good time.'

Robert looked at his Master and saw him exchange some kind of meaningful nod with Heminges, just like the look the other day that said 'Not yet'.

It wasn't long before they were off like dogs after the dullest of scents. Robert and Nathan had rigged up a makeshift sedan chair for Shakespeare, but within fifty yards, Robert's whole body began to sag under the dead weight of his Master. The oak pole dug into his neck so badly that he had to shift it further onto his shoulder to relieve the pain.

Fact was, Shakespeare had confided in Robert earlier that his legs felt odd. He claimed his knees wobbled and his right foot dragged. Robert knew better than to suggest other potions, for he saw full well that the answer would be no. Instead, he chivvied Nathan along to make up this sedan chair to carry Shakespeare through the streets of London pasha-style. He doubted if Susanna had divined that her father were feeling poorly again – Nathan had told her that it were for the theatre of it all, and that London craved Shakespeare's theatre through the streets any time of day or night.

'God's bodkin, man! Be tender with me!' Shakespeare cried from above.

Robert turned to Nathan and rolled his eyes. 'Aye, Master!' he shouted up to Shakespeare.

Robert took a deep breath. He'd just about had enough of whatever game it were the Master was playing. Hadn't Shakespeare promised him that once they got to London all would be clear as crystal? And now things were as murky as a beetle's back, though in truth, that wasn't wholly the Master's fault. Still, it seemed to him that the only crystal the Master knew of was the crystal ball in that Tronco's parlour at Lambeth Palace. Imagine, hauling them all off to some stargazer to find Ben Jonson, or whoever it were that'd stole those manuscripts from Susanna! And what for? That's what he'd like to know! Then a thought hit him square in the nose – what if Tronco told them that Susanna had stole the manuscripts, and they had been taken from her by some mysterious hand?

Before he could puzzle through the answer, Will Davenant came rushing up and shook his arm.

'Look ahead,' the boy panted.

A crowd of people had closed in and Robert couldn't see what Will was pointing at. He craned his neck and jiggled from side to side. Suddenly, he and Nathan fell out of step, and his pole sprang loose from its crutch. The sedan-chair toppled precariously in a wider and wider arc until he feared his Master would fall and break his neck.

'Robert!' Nathan cried, trying to right the sedan-chair.

'God's death!' Shakespeare swore. 'Help! Help me!'

The others reeled round and made to run back. But Robert weren't having anyone right his wrongs but himself. With a huge cry and tug and heave of the pole, he housed it back into the crutch. The sedan-chair wobbled like a tree that swayed in a strong wind, but soon enough calm was restored.

'Are you trying to kill me, Robert?' Shakespeare asked, leaning over the side.

'Sit straight, Master!' Robert ordered, feeling quite green-sick with worry.

'Eat your peas,' Nathan shouted.

'That's no answer! Are you trying to kill me?' Shakespeare repeated as he leaned further over.

'Will!' Nathan cried. ''Swounds man! Sit still.'

Susanna ran up to them followed by Heminges and Condell.

'Father, behave yourself! Listen to Nathan!'

Heminges and Condell remonstrated with Shakespeare. 'For the love of life, will you stop acting like a two-year-old, Will?'

'But, I ...' Shakespeare began, then shut up, as he saw Will Davenant mouth 'Sorry' to Robert for having begun the near disaster.

Robert was crestfallen. Susanna looked to him. 'Are you hurt?'

He shook his head. 'Only my pride ...' he murmured.

Will tugged at Susanna's sleeve. 'It was my fault. I wanted Robert to see the bawdy basket, look,' he pointed to a watchman leading a cart coming up the side road.

A throng of hawkers had gathered around the watchman to make sport of the downtrodden woman, caged in the back of the cart. She was probably no older than Susanna. Her clothes were covered in stains, most likely from rotted vegetables thrown at her earlier in the pillory. A man walked next to the cart guarding the woman, and hissed obscenities at the crowd as if they were vermin.

'Love powders, buy my love powders,' one of the hawkers shouted, mocking the caged woman.

'No, *my* powders work best ... one dram and whoever sees you first will fall in love with you,' another mocked. The man walking next to the cart looked daggers at him. 'Haven't you done enough harm, all of you? All your talk and promise of true love! Now look at my wife! Look!' he cried.

The hawker glared at him, then turned away with a flick of his tattered gown, crying out to the crowd, 'Love powders, five pence, only today!'

Susanna was shocked. The caged woman was no doxy but that man's wife. As the watchman passed, the woman's dead eyes fixed on Susanna. She gaped back at her, wondering if she hadn't escaped Stratford and her husband, she might be that woman. She lowered her eyes and read the sign the woman wore around her neck and read 'bawdy basket.' She gasped. Well, not as yet ... but if her husband ever found her with another man, he might insist that she undergo a public punishment such as the one she saw before her eyes now.

As the cart trundled up the road, and they were heckled by the crowd, she saw for the first time that there was a man without shoes or stockings who was chained to the back of the cart like some poor beast. His sign read 'upright man.' It swayed around his neck from side to side with each laboured step. Just as she read it he was pelted with a rotten egg, but the upright man acted as if nothing had happened and simply walked on. Was he the lover for whom the woman had bought the love powders? The procession passed on with the crowd taunting them and shouting insults. Susanna stood frozen, unable to tear her eyes away. She wondered again if one day that might be her fate.

Robert was aghast at the sight and had to look away. Then he saw John Heminges staring kindly at Susanna, more kindly than ever before. Bawdy baskets may be two a penny, Robert mused to himself, but everyone could see that the woman in the cart had her husband standing by her, protecting her in an odd sort of way, with her lover trailing behind. He pondered if Heminges must think

Susanna saw something of herself in their plight. Did his Master share Heminges's thought, too?

Suddenly, as he sometimes did to begin a performance, Shakespeare shook his head proudly and sat erect. Susanna looked up at him. He grinned broadly, then stretched out his arms and cried at the top of his lungs, 'Tronco sees all! A Queen among mortals, the goddess of stargazers! O, Tronco, giver of the milk of all human kindness!'

At first Susanna was puzzled. But then she saw how the crowd that had been hounding the bawdy basket and the upright man turned and recognised Shakespeare. Their mood changed in a trice. They ran after her father now, hailing him as their hero, their voice, their friend. Whilst Shakespeare revelled in their accolades and bade them to follow, the woman, her husband and her lover were allowed to escape into the distance without further interference. Susanna smiled up at her father, thankful to him for his tenderness to the woman, a mere stranger. She gazed back at them wondering what would become of them – and indeed her.

And all the while Henry Condell led their little entourage like the Pied Piper. Will Davenant was at his side. The same crowd who had jeered the bawdy basket, now cheered them on.

'Come. Your father needs you,' Heminges said.

Susanna turned and followed meekly in Heminges's slipstream.

By the time they joined the others at the Thames embankment she had mostly recovered from the shock of seeing that caged woman. She was deeply thankful that Heminges hadn't sought to fill their few moments alone with questions or idle chatter. Instead, he allowed her to order her own thoughts. She looked up at him furtively. There was a stillness and kindness in him she'd grown to trust and admire.

Chapter 25

Robert and Will pulled faces at the wherryman. How dare he stare at them so, Robert huffed silently. It weren't *his* fault he had to balance the Master's chair on his head and hold Will Davenant on his knee. Who were this wherryman anyways to look sidelong at them? 'Sides he were too tall for a wherryman any road up. Why if he tried to sit in his own boat, Robert mused, there'd be no room for no one nor nothing.

Whilst Robert thought up insults to hurl at him, the wherryman studied his passengers, all shoe-horned into his tiny boat as he steered them across the river to Lambeth. He frowned, puzzling something through. Suddenly, he blurted out, 'I got it. You're the King's Men.'

Heminges and Condell rolled their eyes.

Oblivious, the wherryman grinned, 'And I'm a playmaker! Name's Philip, gentlemen … at your service.' He doffed his cap and made a low bow, rocking the wherry.

Susanna latched onto the side and stared at Robert.

'Not another,' he glowered, as he righted the chair wobbling atop his head.

'Will, did you hear that? We've a playmaker wherryman on our hands,' Heminges jested.

Shakespeare looked the wherryman over.

Robert muttered to Susanna, 'The world seems over-full with playmakers.'

But Susanna remained quiet, her eyes trained on her father.

Shakespeare nodded at the wherryman. 'Let me guess – you have a play you'd like us to read?'

Robert whispered to Susanna again, 'More fuel for our hearths?'

She smiled slenderly at the memory of the Stratford playwrights.

'Master Shakespeare,' Philip the wherryman began deferentially, 'it would be an honour if you would be so good as to ...'

Shakespeare stretched out his hand to take the wherryman's scrawlings. Philip delved deep into his doublet and pulled out his play from an oilskin he carried next to his heart. With a grand, glimmering, toothy smile, he handed it to Shakespeare.

'It's a bristling tale, Master Shakespeare,' he nodded energetically. 'It's got everything – love, hate, war, famine ...'

'A comedy then?' Shakespeare asked.

'Just so!' Philip could barely contain his joy. 'I can hardly believe the great Shakespeare will be reading *my* play – I'll be set for life, I'll be rich, famous, my father will no longer shiver whenever my mother mentions my name.'

Whilst Philip waxed even more lyrically – arms waving, eyes shut – Shakespeare tossed the play onto the bottom of the boat without a glance at its title page.

Moments later, they docked at Lambeth Palace. John Heminges took the lead with Henry Condell, followed closely by Nathan and Will. Susanna trailed behind them, contemplating the palace with awe. Never in her fondest dreams did she imagine she would be knocking at the Archbishop of Canterbury's back door. Odder still to her mind was that a stargazer should find sanctuary in the Archbishop's palace. But, as Heminges explained, it was a favour to Tronco's dead husband, Dr Simon Forman, for all the good he'd done for the Archbishop and his parishioners over the years.

She glimpsed Robert and Nathan jostling Shakespeare into his chair at the water's edge. Philip the wherryman gazed longingly at them from the quayside. Then she heard footsteps from within, and the door creaked open. She turned and was surprised to see a thin, grey-haired vicar welcoming them to the refuge of the stargazer.

'We've an appointment to see Madame Tronco,' Heminges announced.

The vicar surveyed each of them with a cold appraising eye. 'Follow me.'

After a few twists and turns through a stone passageway, they were shown into Tronco's parlour. Nathan and Robert helped Shakespeare into the imposing throne-like armchair at the end of the table. Condell, Heminges, Nathan, Will and Robert sat too. There were two places left vacant – a richly upholstered armchair at the head of the table and a high-backed chair next to it. Heminges sat next to the high-backed chair. But Susanna wasn't minded to sit just yet, particularly as she didn't know anything about this Tronco woman, other than she was a stargazer whose husband was a doctor of sorts – though never a physician Burbage had said mysteriously.

Her head began to ache at the thought of meeting this Tronco. What if she was a charlatan and made up some nonsense about where the manuscripts were? Worse still, what if she really knew what happened and claimed that Susanna had taken them? The more she thought on it, the more convinced she was that a visit to an astrologer was not a good idea.

She wandered around the parlour, trying to calm herself, gazing at the queer objects. O, the large crystal ball in front of the vacant armchair was to be expected, but there were stuffed bats dangling hither and thither, and many coloured healing crystals in Oriental pots dotted around the room. There were African-looking charms made of bone and teeth, Indian plumes, silk robes from China adorning the walls, an Arabian cloak hung over a wire frame the size of a man, a falcon's head made with fine downy feathers, an ancient lute with only one string propped against a bookcase, a twisted unicorn's horn, silk shoes from exotic places set alongside porcelain dolls. Rich silken tapestries were tossed carelessly over the furniture, and everywhere dozens upon dozens of candles flickered. It was at once both the oddest of rooms and the most beguiling.

Susanna became aware of the sound of metallic jangling and wheeled round. Standing before her was an old woman. Her face was smooth as silk, but her neck fell into tidy folds of wrinkles. She wore a white Arabian turban with designs that looked like some strange sort of lettering. A loose-fitting, shimmering cloak fell in obedient pleats around her, making Susanna feel that this was a woman who commanded respect, even if she might not deserve it. The jangling noise chimed from hundreds of silver bracelets that clambered up her arms.

Tronco let out a throaty cough and cast a malevolent eye at Susanna. As if responding to her silent command, she melted into the high-backed chair beside Tronco's. Susanna looked furtively around and saw Henry Condell squirming uncomfortably. Nathan seemed afraid, and without realising it, suddenly tried to cling to Robert's arm. But Robert wasn't having any of it, and brushed him off like some pest. Poor little Will sat, wide-eyed, mouth opened, gawping in disbelief at the stargazer.

Tronco turned her head, scrutinising each of them in turn, that is, until her eyes lit on William Shakespeare. Her face flashed with joy.

'Eureka! O, Billy, my little Billy!' Tronco sprang to her feet and raced over to him. She grabbed hold of his face, then nearly smothered him with a well-intended bosomy hug.

As suddenly as she had begun, she stopped and lifted his head so she could look into his eyes. 'Hold on there, Billy. You're not dead – and don't you go telling me the cards lied.'

Shakespeare opened his mouth to speak, but she held out her arm to silence him. She touched her finger to her forehead melodramatically. It seemed to Susanna she was more of an actor than a stargazer.

'Don't say? Why I never! Really? Truth to tell?' Tronco spoke to some unheard voice.

Susanna turned to Heminges and whispered, 'Who is she talking to?'

Tronco heard her and strode over, pushing her stargazer's face into Susanna's menacingly. Susanna inched back towards Heminges. She heard a chair scrape and slid her eyes towards the sound. It was Robert, rising up to protect her. Nathan grabbed hold of his shoulder to hold him back.

'Sssh! All of you! The spirits are abroad,' Tronco proclaimed. Her arms were raised to the heavens, bracelets chiming their tune.

And with that, Tronco eyed each of them sharply then walked back to her armchair. She flipped up her cloak and skirts, and sat down as if some invisible hand had pushed her. Heminges nudged Susanna. When she turned, she saw he was smiling reassuringly.

'Dear Tronco,' Shakespeare began, clearing his throat. 'I thank you for seeing us at such short notice. I'll get straight to the nub. We suspect Ben Jonson is in hiding and that he's stolen my manuscripts.'

'That's not exactly so, or maybe it is, but we don't know it was Jonson for certain,' Susanna corrected.

Tronco ignored her and grabbed hold of a deck of tarot cards and began to shuffle them. She looked over to Susanna suspiciously, then to Heminges. Tronco flipped over a card and looked at Susanna once more, clicking her tongue against the roof of her mouth.

'Shame, dearie. If he were my good husband, I'd help him pack up his things–'

'Stop!' Susanna, slammed her palms on the table and stood. Robert stood to make a lunge for Tronco again, but Nathan, ably assisted by Will, held him back.

'My life is none of your affair,' Susanna hissed, her blood fairly bubbling up inside.

'What touches the truth is my affair,' Tronco shrugged.

Susanna was fit to burst. She was certain that Tronco had somehow seen the truth of it all and feared she'd reveal her treachery. 'Then, your cards lie', she said.

'Only people lie. Ask your father.' Tronco gave Shakespeare a knowing wink.

Her eyes seared with Promethean fire, but Shakespeare's chestnut eyes were soft as velvet and cool as if they could douse any flame. They begged Susanna to sit down, gently. Slowly, she obeyed. Heminges feathered her hand with his fingertip, and her anger died at his tender touch.

'Tronco, you're diverting us from our purpose,' Shakespeare said. 'As Susanna rightly put it, we need to know where the manuscripts are now as well as that rogue Jonson. Even if he's blameless, I've unfinished business with him.'

Tronco nodded and put away her tarot cards. She pulled her crystal ball close, the bracelets along her arms jangling their otherworldly tune. With a well-practised motion she ran her hands over her crystal ball, as if trying to clear a cloud, and stared deeply into it. Suddenly, her eyes bulged as if she saw something unspeakable in it. She pushed it away, shuddering.

'What is it?' Shakespeare asked anxiously.

'Tronco, did you see who stole Will's manuscripts?' Heminges asked.

Tronco stood and paced the room, her thumb to her lips as she reflected. 'Can't say for sure,' she muttered, her hawk's eye trained on Susanna.

'All we want to know is where the manuscripts are now,' Susanna pleaded. 'Not some journey they may or may not have taken along the way.'

'Tronco,' Heminges began, 'these are the only manuscripts with all Will's personal notes. If we don't find them–'

'I know, if Jonson or those unscrupulous printers over by St Paul's Walk publish them,' Tronco nodded, 'Shakespeare here will lose his reputation, his legacy, and the rest of you, your fortune. I know all that.'

Susanna wet her lips, staring nervously at Robert. He urged her with his eyes to say something, anything, to Tronco.

'All that matters,' Susanna began falteringly, 'is that we have a trail to follow to get my father's manuscripts back safe and sound. You may see other things, Tronco–'

'I *do* see other things.'

'But for now,' Susanna cleared her throat, 'before the thief can get away, before it eats away at my poor father, we need to find them.'

Susanna gazed over to him. He gave her an impotent, pained smile. O, would that she could lessen his pain with her own anguish. She looked away, fearful of laying bare the remorse that burst in her heart.

The old woman stood cross-armed. Heminges sighed and reached into his doublet for some coins and slapped them on the table. Tronco stared at them. After several moments, she sat down and pulled the crystal ball to her once more.

'It's cloudy,' she said.

'How cloudy?' Shakespeare asked, his eyes suddenly sharp as quills, dark as ink.

'Like a London fog.'

He nodded at Heminges, who reached into his doublet again and tossed some more coins on the table.

'What do you see?' Heminges asked.

Tronco gazed at her crystal. 'Frosty truths and hot lies.'

'Don't speak in riddles, tell us clearly,' Shakespeare urged.

'Where's Jonson?' Heminges asked.

Tronco raised an eyebrow, still peering into her crystal. 'Hiding.'

'Where?' Shakespeare asked.

'With his accomplice.'

Shakespeare looked as if she'd slapped him. 'Who?'

Tronco cocked her head at him. 'Billy, honestly. I'm a stargazer, not his keeper.'

They were all agog. Susanna had no idea what Tronco might say or do next.

With that, the stargazer stood again and nodded at Shakespeare. 'Nothing is as it seems in this affair. That's the truth today, or mayhap the future tells lies. Who knows?'

Tronco turned away, 'Good to see you, Billy. Come again before–'

She peered at Susanna, beckoning her with a flash of her eyes, for a private word.

Of course, she'd have to go, Susanna told herself. As she rose up, she felt her knees turn to wax and feared she'd stumble. As soon as she came within whispering distance of the stargazer, Tronco gripped her arm and breathed in her ear, 'Your secret's safe for now. But you'd best hurry, Will Shakespeare's eldest daughter. The end of this little drama is nearer than you think.'

Before Susanna could say a word, Tronco was gone.

Chapter 26

'Cheat,' Nathan growled.

'Am not.' Will Davenant stuck his tongue out at Nathan.

Heminges stood staring at the fire. Condell and Burbage were engrossed in a game of chess.

Nathan glowered at young Will. 'There's no way on this great globe you could roll sixes as many times as you do without cheating.'

Robert stood behind Will, his hands on the boy's shoulders, and peered over to Heminges. How he hoped something would happening between him and Susanna. Something good, Robert thought.

'Don't you go helping him, Robert Whatcott,' Nathan warned.

'I'll have you know, Nathan Field, that I'm no bad influence on the boy. And I'm not the one who was teaching young Will here how to palm the good dice for the loaded ones.'

Heminges sighed like a bellows.

Robert looked over to him again. Whatever happened, Susanna was a married woman, albeit badly wed. Worse still for Heminges, Robert couldn't be sure that Susanna would feel anything for any man as she'd never known love other than that of a daughter for her father – and even that hadn't been as she would have liked.

Heminges saw Robert eyeing him and gave him a thread-like smile. 'Think I'll take a stroll,' he said softly.

Robert nodded. Burbage and Condell looked up as Heminges crossed the hall. Condell turned back to the chessboard.

'There'll be trouble, mark my words,' he said, shaking his head.

'You old love-monger ... checkmate!' Burbage exclaimed, knocking over Condell's king.

Susanna needed to keep busy. Anything to take her mind off stargazers or soothsayers or whatever they thought they were. Truth to tell, she felt like some idle moss attaching herself to the boots of her father and his players. Well, she was no idle moss, she told herself, grabbing hold of the pitchfork that leaned against the stable wall. Until now, she hadn't passed a day of her life without doing some kind of chore from morning till night. Besides, it made her restless to do nought but fret about how she'd get those manuscripts back or beg forgiveness for all the wrongs she'd done to her father and his men.

She thrust the pitchfork into the bale of hay and scattered it to for the horses. How could she beg forgiveness like some callow youth if they couldn't find the manuscripts? This whole misadventure had started off harmlessly enough. She only longed to see her father perform. So what if she was also running away from a life of woe? Yet, with each twist and turn along the road, her compass had gone out-of-joint, the tables turned, and now she was a wrongdoer. It felt like she was a character in one of her father's plays, where he could move the characters about and make them do as he bid.

O, why had he stoked her Promethean fire, making it unquenchable, with that comparison to her mother, just as he'd made her part of his circle of friends? And why had he opened her eyes to his world of magic? Why let some tiny grain take seed inside her heart for his realm of theatre and the men he called 'family' if her father thought she was truly like her mother? But above all these questions burnt the one about how she could have sought revenge against her father instead of grabbing hold of his love? She heard the vicar of Holy Trinity Church's sermon echo in her head: *When you dig for revenge, you dig two graves.*

'Ahem.' It was a man's voice.

Susana turned slowly to see John Heminges leaning against the doorway of the stables. His manner was relaxed, friendly even. She laid the pitchfork down and gazed at him quizzically.

He turned and looked up at the night sky. 'A fine evening,' he said.

She walked over to the threshold and looked at the stars twinkling in their firmament. It was a clear night and the moon was three-quarters full. But gazing at the stars reminded her of Tronco once more and their afternoon in her parlour.

Susanna shook her head. 'A fine troupe of hangers-on and heretics the King's Men entertain.'

'You mean Tronco?'

'And yet, I fear she is not the most extraordinary of your playmates.'

'Perhaps,' he said and smiled warmly.

Susanna felt her face flush. 'And what of you?'

He shrugged. 'I'm not extraordinary.'

'Neither am I.'

'O, I beg to differ.' He leaned forward and kissed her tenderly.

Susanna had never before felt the thrill of a kiss she'd longed for. And yet, here she was – kissed by and kissing a man she'd grown to love. Heminges caressed her cheek with his hand before slowly pulling back.

'You are a most extraordinary young woman, Susanna,' he smiled.

Later, she stood at the top of the stairs, her face still glowing with the words that John Heminges had spoken. She wanted to share this wondrous news with her father, to tell him all that had happened, and to throw herself upon his mercy. Determined to avow all, she turned towards his bedroom and knocked on the door. Not hearing any reply, she inched it open. Shakespeare was fast asleep, his candle still burning. She stepped inside and moved closer. Seeing him asleep, helpless, made her love him all the more. Somehow she would prevail.

She bent down and blew out the candle.

Chapter 27

Gamaliel Ratsey tied up his stallion outside the inn and nodded to his men. His doxies dismounted their steeds and made to come with him, but he wagged his finger.

'It's for men only here, loves,' he whispered.

The doxies looked at one another and pouted. Ratsey blew them each a kiss.

'Now be off with you.'

He turned on his heel and wended his way through the back alleys of Blackfriars to a secret rendezvous. Snout, Teacake and Fang followed in his wake, ensuring that there would be no ambush from the rear. Though the streets were malodorous and too narrow to ride a horse through, Ratsey navigated these alleyways as if they were as familiar to him as his name. After several twists and turns to left and right, he came upon a crisp, clean whitewashed home with the sign of the cardinal's hat above. The brothel's doxies leaned seductively in the doorway, and he ran his eyes over them with pleasure.

'Later, ladies,' he smiled, doffing his hat. Snout, Teacake and Fang gave lascivious half-smiles at them as they passed.

Ratsey shouldered past a country bumpkin who had a man following sharply on his cloak-tails. He heard the familiar line, 'Sir, God save you, I see from your clothes that you are from my country of Herefordshire. You are welcome in London.'

Ratsey scoffed to himself, *Another cony about to fall victim to his conycatcher.* His business was of a much more lucrative nature than trapping unsuspecting conies. He continued on and made for his favourite ordinary just down the road.

The sweet airs from the virginals and lute rang out onto the street. That's what Ratsey loved about this gambling den. It deceived by hinting that its customers were there for their leisure and refinement, when all that the likes of him were truly after was the thrill of the chase among the fashionable gentry of London. Dice and cards were the principle means of entertainment here. Dice-play had always been his preferred means of helping the well-turned-out young gentleman part with his money. And there were no false dice here, never. This was a gambling den of an exotic quality where cheating was only acceptable if it remained undetected.

It was a subtlety lost on many. Ratsey clicked his tongue as he walked past a young rake palming his dice with a flourished sleight of hand. He glanced over his shoulder to Teacake, Snout and Fang, and they nodded at him, peeling off to watch the cack-handed cheat. Once the rake fleeced his prey, Teacake would nip his winnings. This was no ordinary, filled with tobacco smoke as thick as the night, where the wealthy dipped a toe unwittingly into London's underworld. This was an extraordinary, where only the most especial of cunning gamesters practised to slur a dice surely or stop a card cleanly. It was Ratsey's home from home.

He smiled and nodded to old friends and enemies as he made his way from the front of the establishment to its select back rooms. It was here that the old Queen's groom-porter used to dole out his permissions sparingly to owners of new gambling houses, for she had been unable to stem the tide of gambling in her day. Today, it was where the King's groom-porter minted his own brand of money, selling gambling house licences to anyone who could meet his price. The feat of losing one's riches in all legality to knavery was the man's speciality. Ratsey tipped his hat to the King's groom-porter, and he nodded back with a greedy glint in his eye.

But Ratsey's business was of a more agreeable nature that fine, late afternoon. At a table nearby sat an older, but nonetheless, resplendent woman sipping her sherry sack from a silver thimble. Standing behind her were her two magnificent Amazonian ladies-in-waiting. Ratsey doffed his hat at her and her women.

'Countess,' he bowed deeply.

The Countess smiled back.

'And how is the Countess of Pembroke this fine spring evening?'

Mary Countess of Pembroke lowered her eyes and motioned for Ratsey to sit opposite. She edged forward in her seat. 'Reprobate,' she whispered.

'At your service, Madame,' Ratsey replied, obeying.

The Countess sipped her sherry sack, eyeing him above its tiny rim. Those calm, beautiful russet-brown eyes had seen and known so much in their day, Ratsey mused. She had been the queen of poets, a poetess herself, adorned and adored by men throughout the land and beyond. She was the keeper of the candle of her poor, dead brother's works and ensured that he – the great Sir Philip Sidney – would live on. Personally, Ratsey thought Sidney was overrated and his sister not appreciated enough. But then he always had melted at the mere thought of the Countess of Pembroke.

She put down her thimble and gave the scantest of nods to her ladies. They immediately stood back, just out of whispering distance. Ratsey eyed the Countess with relish. Here was a woman who knew how to live. Her silk and satin gown was made of the finest imported cloth. The jewels she wore on her fingers and arms rivalled the King James's Queen. Indeed, Mary's necklace was said to have come from the old Queen's own collection, given to her in thanks for her support by a grateful King James at the time of his succession.

The Countess smiled seductively at Ratsey and stretched out her gloved palm.

'A kiss is so much sweeter on the bare hand,' Ratsey said tilting his head.

She smiled broadly, and slowly, tugged at the fingers of her glove until it was removed.

He held her lily-white hand. 'Both gloves will be required, I believe,' he teased.

The Countess feigned a pout, but readily peeled away her other glove.

Ratsey held out his hand and she placed both of hers on top of his. He leaned forward and kissed them gently, fancying they smelled of a fresh summer's eve.

'Enough foreplay, Gamaliel,' the Countess quietly ordered.

He looked into her still, stunning eyes. Older women who retained their allure were a weakness of his. He sighed, straightened himself and reached into his doublet. He took out a small pouch, and pulled the ties open. He kept his eyes firmly on the Countess's as he poured the diamonds from the benighted jewelled cloak he had stolen from that hellcat of a woman. Though he knew her supposed employer was Shakespeare, he was as yet unsure how she fitted into his favourite bard's web of friends. And until he did, she was safe.

Countess smiled broadly at Ratsey, as he filled both her hands with the diamonds that had been torn from that accursed cloak. Her eyes sparkled and her face flushed with delight. She raised her gaze to Ratsey's and mouthed 'Thank you' before gently pouring the diamonds back into their velvet pouch.

The Countess reached for her own leather pouch and gave it a quick shake. He could tell from the tune it made that she was rewarding him with a generous sum, as the rattle of gold was his private music of love. Ratsey handed her the diamonds, pocketed the Countess's pouch and bent forward to kiss her hand again.

'You wouldn't try to cheat me, would you Gamaliel?' she asked in a whisper.

Ratsey stood up. 'As if …'

Packing away her silver thimble, the Countess asked, 'So, have you seen Jonson yet?'

He shook his head, trailing her every move. Such beauty, such brains …

'You know that your wish has always been my command,' he shrugged.

The Countess smiled graciously, and nodded that he had her permission to take his leave.

Within the hour, Ratsey, Fang, Teacake and Snout were propping up the bar at the Mermaid Taverne.

'I like this ordinary best, Ratsey,' Snout said, taking a long draw on his ale.

'Don't use my name,' the highwayman hissed, treading heavily on Snout's foot. 'Not ever in public, you hear?'

'Yes Ratsey,' Snout nodded with a frozen smile.

Ratsey shook his head and turned his back towards Snout, only to see Jonson staring at him from a nearby table. How long had the bricklayer been there, he wondered? 'Stay here. I'll be back,' he said to his men.

Fang, Teacake and Snout glanced over to see where Ratsey was going. Teacake nodded to his partners in crime. 'When I give the word, we snarl and look dangerous, got it?'

Fang and Teacake scrunched up their faces, practising their fearsome looks.

Ratsey took his ease next to Jonson. 'Afternoon, Ben.'

'Afternoon.'

'I've come to town to be paid.'

'What for? You failed, Ratsey.'

'Ah, but I haven't. I have them.'

'The manuscripts were stolen back,' Jonson hissed through gritted teeth.

Ratsey frowned. 'What gave you that idea?'

'Me. Saw them. Read them. Held them. I ought to hoist you by your codpiece and make you sing soprano,' Jonson growled.

Ratsey lifted a brow, wondering just how Jonson might achieve that with his men not ten feet away. 'Where did you do this seeing and reading, Ben?'

'Oxford. In Will Shakespeare's room.'

'So you have them, then?'

'No,' Jonson shook his head. 'And just for lying to me, you can steal them again.'

'Hm. Fair enough. Where are they?'

'How should I know, toe-rag?'

Ratsey gripped Jonson by the throat. 'That's very rude.'

Teacake called out, 'Now!'

By the time Fang and Snout turned to snarl, drawn pistols and swords and rapiers from the Mermaiders glinted in the candlelight.

Jonson smiled as Ratsey released his grip. 'This is *my* ordinary, Gamiliel.'

'So I see, Ben.'

Shakespeare drummed impatiently on the table. 'Inspiration awaits no one,' he muttered. Suddenly he let out a shout, 'Robert! The arm is itching to write. Quick before it deserts me again. I've a play to finish.'

In the box room nearby, Robert sighed and reached for Shakespeare's writing kit. 'More like twitching to write, it seems to me. Let me see … quills, paper …' he said as he grabbed each item, 'so, where's the bleeding inkhorn?'

Shakespeare called out, 'I become as the fasting tiger, Robert … hungry to write!'

Robert searched amongst the detritus of the writing box. 'Anon, good Master! Anon!' What were wrong with his Master? He'd become so impatient of late and writing at all times – day or night or in between. Sometimes Shakespeare seemed angry, just for Robert being there to help him, and other times, he said things that made no sense. If his Master didn't stop writing, or fretting about writing, he'd be all writ' out! But a manservant must do as he was bid and not question these new ways, and so he kept looking for the inkhorn.

Shakespeare sat back and whispered to the heavens, 'So much to say, so little time.' He looked out at the sun setting over the rooftops of London. Soon, the pinks would become purples then oranges before they would give way to the rising darkness and another day would be gone. 'Robert!'

Robert turned over the last scrap of paper in the box, and stared at its empty bottom. The inkhorn had vanished. He let out a hefty sigh. That were the inkhorn old Master John Shakespeare had given his son when he first set out on his travels. It were the Master's prized possession – his good luck piece for writing. There would be blood on the floor, and it would be his, he cursed to himself. Robert sighed again, and walked through the door to his Master's bedroom like a condemned man.

'Ah – decided to join us at last?' Shakespeare asked acidly.

'Master, I can't – no matter where–' Robert babbled.

'Speak, man, I don't bite!'

'Can't find your inkhorn,' Robert blurted out, setting down the paper and quills.

Shakespeare's eyes widened.

'I've searched through everything in your writing box, Master,' Robert avowed, holding his hands up in surrender, 'I've yet to lose a lock of your hair before Master Shakespeare, I–'

Shakespeare hid his head in his hands. 'The bed pillows, Robert.' His voice was soft, suddenly overflowing with milky kindness. He motioned towards the bed as if to make Robert hear his words clearly.

'Beneath the pillows, dear friend,' Shakespeare said, still holding his head. 'Wrapped up in a kerchief. I completely forgot. O, Robert! What's happening to me?'

Robert lifted the pillows and saw the kerchief all bunched up. He brought it over to his Master.

'A thousand regrets, dear Robert,' Shakespeare said, unfolding it to reveal the inkhorn. 'Even then, I owe you more ...'

Robert was relieved and cross with him all at once. 'But–'

'I lose my memory at times. It happens more and more these days.'

'You're just worried 'bout the manuscripts, Master.'

'Perhaps, but there are other matters troubling me.'

'Your sickness?' Robert asked.

'Yes, of course, but there's even more.'

'Pray, tell me.'

Shakespeare hesitated before he looked at Robert. 'I've not been honest with you.'

'That is not for me to say, Master.'

Robert lowered his gaze, ashamed that he'd been wondering why the Master had changed his ways with him. Then suddenly Susanna's secret burned in his brain, and he thought, he hadn't been honest with him either.

'Yet it is for you to know,' Shakespeare said with a pleading eye.

Robert felt his cheeks flush. He saw his Master was deadly serious.

'You are a prince among men, Robert Whatcott.'

Robert was puzzled. His Master must be sickening again. He were never a prince. Should he call for a doctor?

'I see I puzzle you,' Shakespeare said, laying out his papers and quills just as steadily as he'd done hundreds of times in years gone by. 'I promise, it's not the sickness that speaks. But I fear I must ask you to be patient with me a while longer. I promise your forbearance shall be rewarded.'

Robert thought for a moment. A light seemed to shine in his mind. 'You mean?'

Shakespeare nodded. 'The time is now.'

Robert felt as if an anvil had been lifted from his shoulders. He beamed at Shakespeare, and his Master grinned warmly back at him, deep-searching Robert with a clear and lively eye.

It was an exhausted Robert who slumped down in the armchair before the fire in the great hall. He'd been at his Master's beck and call for the last few hours. And now he held his Master's secret in his heart and head as well as Susanna's. How it made for a heavy burden, a dizzying dilemma even, for it demanded much of him in ways he didn't like. It demanded he dissemble with Susanna as well as his Master, leaving him friendless and possibly jobless. And what for? Just so Master Shakespeare won't say as he should, *I've done you wrong Susanna* in five simple words? Or coz Susanna feared the shame in her own heart would make him hate her? It seemed to him that both father and daughter trod on their brains and used their feet to think!

'Fetch me this, then t'other...' Robert muttered aloud. 'Robert go on this errand or t'other or a journey to the world's end if you will. It's all the same to the Master. But when I says the time has come to be forthright with her, he says shush. And when I says the time for writing his fine words has passed and it's time to speak the words you have in your heart, he says keep your lips still, coz you don't see. But I do see. It's them that's blind and I'm led by a madman. But I'm just Robert and the Master won't listen to me, so I talk   myself   mad.'

Susanna walked into the great hall and heard Robert muttering to himself as he stood to add another log to the fire.

'Does he not think a daughter's love a jewel worth saving? But no, he says … not your way, Robert.'

'Ahem,' Susanna cleared her throat.

Robert wheeled round, his face bright red.

'Uh, Susanna, er … how long have you been listening to me?'

'What's this murmuring about?'

'Uh, er …'

She cocked her head to the side.

'Ask me no questions, I'll tell you no lies!' Robert blurted out.

'Then tell me you've not been speaking to my father about *you know what.*'

He opened his mouth, but no sound came out.

'Tell me, Robert.'

'I tell you I've not revealed any secrets.'

Susanna approached him. 'Then what have you been talking of with him – or saying to that fire there?'

Damn. O, damn his chattering and muttering aloud. 'That's a question asked,' he said.

Susanna gazed long and hard at him. Was it fair of her to ask him to betray a conversation with his Master? Surely his promise of a secret kept was good enough?

'I believe you,' she said with a nod.

Robert breathed a sigh. He hadn't betrayed her or the Master and he hadn't lied, but he'd not told the truth either.

They stood for some long while in silence, staring at the flames dancing in the fire. The green oak crackled and spat from time to time, and the golden blaze slowly tamed. Blue flecks rose above the burning wood as the fire mellowed.

Finally, Susanna plucked up the courage to say what she had originally sought him out to ask. 'Robert... have you seen John anywhere?'

'Why?'

'He should have returned a while ago. He went to talk privately with Ben Jonson.'

Whilst her question hardly came as a lightning bolt, Robert had his orders on what he could and couldn't say, and he knew he could say nothing.

'John who? I know many Johns.'

Susanna wrinkled her brow. 'Heminges, Robert. John Heminges.'

A plague on them all, Robert cursed to himself. How could they expect him to resist her directness? He who'd cared for her since she was born. She was sure to see through any veil he'd try to draw over something as tiny as a dormouse, much less something as big as where the King's Men were. But there was nothing for it. He must obey his Master or suffer the consequences. Yet how could he possibly dissemble like an actor?

Suddenly an idea popped into his brain. He let out a plaintive moan and began to rub his head, feigning pain. Surely Susanna would leave him be if he had a painful head?

'O, Lord, how my head aches! What a head have I! It beats as it would fall in twenty pieces!'

Susanna could see he was feigning illness, but decided to play along in his game. She felt she owed it to him. 'In faith, I am sorry you are not well, dear friend. Here,' she said, 'let me rub your sore temples.'

Just as she began to rub his temples, Robert cried out, 'Ah, my back, my back!'

Without a word, Susanna began to rub his back. She could scarcely keep from giggling. The darkness that hovered in her soul began to lift.

'O, Mistress–' Robert opined, 'I am weary, give me leave awhile.'

He tore himself away from her, backing out of the hall and bowing low, his hands sweeping the floor in overblown, theatrical gestures.

Susanna smiled. 'Robert! The whereabouts of John Heminges?'

'Alas, fair Susanna, I must away. I bid you farewell and good hunting, my lady.'

She stood alone by the fire, perplexed. She knew she had just seen some mightily awful playacting… but why?

Unbeknownst to her, Shakespeare was sitting in bed upstairs, writing furiously. Page after written page piled ever higher. The words *that she should dream knowing the full measure of a life well-lived* flowed from his quill. He thought for a moment then wrote: *I shall outstare lightning for you and take away your fury to restore your heart.*

Precious seconds stretched to minutes, and minutes to an hour. Still his arm held out, and his mind flowed with poetry for her. 'Susanna may never forgive me, but I shall make her journey worth her while, that she would have her chance at a life well-lived,' he whispered aloud, looking at the dozens of pages piled beside him.

Will Davenant knocked lightly and entered. 'This journey must be worthwhile for you as well,' Shakespeare nodded, handing him the papers.

Will smiled and peered down at the pages.

'Remember, no peeking,' Shakespeare said and grinned.

Chapter 28

Sitting in the medieval inner bailey courtyard, Susanna wrapped the shawl tightly around her. Chaos slept peacefully at her side. A northerly wind swirled in the enclosed space, blowing its chill into her bones. She looked up and saw the lights flickering inside the gatehouse that bounded her above on three sides. Beyond, clouds gathered round the moon as if trying to steal its warmth.

Unbeknownst to her, Robert peered down at her from the gatehouse, thinking how lonely she looked sitting on the edge of the makeshift stage beside her dog. He gnawed at his lip, upset that he'd told her nothing, coz in his beating heart he knew it weren't the right thing to do. When he looked up and saw John Heminges pacing in the passageway opposite, also gazing at Susanna, he wondered what he knew about the Master's plan.

'I feel peculiar again,' Shakespeare breathed into Robert's ear.

Robert turned and saw at once that his Master was ill. 'I'll fetch the doctor.'

'No.'

'The apothecary?'

Shakespeare shook his head and suddenly crumpled in a heap on the floor.

Robert gasped. He flung the window open. 'Susanna! Master Heminges! Come! It's the Master!'

Susanna mopped her father's brow. His cheek twitched badly and his writing hand was curled up in a knot. She raised her eyes to Robert, who smiled slenderly.

'These little fellas here will do the trick, just you see,' he said.

Susanna forced herself to look. Leeches wriggled on her father's writing arm, drawing blood as they snaked upwards.

Shakespeare gave a jagged breath and batted his eyes open.

Susanna bent down so he could see her. She whispered, 'O, Father can you forgive me? Please, forgive my utter stupidity?'

'What for?'

'In all our worries about the lost manuscripts, I clean forgot I had the recipe for your medicine.'

'Your husband's?'

'Yes.'

'I wish I'd never taken it,' he mumbled.

Susanna frowned. 'Don't be silly. John has gone to the apothecary's. He should be back with the medicine shortly.'

Shakespeare tried to raise his head, but the effort was too great. 'I'm ashamed,' he slurred.

Just then, Heminges ran into the room clutching a large bottle.

Susanna grabbed it from him and held it up to the candlelight. 'It looks different somehow.'

'Just give it to him,' Robert pleaded.

'Get those wretched things off his arm,' she ordered uncorking the bottle.

Heminges and Robert squeezed the leeches off and propped Shakespeare up on his pillows. Susanna deftly administered about half the medicine. Then they waited – and waited. No one said a word. No thought passed their minds, save that William Shakespeare must live. Minutes eked out the time into an hour before her father stirred.

'Soon there will be no more gilded butterflies ...' he whispered, eyes closed.

The three of them sighed in relief. Susanna knelt by his bedside and curled her hand into his. She was reassured when he squeezed it to his chest tightly.

'He'll recover,' she nodded to Robert and Heminges.

Shakespeare opened his dark eyes. Susanna smiled, wondering what she could say. Her thoughtlessness had nearly killed him, and she feared she'd drown in her own distress for all that she'd done. He'd slept some hours and she felt unduly blessed that she was there when he awakened from that faraway place where those afflicted by falling sickness travelled alone.

'Susanna, forgive me?' he asked in a thread-like voice.

'Forgive you? But I'm the careless one, Father. I've been thoughtless – '

'Stop, please. I am the careless one. A daughter's love is a jewel worth cherishing. I tossed you away into a loveless marriage. I, of all people, should have known better. I knew how it felt and what I might be doing to you. Forgive me?'

'It is a father's duty to see his daughters marry well,' she shrugged, making light of her pain.

'But we'd not known him long enough, and he dazzled me with his cures.'

'He dazzled us all, Father.'

'They say love is nothing, you need an occupation and money to live. But to live without it, is everything,' Shakespeare breathed softly. 'And so, I kneel down and ask of thee forgiveness: so that we may live, and pray, and sing, and tell old tales, and laugh at gilded butterflies.'

King Lear and Cordelia again. This time, the words flowed freely from her lips in reply, 'We are not the first who with best meaning have incurred the worst, father.'

Susanna searched his face. He understood what he'd done after all, and was shamed by it. Now was the time to avow her lies and failings.

'Father, I have a confession …'

But before another word was said, Susanna saw that he'd drifted off into a peaceful sleep.

Chapter 29

Susanna stood next to Heminges in the queue. Robert hovered behind them carrying the baskets. The wind had picked up. They'd buy their provisions, Susanna mused, then relieve Nathan and Henry Condell from their bedside duties. Afterwards, she'd cook them all a hearty stew. Then she thought on young Will. He had persuaded them that with his being little, and streetwise, he could pass into places where no one else could go and overhear all manner of things, and that people wouldn't be mindful of him. He'd explored enough around Blackfriars to know the haunts and hollows of London's underworld and where it mingled with the players and the playhouses, he claimed. Despite Susanna's objections, it was decided that Will would sniff out the whereabouts of the manuscripts. Above all else, she prayed he would stay safe, as she feared he was trying to make his new father extra-proud of him and would take unnecessary chances. If anything happened to him, she'd —

Heminges interrupted her thoughts as he curled his fingers around hers. She felt a surge of passion rise as their eyes locked.

'Move on!' a shrill voice shouted in her ear.

As they inched forward, Susanna let go of his fingers. She tried desperately to think of something other than kissing him again and holding him close, but when she did her mind trailed back to Will. His plan to help their father made her tremble with unease.

'So, how are your rehearsals?' she asked Heminges, to take her mind off her infernal fretting.

'Not too badly.'

'Why won't you tell me which play it is?'

'Ssh! It's a new one, never before seen.' Heminges touched his finger to his nose. 'Look about you. See how their ears grow long?'

Indeed, when Susanna looked around she saw how people stared at them. It hadn't dawned on her before how naming a new play by William Shakespeare might cause such a fuss. But then, why would she? She'd only just discovered her father in his own world.

'Can I come and watch?' she asked.

Heminges moved her forward in the queue, his hand in the small of her back. 'No.'

Robert giggled. Like two schoolchildren they were. What a difference a day made in their lives. With Master Shakespeare getting better by the minute and the apothecary's brew working just as well or maybe better than Dr Hall's, perhaps the storm clouds would lift from all their lives.

'Please?' Susanna implored.

Heminges smiled. 'It will be best for you to see the first performance. Trust me.'

'It'll be a surprise that way,' Robert chirped.

'A good surprise, right, Robert?' Heminges laughed.

'My father's never surprised me before, so I don't see why he should start now ...'

They reached the front of the queue and Susanna gave her vegetable order.

Heminges pulled Robert back by the elbow and hissed, 'She's not meant to know.'

'I know my mistress.'

'As I know your Master.'

'Who knows what I'm meant to know, tell me that, huh?' Robert dared him.

'Which is?'

'To know what else you shouldn't know,' Robert huffed, stepping towards Susanna and jostling her into the back of another man.

'Morning, Mistress,' a rough voice called out.

'I beg your pardon,' she said. The man turned to face her.

'Beg away,' Jonson leered. 'I know what you do.'

'You do blow an evil wind upon me for no cause, Master Jonson.'

'You've not your father's wit.'

'Others say it speeds too fast, bricklayer.'

Jonson clutched at his heart. 'O, I'm wounded, help me!'

'Scurvy toad,' Susanna scowled.

Jonson stopped playacting. 'Maybe you haven't heard that I'm a dangerous man to provoke.' He waggled his thumb at her, branded with the letter 'T' for Tyburn. 'Only pardoned murderers bear that mark,' he said.

Susanna swallowed, thinking back to the pickled thumb in her husband's oddities at home.

Robert made to come between them. Yet for some unspoken reason, Heminges held him by the arm, a satisfied cat-who-swallowed-the-cream smile on his face.

'O, do I hear the strains of the strutting rooster?' Susanna cupped her hand to her ear. 'No. Must be the crow.'

'Your father's the upstart crow, or haven't you heard?' Jonson looked about him trying to gather an audience, but the Londoners paid him no heed. 'I can crow you his tune if you will?' he added, twirling about, arms outstretched.

Robert quickly glanced around. No crowd yet.

Susanna mocked him. 'You? Why you'd not be nimble-lunged enough to sing a baby's cry!'

The woman stallholder stopped gathering up the vegetables for Susanna and watched them trade insults. So did another woman nearby. Then another and several more. They nodded and winked to Susanna, egging her on, as Jonson loomed over her. 'You took those manuscripts. I know.'

Susanna reddened with confused anger. Surely *he* took them? That is after she did. Still, that wasn't strictly so. She took them three times in all.

'From Stratford? Of course I took them from Stratford – on my father's orders, you wind-swept foul-faced varlet,' Susanna cursed at him, turning his insults into the ravings of a jealous fool. 'And you took them from my father!'

Heminges patted Robert on the arm as a signal for the two of them to intervene. The stallholders grinned. They'd never seen a woman get the better of a playmaker in a war of words.

'Why you–'

'May the devil burn your fingers for your hot lies, Ben Jonson!' Susanna growled.

Heminges pulled Jonson back. 'Why can't we talk this out like fellow playmakers and friends?'

'Mornin' Ben. How are you, Ben? Long time no see, Ben,' Jonson rounded on him. 'Where'd you leave your manners, John, in the brothel on Turnmill Street?'

Now all the men stopped what they were doing and gathered round, smelling a punch-up. As quick as a flash, odds were laid and coins changed hands.

'Where are Will's manuscripts, Ben?' Heminges demanded.

Jonson put his fat finger to his cheek, tapping it lightly, feigning to think. 'Let me see,' he posed for the audience, 'you mean the ones written in Shakespeare's own fair hand?'

Heminges grasped Jonson by the throat and began to shake him. A fist fight never solved anything, Susanna thought as she motioned for Robert to help her pull him back. Besides, how could Jonson say anything if he were choked?

As Robert struggled to grab hold of Heminges, Susanna pleaded, 'John, he's not worth the trouble. He wouldn't know a manuscript from a mackerel if you smacked him with it.'

Everyone – except Jonson – rang out in peals of laughter. Heminges let go and smiled at Susanna. Jonson spluttered whilst Robert shielded them, arms on his hips in defiance.

'Why Jonson's poetry is heavy, laboured even,' Susanna called out to the crowd.

The Londoners sniggered and giggled.

Susanna smiled at Heminges. 'Why I hear he murders words in mortar, like the bricklayer he is!'

Jonson straightened up, pushing Robert aside. He glowered down at Susanna. Heminges took her by the shoulders and moved her away gently.

'The lady has a point, Ben,' Heminges said with a grin.

Rattling his thumb in their faces once again, Jonson scowled, 'Though I wear the mark of a murderer, I'm no thief!'

Susanna sighed, suddenly weary of all the wordplay. 'What quarrel d'you have with my father? I'd heard you were friends once.'

'He steals the very air I breathe,' Jonson bellowed. 'The very air, hear me! Tell your father, the upstart crow, I hope he never finds his manuscripts, but if he does, I hope he chokes on them!'

Before she knew it, Susanna had raised her hand to strike him, but Heminges was too quick for her and grabbed her wrist. Gently, he steered her aside, whispering in her ear, 'I think he's bigger than you and not desperately mindful of striking back at a woman.'

Susanna looked at him. No one besides Robert had ever protected her before. Still, it would have been the first time she'd ever slapped a man. Nonetheless, she hadn't finished with Jonson, she thought. Her anger was on the rise.

She turned back and cried out, 'You hang on this world like a disease, Ben Jonson. The sooner we find a cure for you the better!'

Robert took up the flank whilst Heminges led Susanna away as swiftly as possible, conscious that all Blackfriars had had their good entertainment at Jonson's expense. Problem were, she shouldn't have provoked such a mean-spirited man like that. He scratched his chin thinking. This weren't the Susanna he knew. But now that she'd spoken out so, he couldn't see how they'd secretly track down the manuscripts. Suddenly, he wondered where young Will had got to. The boy had been following Jonson, hoping to discover his hiding place and who the accomplice were that Tronco'd seen in that crystal ball of hers. What if something happened to him? He turned like a wheel with a searching eye for the boy but saw no youngsters at all.

Fear welled up in his heart. Will were only a child, and if anything happened to him the Master would be just as upset as if Susanna had fallen foul of London's streets. Susanna were safe with Heminges, of that he were sure. But if he told her what were on his mind – that he wanted to look for the boy – she'd insist on going too. He looked down at the baskets filled with carrots and onions and turnips, and his face brightened.

'You forgot the carrots!' Robert called ahead to them. 'I'll go back and fetch them.'

Susanna and Heminges glanced at him and nodded.

As Robert turned away, he prayed that he were merely fretting about the boy and that all was well. From the corner of an alleyway that gave onto Blackfriars, Ratsey watched Heminges and Susanna head towards the river.

Chapter 30

Susanna's eyes sparkled with life, and she began to laugh. Indeed, she laughed so hard that they had to stop walking. For the first time ever, she was a woman who was born to joy instead of the sorrow she wore so heavily upon her sleeve.

A gust of wind blew sharply, funnelling its way up the lane. Grit flew into her eyes and she tried to squint it away.

'We'd best take a shortcut through the private park up ahead, Heminges said. 'With this wind,' Heminges said, 'we'll be covered in soot in no time.'

He took her by the arm. Susanna hesitated, blinking away the last of the grit.

'It's all right. We know the owners,' he said.

Susanna looked into the park and felt the lure of its beauty and walked in happily. The sheltered gardens with their unusual plantings, made her feel transported to another place and time. Whoever lived her had to be as rich as the King, she thought. The park was secluded from prying eyes by majestic Irish yews that stood as armed sentinels guarding either side of its avenue. Nodding flowers filling tiny knot gardens and mature rose bushes peeked above the entwined box hedges. Red and white rose buds had begun to appear. Soon it would be high spring.

Susanna grew pensive. She wondered if she might yet regret her encounter with Jonson.

'Don't let Jonson trouble you, Susanna,' Heminges said, reading her mind.

'I don't fear him, if that's what you mean.'

He grinned wickedly. 'Perhaps it is he who should fear you? Jonson is all jealousy, he simply envies your father's way with words.'

'And you, John? Do you envy my father?' she asked.

'Not for his way with words,' he replied enigmatically.

'Then for what?'

Just then a woman strolled into view.

'That's Mary, Countess of Pembroke, the owner,' Heminges sighed, exasperated.

The Countess headed directly towards them, her two statuesque ladies-in-waiting trailing behind her. The tallest lady saw Heminges with Susanna in the clearing between the yews and nodded wistfully to him, as if they were old friends.

Susanna turned to Heminges. He blushed.

'A beautiful day for the time of year, is it not, John?' the Countess asked.

Heminges swept off his cap and bowed deeply. 'Save the wind, of course,' he replied.

The Countess nodded. 'Of course. Ah, and it blows some rain our way too, I see.'

Susanna raised herself from her curtsey and looked up at the gloomy clouds darkening the sky.

'Your Grace Mary Countess of Pembroke, may I present to you Mistress Susanna Hall, daughter of William Shakespeare.'

The Countess seemed to know who he was, for she immediately said, 'I pray your father is recovering.'

Susanna nodded in reply, awed by the Countess's enquiring after his health. Was it not odd for a noblewoman to be concerned with her father's illness?

The Countess turned to Heminges. 'And there's talk in the market place of Shakespeare's missing manuscripts, did you know, John?'

Susanna and Heminges exchanged looks. Her multitude of insults to Jonson flooded back into her brain. She'd never been so embarrassed, for she was certain that this all-seeing Countess also knew of her tirade against Jonson. Decorum should demand that she hide behind the nearest yew yet Susanna understood she'd have to stand her ground.

The Countess must have sensed her discomfiture, for she added, taking hold of Susanna's hands tenderly, 'I am your father's oldest friend beyond Stratford's town limits. May I call upon him on the morrow? It has been so long since we've talked of innocent things.'

Susanna's mouth had dried up but her mind raced ahead. The 'what ifs' were suddenly clear as glass. Those margin notes she'd read – those two words *the countess* – struck her. So, this was she. Susanna's eyes trailed over her fine features. How she admired that perfect smile and graceful manner. The Countess was just as her father had written: *he had found delight there writ with beauty's pen.* The Countess was everything that her mother was not. Where her mother angered at a glance, it seemed to Susanna that the Countess would smile wryly. Where her mother was plain-speaking, her rival would rarely speak her mind. Still, an educated and polished woman such as the Countess didn't bear comparing to her mother, or indeed herself. It was little wonder that her father had been besotted by such a glorious woman.

Heminges nudged Susanna back to the here-and-now.

'Of course, Countess,' Heminges bowed. 'Good day to you.'

The Countess nodded, and with the merest flick of her head, bade her ladies to follow. As Susanna and Heminges stared after them, the tallest one peered back at him and bestowed the kind of smile only intimate friends share. Susanna knew she was green-eyed with jealousy and shocked by the wholly unfamiliar feeling. Perhaps it was more to do with the Countess's floating on air like some goddess? Or maybe it was the realisation that her father had loved this woman, heart and soul? The sad truth was, having met her,

Susanna could never blame him. The Countess was perfection to her eyes.

Shaking herself from her reverie, she knew she had no right to be jealous of any woman who made eyes at John Heminges. It was ridiculous that she should harbour such feelings. Yet the sight of the lady-in-waiting casting an intimate look that held guilty secrets gave rise to that monster within. She'd no right. She was another man's wife!

Susanna looked back, hoping to glimpse her one final time. Instead, Gamiliel Ratsey peered at her from behind one of the yews. Dear Lord! She wheeled round, and took hold of Heminges's arm and pulled him in the opposite direction.

'Yes, you gave us all an enjoyable show with Jonson back there, you know,' Heminges said, picking up the earlier conversation.

'A show that advanced us nowhere. John, please don't look behind us, but Gamiliel Ratsey is hard on our heels.'

Heminges stiffened. 'Then come. I know a shortcut to the Gatehouse from here, and if we hurry, he'll not be able to find us.'

It started to rain just as they walked swiftly into the maze of box that stood ten feet high.

'Quick, through here,' he urged.

As they raced through the maze in the downpour Susanna worried that they were leaving tracks that Ratsey could follow. After all, hadn't she trailed after him in the countryside without the benefit of rain to mark his path? As they exited at the far side of the maze and ran into the street, Susanna was struck by a stitch in her side.

'John, please, slow up,' she begged.

Heminges obeyed, a look of concern etched on his brow.

'I'll be fine in a minute. It's just a stitch.'

The rain drenched them as Susanna stood holding her side. Why were they running away? They had nothing of value for Ratsey to steal. Perhaps he was after some cold revenge for her having stolen back her father's manuscripts? Then it suddenly dawned on her. Her thefts of the manuscripts had reduced all who surrounded her to villainy. She felt sick with her wanton disregard for others. Not that her husband deserved better, mind – but Robert certainly did. And what had the King's Men ever done to her that she should punish them along with her father by purloining the manuscripts again?

All she had accomplished was to shame herself and most likely lose the love of her father she had so longed to win. What would Heminges and the others think of her when the truth was known? At that moment, she knew she had to abandon hope of her folly remaining secret. But what if young Will succeeded in finding who had stolen them this time? Susanna closed her eyes. So many questions and no answers.

Heminges placed his cloak over her shoulders. 'Feeling better?'

Susanna willed herself to tell all. Instead, she merely nodded.

Chapter 31

Robert shook the rain from his cloak and bounded up the stairs. He could scarce believe the man's cheek. Here he were trailing after Ben Jonson, when without a by-your-leave that bricklayer turned round and chased after him. 'O, fool that you are, Robert Whatcott,' he moaned aloud. 'You led Jonson straight back home, and now he'll burst in all hellfire and brimstone to upset the Master.' He had to warn his master quickly, for Jonson followed close behind.

He pushed open the door to the great hall and stopped dead. Condell, Nathan and Burbage were seated at the table with Shakespeare. Will Davenant plunged a hot poker into their tankards to warm their small ale.

'Master – you're better?'

Shakespeare smiled at him. 'Thanks to you and Susanna. Where's she gone?'

'Off with Master Heminges,' Robert wrinkled his brow wondering why young Will had stopped following Jonson. 'Will?'

The boy looked up. 'I'll get some small ale for you too, Robert?'

'And Jonson?'

Will gazed at the others to see how he should answer. Shakespeare, Nathan, Condell and Burbage all lifted their tankards in unison for a long hard swig of their ale.

Meantime, in the street below, Ben Jonson glared up at the glistening stone walls of Shakespeare's Gatehouse. He leaned heavily against a nearby market stall, the rain overflowing from the brim of his hat.

The wind whipped his cloak into the air. A cat tried to shelter beneath it, but when Jonson felt it rub against his leg he kicked it away.

Just then a stranger approached him. 'I see you are a man after my own heart,' he said. 'I hate this fashion for domestic animals.'

Jonson sneered at the stranger dressed in drab Puritan country clothes. He looked a right cony. 'Be off with you. I've business here.'

'But I seek–'

'I'm no conycatcher and have no time for country parsons.'

The stranger looked hard at Jonson. 'I had expected a warmer welcome.'

Jonson leered at him and jested. 'O, these bedevilled Londoners, right? All alike to a man – full of their own importance and godless thespians playing to an audience, right Puritan?'

The fellow pursed his lips as if he'd sucked on a lemon. 'I'm a Puritan on a mission, I'll have you know, sir, and I'm sick and tired of being lied to, cheated and plain hoodwinked. I'm seeking the great playwright Jonson. Ben Jonson.'

Jonson stood back, eyeing the pilgrim from toe to head. 'What for?'

The Puritan stood proud. 'I've private business with him.'

Jonson nodded, barely disguising his disbelief.

'I seek Jonson for the truth, and I have little time for such games,' the Puritan said acidly. 'I'm tired and muddy from my misadventures. First to Oxford on a wing and a prayer, then off to Norwich chasing wild geese, and now here! One day God will smite down all you sinners for your wicked ways.' The stranger flicked his cloak as he turned away, splattering mud across Jonson's face.

'Why, you – pilgrim!' Jonson cried, wiping the sludge from his cheek. 'What business would a hopeless pilgrim like you have with a monumental talent like Ben Jonson? More to the point, what business could *he* have with you? Pilgrims hate the theatre – and pilgrims hate fun.'

The stranger stood open-mouthed. Jonson was florid with rage. 'You …unmuzzled weather-beaten preacher of doom.'

The stranger reeled towards Jonson, a fire igniting in his eyes. 'I've not come all this way to wallow in Sodom. I was told that Ben Jonson was Shakespeare's enemy once again.'

Jonson stood stock still. 'Could be ... what affair is it of yours?'

'Because he would tell me the truth of where Shakespeare lived. I've been in London a day searching hither then thither, misguided and misinformed of Shakespeare's whereabouts by his friends. I require his foe to tell me the truth.'

'And why do you hate Shakespeare so much, other than he's the darling of the playhouses?'

'He's my father-in-law. I don't hate him. I come to cure him.'

'Dr Hall?' Jonson enquired, incredulous. 'Dr John Hall?'

Hall nodded.

'Dear Friend!' Jonson exclaimed, embracing him in a squelching bear hug. 'Do forgive my outburst, please. Why, Dr Hall – I am mightily pleased to meet you at long last.'

Hall stood back, bemused. 'It is ungodly to make such a public show of greeting to a stranger. Pray, are you Ben Jonson?'

'Course I am.'

Hall looked down at his bag and saw it was still clamped tightly shut, then tapped at his pockets. The jingle of his money pouch proved reassuring.

'I've not robbed you, if that's what you fear.' Jonson winked and hugged him again.

Hall looked at him as if he were a madman. 'What is it with you theatre people? All touching-feeling one minute or frozen like stone statues the next!'

Jonson removed his arms as if he'd been scalded.

'Where does my father-in-law dwell?'

Jonson smiled slenderly. 'Come my friend. Let me show you the way.'

Hall saw the seller of oranges nearest to them spit at the ground and glare at Jonson. He turned, only to see another stallholder snarl at Jonson. 'Beware your purse, pilgrim!' he called out.

Hall rounded on Jonson. 'Are you or are you not this Jonson? This friendly foe of Shakespeare's?' Hall growled.

The shoppers and stallholders smirked and shook their heads.

'Mustn't have been at the Mermaid yesterday, pilgrim,' someone shouted.

'Jonson and Shakespeare friends?' another scoffed.

'Depends on their moods,' a third called.

'Or the winds,' another cried, bent over in peals of laughter.

Hall wheeled round and round as each one peppered his confusion.

'Jonson is Shakespeare's friend so long as Shakespeare don't write,' someone else hooted above the uproar.

'Can't you Londoners answer a polite question without riddles?' Hall shouted in frustration. 'Can anyone tell me if this man is who he says he is? Ben Jonson, the playwright?'

Jonson raised his brow. The mocking stallholders stood silent, as he stared at each of them. One by one they nodded at Hall, as if the gift of speech had fled their souls.

Hall sighed, smoothing down his pilgrim's suit, 'At last, an honest answer to an honest question.' He gave a curt nod. 'Then I shall come with you, Master Jonson.'

Jonson gave a wintry smile. 'Then let's away.'

From an alleyway leading onto Blackfriars another pair of interested eyes observed. Gamaliel Ratsey had found the encounter between the pilgrim and Jonson most illuminating. As illuminating as those sparkling diamonds, he ruminated. He stroked his beard, wondering if …

Susanna tongue-lashed herself a dozen times in her mind as she made her way back to the Gatehouse with Heminges. She had been unworthy, ungracious and unforthcoming with everyone. Now she was stuck in that role as any poor player would be. But, they hadn't written this script for her, *she* had, and she must rewrite her role, somehow. She must work to gain their trust and prove herself a person worthy of their praise and love when the curtain fell. Everything rested on finding the lost manuscripts.

She was pleased to see how Heminges held her in his eye as they ambled home. So this was love? Or was Cupid hoodwinking her as he did her father's characters? Had she borrowed Cupid's wings to soar above the ground under false pretences? This tender love she felt would soon be rough and rude and boisterous and prick her like a thorn once they knew of her treachery.

Of course she'd no right to have such feelings. No right at all. She beamed back at him. She was a liar, a cheat, a thief and a married woman. But come what may, she wanted above all else to enjoy this moment for its unalloyed sense of the present.

Richard Burbage reached across to Henry Condell's plate and helped himself to some of his eggs, as Henry chatted to Shakespeare. Burbage scoffed the eggs down before his friend could notice.

'I know your objections, Will, and why you don't want to travel so far, but I've booked the Tabard Inn, and you've announced it,' Condell said. 'Besides, it's just right for this play, I promise.'

'But Henry, why can't we play here at the theatre here at Blackfriars?' Shakespeare took a small bite of his buttered bread. 'The playbills have yet to be printed.'

'The playhouse has been empty for months, you know that,' Condell said, stabbing his fork into an empty plate. 'It would take at least two weeks or more to patch the leaks in the roof and rid it of its bad humours. If the Master of the Revels came to inspect—'

'I know, I know. It's just ...'

Condell's eye twitched. 'Will, you're the one who said we had to stage this play with all haste, and for good reason. The Tabard is small, granted, but beautiful. It's available and it's convenient. Besides, it fits the action better than any other theatre or playhouse or inn yard I know. It has all those entrances and exits we'll need.

No, Will. I have to insist. The Tabard is the only stage that fits the play.'

Shakespeare shrugged and took another bite of his buttered bread. Condell looked down at his empty plate and frowned. Burbage wiped his mouth on his sleeve, pretending not to notice Condell's confusion. Further along the table, young Will was dishing out scraps of bread to Chaos.

Robert shook his head at them. They were like small children, each and every one of them – small children of the same family. It did his heart good to see such a sight, especially as he never thought he'd live to see the day dawn again with Master Shakespeare talking in good health. An urgent knock at the door interrupted his thoughts.

'When folly knocks–' Shakespeare pronounced. Everyone laughed at the echo of Agnes at the Mermaid Taverne.

'Must be the owner of the Tabard, come for his money,' Condell called after Robert as he rose to answer.

'Tell him to wait,' Shakespeare said. 'Show him into the small library, Robert.'

'Aye, Master,' Robert answered, pulling the heavy oak door open.

Robert's world suddenly crumbled. Standing before him was Dr John Hall, dripping wet, glowering at him. Behind Hall, stood Ben Jonson, smirking.

'O, dear Lord,' Robert heard himself exhale hoarsely.

As the rain bucketed down, Susanna and Heminges ran the last few yards to the Gatehouse door. They burst inside, laughing and shedding their sodden cloaks.

'It's not a question of shaking the water off these, I fear,' Heminges said, holding Susanna by the shoulders.

'No, it's not.'

'We should leave our cloaks on the pegs down here,' he said, slowly bending towards her face.

'Mm,' she answered, tilting her head to the side.

As his lips feathered hers, she wondered how she'd lived all these years without the love of a good man, and prayed once more that this moment would never end.

They held each other tightly, Susanna as much in fear of letting go as in passion.

Suddenly, at the top of the stairs she heard her father screech, 'NO!'

They pulled back at the same time, eyes wide with fear. Heminges bounded up the stairs two at a time, with Susanna trailing behind. 'Dear Lord, please don't let him die,' she murmured.

By the time she reached the door to the great hall, Heminges was standing still, blocking her view. She inched around and gasped.

'Ah, my good lady wife,' Hall nodded, towering over Shakespeare.

Her father sat at the refractory table, head hanging, his plate of food and tankard lay topsy-turvy down on the floor. In front of him was the large box of her husband's medicines and several smaller ones beside it. She looked at Robert and needed no words to explain what was happening. Standing by the table, with their chairs all helter-skelter behind them, were Nathan, Condell and Burbage, whose arm was wrapped around young Will to protect him. Chaos whimpered in the corner, as he did at home whenever Hall kicked him.

'Have you no words of greeting for your husband, good wife? Especially when I greet you well? Funny, we were just talking of you.'

She stared at him, wishing him gone. Alas, he remained standing before her, a waking nightmare.

'My father is unwell, John. Unhand him,' Susanna commanded.

'Unwell?' Hall bent down and raised Shakespeare's chin between his thumb and finger.

Susanna saw her father's grief at once. He blames himself, she thought, when all those years ago he only wanted the best for me.

'If you're unwell, that would be because your daughter didn't bring enough medicine, isn't that so, Father Shakespeare?' Hall intoned mockingly.

'There was no need for you to bring more medicines yourself, husband.'

'Ah,' he said reaching into his doublet and handing her a letter. 'But there was.'

Susanna crept towards him and snatched the letter.

'See how your father writes to me in his own scrawl?'

She read aloud:

> 'John, I thank you for the box of medicine but need more. Indeed, I need to speak to you about my illness. Come to Oxford. Ask for me at Magdalen College. WS.'

Tears welled up in her eyes. Her father's astonishing words rendered her speechless. 'Seems your father was unaware of your theft, Susanna,' Hall gloated.

'I, I ...' she began, but the words choked her.

'And equally unaware of your shaming me.'

She breathed slowly to stop herself from sobbing. He was the one who had shamed her. 'This is between us alone, husband.'

'Stealing,' Hall wagged a finger at her, 'is a crime. The punishment in some cases is hanging.'

Susanna's eyes widened. She searched her father's face for help, but could see his mouth drooping and knew his speech had fled from him once again. Turning to the others, and finally to John Heminges, she realised that they were all utterly powerless in their own ways.

'I–'

'Theft of my medicines is a serious crime. Theft, mind you, is a crime I could levy at all the Shakespeares: your father stole your life, just as you stole my recipe and medicines to give to these London apothecaries. You stole my pride, Susanna.' Hall glowered at her. 'Robert, over there, ran off with you and everyone calls me a cuckold. I'm the laughing stock of the county, d'you hear?' Hall shouted.

Susanna was too grievously wounded to speak.

'Then there's your mother and sister harping on about ruddy stolen promises!'

'Why you–' Heminges growled at Hall.

'John, no,' Susanna called out.

'Ah, so you're my wife's other lover sighing like a furnace to her. Well, too late, the bargain's sealed, lover boy!' Hall hissed.

Heminges made to lunge at him, but Nathan stood in his way and Condell held him by the shoulders.

Hall glared at Shakespeare, 'Though why I agreed, Father Shakespeare, I can't think.' Slowly, he turned his wintry gaze scorching Susanna. 'You see, good wife, your father has sold you to me once again for his medicines. But the bargain's not complete until you fetch back my recipe from that horn-thumbing apothecary you used.'

'Father? You bargained me away for your medicines?' Her voice was as thin as a spider's thread.

She looked at her father, wishing it wasn't so, but knowing it was.

Shakespeare struggled to raise his head. Then his eyes narrowed to pinpricks and with the force of a sudden gale, he scythed the boxes of medicines off the table, growling, 'NEVER!' The phials shattered on the flagstones.

Exhausted yet revitalised by his effort, he seemed to find his words. 'I'd rather die first, Susanna,' he whispered.

She didn't know what to believe.

As if reading her mind, he rounded on Hall. 'Go back to your holy hell! Leave us be!'

It was the permission to act. The King's Men and Robert closed in on Hall.

'Susanna, I didn't know how horrid – I told him he should never darken your door again … O, my poor girl, why didn't you say?'

'Was there a bargain, Father? Me for the medicines?'

'HE LIES,' Shakespeare cried. 'He lies,' he repeated in a whisper.

Hall smirked. 'Do I? That's not my recollection. Though I wonder if I would have fared better with two geese and a heifer.'

'LEAVE!' Heminges shouted. 'Take your filthy lies and go. Go to perdition with your helpmate the Devil before we help you on your way.'

Hall smirked again at Heminges and sauntered towards him.

Suddenly, Heminges walloped him in the chest and then in the face. The King's Men cheered him on. Susanna turned to her father. Tears streaked his face.

Out of nowhere came that spider's thread voice in her head, entreating her to run. Run away from your shame. Run to find peace. Run away from it all, it cried louder and louder until the slenderness of it became a roar.

Whilst her husband and the man she loved scuffled, and Shakespeare stared down in shame, Susanna listened to that voice and ran from her father's home.

Chapter 32

Susanna's head exploded with a thunderous anger. As she fled down the rickety staircase all she could think of was escape. Escape from the lies that passed as truth and the man who passed as her husband. But what of her father?

The shame of it all burned inside. He'd apologised for telling her to marry Hall. Most fathers wouldn't see their own errors, she knew. A daughter's duty was to marry as her father bid and have done with it. Love rarely entered into marriage. She only had to look at her own parents to see that. The shame of it lay not in the loveless match, but in the fact that her father made her believe John Hall loved her and wanted her above all others.

He had reassured her that he sought her happiness and that Hall would cherish and honour her for the rest of their days together. Now she saw clear as glass she'd been too ignorant of men to know that her father played the puppet-master with her to his own selfish ends. Even then, his mortal fear that others would learn of the falling sickness in the Shakespeare family preyed heavily on his mind. Fact was, there was much to commend in her husband's words that her father had wanted a tame doctor to disguise and dissemble his fears. So, if the prize or price for the good doctor's silence and services was Shakespeare's daughter, then so be it.

How could she be expected to believe her father now, when in the past he had bent the truth to his will? Susanna flung open the front door to the Gatehouse and raced out. The rain pelted down her back and her feet skidded on the cobbles underfoot. She felt like some hunched small ship, tempest tossed, about to sink in a storm. But her anger steered her forward as she ran.

It was only twenty yards or so before she felt faint, her mind soaked through with memories. From somewhere buried within came the time her father had taken her punting on the Avon and a summer shower doused them. Then she recalled when her brother Hamnet painted her father's face with willow bark as he slept in a glade. Then playing in the meadow and trying to guess what animal their father was pretending to be. She stopped to lean against the stone wall to catch her breath, the rain cooling her face and mind. Dear Lord, she prayed silently, please stop the memories, they confuse me.

Here she stood, just as she had all those days ago in Stratford-upon-Avon, bolting from what should have been her home and refuge. Here she was, without a change of clothing, without the least little belonging. She had nothing, coz she was nothing. She broke into a run up the crowded Blackfriars byway, fearing the memories would drown her. She needed to be rid of them. She needed to forget she was Shakespeare's daughter and Dr John Hall's wife. Most of all, she must forget any notion of John Heminges.

She turned the corner and spied the tiny church ahead. The rain drove harder and her wet clothes clung heavily about her. She made for the church, deciding that, for now, this place of worship was a far better sanctuary than any other in London. Besides, her father would never look for her in a church, she scoffed as she pushed open the lichgate.

The door to the church was ajar. As she entered, she heard the rain beating down on the roof, resounding in a hundred tiny echoes within the stone walls. It was a plain church, whitewashed from floor to ceiling and without any signs that it had once been a place of high Catholic ritual. As she moved slowly down the aisle to the transept and altar, she asked herself if John Heminges had been part of her father's merry plan too.

She raised her eyes solemnly to Jesus at the altar – the sacrificial son. Sorrow overcame her and she fell to her knees in desperate prayer. 'Who can tell me who I am?' she moaned, collapsing on the cold flagstones.

Robert dashed out after Susanna. No one saw more clearly than he how she'd been betrayed. O, Dr Hall were the guilty one to be sure, but so were Susanna's mother. He felt a chill run up his spine. Hall hadn't been privy to the rows all those years back between his Master and Mistress Anne. Course when Susanna had Hall's proposal, Anne determined like one of them furies that her firstborn should wed as soon as the law would allow. The Master were set against it, but he gave in – Mistress Anne ranted it were as good a match as a strong-willed girl like Susanna could get. The Master hadn't seen that his wife would do anything to be rid of the daughter she'd never loved. It were like that tale of an eye for an eye. To Mistress Anne's eye, Susanna had cost her a life, so she'd cost Susanna hers. Robert frowned at himself for knowing all and saying nothing these long years. But why should he? To hurt Susanna? Or was it to protect her from what she'd always known – that Anne blamed *her* for a life of broken dreams.

Mistress Anne were why his Master'd allowed the marriage to that pompous pilgrim Hall. But, maybe it were for the family honour too, as Hall claimed. Maybe it were so the Shakespeare name wouldn't be dragged through the mire with the curse of these falling spells. It'd always niggled like a flea bite at the back of his mind that Dr Hall would one day reveal all about the Master's suffering from the Falling Evil. And if Hall threatened such a thing, how could the Master prove otherwise, with him being a doctor and such like?

Then again, maybe it was too easy to blame Mistress Anne? That the family honour and livelihood were at stake he'd never doubted, for precious few wanted to have anything to do with someone afflicted by the curse of the Falling Evil. Some said it might be catching. Others that it were the sign of the Devil on earth. But for most, it were plain terrifying to watch a grown man or woman fall under its spell and writhe and wriggle and holler and cry out and foam at the mouth like some stray dog – then minutes or an hour later be right as rain. Robert had to admit it were a mighty worrying spectacle.

Whatever the Master's reasons, facts were that Hall's marriage to Susanna were no bargain where money passed hands. Dr Hall had seen a way to become a big fish in the small Stratford pond, and had jumped in gladly, telling the Master to please bait the hook and listen to Hall's counsel or drown. But whatever the rhyming of it all, things had changed. Robert had seen since Oxford how the Master stopped thinking of the cursed family honour if it meant sacrificing Susanna to that prig of a Puritan. Someone needed to stop her pain, even if that someone was a lowly manservant like him.

By the time he sprang out of the front door, Robert heard what sounded like a great barrel tumbling down the staircase after him. He stepped aside, to see Dr John Hall catapulted through the door by Heminges's boot up his backside. The doctor landed head first in the horse trough opposite the Gatehouse. Robert hesitated – half hoping Hall would drown there and then. When Hall heaved himself up, dripping in horse spit, Robert sighed. There was precious little justice in this world.

Heminges bounded out of the Gatehouse door and ruffled away the red Moroccan leather casebook from Hall's doublet. Robert smiled. Without that little book, Dr Hall would have no proof that he'd ever tended to his Master in such and such a place at such and such a time. Now why hadn't he thought to do that himself?

Robert turned away, lighter of heart, and raced up Blackfriars in search of Susanna. Heminges had the doctor just where he belonged. Time to stop wondering on the mystery of things and bring Susanna back to them. Was he too late to persuade her that his own story of what happened back then was the truth?

Heminges slammed the Gatehouse door behind him. John Hall stood in the horse trough, spewing out brown water.

'That went well,' a deep voice said.

Hall turned to see Ben Jonson and a dark stranger ambling up to him.

'He's bound to know where the manuscripts are,' Jonson murmured to Ratsey.

Ratsey smiled. 'Only one way to find out, eh Ben?'

Ratsey nodded to his man Teacake, who was lurking in the side street. It was just the kind of opportunity he liked to call 'the proverbial gift horse.'

Robert scoured Blackfriars and the alleyways running off it, but without luck. He asked stallholders and passers-by if they'd seen a woman running without a cloak or shawl. Everyone shook their heads. As he searched the inn at the top of the road, he sighed, thinking he'd never find her.

Then the barmaid nudged him and pointed at the street through the open door. 'Is that the girl?' she asked.

Without a word of thanks Robert sprinted off. 'Susanna! Wait!'

Susanna twisted round. When she saw Robert she ran the other way. The rain had become a mist but the road was still slippery and he stumbled on the cobbles as he hurtled after her. She were younger and stronger than him, and would soon escape again if he didn't outsmart her. It should take her longer by the main road than the byways, he reckoned, so he ran down one of them, praying he'd be in time to stop her.

He mustn't fail, he couldn't fail. He felt the blood pulse in his legs as he willed himself to sprout wings like one of them Roman messenger gods the Master went on about. He sprinted through the narrow lanes, some no wider than an arm's length, at times bumbling into people but running on regardless, like some fleet-footed thief. He had to save Susanna and beg her pardon for them all. He'd never seen her so happy as these past days, and he wanted her to have that kind of joy again.

He scrambled back onto the main street just as Susanna rounded the corner. She fell into his arms before she could stop.

'Leave go of me, Robert Whatcott,' she struggled.

He wrestled with her, both of them dripping wet, his hands slipping on hers. 'Susanna, if you'll just listen to me.'

He saw some of the townspeople elbow one another to gather round them. They must have thought it was a domestic, for the men gave Robert a thumbs up and the women scowled.

'I'll leave go if you stop long enough to listen to me,' he urged her.

'Stop long enough?' she asked. 'And where do you think I might be going? To meet the King? I've no one and nowhere, Robert Whatcott, can't you see!'

He saw her eyes shine bright with tears. He took her to the corner of the street and leaned her against the wall so she could catch her breath. She were well penned in and couldn't run off easily. Then he released her measure by measure.

Susanna barely knew where to begin or what to say. 'How could I have been so witless? He wears my heart out!' she wailed. 'How could I be blinded by the beats of his betrayal?'

How indeed? Robert thought.

'And how could you not tell me? I thought we were friends.'

His heart fairly broke seeing her at the edge of despair. Tears stung his eyes. He cleared his throat to push them back. 'We *are* friends, Susanna. So, believe me when I says, it's not as your husband pretends.'

She searched his face. 'Did my father have no scruples in bartering me to that man for his potions? What kind of moral medicine did he have me take for his follies?'

He held her by the shoulders and shook her gently. 'O, Susanna, I wish my horse had the speed of your tongue. Listen, please. Your fears blind you to the truth.'

'No, Robert. I've listened enough. How could he have sent for John Hall from Oxford?'

'He didn't know about what happened in Stratford until after he wrote that letter. I should know coz I told him.'

Susanna was shocked. 'You knew about his letter to my husband?'

Robert was silent.

'And you said nothing?'

He swallowed. 'When I told all to your father, he regretted bitterly what he'd done. We laid false trails for Dr Hall in the hope he'd never think to come to London.'

She shook her head. 'My father dresses his love in many guises. Well, I'm not made for such shallow follies. I was a fool to think he could have cared for me, and I blame myself for allowing him to take me in yet again.'

Robert saw from the set of her chin and the determined, look in her eye that he had lost the battle. He hung his head in pity for them all.

'I cannot stay for the great William Shakespeare to pile his ridicule on me any longer, Robert. Tell me, what will he do when he discovers, as he surely must, that I stole his manuscripts in Oxford? No, Robert. I'm finished here – one way or the other.'

'It's not as Dr Hall told it, Susanna. You forget I were there back then.'

'O, Robert, surely you see I must leave?'

He was shocked to realise she wasn't listening.

'And you must help me.'

'As much as I'd like to, I cannot,' his voice cracked. 'It would be a hopeless betrayal.'

'O, you mean as he has betrayed me?'

Her eyes flashed at him. There was no more to say. Susanna regretted her words almost at once. Robert was the only one who cared enough to come after her, and all she could do was gnaw at his hide for it.

'Robert, surely you see I've no choice?'

He lowered his gaze. He hadn't the words or the quick wit to hold her back. Reluctantly, he nodded.

'And you must tell no one, hear?'

Though it broke his heart, he had to agree.

'Good. Then, dear friend, for you are a dear friend, go fetch my things. I've no one else to help me. Pray, don't betray me.'

He thought back to the past week, how things had changed, how his eyes and soul saw Susanna better for all the wrongs done to her and all the wrongs she were now doing and how if he agreed with her, it would be one final betrayal. And yet, if he didn't help, she'd turn and take flight, and none of them may ever see her again. Think, he urged himself. Think hard and quick like you've never done before. A plan fleeted across his throbbing brain and he grabbed hold of it. He realised it were the only way to help Susanna see beyond her prig of a husband and the past she believed in, but that'd never been.

Robert nodded once more.

Chapter 33

Heminges stood beside Richard Burbage. Both men stared down into the inner bailey courtyard at William Shakespeare gently tapping his knuckle against his lips. He'd been sitting in the same position, as if thinking, for over an hour. He was soaked through by the fine drizzle.

'Shouldn't we go to him?' Burbage asked.

Heminges stared blankly.

'John?'

Heminges looked at Burbage. 'I've no idea.'

'But we can't just … leave him in the rain?'

Heminges saw young Will step gingerly into the courtyard with Susanna's dog. The boy held out Chaos for Shakespeare to take. After a few moments, he nodded at the boy and hugged the dog tightly in his arms.

'He's with young Will,' Heminges whispered.

'But the boy's sorely pained too,' Burbage shook his head.

'That's the right time for a father to comfort his own son. Besides, young Will is also best placed to get Shakespeare to see reason and come inside.'

'And you, John? I mean, will you see reason?' Burbage asked.

Heminges shrugged. 'It's a bit late for that.'

Young Will prayed he'd find the right words to comfort his father.

'She'll be back.'

'No, she won't. The wound cuts too deep.'

Young Will shrugged. 'She'd never leave her dog.'

Shakespeare stroked Chaos.

'She'd never leave me,' young Will said.

Shakespeare looked at his son. 'What makes you think that?'

'She promised, an' unless I'm mistaken, Susanna would never break a promise.'

A thin smile crossed Shakespeare's lips. 'Sometimes we break promises without meaning to. Sometimes we're not left with a choice.'

'Like leaving me in Oxford with my mother?'

Shakespeare closed his eyes and sighed. 'Your mother wanted you to have a father around you all the time as a role model.'

Young Will smiled broadly. 'Well, she got her wish.'

Shakespeare opened his mouth to speak, but words failed him. Young Will saw the pain in his father's eyes and understood that he never wanted to abandon his children, but it happened nonetheless because of how he had to make his living. He slowly took his father's hand in his and squeezed it.

'Susanna will come back, mark my words. And all will be good again in the world,' young Will prophesised.

Heminges and Burbage watched them from above. 'Looks like young Will is weaving his own magic,' Heminges said.

'Hm. But even if he can get Will to see reason, can *we* make Will see that this game of his with his daughter must cease,' Burbage sighed.

'It's Will's gambit, and we've all agreed to let him direct the new play,' Heminges said sadly, watching Shakespeare rocking Susanna's dog back and forth like a baby.

'But it's no play worthy of the name 'Shakespeare,' John. This is real, and it's turned sour as vinegared mustard. Admit that at least?'

'Where's Henry?' Heminges asked, ignoring Burbage's question. 'I have an idea.'

'He's gone to find Robert.'

'And Nathan?'

'Gone with Henry.' Burbage shook his head. 'All our planning ... Will's planning I should say ... has turned to dust.'

Heminges shrugged. 'Only time can tell us that.'

A small post-chaise hurtled through the open countryside, heading due west, its driver whipping his horses repeatedly and cursing their late departure from the bedevilled borough of Blackfriars. He wiped his lips with the back of his hand, and flicked his reins. They had another hour or so of daylight, and would have to stop short of their destination if he couldn't make up for lost time.

He mouthed toothlessly, mocking the object of his derision. 'O, tarry! Tarry please? says the little woman. What for, says I? For the expectation of plenty, says she ... O, tarry! Tarry, driver please! Wait for my man to come with my things, for I shall die of cold in this place without them, says she. Die of cold? Puh!'

The driver spat over his shoulder to ward off some evil spirit and flicked the reins at the horses again.

'Too cold for hell, says I, why hell is other people! So she looks up all simpering like at me and places a shilling in me palm. So I tarries – and now we'll have Beelzebub riding on our backsides if we don't get to Windsor before nightfall!' The driver spat over his shoulder again and cried out to the horses cracking the reins harder, 'You sluggard jades! Make haste! Put the wind to shame!'

Susanna heard his cries from within the carriage and winced. Those horses were being whipped because of her. Why had Robert taken so long? Surely he hadn't betrayed her? When she searched his face for the truth, she'd no time to tell. The coach driver had bundled her into the coach and whisked them away. Still, that was over an hour ago. Surely if Robert had said something, she couldn't have escaped this far without her father trying to stop her? She saw the lengthening shadows playing in patchwork patterns through the tree branches. The child within half wished that Shakespeare would try to stop her. At least it would show he cared. But if she were true to herself, she had to admit that John Heminges's indifference stung as much as her father's lies.

Susanna looked glass-faced at the two men sitting opposite. Puritans, she smirked, one fat and young, the other old and nought but skin and skeleton. The two of them could be twins dressed with their drab grey overcoats and breeches and their buckled boots shined to within an inch of their lives. They mirrored each other in their mannerisms too. The first thing they did when they climbed aboard the coach was to spit and polish their boots till they could see their faces reflected. Not the sort who would have thought kindly towards her need to have her belongings and make them all late for the first stop beyond London.

She looked to the women seated beside her. The one in the middle was young and smelled of oysters. The oyster-seller seemed sullen, her mouth turned down like a haddock's. The older woman by the window was a good housewife with a confident smile, sturdy and ready to defend her corner if needs be. Both balanced baskets of food on their laps. Just then, they hit a rut in the road and Susanna grabbed the side of the carriage. They all bounced up in the air and crashed down again.

'Dear Lord!' the young, fat Puritan exclaimed.

'The Lord has nothing to do with it!' the old skin and skeleton one replied. 'I'll not have you use the Lord's name to swear lustily, especially before these ladies!'

The young, fat Puritan tipped his hat and bobbed his head up and down.

The good housewife narrowed her eyes at them, biting her tongue.

Susanna looked out of the open window at London receding in the mist. As she rocked from side to side with the motion of the carriage, she reflected back to that first fateful day in Stratford-upon-Avon and how it had begun much like any other. How extraordinary that things turned out as they have, she mused. Who would have thought that she would have seen her father's world better? Who would have said that she'd feel an unquenchable ache in her gut for an actor and dear friend of her father's?

She asked herself if she was unhappy that she had declared her independence from her husband and her life as she knew it. She stared blankly out and thought of John Heminges the first time he clapped eyes on her, and his suppressed look of shock, and her avowal of all her woes to her father when he feigned illness to get her to tell him all and how she had run off then to find Jonson fiddling with the manuscripts. Then she recalled on the road how Robert – dear Robert – had thought she might kill him when she began waving that pistol around between him and the ruffler. And she thought how these last days had made her feel so alive. Then, she remembered today and her husband and how her new enlivened world had shattered. What would happen next? Where was she running to now?

Will Davenant scratched his head. 'Want to play cards?' he asked.

Shakespeare shook his head. 'You cheat.'

'Dice?'

Shakespeare stared down at the ground, stroking Chaos. 'Like I said, you cheat.'

'I don't like repeating myself, but you're a bad listener. *She'll be back, you mark my words,*' young Will said, this time with an unconvincing smile.

It seemed forever before Shakespeare lifted his head and looked him squarely in the eye. 'Why?'

The boy beamed at his father. 'Coz she promised, coz we're here, and coz she loves us.'

Shakespeare looked at him as if he had said something confusing.

'Come. Let's go inside and get spruced up for her,' Will went on. 'I'll bet she'll be back in time for dinner.'

'Will?' a lady's voice called out.

Shakespeare and the boy both raised their eyes. Mary Countess of Pembroke stood in the archway, flanked by her ladies-in-waiting. The King's Men and Robert stood behind them ready to ride out, their horses stamping at the ground in the road beyond.

'Mary ...' Shakespeare's voice trailed off.

She stretched out her arms. 'Come, let's sit by the fire and talk of innocent things, as we always promised each other we'd do again.'

He stood up, supported by Will, and shambled towards the Gatehouse door. The Countess took his other arm and followed, nodding away her ladies. 'Besides, I've brought you some gems for your jewelled cloak you once spoke about.'

Heminges, Burbage, Condell, Nathan and Robert looked on after them.

'Will they be safe with all of us gone?' Condell asked.

Heminges nodded. 'Mary has arranged everything. Come, let's be off.'

Robert urged them on. 'I'll stay to look after the Master. You've no time to lose, gentlemen.'

Heminges smiled weakly. 'We shall prevail,' he said.

'Hurry,' Robert begged.

Heminges motioned for the others to mount up their horses. As Robert watched the four King's Men ride out, he were less sure than Master Heminges, but then, he knew Susanna and his Master better than most.

The Countess of Pembroke stood to the side, watching Robert minister to Shakespeare. Tiny wrinkles of grave concern were etched on her face.

'Where's that knave, the *good* Dr Hall?' Shakespeare asked as Robert settled him into the armchair in front of the fire.

'Gone, forever, Master. His casebook on you has been destroyed,' Robert replied.

'Gone? And Susanna? Where's she gone? Where, tell me that?'

Robert cleared his throat and went to fetch another blanket. What could he say? The Countess followed him with her keen eye.

'They've gone to fetch Susanna back, Will,' she said reassuringly.

Shakespeare looked up at her with wounded eyes.

'I thought him a man of means, a man of faith. I thought she would be content ... that he'd care for her. How was I to know he'd twist and turn my words to another meaning and stab me with them as a knife in the back?'

'I know, Will,' the Countess said, kneeling beside him. 'But she's not had a life well-lived, has she? First her mother, then her husband?'

Shakespeare shook his head, fixing her with his glistening eyes. 'She feels only pain,' he muttered.

'She sees only what suits her burden. That means, dear heart, that blaming you fits like those jewelled gloves you made for me in our salad days.'

He reached out to touch her face. 'Her burden is mine. Her burden   is   me.'

Robert walked over to them, clutching another blanket. He feared Shakespeare would catch his death from sitting in the rain. But more than that, he feared that no one but his Master could tell Susanna the truth – a truth she would not be disposed to believe now that Dr Hall had puked his poison. He had to tell the Master what he thought, for he'd seen her at that church and felt the fear in her heart.

'Forgive me please, Master Shakespeare, Countess, but Susanna cares not for your sorrows or penance. She lacks the will to trust you. And after what Dr Hall said, she feels like she's dancing in treacle.'

Shakespeare craned his neck to see him better. After several moments, he nodded. 'I've paid too dearly for my follies. O, Robert, what have I done?'

Robert looked to the Countess. With a nod, she urged him to continue to speak.

'You begot her, bred her and loved her, Master. Since Oxford, you tried to make amends in the ways you thought best.'

> With a heart-wrenching sigh more akin to a groan, Shakespeare cried, 'I abandoned her.'

The sun was sinking rapidly in the west. Susanna felt the eyes of her fellow passengers bore into her. The fat Puritan piped up, 'Well, if some of us had been ready to travel, we'd be in Windsor by now!'

She narrowed her eyes into slits and was about to give him a proper fig when suddenly the driver called out 'Woah!' at the horses to slow down. The coach lurched to a stop. The Puritans latched onto one another, the women grasped at the walls of the carriage. Then a pistol shot rang out. The Puritans shrieked in panic. The women grew all wide-eyed, their heads trembling in terror.

From his bench above them, the driver called out, 'Everyone out, with your hands held high! We're being robbed!'

'O, not again,' Susanna muttered.

The Puritans, gentlemen that they were, allowed the oyster-seller and the good housewife out of the carriage first. They motioned for Susanna to go next, but she shook her head.

'But we insist,' the fat one said. 'Ladies first.'

'I've been robbed twice in the last week, so I know the way it works,' she said with a flinty look. 'You two first.'

'I knew she was a bad omen!' he complained as his skin and skeleton companion pushed him through the carriage door.

Susanna cast a withering look at the skinny one, as he scurried out.

'Is that all?' she heard a muffled voice ask.

'There's the "Tarry Please Lady" to come too,' the driver bellowed helpfully.

That was her. She stepped down from the carriage.

'Hands held high!' the driver shouted at her.

Susanna saw the others with their hands up, so she did the same. The highwaymen stood with their backs to the setting sun and she couldn't see their faces.

'Is that it?' the head highwayman asked again as he dismounted and walked towards them.

'Aye,' the driver replied, his voice cracking.

The highwayman walked closer to Susanna as if she were the main object of his robbery. Still, she couldn't see his face, blinded as she was by the low-slung sun. The others remained mounted and silent as he turned, as if in slow motion, to the north. His greying curly hair and his broad shoulders suddenly became familiar to her. She put her hand up to shield her eyes. There, mounted before her were Nathan Field, Richard Burbage and Henry Condell. She turned round to the first man, and saw that it was John Heminges. Her heart raced. They had come to fetch her after all.

But they couldn't just dance back into her life, as if nothing had happened. She tried to climb back into the carriage, but Heminges held her by the arm.

'Leave me be, John.'

He pulled her gently from the carriage step and turned her round to face him.

'Pray, let me go.'

He bent down, nearly touching her cheek with his lips. 'I've come to beg you to return home with us,' he whispered.

'But it's not my home. I have no home, John.'

'Then what do you have to lose? Why flee? Stay. Please.'

Susanna wiped away her tears with her free hand. 'Why do you torture me so? You know, it's not where I flee to, it's where I flee from!'

He tugged tenderly at her arm and gestured towards the King's Men.

'*We* wish you to stay, Susanna.'

She stared at Burbage, Condell and Nathan.

Heminges leaned in closely again and whispered, '*I* wish you to stay. You see, I love you.' He let go of her arm, and waited.

Susanna gazed deeply into his cornflower-blue eyes. She saw immense pain. Did he fear he would lose her? Or was he bringing her back for her father?

Just then, another group of riders rode out of the woods. All heads turned towards the incoming horsemen.

'I don't believe it,' Susanna murmured under her breath.

Ratsey was descending on them with his unlikely mob, Teacake, Fang and Snout. Armed with pistols, daggers and halberds, they'd come to transact their nefarious business. Ratsey pulled on the reins of his horse and pointed his pistol.

'Ah, John, I see you found our prize first!' He flashed a gleaming white smile at Heminges before nodding to the other King's Men.

Ratsey dismounted and doffed his hat to Susanna. 'And you, my worthy opponent, we meet again.' He sauntered towards her. 'Though I didn't know the last time we met that you were Will Shakespeare's daughter. You should've said.'

She felt her eyes grow wide glancing from Ratsey and his men to her father's friends. 'You know each other?' she heard herself ask.

Heminges cast an ashamed look at Ratsey. 'It's a long story, but the short answer is yes. The Countess intervened with him on our behalf.'

She stood motionless, feeling utterly brain-addled.

Ratsey smiled at her. 'Let's just say I'm called upon every now and again by the great and the good of the land for my special services.'

Susanna was speechless.

'I see you are afeared,' he shook his head with feigned sympathy. 'Have none.' He waved at his men to dismount. 'Well, what's it to be, Mistress?' Ratsey asked. 'Will you accompany the King's Men or mine?'

Chapter 34

Susanna looked at the Puritans, the post-chaise driver, the oyster-seller and the good housewife. They all gawped back at her in amazement. She smiled back, truly no less surprised than they were. How odd, she thought, that Ratsey should be the one to force her make up her mind to return to Blackfriars. She mounted up behind Heminges and laced her hands around his waist. He motioned to the others, and spurred his horse to move on.

Of course, she knew Ratsey's immediate payment would be to make the most of this golden opportunity, though he would find his takings from the carriage rather slim. Still, the oddest part of the whole saga of her journey to London was that Ratsey had been seeking the manuscripts all along. It seemed when he'd robbed her on the road to Oxford, he'd been hired by Jonson. Something about keeping her father from publishing his plays first and stealing Jonson's very air. Yet once the Countess worked her magic on Ratsey and told him straight up what all the fuss was about, Ratsey simply switched sides – as any highwayman might do – sniffing more gold on Shakespeare's side of the deal. Besides, Ratsey professed, he liked her father's plays better.

All the way back to London, Susanna felt their horses weren't speeding fast enough to reach her father so she could confess her own sins. At the same time, she hoped they'd slow up some so she could hug Heminges tighter and feel the warmth of his body next to hers. He loved her, and had come to claim her as his own.

Susanna's mind was at the same time settled and confused. From what Condell had said, her husband would bother them no more. How or why this came to be, she didn't care ... only that it was so. And Burbage insisted to her that Shakespeare disavowed any bargain had occurred before she was married, as Hall claimed. Besides, Heminges chimed in, he couldn't imagine Shakespeare forcing her to marry such a humourless Puritan for any reason, that is unless he believed Hall would truly care for her.

Susanna closed her eyes and allowed the wind to cool her overheated mind. She wanted to believe them, but a lifetime of mistrust had grown up between her and her father. Still, she had to admit that if her husband had coloured the truth to suit his own ends then her father was outrageously maligned. She wouldn't put it past her husband to hold her father to ransom over his falling sickness – as a doctor his medical knowledge certainly gave him untold power over the family. O, if she could only be a spy of time and hark back to what her father had truly said or intended! If only she could be sure he meant her no dishonour or harm.

The daughter's speeches from the beginning of *The Tempest* suddenly sprang into her mind: *you have often begun to tell me what I am, but stopped, and left me to a bootless inquisition ... your tale, sir, would cure deafness* ... And just as suddenly, all was clear. Shakespeare had repented long ago. He had made the daughters in his plays objects of love, grievous disappointment or hate. They were never indifferent creatures. He had recreated most of the dark twisting alleyways that took families in their winters of discontent onto tortuous journeys through leafless forests. Shakespeare had seen what he'd done to her, her mother and sister long before she'd come to London. His work was his repentance. Without her needing to teach him, he'd learned backhanded lessons about the turmoil he'd created. Had he written to her asking for forgiveness in each line that spoke of a father who had hoped for more, but given less? Yet, why hadn't he wanted her to see his life's apology performed for all his sins and secret loves until after his death? And did he believe his end was near?

'Hurry, John,' she called out. 'I must beg my father's forgiveness yet again!'

Chapter 35

The daily clatter of the city passed virtually unnoticed at the Gatehouse. In the street below the hawkers were already busy at their work, crying out 'A NEW PLAY BY WILLIAM SHAKESPEARE!' Passers-by grabbed at the playbills, even if they weren't readers, as if these papers were some sort of treasure map to be hoarded and kept away from others. There was little doubt, as they scurried to finish their shopping, that many would try to squeeze into the Tabard Inn. Still, most knew the Tabard was more intimate than Blackfriars Theatre or The Rose or The Globe, and so they rushed through their chores, not to be turned away.

From the window embrasure, the Countess saw their excitement and sighed. She glanced over her shoulder at Shakespeare and whispered, 'You are the brightest light in my life, my dear friend, and always will be.'

'How can I thank you?' he replied.

'By succeeding, as always.'

'I'll do my best, Mary. Ready?'

Shakespeare held out his arm for the Countess and together they walked slowly from the great hall.

Susanna's fingers ached as if she'd been sewing for weeks, she reflected as she re-threaded the needle. The costumes needed updating, John had told them, and so she volunteered to change the ruff collars from the old Queen's day to the long, flat ones in fashion now. She'd also repaired the jewelled cloak. It was the least she could do. There was a knock at her open bedroom door.

She looked up to see Robert smiling at her.

'Just finishing now,' she mumbled, taking the thread between her teeth to break it. 'There.' She held up the doublet. 'What do you think, Robert?'

'It will do very nicely,' he said. 'I'll send the carter round to the Tabard with these whilst you get ready. I'll be waiting downstairs in the carriage.'

The Tabard's innkeeper stood at the archway taking coins from the expectant groundlings. Further along, his good wife hawked cushions for tuppence more to those who were seated on benches, but she had few takers. Once inside the inn yard, a buxom barmaid offered the expectant crowd the Tabard's finest small – very small – ale which foamed like Thames water. A shabby old man took a swig and spat it out. 'That's cow's piss!' he cried, scraping his tongue against his teeth.

The barmaid smiled. 'O, so you've drunk cow piss before?'

His neighbours guffawed.

'I've been here afore for plays,' the old man croaked back at her, 'an' there's never been a cow pissed in yer ale.'

The innkeeper's wife sidled up to him, hands on her ample hips. 'It's been watered down on the orders of the King's Men. They don't want no drunken brawling for this play, hear?'

Henry Condell watched from their tire room above and shook his head. 'This does not auger well ...'

Burbage slapped him on the back. 'You would say that, Henry, wouldn't you?'

***

Robert and Susanna sat in nervous anticipation, each looking out of the window as the hackney carriage hurtled along the embankment of the Thames. These last days had blurred together, just like the people and places they now passed. She thought back to her pleading for her father's forgiveness, owning up to stealing the manuscripts in a moment of pique and throwing herself on his mercy. He replied that it was from her that mercy should be begged, and even if he never found his manuscripts again, he had won a far greater prize in the love of his daughter. His understanding made her shame the greater, but neither he nor the King's Men sought to blame her for all that had happened.

She thought back to another special moment as she'd changed her clothes before leaving for the playhouse. Looking at herself in the mirror in her bedroom, she felt she should pinch herself black and blue to count her blessings. The Countess smiled sweetly at her reflection. 'It suits you,' the Countess purred.

The last time she'd worn the Rosaline gown Susanna had felt like an interloper. Nathan had wanted to grab it off her. Today, she was one of them.

'You are beautiful, Susanna,' the Countess said, 'just as beautiful as your father used to tell me.'

'How can I thank you for all you've done? For helping him – me – even for persuading Ratsey–'

'That's odd. Your father asked me the same thing,' the Countess mused. 'I've done nothing. We all have our parts to play. I shall play mine well today, as shall you.'

Susanna gazed out the window at the people scurrying on the pavement. They all seemed to be heading in the same direction as the carriage. Surely they couldn't *all* be going to the Tabard for the play? Just then Susanna spied a little girl with a bright red cloak rolling her hoop down the street pursued by a pig and a dog. Her father had once brought her back a bright red cloak just like the one little girl wore, so very many years ago. The first time she'd put that cloak on, she promised herself she'd see her father perform one day. And now, that promise was about to come true.

Robert peeked at Susanna as they rocked with the motion of the carriage. How quiet and still she were. Then he smiled. Susanna had blossomed into the woman he'd always hoped she'd be in a matter of days.

Inside the Gatehouse, the only sounds that could be heard were the ticking of the wall clock and the murmur of the horses and people rising like a mist from the streets below. Suddenly, there was a metallic click and a creaking of the front hall door as it opened a crack. A tall, shadowy figure stood for a moment in the doorway, listening. The hush within was at once oppressive and welcoming. His skin bristled with goose-bumps. It was now or never. And so he entered.

Philip the wherryman sloped into the great hall. 'It's not like I'm stealing anything,' he muttered. He looked around at the hammer-beamed ceiling, the linen-fold panelling and the paintings on the walls, awestruck. 'Nope. I'm just breaking into the home of greatness to return what's rightfully Shakespeare's,' he whispered.

Philip delved into his doublet and took out the oilskin that protected his treasure. He deftly unwrapped his prized package. Gazing at it one last time, he pressed his lips to it along with a letter addressed to Master Shakespeare, and placed it on the table.

'Just think Philip, me boy – no more wherries, no more lying to family and friends in the country that you're already a great playmaker. The name of Philip Massinger will figure amongst the greats in the theatre alongside Master William Shakespeare. Once he reads this, he's sure to reward you for your masterpiece,' Philip murmured as he tiptoed back to the door.

Robert blinked, agog. It seemed that every orange seller, cutpurse, bawdy basket and Winchester goose in the capital were pressing forward to see the last of Shakespeare's plays. Their carriage slowed as they crossed London Bridge, then suddenly, lurched to a stop. Robert and Susanna exchanged worried glances.

'Surely not again …?' Susanna sighed, leaving the rest of her sentence unspoken.

Robert poked his head out the window and heard laughter. Then a booming voice called out above the crowd, 'The playhouse is the Devil's whore!'

Robert inched his head back in. 'Puritans,' he shrugged.

Puritans, she mused. How could she have been so idiotic to have married one? Did she truly hold herself in such little worth?

Someone from the crowd cried out, 'Better the whore you know and love than the one who promises you hellfire and damnation!' Shrieks of laughter rose above the Puritan's reply, and by the time Susanna peered out of her window, the preacher was borne away plaintively on the shoulders of some men. Once more, the carriage lurched forward.

As Susanna and Robert reached the Southwark end of London Bridge, inside the Tabard's tire room, the King's Men and Will Davenant stood looking down at the crowd. Outwardly they were silent. Inwardly, they were a tempest of emotions.

Nathan, dressed as a girl, looked at the boy. 'Young Will?' Will turned.

'You'll be just fine. The first play is always the hardest.'

'Thanks, Nathan,' the boy replied.

Henry Condell repeated his calming phrase over and over. 'The play's the thing,' he chanted to himself. 'This play is the thing. Not as good a thing as plays past, but a noble thing all the same. The play is the thing, and from it … all will be good again in the world.'

'Stop muttering', Richard Burbage hissed at him. 'You know, Henry, one day, your nerves will be the death of me!'

Burbage rolled his shoulders back and moved his head from side to side. 'Breathe deeply in, breathe deeply out. Concentrate on your lines … though why I'm not playing the lead is quite beyond me. It's what the audience expects, and it will be a grave disappointment to them all. Alas, it's Will's casting wish, and I'll not go against him or kick up a fuss – this time.'

John Heminges peered out at the inn yard filling up. There were shouts for 'more ale' and laughter from the expectant audience above the apple-sellers' and oyster-sellers' cries.

'They say it will be a full house, with standing room sold outside, too,' Shakespeare said, placing his hand on Heminges's shoulder. 'Ready, John?'

Heminges looked at his friend. 'As I'll ever be, Will. Are you sure you want to do it this way?'

'It's the only way,' Shakespeare replied solemnly.

Robert and Susanna squeezed by other spectators to take their seats, reserved for them by the King's Men in the centre gallery opposite the stage. She gaped at the crowd, their excitement burrowing into her soul. The audience waited restlessly, some dicing, others playing cards. London's underworld of bawdy baskets and Winchester geese brushed shoulders with its gentlemen ushers and nobility. Above the murmur repeatedly rose the question 'Is this *really* Shakespeare's last play?' Various answers floated to her ears. 'Can't be,' said one. 'Heard he was poorly,' said another. 'Shakespeare will write from beyond the grave,' a groundling proclaimed. So this is what her father faced each moment of his waking life … the adoration of his public. No wonder he left Stratford. It was still incredible to her how loved he was, and how people truly cared about him and his work. The last of the audience shuffled in. Susanna saw Agnes Henslowe with her Oriental carpet-cloak. She smiled recalling the deal her father had brokered with Agnes to calm her ruffled feathers. If he decided to publish, Agnes would receive the first sixpence earned on publication of the plays.

Further along was the extraordinary Tronco. Even Ratsey and his men Teacake, Snout and Fang were there, lurking by the main entrance. That's when she saw Jonson enter like some bear with a toothache. Ratsey exchanged a few words with him before Jonson growled something and skulked off to take his seat. The highwaymen followed. Ratsey spotted Susanna in the crowd and doffed his hat with a grin.

Moments later Will Davenant entered stage left, carrying a huge wooden rod. The roar of the crowd died down until it was a hush. Susanna gazed about her. She knew no more about the play than they did and was just as excited as they were. Her father's last play would be her first.

Will banged his rod three times on the floor to demand silence. The audience's cries rose in whoops and hollers.

Shakespeare walked on and stood centre stage, slowly turning his head to everyone in the audience and holding them with the sheer magnetism of his eyes. The jewelled cloak was stretched behind him, representing the night sky. Susanna glanced at Robert, who judging by his face, was just as surprised as she was. When she looked back at her father, she saw he was gazing up at her. He raised his arms high, commanding the entire playhouse to silence. He was instantly obeyed. In his richest, most velvet of voices, he began:

'The last of my plays I give you this day

Breathes magic in a world where you are tossed

Here the wild waters and tumbledown skies of a shipwrecked life

Give way to a tale that is rarely told.'

He paused, sucking his audience into his world like a vortex.

'An abandoned child, and her father lost,' he continued.

'Search their souls and stars, to see their lives better at any cost

That they may find the truest gift of love.'

He raised his eyes to Susanna once again. They shone like stars. He mouthed the word 'Sorry' before continuing.

'It is a tale of love lost and perhaps never found, of an honest maiden tossed upon a stormy sea. It is a tale told by an idiot, her dishonest father, who had made the way rutted for her, for he never wished her to see him as he really was. Yet through her strong heart and her devotion, he becomes deserving of her love.'

The audience erupted into wild applause. Shakespeare took his bow, and as he straightened he lifted his watery eyes to Susanna again.

A girl actor entered stage right as Shakespeare faded off stage to the left. As she came on, the crowd gasped. The King's Men had flouted all the laws by daring to use a real girl. Susanna had never seen her before, and how the audience marvelled at their audacity and pluck with their swooning sighs.

Silently, the girl tossed some playwrights' scripts onto the hearth and went to another part of the stage, where she began to read. Her mother, played by Nathan, entered the room and scolded her. Then there was a knock at the door and a rider appeared. The girl actor raised her eyes, and saw Richard Burbage, in the guise of Robert, walk past her and take a letter from the rider.

Susanna felt her pulse quicken.

Her Mother read the letter aloud, 'You must bring the medicines and manuscripts to Shakespeare in Oxford? The medicines yes, the manuscripts – never!'

The girl, named Rosaline, cried out, 'Mother, please!'

Then her mother locked away the plays in a cupboard, dropping the key down her bodice. Burbage and Nathan exited stage right.

Susanna gasped involuntarily. So this girl actor was *her* ... not some Rosaline. She turned to Robert but saw he was absorbed in the play.

Suddenly, Henry Condell glowered onto the stage, crying out at the girl, 'You are my chattel woman! What in the Lord's name are you doing?'

The girl cowered. 'I must away husband, for our manservant Goodfellow, is begged to bring your medicines to Oxford.'

Susanna's vision blurred. How odd that after all that had come to pass, she could still feel her mother's hatred searing her skin that fateful morning. Yet she no longer feared her husband. As her story played out, other memories surged on like a rolling tide.

'Master Shakespeare!' Will Davenant, playing himself, said as he shook the sleeping John Heminges who played Shakespeare. 'It's as you hoped! Robert has come with your medicines and manuscripts!'

'And Susanna?' he enquired. Will nodded happily.

He raised his eyes to the heavens and cried out, 'Finally. It worked, Will. D'you hear? It worked! She's come to Oxford!'

Susanna watched, thinking that the words must be wrong. This wasn't her story. Her father hadn't expected her to come to Oxford, had he?

By the time she looked back at the stage, the girl actor was sobbing on Heminges's chest.

'My mother, my sister Judith and my husband hate me, Father. They think I'm a person of no worth. And why? Because I read and love your plays. I read them so I can be near you again. Sometimes I fancy I'm Ophelia, at others, Cordelia …'

'But never a Juliet,' Heminges as Shakespeare sighed.

The audience gasped. Susanna looked around to see how everyone present worried for her and seemed to want her to succeed somehow in her cock-eyed quest. She suddenly felt humbled.

She recalled that cool dawn like a sweet kiss on her skin as she and Robert headed downriver towards Oxford. How they floated in that tiny boat. How she squinted, she recalled, at her father's margin notes littering his manuscript pages. In *Love's Labour's Lost* he had scribbled 'make Rosaline more like Susanna' several times. In *A Midsummer Night's Dream* next to Titania's name he wrote 'Susanna!' *Othello* carried the mention next to Desdemona's name 'make her loyal and loving despite the jealousy. Make her Susanna.' Shakespeare had given heroine after heroine character traits he attributed to her be they true or false. How she ached at the devastating beauty of each word that made up every line of her father's plays. Then she saw re-enacted before her, on the river journey to London itself, John Heminges reciting Enobarbus's speech about Cleopatra.

Susanna flashed her mind back to the loss of the manuscripts, to that morning in the prop room at the Gatehouse when she discovered they were gone. How easily her father had forgiven her for her sins, though she was undeserving.

Suddenly, Heminges as Shakespeare cried out,

> All the world's a stage,
> And all the men and women merely players;
> They have their exits and their entrances,

And one man in his time plays many parts.

He looked directly at Susanna in the centre of the gallery. His speech was not only to her, but for her:

You do look, my daughter,

In a movèd sort, but know this …

You are loved. You have always been loved.

Your home has been here.

H clutched at his heart. Without giving the audience a chance to react, he continued:

As the light fades from my eyes,

I was moved to prove this to you,

To hold you to me in the only way I know,

To make you a play within our play of life.

Murmurs rose from the spectators. Susanna looked around perplexed, then her father entered the stage from the left. As he came on, Heminges bowed out. But instead of addressing his beloved audience, Shakespeare seemed only to have eyes for her:

Whilst all our yesterdays have lit the fools the ways to dusty deaths,

The poorest death of all is a lingering one, to die unloved.

We players lead strange lives, where those we hold dearest, come last.

Where we crave public plaudits, and return to cold and empty homes.

As the light dims in my eyes, I avowed to lay a trap,

So I may die loved by you.

To die a father to the daughter who never knew she was Rosaline, Titania, Viola, Desdemona, Ophelia and many more, all rolled into one …

But never a Juliet.

And I am to blame.

The audience sighed like a bellows. These were names they all knew and loved. Whilst they seemed to understand his meaning, Susanna became more puzzled. Tears blinded her to John Heminges approaching her through the audience, carrying the large leather satchel.

Shakespeare, however, saw everything. He stepped forward to the front of the stage and knelt as a penitent:

I am the actor who feigned his own illness, at times, to bring you closer before

Death claimed me. I am the man who had a lifetime of wrongs to right. I am the father who prayed you would read my plays and who was so undeserving of your praise and love. I have plotted and twisted like a fish on a hook at every turn, but never expected your many kindnesses, or merited them. How could I have hoped you'd love my work as the sweet dew from heaven, or that you'd need to hold them tightly, ever so close to you? It pained me when you tried to return them, so I had to stop you. For they, and all I have become that is good, belong to you.

Susanna gasped. What was he saying? From the corner of her eye, she saw the audience parting for Heminges as he approached her. Somehow, he was holding the satchel.

Shakespeare called out to her:

I see I have confused you … be not dismayed,
For succour is at hand.
My words have been your loves, your laughs
And the root of your sorrows.
My words are all I have to give,
And I gratefully give them all to thee.

Heminges stood next to Susanna, the flame of love burning brightly in his eyes. He stretched out his arms, handing the satchel to her. Without a word, still confused, Susanna opened it. Her father's manuscripts were inside.

Shakespeare whispered from the stage, 'Susanna.'

She clutched the satchel to her chest and smiled at Heminges through her tears. He held her to him and together they turned towards Shakespeare.

For the first time since his second entry, he addressed to the audience.

> Be not dismayed friends, for you are witnesses
> to a father's love letter to his long-lost daughter.
> You are the bleary-eyed jury of his gift of love.
> So be of good cheer and leave here to love those you

cherish,

> And all shall be revealed in your hearts.

Susanna looked around her, stunned to see tears streaking the audience's faces. She turned to her father, spellbound.

He nodded to her and concluded:

> And so our revels now are ended. These our actors,
> As I foretold you, were all spirits and are melted into

air, thin air.

> And, like the baseless fabric of this vision,
> The cloud-capped towers, the gorgeous palaces,
> The solemn temples, the great globe itself,
> All which it inherit, shall dissolve,
> And, like this insubstantial pageant faded,
> Leave not a rack behind.
> We are such stuff
> As dreams are made on.

The beacon Will Davenant held aloft was extinguished and the inn yard plunged into an umbered night. The audience remained still, waiting. Moments later, dozens of ushers lit the tapers around the Tabard's yard to reveal the evening's cast assembled together onstage for their bows. The audience was in a trance, unable to move, hoping for more. A groundling looked from side to side, and decided that the play must be over and began to clap. Soon he was joined by rapturous applause and cheers.

As the theatre erupted in pure joy with hats tossed in the air, Heminges held Susanna away from him and knelt down, just as her father had done on the stage. The actors on stage accepted their plaudits with mild confusion. Condell leaned into Burbage and asked above the din, 'What's going on?'

Burbage could only shrug. 'You wouldn't understand, Henry… It's what they call a happy ending.'

'Huh?'

'Just dance your jig, Henry.'

John Heminges spoke softly as the spectators clapped and danced about them. He had his own gift for Susanna, words of love just for her:

'Speak but only one word to me, and I am satisfied.

Say you can love me, pronounce it faithfully.

If love be blind, let it shine tonight

if love be bold, forgive me, love me, hold me to you,

forget all hollow perjuries, and hurt not the lover who vows to cherish,

Your wit, your beauty, your heart and mind,

O, Rosaline, please say you're mine.

Susanna, the time for running and looking away has long passed.'

She reached up to Heminges's cheek, touching it gently with her fingertips. 'We that are lovers run into strange capers,' Susanna breathed in his ear. 'Though we are star-crossed, and storm-tossed, I love you and am yours.'

Susanna folded herself into his arms and they embraced, whilst the audience and the players of the Tabard played on.

Chapter 36

The raucous music at the Tabard Inn had fallen silent, their revels ended. Yet Susanna knew she must face one last, crucial hurdle, she told herself as she walked back into the seemingly empty inn yard.

Sitting centre stage in a tattered armchair was her father. Robert, ever-faithful Robert, stood by his side. Her footsteps were no louder than a sparrow's hopping along a branch, but Robert heard them nonetheless. He looked up at her, his eyes glistening as he laid a hand on Shakespeare's shoulder. His Master slowly raised his head and looked lovingly at him.

'Thank you, dear friend, for all you've done,' Shakespeare said.

Robert shut his eyes for a moment, overcome. Then he walked towards Susanna, and with a pleading eye, he said, 'Forgive me?'

She smiled. 'What's there to forgive? That my ears were deaf to your entreaties?'

He reached out his fingers to hers and gently brushed them.

'I've loved you as my own daughter, so allow me this last advice. Be gentle with him. He fears you were displeased by his words.'

Before Susanna could answer, Robert ambled off.

She looked at her father. His eyes widened with wondrous surprise at her approach. She knelt beside his armchair and said, 'I see love in your tired eyes, Father.'

He took her hand in his. 'I'm sorry, Susanna. I wanted you to think I was in health, that I wasn't dying when the play ended. Alas, I was acting so well, that I fooled myself.'

'Father …'

He took a jagged breath, trying to hold back his own sorrow. 'I wish I could write us a different ending.'

'Father, please …'

He shook his head. 'This is life, with its laughter, sorrows and pain.'

'Why didn't you tell me you knew all along?'

'Knowing and hoping are two different things. Why did you think I sent you to pack up the costumes in Oxford? It was meant to give you inspiration – for you to see yourself as I do. For you to see better how beautiful you are – outside as well as in–'

'And for me to hide the manuscripts in the clothes chest?'

Shakespeare smiled.

'Why the elaborate game?' she asked.

'Unless I apologised for all the world to hear, I feared you would have taken flight again. Worse, you would have hated me forever. So, I made your adventure mine as well. All I want is for us to enjoy whatever time we have left together, with you knowing beyond all doubt that I love you, and always have.'

'Whatever time we have, it will be well-lived and better-loved.' Susanna stood and hugged her father to her. He buried his head in her skirts like a schoolboy unwilling to be parted from his mother, and hugged her back. It might have been minutes or an eternity before he pushed her away so that he could look into her eyes.

'Forget your husband. Don't fret away one second on what others may think. Go to Heminges. Profess your love. Love each other now and into a long future. Please forgive me, I've been foolish.'

She deep-searched his face, engraving it in her mind's eye, for the times when he would no longer be with her. 'Father, when thou dost ask me blessing, I'll kneel down, and ask of thee forgiveness: so we'll live, and pray, and sing, and tell old tales, and laugh at gilded butterflies...'

Susanna knelt down at her father's side once again. She broke into sobs as she laid her head on his lap. Slowly, Shakespeare rested his hand on her head as if in blessing, and smiled.

Epilogue 1618

Susanna breathed in the summer breeze. Could there ever be anything more beautiful than an English summer in the countryside? She flicked the reins of the chestnut mare drawing her rickety cart and thought back over the previous years. She smiled. As the cart wended its way through the verdant valley, the clatter of stage scenery, musical instruments and racks of costumes rang out.

Susanna and her father enjoyed a wondrous year together in Stratford, before his passing in 1616. In that year, her mother and father talked often of their good days and bad. In the end, Anne Shakespeare doted on her husband as if he'd never left home. Her penance, she said, for all the anger and wrongs she'd done him was to forgo her dower's portion, save for their second-best bed – their marriage bed – that she would sleep in and dream on until her own passing. 'Course Susanna never wanted her to give away such riches, and so she pretended that her home was now with her mother, hoping those gossiping Stratford tongues would never be the wiser. Anne didn't care, she claimed, for she'd accepted her part in trying to make Susanna as unhappy as she, and felt her daughter merited all the wealth that came her way. Peace had broken out between them and Susanna insisted that no more Shakespeare plays or other works would be published in her mother's lifetime. Anne was thankful that the ghost of such misunderstanding and anger had finally been laid to rest.

Dr John Hall lived on at Hall's Croft whenever he wasn't abroad curing what sick people he could. Her doctor husband treated her with respect now, nodding and bowing or smiling when they met, and he'd come to understand how poorly suited they'd always been. He never spoke of his time held prisoner by Ratsey, and she never asked. Not long before Shakespeare died, he even begged her forgiveness for his pretending to love and care for her. Her father had lived to see them reconciled and living – albeit in different homes – in his final year.

John Heminges was a frequent visitor, too, and came with a boy he called his 'adopted son' – Will Davenant. There was no need to rub salt in Anne Shakespeare's newly healed wounds, he said. Nor was there any reason to deprive Will of his son, or the boy of his father. 'Course no one besides her parents, Will and Robert knew Heminges shared Susanna's bed when he came to stay. After making love that first night at her father's home, he held her in his arms and they gazed out the window at the stars from the 'second best' bed. Heminges kissed her forehead and asked, 'Do you feel you're a Juliet at last?'

Susanna hugged him to her. Finally, she knew a passion beyond reason, a love without boundaries. 'Yes,' she whispered with a kiss.

And so, when Shakespeare died and willed most of his property, including his family home to Susanna, she and her husband continued as they meant to go along – in their separate lives in 'his' and 'hers' houses a mere two streets from one another. Over time, a certain friendship blossomed and took root, killing off the memories of those long years they had shared so poorly.

Anne Shakespeare took Susanna aside the morning after her father's passing, and before Heminges would find a reason to leave. She sat her daughter down and said, 'Don't waste another minute of your life here, my girl. Don't follow your mother's mistakes – go with your man. Become a player, beloved as a wife in all but name, but please, do what you will. Live a long and happy life with him and always know that I will look after things here for you.'

And so it came to pass on that dazzling summer's afternoon in 1618, a travelling theatre troupe reached a sleepy Herefordshire market town and handed out its playbills for a licensed performance. The townspeople were urged to gather at the field on the edge of town for *Rosaline Or Love's Gift* – the last play by William Shakespeare.

'It was Shakespeare's gift to his daughter,' the boy handing out the playbills announced proudly.

Like so many market towns before them, the people simply couldn't resist a reminiscence of their beloved, departed Shakespeare, so they flooded to the field where the play would take place. A makeshift stage had been erected, and several play-wagons acted as backdrops. The boy who handed out the playbills walked commandingly on stage and thumped his long wooden pole three times.

From the left of the stage, Robert Whatcott entered. He held the audience as best he could with his gaze and began to speak:

'I am Rumour, come to tell you a tale.

Faithful listeners of my art so fair

This last of my plays I give you this day

Breathes magic in a world where you are tossed

Here the wild waters and tumbledown skies of a shipwrecked life

Give way to a tale that is rarely told.

Susanna, her father's daughter to the end, stepped on stage playing Rosaline with Will Davenant at her side. Philip Massinger, the wherryman, stood in the wings to the right holding the doorway they would use in the next scene, whilst Nathan stood off stage to the left, awaiting his entrance. This was to be their final performance of Shakespeare's last play. Together, masterminded by Philip the wherryman, they had written a new play that the troupe would perform in the next town, providing the bailiff agreed.

Amid the hoots and applause of the audience, John Heminges entered stage right, pursued by Chaos the dog.

Author's Note & Acknowledgements

Above all else, I owe much of this book to William Shakespeare, the man, and to his quill dipped in the magic of words and deeds he invented – words that still touch our hearts and minds nearly 450 years after his birth. I sincerely hope that you have enjoyed this novel, and Susanna's world, I've endeavoured to recreate for you. I've specifically not provided a glossary of seventeenth-century terms, because often half the fun of their meanings is in the guessing. For those desperate to know what they mean, many can be found in the *Complete Works* (Jonathan Bate & Eric Ramussen, eds.) or online at www.shakespearedefined.com/thesaurus.

I'm sure many readers will wonder who was real and who was made up in the story. Everyone was real, but it is a novelist's prerogative to take some liberties with the detail of their lives, particularly when so little is known, as is the case with Susanna and her father. William Shakespeare, so the legend goes, died on his 52nd birthday on 23 April 1616 'at the height of his powers' – three weeks after a slap-up orgy of over-eating with Ben Jonson. Not one manuscript, note or letter survives from William Shakespeare: only six signatures on legal documents. Such wholesale destruction of personal documents leads me to believe that his heir destroyed them, as many heirs did – and still do – to protect the memory of a beloved public figure.

Shakespeare's daughter, Susanna Hall, was his primary beneficiary, and had certain rights to any manuscripts in his possession. Robert Whatcott remained Susanna's faithful servant until his death. The playwright William Davenant claimed to his dying day that he was William Shakespeare's natural son. William Davenant, unlike Shakespeare, is buried at Westminster Abbey. Ben Jonson and Shakespeare were the worst of friends and the best of foes – often bickering in verbal battles that were, at times, close to the knuckle, and at others mere words said or written in jest between friends. Nathan Field and Philip Massinger became writing partners around the time the novel is set, though Philip was never a wherryman. Other characters also existed. Gamiliel Ratsey was the most feared highwayman of his day, though he was hanged for his crimes some ten years earlier. Agnes Henslowe, as her husband's beneficiary, had some rights to a number of plays Henslowe commissioned. Tronco, Dr Simon Foreman's widow, took refuge at Lambeth Palace to avoid arrest. John Heminges and Henry Condell compiled the Folio of all Shakespeare's surviving plays, sonnets and poems. Only 228 first folio copies survive today. As for Susanna and Heminges? No one can say …

One of the catalysts for writing the novel was a question I asked at the Shakespeare Birthplace Trust: where did Susanna and her husband live after she inherited her father's home. No one could give me an answer, so I wondered – 'his' and 'hers' houses? Hmm…

This novel is based on facts that are widely known, as well as many others that form part of my five years' research into Shakespeare the man. Unpicking fact from fiction is not always easy in the case of Shakespeare, since much of what we know about his life is based on literary scholarship into his plays, the theatres and the playing companies rather than who he was or what he thought or saw or where he went. More recently, English study has interpreted history as new historicism approaching the historical elements of Shakespeare's life in its unique way.

In my opinion, much of the literary scholarship is undertaken as a means of proving Shakespeare's genius to satisfy academic research – often referring back to the bogus 'authorship question' as to whether a country boy with little Latin and less Greek could have written such magnificent verse and prose. Their approach is different from how historians and biographers would approach the subject being researched. The 'leaps of faith' that the literary scholar brings to the quest for new details in Shakespeare's life, differ substantially from the historian's. Yet in one aspect, both disciplines must conclude that there is no definitive proof specifically that Shakespeare must have done this or that and therefore he wrote such and such in one of his plays. That said, we are all affected by what surrounds us, and it would be unlikely that Shakespeare was immune to the vast changes in society that occurred during his lifetime.

Other than Germaine Greer's book *Shakespeare's Wife*, very few scholars have sought to discover facts about Shakespeare's family. Only the play by Peter Whelan, *The Herbal Bed*, performed by the Royal Shakespeare Company, about the accusation against Shakespeare's daughter for 'running at the reins' examines Susanna Shakespeare Hall. The interesting thing to note from this true historical incident is that the faithful Robert Whatcott testified in her defence. She was found 'not guilty.' (Of course, no one has ever questioned if Hall had been the 'fornicator' who may have infected her, so that became a feature I was keen to include in the novel.) For readers interested in the younger sister, Judith, who is virtually absent in this final version, Virginia Woolf's *A Room of One's Own* considers what Judith Shakespeare might have become if she were a man. As I have Susanna intimate, Judith married badly – a local boy, Thomas Quiney, who was the son of a good family friend – but had got another girl pregnant at the same time. The shame of it is believed to have deeply upset Shakespeare, leading him to virtually write her out of his will.

As an historian and biographer, my research has taken me far from the sphere of the plays. I have looked into the everyday concerns of those living in the Elizabethan and Jacobean ages, from war and famine to superstition and religion. Medicine has formed a crucial linchpin for my research.

There is compelling evidence that the Shakespeares suffered from a form of stroke, called Transient Ischaemic Attack, or TIA. Left untreated, TIA can develop into full-blown stroke. My eternal thanks goes to Dr Matt Balerdi who, in consultation with other stroke doctors, has concluded that a compelling case can be made to show that Shakespeare and other members of his family may well have suffered from TIA. This would explain beyond doubt the deterioration over time in Shakespeare's signature, one of the cornerstones of the authorship question.

Stroke was not a recognised disease state until the nineteenth-century, and in the Tudor and Jacobean eras was often confused with madness, severe melancholia, epilepsy (falling sickness or Falling Evil) and tertiary syphilis. In England, epilepsy was deemed to be akin to madness, bringing a terrible stigma to bear on its sufferers. For a number of reasons, I believe that TIA ran in the Shakespeare family – from his father, John, through to William and his brother, Gilbert, and on to Susanna and even her daughter, Elizabeth. Some literary scholars feel that Shakespeare suffered from tertiary syphilis, however, if this were the case, his survival from the probable date of infection until 1616 would have been a medical impossibility.

Shakespeare's Daughter was born from these premises. Every character in the novel was known in one way or another to Susanna Hall. However, what we actually know about her, aside from the 'running at the reins' incident, can fit on one sheet of paper. It was said in her lifetime that she 'had her father's wit' and that she was a dutiful wife. At the time of the story, her only child, a daughter named Elizabeth, was ten years old. (She was the only grandchild of Shakespeare to live to maturity – though she would remain childless.) John Heminges had had ten children but little is known of them or his wife, Ursula. There is no substantial proof that Susanna Hall and John Heminges knew each other well, or indeed that they were lovers.

This brings me to the unresolved question of 'what happened to Shakespeare's manuscripts?' This has been poorly understood or explained. Some believe they were destroyed in the fire that burnt down the Globe Theatre in 1613. Others feel that Shakespeare himself destroyed them. If either were the case, then it is unlikely that the First Folio could have been published as a distinctly separate collection from the quarto versions of the plays. What makes the First Folio so significant is that only eighteen of the surviving thirty-seven surviving plays had been printed prior to its publication in 1623. So, without the Folio – half of Shakespeare's plays would be lost to us forever. You may note that I refer to thirty-nine plays in the novel. The reason for this is that it is generally presumed that two plays at least – *Love's Labour's Won* and *Cardenio* were lost to posterity.

The most interesting unanswered question for me, which led me to fictionalise a relationship between Susanna and Heminges, was the fact that the First Folio had been inserted into the catalogue for the Frankfurt Book Fair in 1621. At the time, Anne Shakespeare was grievously ill, and it was believed she would not recover. But recover she did, and without explanation, the First Folio was withdrawn; only to be reinserted in the Book Fair of 1623, once Anne Shakespeare was well and truly dead. If the Folio had not been ready for the Book Fair of 1621, then surely it must have been ready for the Book Fair of 1622? Much can be made of this in a work of fiction. Had Shakespeare promised he wouldn't see his works published so long as she lived? Had Susanna given her mother that undertaking? Or had Anne prevented it in some other way? I doubt we shall ever know.

Authors have many people standing in the wings propping them up in a variety of ways to assist their works into publication, aside from tossing raw meat through a grill in the study door. In my case, no one shines more brightly than my long-suffering husband, Dr Douglas Ronald. As a non-Shakespearean, he has remarkably and relentlessly supported my research and work for Shakespeare charities over the years. With his keen scholar's eye, he has travelled to Elsinore with me during his PhD thesis years whilst I co-produced the first-ever promenade performance of *Hamlet* at Elsinore Castle, and helped me through my various discoveries and imaginings with good humour and unbelievable patience. Thank you, Doug. In the words of my favourite teenager, Juliet, 'My bounty is as boundless as the sea,/My love as deep: the more I give to thee,/The more I have.'

Scholars and academics who have variously supported me through these long years of gestation include primarily Professor

John Drakakis, Dr Paul Edmondson, Professor Stuart Hampton-Reeves, Dr Chris Laoutaris, Dr Abigail Rokison, Professor Stanley Wells and I thank them all for their input and patience with a non-academic and mere historian and biographer like me. Shakespearean theatre directors and actors too have been generous with their time and advice. Thank you Michael Bogdanov, Sir Trevor Nunn, and our dear friend, Nicholas Woodeson, for your time and energy.

I also thank Stephen Bashford, Michael Carlisle, Dr Amanda Foreman, Suzi Isles Buck, David Lowen, Sir Laurie Magnus, Professor Laurie Maguire, Dr Margaret Pelling, Richard G. Mitchell, Peter Robinson, Sally Robinson and Alison Weir. Anna Swan, thank you so much for your patience and insight in copyediting the manuscript.

Finally, I must mention my mother. Her support has been a real eye-opener. We've giggled like best friends together over the highs, and worked through our options when it came to the lows. Thanks to her, there have been far more highs than lows. To paraphrase the words of Shakespeare, I am 'my mother's glass'... enjoy the view, Mum.

Susan   Ronald,
Oxford, April 2014

Referenced Works of Shakespeare

A Midsummer Night's Dream
Anthony and Cleopatra
As You Like It
Henry IV, part I
Henry IV, part II
King Lear
Love's Labour's Lost
Macbeth
Much Ado about Nothing
Romeo & Juliet
The Comedy of Errors
The Merry Wives of Windsor
The Taming of the Shrew
The Tempest
Twelfth Night

Referenced works of Ben Jonson

Every Man out of his Humour
Every Man in his Humour
Sejanus
The Alchemist

Suggested Reading

All the books below are available in paperback.

1599: A Year in the Life of William Shakespeare by James Shapiro.An amazing journey into Shakespeare's prolific year and times.
Contested Will by James Shapiro. A 'Will-dunnit' story that should knock on the head the snobby authorship question.
The Genius of Shakespeare by Jonathan Bate. A brilliant view of Shakespeare's universality and humanity.

Shakespeare Revealed: A Biography by René Weis. A grounded biography with a vast array of interesting details and anecdotes.

Shakespeare: The World as a Stage by Bill Bryson. For those who want a general background with homespun wisdom and without quotes.

Shakespeare's Wife by Germaine Greer. Though filled with historically accurate conjecture based on other women's lives, it paints a compelling picture of the woman's lot.

The Elizabethan Underworld by Gãmini Salgãdo. The ultimate guide to all things nefarious in Elizabethan England

Made in the USA
Monee, IL
18 July 2021